KEEPING IT REAL

ALSO BY JUSTINA ROBSON

SilverScreen
Mappa Mundi

QUANTUM GRAVITY BOOK ONE

KEEPING IT REAL

JUSTINA ROBSON

an imprint of Prometheus Books
Amherst, NY

Published 2007 by Pyr®, an imprint of Prometheus Books

Inquiries should be addressed to
Pyr
59 John Glenn Drive
Amherst, New York 14228–2197
VOICE: 716–691–0133, ext. 207
FAX: 716–564–2711
WWW.PYRSF.COM

11 10 09 08 07   5 4 3 2 1

Library of Congress Cataloging-in-Publication Data

Robson, Justina.
    Keeping it real / by Justina Robson.
        p. cm. — (Quantum gravity ; 1)
    Originally published: London : Gollancz, an imprint of the Orion Publishing Group, 2006.
    ISBN 978–1–59102–539–9 (alk. paper)

PR6118.O28K44 2007
823'.92—dc22

2007000483

Printed in the United States on acid-free paper

For Stephanie Burgis-Samphire

COMMON KNOWLEDGE

In the days that followed the explosion at the Superconducting Supercollider in Texas, at some unknown point in the Lost Year, 2015, scientists discovered a hole in the fabric of spacetime over the blast site. The collider itself—a ring some eighty-five kilometres in circumference built far beneath the Texas soil—had utterly vanished, and only the surface buildings remained.

The explosion had followed an unknown quantum catastrophe inside the machine. However, it was not the kind of explosion that blew matter to smithereens and laid waste to worlds. Its actions took place in the near-infinitely tiny spaces between one raw energy flicker and the next. It transmuted fundamental particles into new states, altering the fabric of the universe as if changing cotton into silk. In less time than it takes to blink an eye everything had undergone subtle alteration, though the how and the what of it was a matter which is still debated to this day—a matter not helped by the fact that nobody could remember exactly or say with certainty how things used to be. In the meantime there were more immediate problems to deal with, namely, the stable but infinitely mysterious hole inside the circle of the old collider, and the fact that it led directly into another world.

In the five years since the Quantum Bomb, as it is popularly known in Otopia (which was once called Earth, according to records made prior to 2015), a total of five other realities have been discovered. They lie parallel to, or approximate with (all words, definitions, and speculations are being assessed as we write, since nobody has yet come up with a theory that can explain the phenomena completely), the human universe.

The first of these is Zoomenon, the realm of the Elements. Zoomenon is hostile to human life and manifests unpredictably in Otopian space where it interpenetrates with it. Sturdily equipped expeditions replete with hardened adventurers have reported the following: every raw element of the periodic table may be found there in abundance, from Hydrogen to Ununbium; the primary colours may be observed there, randomly moving across the raw rocks and sand of what appears to be the basic Zoomenon landscape, a place not unlike Earth in the Hadean age; there are also beings here, of indeterminate energy composition, capable of forming humanlike appearances—these are named Elementals, since they seem to be personifications of the spirits of air, fire, water, earth, wood, metal. There are others, yet to be understood or met with. How many others is unknown.

The second realm is Alfheim. Since early in 2016 a diplomatic relationship has been established with the elves, as the inhabitants call themselves. The elves strongly dispute the QBomb theory. They claim that they have known of Earth and Otopia since times that predate early human civilisations. Few Otopian technologies function in Alfheim, which is the first of the Adept or Aetheric Realms. It is a pristine Eden, untouched by industrialisation despite the complex civilisations that have risen and fallen in its massive history. However, there are tensions within elf society and frosty diplomatic explorations are the only contact that regularly takes place with them. Their borders are closed to immigration of any kind and they allow only a few of their emissaries out in turn. Common people of Otopia know only stories of Alfheim.

The third realm is Demonia. The demons are, like the elves, life-forms which appear adept in magic. Demon scientists have assisted humans in their discovery of the physically real presence of extradimensional regions (I-space) since 2017, regions of incredible power and vitality which seem akin to spacetime itself, yet coexist with it. This region is known to demons and elves commonly as Aetherstream, though their scientists and researchers have agreed to adopt the human name of Interstitial, or I-space. Demons do not recognise the QBomb event as historical fact either, and also claim a lengthy knowledge of "the fourth realm"—Otopian Earth.

The fifth region is Thanatopia. This unlikely place is bound tightly to the I-space continuum. To cross into Thanatopia requires death and return is not possible to those not greatly skilled in necromancy. Only the Aetheric races possess necromancers, and not many of them. It is worth noting that so far no human of Otopian Earth has displayed anything other than the most fleeting ability to detect, let alone manipulate, I-space. Certainly no one has ever been to Thanatopia, or, if they have, they have not returned and its true nature is a complete mystery. The only human knowledge of it has been given by demon necromancers whose strength in I-space permits them access. Officially we may state that the Undead shepherd the Dead of all realms, though what this actually means is anyone's guess. All other knowledge concerning Thanatopia is classified, and as such may not be printed here.

The sixth realm, which most quickly adopted protocols with Otopia and has generated the most traffic, is Faery. Faery has issued tourist visas since 2018. Faery culture, as with all other realms, is unique and complicated. Faeries assure us they have had a long association with certain regions of the Earth over the more interesting parts of human history and the author is not willing to dispute the point, even—especially—in writing.

For the last two years an increasing familiarity with and acceptance of the six-realm structure has led to a steady popularity of migration and trade across willing borders, but human beings have a lot yet to learn.

One year ago Alfheim closed its borders and cut off trade. It began an exclusionary policy which diplomatic negotiations have so far failed to lift. The reasons for this change of heart are classified information. At the time of writing, in 2021, an uneasy state of affairs exists between Alfheim and the other realms.

CHAPTER ONE

The story of how The No Shows got signed was one of those legends that seem completely manufactured by the celebrity press. *Rolling Stone* ran it as lead story the day their first single was released for download. Lila Black reviewed it as she travelled to a meeting with the owner of Ozo Records, Jelly Sakamoto.

A few months ago Jelly had been the producer of a modestly successful indie music label. He was sitting in his office playing a quick five-minute game of Dune Car Rally on his pod, which had become an hourlong frustrating game of Dune Car Rally by the time his A&R girl burst in without warning and said breathlessly, "You gotta hear this!"

Jelly was used to being told that, but he knew that Lucie was frequently right. Still, no point in breaking old habits. He saved and shrugged without looking up, "What?"

"This great new band. They play their own gear, write their own material, and do this kind of weird heavy rock Mode-X number. The backing vocals are all faeries, the DJ is that chick from Zebra Mondo. And—get this—their lead singer is an *elf*!"

"Elves don't rock," Jelly said, unknowingly coining one of the greatest quotes in the history of popular music and the phrase that would follow him to his deathbed. He added, rather more forgettably, "They pavane and jig, they play the flute and the triangle, they do orchestra, they do chant, they sell shitloads of that. They sing like cats with firecrackers up their asses. The only time they ever get sampled is when they've been pushed through an audio sieve so human listeners don't shit themselves, or when they're slowed down ten times to scrape the frequencies for distortion effects to shove behind Crash bands. So, what? Does she mime? Does she look good?"

"Here." Lucie threw a Berrypic of the band down on the desk. "He sings his own lyrics."

Jelly ignored her and the invitation of the Berry's flashing Play command, got up, and went out, allegedly to the toilet, although he claims in a later interview that he was going to fit some new EarWax with higher grade buffers, in order to protect his hearing.

Lucie hung out waiting, and when she convinced herself he must have gone down the fire escape she stormed out, leaving the Berry face-up on his empty desk. An hour later in came Roxanne, the sales director for Northern Otopia at Ozo Records, the largest music company in the Four Realm Trading Bloc. Fed up of waiting for Jelly, who was notoriously late for everything, she sat herself down in his chair and, glancing down at the Berry, pressed Play.

Twenty minutes later Jelly comes into his own office and she says, "Why didn't you tell me you were going to be sending me a million-bytes-a-minute-shifter? I need another month at the least to prep publicity! Honestly, you'd be late for your own funeral."

Jelly bought Ozo Records on the first week's sales and Lucie ran it for him in her new post as executive director, whilst he fussed around producing a whole lot of other bands and arguing with The No Shows' volatile addict of an agent, Buddy Ritz.

The rest, Lila reflected as she reread the tale, was the talk of the medianets every other day of the week. There was no hotter property than The No Shows at the moment.

Lila Black was undercover. She was pretending to be a bodyguard working for Doublesafe, a company specialising in personal security for celebrities. It was an easy job since she was already kitted out for much more active duties as part of her job in the Otopian National Security Agency's Intelligence and Reconnaissance Division, or Incon. The only difficulty she had was in concealing those parts of her body which were entirely metal prosthetics, but she'd found a silk trouser suit and smart boots to do that for her. The synthetic skin on her hands and arms was thankfully wearing well enough to pass for the real thing. As she took a sidelong glance at herself in the mirror at Ozo Records' Reception, she saw a tall, powerful young woman in elegant black flares. Her silver eyes—the irises and pupils perfect mirrors—could easily be put down to decorative contact lenses beneath the soft swing of her ruby and scarlet hair. There was nothing to show that she was barely half a human being any longer. She enjoyed the feeling, until the receptionist popped her bubblegum and said, "Jelly'll see you now."

Lila walked into the office. It hadn't changed since the *Rolling Stone* shoot, except that there were two more platinum discs hanging over his desk, both printed with The No Shows logo: a heart inside a red circle with a diagonal slash across it. She stood in front of the desk and looked at Jelly as he looked at her. He was a thin, leathery whipcord of a man, brimming with nervous energy, and could barely sit still a moment.

"Doublesafe said you were the best," he said and shrugged, not very impressed. "I got to tell you, I don't know. We're getting some trouble. Letters. Threats. We have a tour to do. You look like kinda lightweight, like a kid could push you away in a crowd, or maybe even a big wind. What you got to say?" He took off his dark glasses and folded his hands under his chin. He had a gold ring on every finger.

Lila shrugged back, also not impressed. "If we get into a crowd, then I didn't do my job. We won't be in any crowds." She was recording the entire conversation, sending it to her Incon boss on a secure, wireless feed the entire time, using the camera system inside her eyes.

"Well, you don't look too bad," he said. "And I know shit about it all, only that I need Zal to survive the tour and make some more tracks. You cool with elves?"

"I'm cool," Lila said. The lie rolled easily off her tongue. She felt her heart rate go up and she would have begun sweating, but her autosystems kicked in and masked all of her nerves with effective machine frost. Drugs and hormones from adapted glands in her neck and brain smoothed her until it was true. She was cool.

"Good. You're hired. You can start now. Go pick him up and take him down to the studios. He . . ."

"I have all the details," Lila said in her most professional tone, tapping the back of her hand where an ordinary person kept their Organiser. "Your office sent me everything already."

"Oh yeah?" For the first time Jelly seemed fazed. Then he grinned, "I like having the mostest people working for me." Then, "Why you still here?"

Lila walked out. On her way to the parking lot she connected briefly with her boss, Cara Delaware, to tell her that the job was successful and to hear Cara say, "Great. You okay? Your reflexes showed some peak stress levels there. We can pull you if it gets too much."

"No," Lila said quickly. She'd reached her bike. Its sleek, powerful lines and instant reaction to her touch on the grips had already calmed her more completely than her AI-self's drug response to her nervousness. The doses themselves had been so low that their effect was already gone and here, where inappropriate reactions didn't matter, the AI didn't bother masking her true responses. The engine purred like a giant cat, making the concrete vibrate under her feet. "I'm fine."

"Then you're activated," Cara said. "Partial cover. Your support team are online when you need them. You're operating out of central offices now. Everything goes through the team. Nobody else. Not even me."

"Thanks. Take care of everyone for me." Lila thought of her dog, Okie, whom she'd had to leave at home to be looked after by her colleagues until she returned. She thought of her family, although they'd been left behind years ago when she stopped being plain diplomatic attaché Lila Amanda Black and became something quite different. There was no telling when she might be back from this job, but she had agreed to one thing for certain when she agreed to live as a cyborg of the AI division instead of die of her wounds and now, no matter when the cover ended, she was never going home again.

"Good luck, Lila." The line cut dead. It was the first time since she had been Mended that she was really and truly on her own. Where Cara and the NSA office had been a constant, monitoring presence fresh zones of silence opened in Lila's head. She smiled and the bike traced an arc of beautiful speed into the traffic heading downtown.

CHAPTER TWO

The bike didn't talk. There were versions that did but Lila didn't want more machines in her head than were already there. Besides, she had every A–Z of Otopia available to her from the memory chips in her skull. The address that the studio gave her for Zal's rental home was high in the Lightwater Hills in the most exclusive area of Bay City. She rode without a helmet, her red curls rippling in the wind as she lay low across the gas tank and sped through the streets.

Her route took her around the Bay itself, where whitecap waves were dashing in ones and twos across the water, over the vast towerless span of the elf-built bridge—the Andalune—and through the dense woodlands which crept from the water's edge to the Heights of Solomon. Zal's house lay over the ridge, the only clue to its presence a heavily barred iron gate set in stone posts that were almost hidden by trees. There was no postbox and no speakerphone. Lila pulled up in front and glanced up at the spikes. Behind the gates the forest thickened and the boughs of the trees leant over the road and shrouded it in darkness. Within twenty metres the drive curved away from her and was lost to sight. In the quiet she heard her engine and the sough of wind in the leaves. She was surrounded by trees.

Using the private contact numbers and her AI-self's communication suite—nested inside her head where everyone else had to use a Pod or a Berry or a Seed to interface—she called to the security people from Doublesafe who were already inside. The gates swung inward silently and Lila moved forward in a steady glide.

The road snaked its way steadily uphill and then into a hollow which lay at the summit of the hill. Solomon's Folly stood there—a giant white stone house facing south. It looked through a cut swathe in the forest, like a firebreak, which ran over simple grassland down and down and down to a crescent of white beach and the sea. It was three storeys high for the most part, and roughly covered an area the size of two football pitches. Pieces of it had towers and other pieces had glass roofs. It had many sides and angles. Some of them were lost among trees, others seemed to teeter on or be built inside large boulders which piled along the north face of the house. It looked like it had been built one room at a time, almost randomly, without thought for anything except a sea view and an obsessive need for privacy, and so it had been. Lila felt almost ill looking at it. It was hideous. It looked as though the hollow had been created by the house's incomprehensible weight, and that everything was sinking into the earth.

She paused before the last descent to gawp and catch her breath. Pine needles and heavy loam and other green and rotting smells were thick in the air because the day was hot and making them rise. To her left and right she looked into the woods on maximum zoom and saw signs of a great number of wood elementals but nothing of the elusive beings themselves. You would expect elementals around elves, and in forests of any size, but you would never expect an elf to live in a house like this. It was a rental property. There could be no other explanation. Lila recorded what she saw and went on down to the main door. It stood open and as she dismounted a man in a Doublesafe uniform came to escort her inside.

A woman wearing a gloriously expensive dress, very understated, and antique Jimmy Choo shoes came to greet her. "I'm Jolene, Zal's

PA," she said and Lila shook hands with her. Jolene was the kind of human Lila associated with elf groupiedom; smart, in control, stylish. It was difficult not to feel inferior, especially without a slick manicure. Lila put her hands behind her back and reminded herself she wasn't here to look great, only to carry out her job. Jolene seemed content with her authentication documents and barely raised an eyebrow at either Lila's gender or her size, so perhaps she wasn't all bad.

"Would you like to see the house first?" Jolene offered, glancing at her watch.

"No thanks," Lila said. "I know the layout."

"And the staff and the grounds and what they eat for breakfast, I suppose," Jolene said, smiling. "In that case I understand it's time you were at work. Is that bike the only vehicle you brought?" She peered anxiously across the vast hallway and through the door at Lila's Kawasaki.

"Elves won't travel in Faraday cages," Lila said, "so that rules out cars, trains, and planes. I don't travel on horseback, and it beats walking."

"So, you have done some homework," Jolene nodded, satisfied. "I'll go and get him."

"It's okay, I'll go," Lila said, stepping around her. As Jolene looked puzzled she added, "Our offices sent you a ring, which you gave him to wear. It's connected to our private network through secure branches not connected to the Otopia Tree. I could find him in the middle of a Bears game at Alton Park. Not that he'd be caught dead there." She hesitated but Jolene didn't smile at this efficient sidestepping of Otopia's global internet. Instead the woman's nervousness returned.

"I really wish this wasn't necessary Ms. Black," she said, "I hope you don't take these threats as lightly as you speak of them."

"I don't," Lila said. She regretted her tone as she walked away. Showing some small weakness in front of Jolene would have gained her more sympathy. Now the woman was faintly antagonised by her.

The hall gave way to several corridors and stairways. Lila went up to the second floor and through a maze of meandering ways to where a room the size of her entire apartment looked out through a glass wall to the ocean, giving a superb view. She couldn't see anybody in it, only a set of pale sofas, a seemingly random assortment of plants in pots, and a coat laid over a straight-backed chair. Very faintly from somewhere she could hear Stevie Wonder singing "Blame It on the Sun." Otherwise the house was silent.

She walked to where her augmented and automated senses told her Zal was. The Doublesafe ring was on the chair, beside the coat. Lila glanced at it with annoyance, verging on anger, but curbed the feeling quickly and concentrated instead on the beauty of the coat. It was elvish-made, of tightly woven raw silk, sparely decorated with magical sigils that were so old they no longer bore any scent or colour of their own. The coat had been bleached by the sun. Only the inside showed its once true shade of crimson. The outside was a dull reddish clay, worn to white in places.

Lila touched the hem of one sleeve as she looked around more carefully. The fabric softened between her fingers and she let it go quickly, only then realising the fact that the feeling that was nibbling away at her insides was fear. She hadn't seen anything elvish since the day she was last completely human. She had gone to some lengths to avoid hearing Zal and his band, or any other elvish sound. She would have been content never to know anything of them ever again. She was glad of the processor that filtered her dreams. She did not want to meet the near-immortal she was charged to preserve with her brief life. She didn't want to touch his coat.

It was at this moment that the fineness of her hearing became more highly attuned. It was not Stevie singing his old song. It was somebody preternaturally quiet who was standing in the shadows, not more than a body's length from her. It was Zal.

Lila made herself turn very slowly, lest she look surprised. Her heart almost burst beneath the control of her AI-self's attempt to regulate it. "There you are," she said lightly. "I'm Lila Black, your bodyguard." And she realised as soon as she spoke that she had foolishly given her real name, not the pretend name of the identity she had been meant to assume.

The flare of her anger fizzed with a curious tang like the citrus twist in a sparkling drink as she acknowledged her mistake. Oh wait, that couldn't have been the zing of wild magic, could it? Couldn't have been the onset of a Game? Elves, humans, and Games were notorious . . . the idea chilled her, but it was too late now. No, it was too faint. It couldn't be anything more than her imagination.

Zal had stopped singing as she noticed him standing there in plain view. He was exactly her height so they stood eye to eye as her anger stung her. She thought he looked slightly surprised but Lila couldn't think straight. She was dismayed at how unprepared she was. It wasn't his looks or his rock star status that made her feel sick with nervous tension. It was the sense of his otherness, the combination of how nearly human he appeared and how inhuman he really was.

He'd made no effort to hide, but she hadn't seen him. His natural magical aura had concealed him from her attention and now her technologically assisted senses could feel the slight charge of it as he stepped closer. This elvish aetherial body, larger than his physical body and moving independently of it, reached out ahead of him and touched her with slippery, invisible coils. His *andalune*, after which the great bridge of Bay City was named, was as natural to him as her own skin was to her. Its curious touch was another kind of glance, nothing more, but the unwanted investigation made her back away one step even under her tightest control and she had to look away. Lila remembered other *andalune* touches like this one that were neither kind nor merely indifferent. And then, almost before it was there, it had gone away, satisfied that it knew everything it wanted to know about her. She could still taste a snap of lime in the air and some half-remembered warning tried to rise in her mind, though she was so slugged on adrenal suppressants it had nowhere to go. Her body wanted to run. Her mind was frozen. She gave him a casual nod of recognition with a dip of her chin, as though she couldn't be more comfortable.

For a second she thought he looked surprised. She saw a moment of curiosity burning in the slight widening of his large, slanted eyes.

"Hello, Lila," Zal said. He didn't have an ordinary elf voice. Their normal speaking tones were very like human voices with subtle harmonies buried inside, but this one was smoky rather than bell-like. He didn't exactly fit the mould of serene snottiness she had been braced for either, although his long ash-blond hair and attenuated, pointy ears were exactly on theme. Lila had never seen an elf with dark eyes before. Zal's were chestnut brown with darker rings around the iris. She was staring into them like any fool for a good half a second before she composed herself. She turned aside and felt her face heat. The feeling she was experiencing was startling, and nothing like loathing.

Zal arched one dark eyebrow at her in a laconic expression of amusement at her clear efforts to repel all his natural glamour and Lila seethed with annoyance.

"I don't require your services," he informed her. He took his coat up and put it on with insouciant ease, then tilted his head, waiting for her to do something.

They always wait, Lila recalled, all trace of blush gone. They have the time. They like to watch and see what silly things humans will do, given the opportunity. He could stand there till Christmas with that false pretend-polite expression on his face.

Lila picked up the ring. It was a stupid thing to have given him in the first place, but Doublesafe hadn't thought past their human security procedures with any imagination. There was no way he would wear it. "Yeah well, you're not paying the bill," she said calmly. She wished she could take the ring and stuff it down his throat, but that would be only a short-term solution. Instead she put it in her jacket pocket and hoped she'd think of something. "It won't make any difference. Until Jelly is happy that all threats on your life are gone, then where you go, I go."

"Until you die?" he asked, both brows up for a second, taunting.

"Or until you do."

Lila saw the ghost of a smile cross his face as he walked past her. His gait was deceptively slow to look at, but he was fast. It was all she could do not to trot in order to keep up.

At the bike he didn't pause, put his hands on the beautiful sunrise paintwork of the gas tank, and swung his leg over into the riding position. So much for the legendary elf aversion to machinery.

Lila knew that this was the moment when she had to take some control if she were ever going to stand a chance. She didn't hesitate: walked up, put her hands on his waist, and lifted him off her place and onto the pillion seat. Then she kicked her leg high over the handlebars without waiting to see if her strength had caused any surprises and sat down very hard and towards the back of her seat, rather hoping to do him some minor damage.

The bike reacted immediately to her touch, reading her intent from the tension in her body, the speed of her movements, and its trace readings from her AI-self. As she took hold of the grips it was already moving forward, and as soon as her feet were off the ground it accelerated rapidly, bending them low as it curved around the tight turns into the woodland.

She felt Zal adjust to the movements easily. He did not grab her, as she'd hoped he might have to because he was off balance. He waited until they were stopped at the gates and then slid up against her and put his hands on her hips.

"Don't be mad, honey," he said, so close to her ear that she could feel his breath warm the long curls of her hair. "I thought you wanted me where you could see me."

"I can see you all I want from here," she said and took them down the last slope at speed, necessitating a heavy sideslide into the road which almost took both their knees out on the hardtop. She was almost certain that he would be able to feel where her real body and the intelligent metal prosthetics grew into one another and that was horrible, more than she expected, but, much more than that, what most concerned her was that despite all her training it had taken barely seconds before she was playing a Game with him when the first rule of engagement with elves, like dragons, is that you never play Games with them. The smart one-liners were a dead giveaway. That lime and lemon zap—had he started it deliberately? No doubt . . . but her brooding was cut short.

As she straightened them into line she saw shadows shifting on her right, where the trees clung to a steep bank. She glanced there and saw the uncertain, staglike form of a large wood elemental looking at them from the shade, branches its bones and leaves its flesh. Such creatures were incredibly rare in Otopia.

The bike was too fast. She caught no more than that glimpse.

Zal didn't say or do any more but he didn't move away either. All the way into town she could feel his body and the almost-skin contact of his *andalune*, warm against her back. She found herself mentally reviewing a still shot of the first moment she'd walked into the room with the ocean view. He'd been watching her, the whole time she'd been in the room, long before she saw him. Looking at what her AI-self could analyse from the images now she thought his look at her was disturbingly acute.

I will not be attracted to him, it's only a ridiculous magical trick, this Game, she told herself sternly. *The entire thing is just one big easy weapon they use to get whatever they want out of humans. Most can't do anything about it, can't even feel it when it takes hold, but I can, and I'm not falling for that old trick. Magical bonds do* not *count as reality and they don't stand up in court. Anyway, all elves stare acutely. It's a species-trait, like the ears and the supercharged nervous system. My job is to find out all about him, to guard him and to find out who's after him, and that's all.*

Which was all true. But it felt truer when they arrived in the studio parking lot and he got off and ignored her completely. This time she had to stride at her fastest to catch up as he vanished into the dim, air-conditioned interior.

CHAPTER THREE

Lila ignored the ride and her various disquiets by forcing them into temporary storage in her AI-memory system. She concentrated as she met the rest of the band, the support crew, the studio execs, the sound engineers, and the various hangers-on who had accumulated to listen to the recording. As she shook their hands she took readings and compared them with the files she had on them already. Data ran like water in her mind, showing her their names and every other known statistic under the sun.

The three backing singers were faery; two of Emerald Nation with beautiful green skins, and one Chalcedonite who was striped like a tiger in tones of dusk and gold.

"He's a Mojave Blue," one of the Emerald girls, the ultra-dark Viridia, told Lila proudly, because he was her boyfriend. He introduced himself as Sand, Sandy for long.

The other faery woman was even more lovely than Viridia, with spiky natural lime hair in a punk style and a slender, willowy shape. Her face was all delicate features, boosted with extraordinary silver and turquoise makeup in the faery equivalent of Goth. "I'm Poppy," she said, with a dazzling smile. "Hey, how are ya? Nice to see more girls around. This place is strictly over-testosteroned, if ya know what I mean. Did you see Zal's letters? They're utterly hideoso. Hey Zal," and she took his arm as he passed her and air-kissed him in the direction of his lips—a gesture he matched with an elegant *mwa*, millimetres from contact. "Catch ya later."

Lila watched Poppy glide just above the floor in that floaty faery way, as though she was as light as thistledown. Viridia and Sand made slightly more effort to stay floorbound, but not much. Their wings were not visible in Otopia, but Lila found that they created a slight buzz of interference with her internal comms, as certain kinds of faery often did. She'd have to be careful around them because they'd made her slow to react.

Zal did some complicated ganglike Hi-Five greeting with the others in the band. From letting Lila make her own way with the guileless bonhomie of the faeries he actually reached back and drew her forward into the studio proper to meet the humans.

"Guys, this is my new shadow, Lila. Lila doesn't like rock, and she doesn't like elves."

"Hey," said the bass player, dark and fresh-faced Luke who was, Lila judged, twenty-five going on fifteen. His rap sheet included two counts of Class B alchemical possession. He gave her a grin and a heavy squeeze on her hand. "Is she like, going *everywhere* with us?"

"What does she like?" asked the girl DJ, giving Lila a competitive and warning-off stare from under the brim of her battered top hat.

"Violence," Lila said sweetly in her best Swiss-finishing-school voice. She withdrew her hand from Luke's hold. He winked at her.

Zal laughed.

The DJ relaxed and nodded, her stiff-faced initial reaction softening into a smile. "Whatever."

Luke said, "Don't like elves? Are you what, some kind of racist?"

"I love elves," Lila said in exactly the same tone as before, her smile fixed. "And I love rock."

Jelly's voice broke in over the intercom. "Can we get on with business before the rental of these fine additional musicians destroys all potential of my third house purchase in New Malibu? Stations people. Instruments. Connections."

Lila retreated to Jelly's side of the glass wall and sat down beside him at the mixing desk. She detected no hidden enmities in the band. Far from it, they were all perfectly easy with one another. A quick surveillance of the rest of the people here gave her no more evidence of any internal rivalries at work. She settled down to watch them do their stuff. They were going to record a Mode-X cover of "The Ace of Spades."

Lila, like Jelly, had no faith that Zal could ever convincingly sing tracks like that. She'd never heard an elf sing anything other than chant or a peculiarly prissy version of "Silent Night." She didn't want to wait around either. Now that she was satisfied that the studio was secure, and with two other guards on duty at the doors, she made an excuse of visiting the ladies' room and took her chance to slip out in order to investigate the rest of the building.

Poppy had been quite right when she said that the letters sent to Zal care of Ozo Records had been hideoso. They were also, as far as Incon were concerned, of possible relevance to national security. Although some of them were crackpot in nature, hating Zal for his race, for his taste in music, or for his betrayal of all matters precious to Alfheim, those were easy to deal with: from elves or from humans they went straight in the bin. But the dangerous ones that had sparked Lila's operation weren't like that.

These few were letters that had been delivered on magical vellum, and what they said changed according to who read them. When the manager of the fan club had opened them they read like regular fan mail. The senders had even included cheques to join through special promotional rates promised through an ad in *Vanity Fair* which had accompanied a big article on Zal. But in Zal's hands the words and letters spun themselves around. It wasn't possible for Lila to read what he saw, but she'd been provided with Zal's brief report on it. The letter read:

Return by the lost way or not at all,
Return by the longest day or not at all:
Else be lost and ever wander,
Life and limb and spirit squander.

It was a general kind of magical threat that any of the non-Otopian realms might have employed, but unlike most spellcast items it bore no telltales of its origin that Incon's aetherial forensics had been able to decipher. Since magic was created through the spirit of the creator, it was technically not possible to have traceless magic. Magic bore the signatures of the maker all through it, like a hallmark. But the letter had proven completely flavourless.

The lost way part referred to the elf-only gateway out of Otopia to Alfheim. The longest day was easy: that was Midsummer Solstice, two days away. The rest of it seemed to indicate less favourable conditions. Other Incon agents had been dispatched into Alfheim to see if they could find out whether it had come from someone there. Lila, glad to be in Otopia, didn't know what she was looking for now, so she looked for anything.

The studio was set up in an underground room, insulated for sound. Above that, on the ground level, the administrative offices filled the space. Most of the areas were populated, so Lila used her day clearance pass on the fire escape door and went up another flight. Through the concrete and steel of the walls it was hard to obtain any accurate scans but she did her best, searching another empty office, a storage cupboard, a room full of old equipment. It was here that she detected a trace of illegitimate radio transmission.

Inside, junk was stacked to the roof. Lila lifted boxes and crates and old packaging. It was covered in dust and soon she was quite filthy but she persisted. The transmitter was behind a filing cabinet which was full to the top with broken mikes, old amplifier stacks, and lumps of electronics that must have been made before Lila was born. She couldn't be bothered to unpack it for its trip to the corridor so, after checking that nobody was near, she engaged her internal hydraulics and lifted the entire thing, sliding it along the carpet on one edge until it snagged on the lintel. Breathing out, sucking her stomach in, Lila sneaked past it into the corner of the room, felt a tug against her leg, and heard a ripping sound.

"Ah, crap," she said and looked down at the burst stitches on her new pants. It was just a whole day of too-late, she thought.

With more force than necessary she bent down and yanked up the carpet. In a billow of dust and dead flies she sneezed and reached down, carefully letting the little finger of her right hand rest against the tiny object which looked like a pebble. Intricate receptors housed where a knucklebone would have been identified it as a faery device, part silicon and part metal. It was using bounce-retort techniques to get a reasonably clear sound pickup from the studio, and was broadcasting on a coded frequency to somewhere quite local. It must have been here a long time for its battery power was almost exhausted. Lila listened through the bug for a moment or two.

She could hear Zal and the band. The raw energy of the music reached up and caught her. Zal's voice was a shamanic, self-destructive growl—*the pleasure is to play, makes no difference what you say* . . . It made a strange, dark exultation rise in her chest, the sensation so clear and quick that she jerked in surprise. Her AI-self picked up frequencies that her human ears couldn't hear. She wondered for a split second if there were lots of dogs and cats in the intended audience, but her AI corrected her. Zal's anomalous sounds were in the subaudible band, not the high pitches of specialized whistles.

Lila stored the information to send back to the lab later, in case it was an important slice of data, and took her finger away from the bug, deciding to let it lie there for the time being. It took a few minutes to replace all the crap where it had been. When she'd done she dusted herself down and tried washing in the ladies. The soap and water did a reasonably good job but there was nothing to be done about the tiny tear she'd made in the outside seam of her trousers where it had caught against the corner of the filing cabinet. She patched the inside with a piece of sample tape which she carried, along with the rest of her field forensics kit, in a capsule container that fitted inside her jacket pocket like a wallet, and went back to the studio.

What she really wanted to do was get outside and trace the broadcast to its reception unit, but that would mean getting too far out of range of His Highness. Lila had to settle for a seat next to Jelly in the recording booth where she watched everyone except Zal do ten repeats of the same song whilst Jelly fiddled levels and mix and his assistants dashed around making much of nothing to do.

During the repeats she watched everyone closely. The musicians were so used to the regime that they patiently repeated everything. Poppy smiled once to Lila and they had to stop that take.

Jelly screamed at her, "Stop grinning! We're self-destructing here, not selling hamburgers!"

Zal looked briefly at Lila through the glass, when he turned around from talking to the DJ between takes of Luke's bass track. He mouthed something at her which she wasn't meant to hear, but Lila could read his lips even if she hadn't been able to instantly recalibrate her hearing filters to pick up the actual sound. It was elvish words saying a thing she was reasonably certain no elf had ever said before.

Zo na kinkirien. I love your pants.

She was puzzled for a moment but pleased she didn't actually look down as she realised the tear on her seam must be visible and that he was taunting her for going off instead of sticking like glue to his side. He'd turned away before she could give him her frosty look.

Jelly listened through his private headphones, jouncing on his seat. "One more time. Everyone except the lord of darkness himself—Zal, you're done," he said through the connecting mike and added. "Ear-bleeding effort ladies and gennlemen." He cued the intricate, slamming drum line with a fingertip and glanced at Lila. "Hey, don't go getting ideas about Zal. You know I have to say it. Every girl comes in here and the boys . . . okay they're like mostly engineers or admin and shit . . . they always end up getting . . . you know what I mean?"

Lila had no idea but she could guess. She nodded, rather interested that this was still standard practice after so many years—warn the new girl off, insult the bodyguard's intelligence, make sure she knows she doesn't count. She smiled vacantly at him with agreement whilst inwardly seething.

"Good. 'Cause you have to like be around him all the time and that's not gonna be a picnic. Don't tell him what to do. And don't tell him what to take. In fact, don't speak, because that all pisses him off and we have to start touring on Monday and I can't hand him over to Jolene all pissed because good tour managers are like rocking horse shit and if she quits we're all screwed. Don't let him go on another god-damned bender. He missed two dates last month, off his head out in the woods somewhere, and it took four days to find him even and we never found whatever it was he took, maybe it was mushrooms or some elfy thing he dug up, you know? And he'll resent you. Oh man, he already resents you. He'd resent you more if you was a guy, though, if that makes it any better. That's all I can say." Jelly paused as the music started and then turned back. "Do you have to shower with him?"

"No," Lila said.

Jelly made a face that said it was a sport he was sorry he was going to miss, and then he slapped his headphones back on.

Lila tested her patience to the limit by sitting quietly for the next hour simply watching, learning that when Jelly said it was the last take, it wasn't. She used the time to sharpen up her intelligence on Alfheim and tried to use the extensive database of genealogical data given her by Incon to try and place Zal.

The only thing he'd ever said about where he came from was in the *Vanity Fair* piece and it read: "There's no reason for me to be here other than the music. I like to sing."

He'd lived in Queenstown, in the north of the Bay City area, for six months before The No Shows got their act together. Before that there was no record of anything unusual. He'd entered Otopia from the Alfheim gateway under the usual restrictions and all his paperwork was in order. Lila thought Zal must be a shortened version of his real name, but the database contained no elvish names beginning with a Z. He was good at talking in Otopian, but so were many elves, who picked up languages and accents like good carpet picks up dog hair. Lila couldn't genome test him without his permission according to international law, so that was out of the question for the time being, unless he were involved in a provable criminal action. It really looked like he was just an elf who wanted to be a rock star. If only that weren't against every chosen or given trait of Elfdom she'd ever known. But then nobody here seemed to have a problem with it, probably because they were all getting rich off it.

Lila was grimly aware that stereotyping had provided the majority of her own attitudes towards his species, and what had happened to her in Lilirien, the Second Realm of Alfheim, two years ago hadn't done anything to broaden her mind. The problem with Alfheim had always been that the elves had very little contact with humans in or out of Otopia. They didn't mix with faery much either, and they had active rules of avoidance regarding demons—it was something to do with the magic systems each used. Ancients and elementals moved freely among elves and were even welcome, but this was because all of them had derived from similar magical roots. To Otopia they were neighbours; cordial and distant, as out of Lila's league as though they belonged to a country club that she could never afford to go to.

To the rest of the elves Zal must look like he was slumming it. She wouldn't be surprised to find all the threats of any substance coming from resentful authorities and individuals there. "Ace of Spades," in its Mode-X format, was comprehensively about as opposed to the serenity and rarefied values of elven society as you could get. Which is why she took the letters seriously. She knew that the elves' protectiveness over their precious culture extended well beyond simply keeping secrets and writing letters.

At last everything had been done according to Jelly's incomprehensible standards. The engineers began to pack their equipment, and the band decided they all wanted to go out and eat, with a view to staying out all night. It was the last thing Lila felt like doing, but it wasn't her place to argue. Only as they settled down in their private dining room at the Lizard Lounge did she realise how hungry she was. She found herself placed next to Jolene and Luke, across from Zal.

"Cool 'tacts," Luke said, grinning at her. "Good hair too."

"Thanks." His flirting with her made her sorry her suit was so ordinary.

"No problem. I was a bit offish before. Sorry. We get a lot of shit about that, y'know?" He passed her a menu as the waitress handed them out.

"I know."

"Yeah, you read those letters?"

"Yes."

"Think they're real?"

"Luke," Jolene broke in rather sharply. "Can we not talk about it now?"

"I was only asking," Luke said and gave a glance at his menu before tossing it down.

"No, I want to know too," said Poppy from the end of the long table.

"And me," Viridia chimed in. "After all, we're the ones who are in the firing line. Well, maybe from some angles."

Lila glanced at Zal, braced for some sarcastic or otherwise difficult response, but he picked that second to take his coat off and didn't meet her eye. She looked back at Luke and then at Poppy. "They're real. Doublesafe has put on extra security at all hotels and venues. I'll be with you all the time."

Jolene rolled her eyes and gave Lila a thanks-for-nothing stare.

Lila tried to reassure her, "You shouldn't worry about it. That's my business."

"Easier *said*, man," Luke said. "D'you have a gun?"

"Several," Lila assured him.

"Where?" he leant back and stared at her chest. Viridia kicked his ankle. "Ow." He laughed and kicked her back.

At that moment the waitress returned. Everyone except Zal and Lila ordered beer. Lila skipped on drinks, not wanting any distraction. Zal drank water. She guessed it wasn't because he was trying to stay sober because he smoked some funny cigarette of Sand's and she could measure the dilation of the pupils in his eyes enlarging by the second. Jolene made a few comments, but he paid no attention to her.

They talked amongst themselves as though Lila wasn't there for the most part. She preferred it that way. It let her watch them closely because she didn't have to concentrate on finding things to say. Poppy excused herself just as the food came and Lila tracked her idly as the humans all tucked into pizza or burgers. The fey ate strange set jellies, and honey from the comb and big lumps of sweet milky pudding. Zal did something Lila couldn't believe she was watching at all.

She hadn't thought he could sing but she'd been dead wrong about that.

She'd expected him to treat her with contempt but, whatever he was treating her with, it wasn't that.

Now she was sitting opposite an elf with unmistakably high-caste features, who could have easily passed for High Snot of the Brotherhood of Ultimate Superiority, a member of an entirely vegetarian *species*, watching him eat raw steak.

Beside her Luke snorted and said through a mouthful of fries, "Like watching Bambi eat Thumper, innit?"

Zal looked at him and he went quiet. Zal looked at Lila, a glance not unlike the way she'd once been looked at by a lion in the zoo at feeding time, the sort of glance you didn't want to linger in. She shrugged and went on with her sandwich. Until that moment she'd really begun to imagine that Zal had stepped out of Alfheim one day and decided to act on a temporary whim for a taste of the lowlife. Surely there must be traumas that elves could suffer that could allow them to be as messed up as any human rock singer or songwriter? And they must have rebellious sons and daughters with a yen for travel? Or maybe he was born with an unusual talent that had never had any outlet in Lyrien and the wider elf nations? But now she had to put all those theories on hold. Even in situations of starvation she had never come across any evidence of elves eating flesh. They would rather die.

After a few more minutes Lila excused herself, checked that the room was secure, scanned outside the building, and went to the ladies. She found Poppy already in there waiting for her.

Poppy chattered excitedly about the coming tour, her hopes of finding handsome groupies, how fun it was going to be having Lila come along, as she fixed her makeup. It was the kind of gush that didn't need a response; fey friendly goodwill, like their badwill, came in seemingly random scattergun blasts that claimed anyone in range.

Lila looked at her own face—she looked clean and her metal didn't show. She looked away again. She didn't like the sight of her new face. In recreating it the surgeons had made her well, even reasonable to look at, but the face wasn't hers. It felt like it from the inside, until she saw the outside.

Lila had once had soft features, round cheeks, a pretty face. Now she was not pretty and she didn't know the word for her look these days. Her hair had grown back auburn on half her head and scarlet elsewhere, because of the magic that had stained her to the bone. They washed it out eventually, but bits of her were gone forever and in their place was this machine, strong and restless and ill at ease with the flesh that was left. They were growing into each other, her AI-self and her real body. It would take years, they said, but one day the joins would become invisible.

"Gods, I know I shouldn't say this," Poppy said, beginning to floss her pale green teeth, "but Zal really *really* likes you."

"How d'you figure that out?" Lila said.

"He watches you like *all* the time. Hadn't you noticed?"

"No," Lila said honestly. Had he been?

"No you wouldn't," Poppy said, ripping a new length of floss. "Not to worry. It's a magic thing. But I can tell."

"Hey," Lila said, feigning interest, though she didn't know what to think. She had the sense that Poppy was one of those girls who very quickly become girlfriends who like to fix up their other girlfriends with their friends and have coffee shop fantasies about the whole thing.

"And Zal doesn't like anybody like that really," Poppy added. "Not like that, you know. Especially not . . ." She paused. "Well, not."

"No, go on," Lila said, lounging against the sink as if she had all day, as if they really were friends already.

"People of nonmagical extraction," Poppy said as fast as she could. "Sorry, I know that's really not the right thing to say." She covered her mouth with her hand.

"No, no," Lila assured her. "It's fine. Who likes everyone? Anyway, I'm an employee." So, like all the others of his kind she'd ever met, he was racist. Figured.

"Yeah, but if you're like with us all the time you're one of us, right?"

Female faeries couldn't stand noninclusivity.

"Right," Lila said, smiling. "Absolutely right."

"Well, good, I'm glad we've sorted that out." Poppy smiled. She really was gorgeous, Lila thought, feeling a stab of envy that was as unwelcome as it was unusual. She reminded herself strictly that she was lucky to be alive.

"Does Jolene have a thing for Zal?" she asked as she held the door for Poppy.

"Oh big style," Poppy said. "Who doesn't?"

Lila followed her back to the table. More beer had arrived, more fancy cigarettes. They were in it for the long haul.

CHAPTER FOUR

It was three AM when Lila was finally alone in her room which adjoined Zal's in the enormous, empty house on the hill. She sat on her bed and stared around her at the unimagined luxury of the place as she listened to him moving around next door, her hearing filters deep in her AI processes grooming every minute vibration as they searched for things that shouldn't be there. Their apartments led off the ocean-view room that she'd first met him in. If she tried hard she could hear the sea. Its soft rhythm was soothing after the night's activities.

After the restaurant they'd gone to several bars. After the bars, two clubs. At the Ebony Bar, Luke had tried to hit on her.

At Lazy Daisy's a group of fans had tried to mob the whole band.

At Voudou Zulu there was an almighty street fight between The No Shows' and another band's fans, and Lila had ended up having to rush Zal through the cellars and out a back alley after punching out the drunk minder of an A-list film star who seemed determined that she'd started the entire thing.

Zal had been laughing so hard she barely managed to get him to walk. He'd asked her if he could drive back. She said no. He didn't argue. She was disappointed at his lack of response and the sulkiness made her angry and her anger made her resentful because it shouldn't have mattered that he didn't care. She rode too fast and nearly took them off the road and into a gully. By the time she'd got herself together they were walking through the echoing hallway. Jolene, who had returned home before one AM, had met them and shown Lila to her room alongside Zal's with palpable irritation. Zal had politely thanked Jolene for all her work—she was organising the whole tour after all— and Jolene had melted under his attention. Then Zal had simply shut his door on Lila. So she went into her room and shut hers with exactly the same finality.

A few moments later, as she stood in her own room, he'd opened the door that joined their two rooms, stuck his head around it and said, "Goodnight Ms. Black," and shut it again.

"Goodnight," Lila had just said to the door and the satin bedsheets and the silk throws and the platinum-coated bath taps in the Italian marble bathroom. She listened all the way out to the shoreline, and then set her sentry senses on automatic, connecting herself wirelessly to the building's security systems, so that her AI-self could do the work and she didn't have to stay awake all night. When she'd finished that she felt the weight of responsibility lift enough to let her relax a little.

Her cases had been placed at the foot of the bed. Their security locks blinked green, untouched. But Jolene had done her homework. The toiletries in the bathroom were the ones Lila always used. The robe and slippers in the room matched the ones she last bought for herself— although the ones put out for her here were of superior quality. A vase of freesias stood on the bedside table, and there was a silver-framed photograph of Okie on the wall, his black labrador coat shining in last summer's sun. Never in her life had anybody taken so much trouble to make her feel at home. Now a perfect stranger had done it because it was the business thing to do.

Lila folded the robe and put it away with the rest of the gifts in the closet, even the picture of Okie. She put the freesias into the huge bathtub that she wouldn't be using—the idea of lying naked anywhere appalled her, even if she wasn't visible to anybody, and besides, a bath was hardly the spot from which to spring into action. She took her own Berrypic from her innermost pocket and looked through her pictures the one time that she allowed herself each day. She was afraid that if she let her mind turn back any more often she'd never find the strength to get up and go forward again.

Lila's pictures: Mum and Dad and Lila and her sister Maxine standing under the trees at Windover just above the golf course that backed onto their garden. Everyone smiling. Rusty and Buster, the two retrievers, standing at the front, tongues lolling in the heat. The sun out, making everyone pink.

Julia and Beatrix, her best girlfriends, at Lila's fifteenth birthday party. In the background Dad walking out of shot holding a giant handful of balloons. Julie and Beatrix excited, holding their first glasses of sparkling wine. On the table the hands of Bryan, Mike, and Sophie from school, the rest of them cut out of shot.

Buster on his own. He's just rolled in a lot of mud and is being given a bath. He is gleefully savaging the hosepipe and water is spraying everywhere.

Rusty and Buster on the couch with Maxine's feet. Why did my family never manage to put everyone in the picture? Lila wondered. But she'd taken this one, so she only had herself to blame.

Roberto at night on the porch, a couple of years ago, the flashlight all shiny on the cellophane wrapper of the flowers he's holding, and next to him . . . Lila skipped past that one really fast. She didn't need to see herself in a ridiculous cocoa-coloured prom dress.

The last one was of the family garden. Nobody in it. It's summer and the roses are out. This is a very bad shot of a nice rose gone all blurred in close-up.

Lila put the slim wafer of the Berrypic back in her pocket. She closed her eyes and tuned to her AI-self briefly. It trawled the Otopia Tree's domestic data drags for her on a nightly basis, picking out all the news about her family and friends. Everyone was fine. Rusty was at the vet's for a thorn in his paw. Julia was getting married . . . oh my god . . .

Lila's eyes flashed open. She saw an image of her own memorial, shiny and fresh, black marble spangled with rain at the summit of the cemetery on Windover Hill. *Here lies Lila Amanda Black* . . .

There wasn't really such a thing, not yet. It was her imagination. Her family believed her missing in action. Her room at home was still there. They kept it in case she returned, knowing she would if she could. Agreeing to a contract of silence with Incon had seemed the easy and obvious thing for Lila when she was lying in bed at the hospital, under heavy sedation. Later, during her long, painful rehabilitation at the clinic, it had seemed less certain. When she realised the extent of her injuries and the consequences of her Mending, she'd made up this image of the memorial as a way of coping with what she came to see as her death. She expected, somehow, to be the same Lila, in spite of the fact that she was now a one-woman walking army, but when she looked inside she didn't find her old self there. Even the pictures had a strange look to them, like they were things she'd been handed from someone else's life. She could never walk back into her old world, but there was consolation of a kind in thinking that it hadn't changed a bit. Except that Julia was getting married and Lila would not be there.

Julia had been her best friend all through school and college and they'd kept in touch through their later lives. They had planned their weddings and divorce settlements in meticulous, ridiculous detail a thousand times. All very silly, but now her heart squeezed tightly.

She heard Zal turn the shower on. One of the guards checked in with her to report everything quiet. Technically she was now permitted to sleep.

Lila took her suit off. When she went to hang it up she found three more the same waiting in plastic wrappers on their hangers. "Cute," she said aloud and left them there. She took a fast shower and examined herself carefully where her skin was grafted to the biometallic structures that had saved her. Some of them were red and angry where she'd sat too long or where cloth had rubbed them, but nothing too bad, nothing worth reporting. Her internal medical systems informed her she needed rest. All adaptations were proceeding at expected pace. Half her body and brain might be metal and synthetics, but that didn't change basic requirements.

Lila was used to the routines of self-checking, tending, and managing herself. She was fast and efficient with the machines stored in her smaller case; a toolkit for self-maintenance. The last one was a power unit diagnostic that tested her reactor block. It was running sweetly. The fist-sized tokamak would outlast her, if nobody blew it up.

She brushed her teeth and then, so that she could sleep properly, checked and cleaned the medical equipment that she carried inside her thigh armour on both sides. Then the guns. Everything moved silently and smoothly. All her systems greenlighted.

She dressed herself with the measured, gentle movements of Zen ritual in black, close-fitting fatigues and put on her upper body armour with its third gun and other supplies, brushed out her wet hair and lay down on top of the hand-painted satin coverlet. Her boots felt clunky and uncomfortable on the soft surface, but that couldn't be helped.

She heard Zal get out of the shower—that took ages, she thought; check for elfy fastidiousness—and then there was silence.

Julia is getting married, Lila said to herself, curling up. She wanted sleep because she longed to escape, but at the same time, she didn't want to sleep. Sleep meant dreams. She lay quietly. Her eyes were sore and tired, so she closed them to let them rest.

Two hours later she heard a tiny, odd noise. She woke hearing it and knowing it was trouble from a distance, alert and fully able, though only a split second before she had been deeply asleep. The jolt of her heart was the only symptom of her sudden transition and even that was soon gone into the smooth, cold world of action. She was only a beginner in fighter terms, but her AI was a master and it seamlessly moved her from sleeping to waking before sliding back to lie in her nerves like an obedient pet. She felt a frisson of anxiety—it was a rebellious pet—but the AI absorbed that too.

Lila slid off the bed and crossed to the door, put her ear to it, and turned up all her sensors. The slight sounds that had disturbed her were very small, very stealthy, and far distant. Her AI-self showed her a plotted location—right at the back wall of the building.

There was no reason for Lila to sneak, but she moved quickly and reasonably quietly out of her room and through the ocean room, where nightlights in recesses close to the floor showed her that there was nobody there. The sounds had stopped. Perhaps their maker had heard her? But then they began again and Lila pinpointed them at the other end of the house, where the second storey backed into the hillside and it would be easy to hop onto the flat roofs of the kitchens once the guards had been passed.

She accessed the house controls, using her Doublesafe code, and turned off all interior lights. Instantly she was plunged into darkness, but she could see relatively well on infrared, well enough that she could better a human attacker, and match a magical one. In response to her action another silence ensued, broken only by the sounds of various sleepers and the natural noises of the night.

Lila checked in with the perimeter guard, but they'd seen nothing. The one at the back of the house was a witch, so she shouldn't have missed a trick out there, even in the thickest forest cover. There were a couple of things that might get past her: an elf, or a faery of one or other kind. Lila hoped it wasn't either of those as she ran the length of the house, passing through rooms in a blur. She passed the guest bedrooms which were semipermanently occupied by the band, but only DJ Boom had come back so far. Her door was locked and there were quiet snores brushing up against it.

Lila reached an end wall with an arched window that overlooked some of the lower roofs and was on eye level with the forest canopy some hundred metres away. Above the black line of trees the stars shone brightly, and the heat rising in vapours from the kitchen vents was almost blinding. Nevertheless she was just able to see the agile, small form of a black-clad humanoid figure jump the gap between the kitchen stores and the main building. There was a soft thump as it landed on a window ledge—so soft it could have been a night bird alighting. Lila strained to see. It went right on up the wall, climbing swiftly. By the quality and speed of movement, its relative quiet, and the fact that it was hard to see—and therefore contained most of its body heat because of an aura—Lila guessed it was an elf.

As she turned to monitor its progress, she heard the front door open and voices talking about the lights—a guard explaining it was only temporary, nothing to worry about. Poppy had come back. The sudden inrush of noise deafened Lila to the sounds on the roof. She did the only thing she could do, and doubled back towards Zal's room as fast as she could.

DJ Boom must have heard her. As she reached that room the door opened. Boom's sleepy shape turned into the corridor, facing the wrong way. Lila was going too fast. She had to leap through the gap between Boom's head and the ceiling in order to miss her—a power-assisted dive that cracked the floorboards when she took off. Lila landed on her hands, flipped once to regain her feet, and was gone even as she heard Boom calling out fearfully and then the slam of her door.

In spite of her speed she was not the first person to reach the ocean room. Poppy already stood there in front of the huge glass wall opening one of the sliding doors which led out onto the broad balcony. She was so occupied with the care of this task that she didn't notice Lila's arrival.

Lila ducked behind one of the settees as she saw that Poppy was expecting someone. That someone dropped off the roof and came in quickly. There was a flash of metal that Lila saw as deep blue against the careless red glare from a chink in the intruder's aetherial self. Poppy showed brilliantly, like a yellow ghost.

"Are you sure about this?" Lila heard Poppy whisper.

The other put their finger up to the faery's mouth and pressed it there for a moment. To Lila's surprise Poppy yawned prodigiously and backed away, but there was no time to think on it.

The new figure darted forward suddenly, towards Zal's door, so focused on its purpose that it barely flinched aside when Lila stuck her leg out and tripped it in midflight. There was a gasp and whoever it was went rolling. Lila jumped, caught a handful of cloth, and felt it rip out of her hand as the other sprang up and turned. It whipped out the knife it had been carrying and faced her for a second, then looked back and forth in clear indecision. Lila took her chance at that moment and dived forward at full stretch. She landed on top, the attacker's knife hand trapped between both of hers. She dug her reinforced fingers into the narrow wrist she was holding with maximum strength, and was rewarded by a gasp of pain. The knife fell.

Then Lila felt Poppy's hands on her shoulders, rather fumbling. The faery's proximity sent a slow shudder through her circuits and Lila felt like she was moving through treacle. The body underneath hers made a great, fishlike effort and wriggled free. It caught up the knife again. Lila threw Poppy off backwards onto one of the sofas and heard her land there with a protesting cry, but already the black-robed elf was halfway back to the balcony.

Lila freed a line in the palm of her right hand and made a desperate cast. The coils of thin braid, weighted at their flight end, wrapped around the figure's waist in a whip action. Lila yanked on half power and the figure went down on the carpet and began struggling to slash the cord. Before Poppy had a chance to recover herself, Lila spooled back the line and jumped down across the small body to pin it flat with the simple fact of her weight again. The elf stopped trying to cut the line and instead made a desperate slash at Lila's face. Lila leaned back easily only to find Poppy's hands over her eyes suddenly. The faery tried to pull her sideways, off her prisoner, but only succeeded in hurting herself as Lila was far too strong for her. As Lila brushed Poppy's hands away the elf made a lunge and she felt a sharp, fiery pain score across her side. Lila trapped the offending arm on its retreat, catching it between her own arm and her damaged ribs, and punched the elf hard in the guts. They doubled up with a near-silent aahh of agony and released the knife a second time. Then Poppy hit Lila's head with a plant pot.

Lila found herself sitting in a scatter of soil and broken crockery, holding the knife. The door to the balcony stood wide and she could hear the sea. There was no sign of her attacker.

"Oh cat's piss," she heard Poppy say despairingly from the settee. "I just *knew* you'd ruin it."

Lila got up, went across, and pulled the faery up by one arm. Poppy slowed her down again, but now it hardly mattered since Poppy had clearly quit any ideas of further violence. "What the hell was that?" Lila hissed at her.

"That *is* you, Lila?" Poppy said. She sounded terrified.

Lila coded the house to put the lights back on. "Of course it's me! Who were you expecting? The Lone Ranger?"

"It's not what it looks like," Poppy sniffed, frowning and crying at the same time. She didn't want to meet Lila's gaze and added without any conviction, "Let me go. You're hurting me."

Lila tightened her hold and brandished the knife in her other hand. "What's this for? And who was that?"

"Oww! Please!" She plucked at Lila's fingers. "It was nothing really. It wasn't going to hurt anybody. It's a magical weapon, you see? It was charmed to put him to sleep so that he couldn't go on the tour and they wouldn't be able to get him. It wouldn't have really hurt him. Now you've spoiled everything."

Lila let her go. "I've never heard anything so stupid."

Poppy rubbed her arm and looked around but nobody had yet come running. "Please," she said quietly, "Can't we forget it? Just between us. Don't tell him. Please, Lila. There's nobody else. Just the two of us. It was her and me. We're the only ones in on it."

"Who was your friend?" Now Lila could feel a trickle of blood on her skin. She felt unreasonably, unexpectedly tired.

"Nobody."

"Consider yourself under arrest."

"All right, all right!" Poppy rubbed her face and stamped her foot in pique. "It was his cousin. Okay? His cousin from Alfheim. She doesn't want him dead either—only one of his family that doesn't. You'd better leave her out of it, please, Lila, she's only twelve." The faery looked at Lila with desperate, beseeching eyes.

"Twelve!"

"*Please*, Lila." Poppy was floating two feet over the floor with anxiety. Her hands were together, begging.

Lila was suddenly too exhausted to move. Even her anger wasn't enough to keep her awake. "Poppy," she managed to say, slurring her words. "Help me." And then she fell over, her eyes closing of their own accord, and she knew no more.

CHAPTER FIVE

It was sunny. The sky was blue with streaks of high cloud. The warm air was full of the sound of splashing and the smell of freshwater and seawater alike. Lila was awake but could barely open her eyes. She was lying down on some padded kind of flat couch, and couldn't move. She could feel her body, but only the human parts. The robotics were utterly dead. There was no reaction to her thoughts to summon it to life. She struggled to make a connection, wishing she could rouse it as effortlessly as it roused her, but she realised that the power was out. What she could feel was heavy, the way she felt during the worst attack of 'flu she'd ever had. The only reason she could see anything was because one of her eyelids was slightly open. The blinding glare hurt because the apertures on her irises were set wide-open, where they'd been when the sleep charm had taken effect. There was nothing she could do. A tear formed and ran down her temple. Compared to the clinic it wasn't so bad though. And miraculously there had been no dreams. Water was running nearby.

After a minute or two she gathered that she was lying on a sun lounger beside the large, unevenly shaped swimming pool at the front of the house, not far from where it was fed by streamwater from a little forest cascade. The light was very warm but the air was full of the forest cool, so it was still early in the morning, perhaps before seven. Lila tried moving, nothing happened.

As the minutes passed she became able to sense more, through what remained of her human organs. It began to dawn on her with a creeping, stomach-churning horror that she could feel the breeze blowing a light, flappy fabric against her skin. It told her she was wearing a robe with very possibly nothing underneath it. No, surely a swimsuit? Or something. But that hardly mattered. The bare fact of her cyborg change, which she had wished to hide completely until some unspecified future of confidence and acceptability, when she might be able to reveal it to someone trusted, was on full show. Shame and fear flooded her, but even they could not make her move. Only her breathing and her heart were active and they didn't respond to her feelings at all, as though she really had slept the sleep of a thousand years.

Then a shadow fell across her—bliss for her eyes at last. She smelt a bright, mineral fragrance like bath salts.

Poppy leaned over her and carefully pushed a pair of sunglasses onto Lila's nose, settling their arms carefully over her ears. "There," she said, with the playful voice of somebody dressing a doll. "Nobody from the house will ever know you're not out here just taking some rays." She dabbed the tear from Lila's face with the tip of her finger. Lila heard her straighten up and the edge of Poppy's fragile robe brushed across her bare hand. It was agonising to be able to feel everything but be able to do nothing. Lila was desperate to know what had happened, but she didn't have to wait.

"Hey!" Poppy called out across the pool. "Zal, how long will this take?"

No, no, no, Lila was moaning, somewhere deep inside. Just when she thought it couldn't be any worse—it was. Part of the reason she'd been sent to this assignment was because Incon suspected that extremists from Elfland had picked Zal as a target through which to get some publicity for their cause. Their real motivations however, far from being directly related to rock stars or even dissident elves, were set against the furtherance of Otopian technologies, particularly nuclear reactors and cyborg systems, which they saw as abominations. Their views were the sharp end of a general trend among elves against high technology. There was no more repellent vision for an elf than a natural being invaded by inert machinery, except possibly something Undead. Although her pride and the shreds of her vanity surely burned at the idea of Zal now having a good reason to loathe her, Lila was sick with the realisation that her cover was almost certainly blown. So much for her great spy skills.

The sun came back full force as Poppy moved away. The light was like a lance straight into her brain. Lila wished herself asleep again—for a million years.

Zal's voice spoke from somewhere slightly below them both and to her right. "The counteragent should take it off in a day or so."

A day! Lila cringed. She could not, would not even let herself think about being Poppy's new lifesize robo-Barbie for an entire day, though before she could squash the idea she had already seen herself dressed and redressed and stood up as a piece of living statuary somewhere embarrassing while Poppy talked the entire time about what great fun it all was. The only possible mercy was that faeries in their human forms were generally so congenial that they wouldn't let her come to any harm. Even so, it was unbearable, but Zal hadn't finished . . .

"I can speed things up, probably." She heard him get out of the pool and then he moved into her field of vision as he stood up. He was a lithe silhouette, dripping with diamonds.

"She's gonna be *so* mad," Poppy whispered, close to him.

Lila could see Poppy as a green-tinged shadow surrounded by diaphanous cloth that floated on the air. She was so close to Zal that there was only a tiny strip of light between them. Poppy's outline jittered and she sounded strung out.

"Please Zal," she said. "You can talk to her. She likes you. She'll be cool. I'm so tired. I have to get some sleep. Oh come on, don't look at me like that. You already forgave me, remember? Pretty please? I'd do it for you."

Zal snorted with laughter and folded his arms across his chest.

Poppy's tone changed from pleading to pretended anger, the kind that only very good friends can exert with one another. "You are so bloody High Elfy sometimes, you bastard. Come on."

"Only if you swear you won't take any more pixie dust until the tour's over. That's why you can never sleep. And fixing it gives me a headache."

"I swear, I swear!" Poppy danced from foot to foot.

"And no more enchanted knives and midnight assassination attempts with school-age conspirators? Making me rescue my own bodyguard? Wiping the mess off your face?"

"No, no, no! Come on, Zal. I'll do anything, anything, baby, cross my heart, pleeze! This is the last time. I promise. I'll be so good."

"You're full of it," he said wearily, and took her in his arms and kissed her. He picked her up and they moved out of sight.

The sun blasted Lila, although the glasses cut the worst of it. She fought just to move one finger. Nothing.

"Mmmnn," she heard Poppy sigh. "That's perfect. One more time till I can't hear the sea . . ."

Lila remembered Poppy yawning in the same tone the night before, at a very un-yawny moment, when the other elf, the cousin, had touched her.

"My reverse prince . . ." she heard Poppy sigh.

"Pixie shit," Zal muttered, almost beneath hearing.

Wood creaked. The trees soughed in the wind. Lila's robe flapped and her hair moved. Heavy fabric rustled not far away. Lila wondered—she thought Poppy and Zal were going to do something else, but had he put her to sleep? Was it a feature of elf/faery interaction she'd never known about before? If only she could see . . .

Zal's shadow fell across Lila's face. She tried to close her eye, but it didn't.

He sat down next to her and she felt something brushing over her forehead—a feather. Zal hummed something wordless, tuneless, a mesmer that seemed to circle as the feather circled, and a tingling sensation spread down from her forehead and all through her. Occasionally he stopped and flicked the feather away from them both, as though shaking water off it. The tingling stopped.

Then he got up and stood astride her lounger, feet on the floor. She blinked and could see a little better.

Zal bent down so that his face was only a short distance from hers, his hands on his knees. His long wet hair fell across her chest and the water from it spread out, suddenly cold, through her robe.

"I know you can hear me," he said, and she thought he was smiling. "I have to do this last part to wash the charm right out." He held up the black feather. "I want you to know that it's perfectly justified and that I'm not just feeling you up, although I am doing that too." He reached down and separated the front of her gown.

A fury, alternately cold and hot, started burning in Lila. She privately promised herself that she would make him pay for this, and soon. How dare he?

He slid his hand down softly across her breast, over her ribs, and pressed the feather against the place where she was cut by the knife. It suddenly stung with agonising sharpness and Lila felt new tears spring into her eyes. Zal said something in a language she didn't catch, though she was reasonably sure it wasn't elvish. She could feel his *andalune* aethereal body suddenly concentrate itself around the place. The touch of it was more intimate even than his skin on hers and it made different tears rise and replace the angry ones, though she didn't like that it had that power and she still fiercely resented his invasion, even if it was so wretchedly caressing and kind.

Then Zal took the feather off. Lila saw it crumple into dust and be swept away on the breeze as he put his finger on the bridge of her shades and slid them down her nose. Lila glared into his dark, slanting eyes. He grinned at her. "You should have let those two idiots have their fun," he said. "The day I get sneaked up on by a twelve-year-old is the day you can drown me and throw me in a Dumpster."

Lila ran a startup on main power. It responded perfectly. The tokamak was a second sun, deep in her belly, vivid with raw energies.

He sighed. "Poppy wanted me to tell you that your secrets are all safe with her, so long as she's not under arrest."

"And you?" Lila found her voice fully functional.

"I'm sure we'll come to some arrangement, Agent Black."

Lila opened her eyes wide. Zal blinked and flinched as the sun reflected off her silver irises and in that instant she put her hands on his chest and threw him backwards into the pool. It was a good throw—five metres. Nothing wrong with the machine. She stood up and belted the ridiculous faery robe.

Zal surfaced and shook the water out of his hair. He glided away from her on his back towards the far side, watching her with that maddening catlike calm. She saw his eyes trail her up and down quite slowly.

Lila looked down. The prosthetics of her legs and the way they had been grown into her made them look like chrome stockings. The robe was obviously one of Poppy's—it didn't so much conceal anything as hint at concealment, but then give it up as a pointless effort. She saw her own arms, where they were real skin, crisscrossed with pink and silver scars, stained with red like splashes of paint. She glared across at the faery, but Poppy was asleep, all but entirely hidden under an outsize bathtowel.

Zal got out of the pool. "Don't thank me," he said to her as he walked past, almost but not quite brushing her arm. He didn't glance at her.

"*Thank* you," Lila said through gritted teeth. She followed him back into the house.

Zal went into his room and shut the door on her. She guessed he was going to go back to bed.

She found all her armour and clothing laid on the floor of her room. Nothing was missing. There was a small tear in the vest where the knife tip had punctured it. The knife itself was on her mahogany side table. She was examining it when there was a knock at the adjoining door.

"Lila?" It was Zal.

She waited until she was fully dressed in her fatigues and then opened it.

He was still standing there, dry and fully clothed. He didn't seem angry or upset. He handed her an envelope and she recognised the faery vellum with a sinking feeling.

"Another letter?"

"They're not big on e-mail in the magical nations," Zal said, watching her take the sheet of paper out and open it.

It was in the highly cursive elvish script but she could read it. She could not read the magical symbolism that wavered in the air above it, crackling with static electricity that made the connectors in her fingers tingle. "Thanks," she said, betraying none of her dismay at its vitriol. "I'm going to send it in for a complete analysis."

"You needn't bother," he said. "It's from the Jayon Daga, the Elvish Secret Service. The usual. *Go back where you came from or die.* With the added charm of their special seal."

He wasn't mentioning the chain of curses that circled the edge of the page, nor the hatred directed at him through the charms which he must have felt as soon as he touched it. Lila was grateful she only had to see the words.

"The seal means this is the last warning," Lila said with dismay. She knew about Daga seals. She'd hoped never to see one again. "I need to talk to Jolene and," she hesitated—yes, he'd said Agent Black, no, she wasn't ready to admit everything, "and to my bosses. I don't think we can carry on."

"We are carrying on," Zal said with complete confidence. He reached for the letter but Lila twitched it away from him.

"It's not worth dying for," Lila said, stating what she thought was
the obvious.

"Compared with what?" Zal stepped back suddenly, and beckoned
her in. She hesitated, still smarting from the events earlier, but swallowed her feelings and obeyed. He made a vague gesture that she
should take a seat anywhere. She didn't want to risk making prolonged
eye contact because she knew that would only tend to make her agree
with whatever he said, so she walked around instead and made a
minute search of the entire room, wondering at what had prompted
him to make this concession.

She found out nothing, only that he was tidy and that everything
was elven-made including his regular clothing and stage clothes. On
the wall opposite the bed was a huge larger-than-lifesize original
painting of a dramatically sprawled female demon. It was by Laetitia,
the faery artist. About the demon other figures seemed to hover in
forms that might be of any of the Severed Realms, but they could have
been steam rising from the demon's crimson skin. The erotic charge
was a bit of a shock amid the leaf tones and neutrals of the rest of the
place. Lila tried not to stare, although it was very beautiful. She sat
down on the edge of the bed and waited.

Zal leaned against the table beneath the painting and said, "I'll
spare you the speech about not fitting in. I'm sure you can imagine
what it's like to be different to everyone else, never meeting their
expectations. I'll be surprised if they're the only ones out to stop me.
But they're not going to. You can help me, or you can leave."

"It's not that simple. There was only a vague threat until today. If
they stick to their usual ways, there are now a pair of elvish assassins
out to get you who think they have a free shot any time after midnight
tonight." She made herself face him. "I want to report and check back
with my office team and then go back to the studio and check something there. I don't think there's anything here to worry about until
the clock strikes twelve, not from them at least. JD are very rule-

oriented. I need to get some more gear too. Under the circumstances, I think you should leave here by this afternoon and stay in separate locations from the rest of the band unless you're on stage. I'll be back for you in two hours. Until then, do nothing, go nowhere."

He nodded, "And if I say no?"

"Then I quit."

"I don't think that's up to you now, is it?"

"It's up to me," Lila said. "There are other agents who'll do it."

Zal smiled when she made herself break with his gaze. "Well, I want the girl secret agent who looks like a million dollars. No, it's probably several billion dollars, isn't it?"

"More than you can afford," she retorted.

He gave her a glance that left her in no doubt he was mentally undressing her. "So, if the Jayon Daga are coming, and I only have sixteen hours left to live, how do you feel about charity?"

"Ask me in fifteen hours and fifty-eight minutes," Lila said sweetly and walked out, cursing herself this time because she could not or would not—she wasn't sure which—stop playing the cursed stupid Game.

CHAPTER SIX

Lila rode up to the studio building, passed it, and parked a couple of blocks away. She walked back and introduced herself to the receptionist, explaining that Zal had left something behind and she'd come to collect it. The man let her in without a comment, and gave her a guest badge to let her through the inside doors unescorted. It never ceased to surprise her how easy it was to get most places. She would have sacked him on the spot.

Yesterday the actual studio where the musicians worked had been so full of people and instruments she'd had no chance to do a proper scrub search for spying devices or other things. Now it was briefly empty during a lunchbreak and she let herself in and allowed power to run through her specialised sensors. She could clearly see and hear the bug upstairs, its radio signals and the electromagnetic frequencies of its small operations converging to a focused point. There were no other electronics out of place. Temporarily satisfied, because there were no plans to come back here soon, and so no reason to be particularly worried, Lila went back to her bike and called for assistance from the office. She could not dislodge the nagging feeling that she had missed something important and she wasn't about to let it go—the receptionist's attitude had been the cap on a slowly filling bottle of discontent—but if there was something it must be magical, not physical, and she couldn't detect it. As she waited for one of her colleagues she walked the local streets, looking for any devices that might be responding to the bug.

Her hopes were soon fulfilled. An old sedan car, slumped across the curb one block west of the studio, was sending a brief ping response to let the listening device know it was around. Lila walked past it, as though on her way somewhere else, and glanced in casually. It was unoccupied. The receiver was inside the stereo unit. She checked the street and stepped across to the nearest door, sliding her fingers around the handle. The car unlocked itself as the frequency picker in her hand acquired the right signal and she let herself in and sat down in the soggy leather driver's seat.

The stereo was of the very old style that were all one with the dash, but closer inspection revealed that it contained a recording unit which even now had a Berrytone installed and running. The Berry's hard disk was three-quarters full and Lila reckoned it could hold at least seventy-two hours' worth of noise. That being so, and given the age of the bug itself, Lila was prepared to bet that the Berries must be collected regularly and the car moved around. It was the kind of gear you used in a lengthy surveillance; human, rather old, rather reliable.

She quickly searched under the seats, and in the glovebox, but the car was reasonably professionally maintained—there was nothing to find. As a last resort, and in the absence of any signals that might indicate booby traps, she decided to pop the trunk. She got out and walked around to the back of the car. Kids crossed the end of the street, but none came towards her. Explanations for the recordings—anything from tax to blackmail to bootlegs—were running through her mind as she opened the lock and lifted the lid, and so she was completely taken by surprise when a small black shape leaped out at her. It shot out with such desperate velocity that it struck her shoulder a hard blow. She heard claws rip her suit and snag in the armoured jerkin she wore as she whirled to see a cat land easily on the road behind her.

The beast turned to hiss at her, and even though it was noon she could see the faint smokiness of working magic around it. In the blink of an eye it became more like a weasel than a cat, and then suddenly more like a rat, changing shapes as it struggled with its own surprise and the fact that it found itself in daylight. Lila made a grab for it, but it was too fast. In a second it had broken up into a watery slither of shadows and flowed down through the rim of a drain into the comforting blackness of the sewers.

Back on the underside of the trunk lid Lila could see faint bloody markings starting to vanish as their spell was completed. Whoever had left the charm would soon be receiving information as to who had disturbed their gear. Small, dark magics like this one were common in the criminal world. Faeries had no respect for law or order and humans bought them from the fey.

Lila's scalp smarted and she realised with annoyance that the creature had managed to snag a few of her hairs. She had to bite on her frustration that her help hadn't appeared sooner so she could have caught and traced the charm, but she had no ability with aetherial creations of any kind, being simply human and simply machine. All she could do was watch the telltales flicker and die in the daylight, shut the lid, and leave the car to continue doing its work.

Back at her bike she met the faery special agent she'd requested. Malachi was a Rowan spirit, belonging to the Anthracite nation, his skin and hair as blackly sparkling as pure coal, his eyes a surprising ash-berry red, which meant he was often mistaken for a demon by humans; something which always delighted him. He was well used to running around after his human colleagues and seemed pleased to see her out of the confines of the office and the medical suites where she'd spent most of the last year. Lila had always found him trustworthy and kind. They chatted for a few minutes, catching up before she briefed him.

"Just a feeling? Sure you haven't got the . . ." and he shivered his hand back and forth to indicate a feel for magic.

"I'm sure. Call it intuition."

"If there's nothing to see, I'll have to put it down to the usual."

"Cheese, chocolate, pickles." Lila smiled, feeling better with the old joke. "Haven't had any in days."

Malachi got in and out of the studio on a faked engineer's ticket and the diversion of his fey charm and returned in less than twenty minutes. His face was serious and he was almost trotting, his shiny shoes clipping the pavement like a tap dancer's as he reached her.

"Your gut must have faery sympathies, or something else," he said. "There is something there, trouble is, I can't say what." His reflective skin and hair seemed to run with sunlight as he gave her a helpless shrug. "It's very deep and very old and . . . I got this feeling off it that —this sounds crazy—that it was there before the Bomb. Way before the studio."

Lila stiffened. Before the Quantum Bomb there had been, allegedly, a single world with a single history. After the Bomb it had been divided into the Severed Realms. Each of the new realms lay alongside the first world, which had been Earth and was now called Otopia. Each realm had an immediate history as long as or longer than the Earth's. And experience and archaeological study had taught Lila that the Bomb had peppered the time of all realms with fragments of things: the past, the future, objects, persons, and above all, magic or I-space energy. Before the Bomb that kind of thing had existed nowhere but in human imagination. But Before the Bomb was a matter of extreme debate and political difficulty. She could feel her old diplomatic hackles rise at the thought of discovering an artefact that would cast doubt on the human version of history.

"If I hadn't been looking, I'd never have seen it," Malachi said uncomfortably. "I'm not sure—it could be an echo fragment of the explosion, you know? Like a geological fault? Trouble with Bomb fragments is that they often look like they're something they're not, especially ejecta from so close to the original site, which is, unfortunately, pretty much everything from Bay City to Old Salt Lake. I need more help to find out. Probably have to dig down."

"But if it's been there that long then it's very unlikely to be anything to do with rock stars and their publicity is it?" Lila said, rather surprised at her own spitefulness as she spoke the words.

"Getting up your cuff is he?" Malachi asked with a smile, glad to be changing subject.

"Nothing I can't manage." Lila checked the time and got back on her bike. "Give you a ride back? I'm going to see Sarasilien."

"Darling!" Malachi objected and pointed to his smart clothes. "I'm strictly a car boy. Say hi to the old charlatan from me. And put a helmet on."

Lila waved and tried not to notice how Malachi had failed to completely quell her disquiet. She spun the bike around in an entryway and, as she passed him on the way back, saw him studying the ground of the parking lot outside the studio with such absorption he didn't lift his head, only his hand in a farewell.

Her ride to Incon's facility was hot and dusty and full of lazy midday traffic. Lila was later than she meant to be when she finally rode into the subterranean garage of the undistinguished office block on the city outskirts. She took the express elevator down, bypassing the street levels and the administrative floors. Barely was the dust out of her hair before she presented herself before her—she didn't know what he was anymore; healer, friend?—before Sarasilien, the only elf agent within the NSA, and the one who had saved her from death of her magical wounds.

His rooms were the largest and most peculiarly appointed of all the strangely outfitted rooms in the building. Technology and magical instrumentation fought for space across several tables and desks. Sand trays and inkstands lay under the glow of virtual keyboards, marked with the awkward runes of a dozen magical languages. Giant-sized Berrypics covered the walls with manuscript, evidence charts, duty logs, and glorious vistas of other realms. Server racks hummed quietly. Magical test rigs, filling the air with strange, light-bending architectures, funnelled I-space contingencies out of the room and out of the universe. Sarasilien's tall, blue-and-grey-clad figure stood at one of these.

To Lila, even though they bore no physical resemblance, the elf's tall, elegantly spare form and long, silvering chestnut and gold hair immediately reminded her of her father. When he turned to greet her, the strong slanting of his features on their angular bones and the sudden small movements of his long ears—their attenuated tips were as high as the crown of his head—should have put paid to that impression, but they didn't. She couldn't even detect a trace of warmth in him as he came towards her, silver stitches in his clothing glinting, his face as stern as a patrician statue, manner as composed as a king's.

Sarasilien's *andalune* body had always been tightly controlled—he kept it completely subdermal for most of his time in Otopia, she understood—but, since encountering Zal, Lila was suddenly much more aware of the possibility of its presence, and curious, since she had never witnessed Sarasilien displaying it. His control of it was, she knew, a sign of extreme self-mastery, a thing as rare in elves as any race. Its absence had been a key factor in the comfort she felt with him before. Now, that comfort seemed to be gone.

Her awkwardness with him made her self-conscious, and that made her more awkward. She was suddenly ill at ease before his calm, and cast her eyes towards his boots rather than his face. She thought suddenly of Zal, though Zal had never once made her think of Sarasilien. Her reasons for being here, at all, were suddenly unclear to her. Now that she saw him she became more sure that the need she had to talk to him was nothing to do with the case, but entirely personal, and that seemed like a weak and insubstantial reason to be here.

"Lila," Sarasilien said and lifted her chin with his hand, so she must look at him. "Are you well?"

His concern manifested as a much slighter expression than it would have merited on a human face. Even when moved deeply, his face showed only hints of what he felt. But Lila was tugged by the care, more than she wanted. "I'm fine. Sorry. It's been tougher than I thought."

Sarasilien looked down into her eyes and the ghost of a smile made his lips turn at the corners. His cheek dimpled very faintly and she saw the tips of his long ears turn more closely towards his head. He was really very glad to see her. "You look well, although your presentation has more of the urchin than the goddess about it. Town must be busy."

"It was," she agreed and then she stepped forward impulsively and hugged him. She had missed him. She'd had no idea how much until that second. Perhaps it was to be expected, after they'd worked so closely for so long to get her fit again, mentally and physically at least. Emotionally she clearly had a way to go.

She felt his *andalune* body very briefly on the exposed skin of her hands and face, like a breath of air that had come off the tops of a cold and lonely mountain. After a second of his normal reticence he embraced her back, and then he set her from him, not unkindly. "What brings you here?"

She sat down on one of the guest chairs, looking around the familiar room with its oak-panelled walls, library bookshelves, and the largest of all the Berries, showing the white-capped mountains that Sarasilien called his home, very far from Otopia. "Isn't seeing you enough?" she asked, not certain she could tell him everything on her mind.

"Yes, but that's not the matter." He was standing close by a book table suitable for viewing very large volumes. He closed the one that lay open there and folded his hands in front of him.

Lila was sure she had his full attention and it daunted her. "I don't think I can carry through this job," she confessed.

"Why not?"

"I don't know. It's too much like facing everything too fast."

"Because Zal is an elf?"

"Because Zal is *not* an elf," Lila countered, glancing into his green eyes and seeing the sympathy she was looking for, bound inside a world of strict expectations; emerald in ice. "I was ready for him to be like you. Not as kind. Even like the Daga agents maybe. But like you. And he isn't. And he is. Oh, hell . . . I'm getting this all wrong!"

"Tell me the facts."

That was more like it, Lila thought, wishing she'd done that to begin with. She found coherence now she was on familiar ground. "A lot of the hate mail the band receives is standard stuff, nasty but not dangerous. The letters that made Incon decide to act are still coming —I brought them." She took them out of the pocket of her armoured vest and the dagger with them and held them out to Sarasilien.

He took them, careful not to touch the knife but balance it on the envelopes. He set them on the book table and with one finger pushed them apart. As he inspected them and began to open the letters Lila continued.

"I can't read magic, despite everything we've tried. I can't do that and I don't think he tells me what they really say. And the knife . . ." She explained the whole story of that incident as Sarasilien read the letters, one after another. She could see him controlling his reactions carefully so that barely a twitch of one ear betrayed him. Nonetheless he sighed with relief when he was able to put them down.

She didn't tell him all about the knife. Not the part about Zal touching her or the remark he'd made. Or the Game they were playing. She willed Sarasilien to guess it, so that she didn't have to admit making such a stupid move, so he'd take her off the assignment and she could avoid the shame. But her will had all the effect of her efforts at sorcery.

Sarasilien examined the dagger very closely indeed. He spoke to it and Lila saw words deep within the metal rise to the surface at his command. Wisps of black and silver ran along the edges of the blade and dripped into the air at its tip only to swirl and vanish quickly. As he went to put it down, the knife twisted somehow in his fingers and she heard him take a sharp, short breath.

Blood ran down the knife together with the white and black, the orange-hued scarlet of elf blood quickly deepening to crimson as it fell and bore magic with it onto the letter paper underneath. Immediately all the pages burst into flame.

Sarasilien spoke a single word and the burning pages and the bloodied knife became frozen in space and time, as though in a photograph. He muttered over his finger and went into the bathroom suite that led off his rooms to tend it. When he came back he sat down beside Lila on the other guest chair and looked into her eyes. He seemed very sad and she braced herself, for she'd never seen him make a mistake before, and although the cut was small and the sleep charm already used up, she was afraid.

"You did well to get them here. The blade was spelled to want to cut elf flesh. It was a magic of higher than the Seventh Level. I don't doubt that if it had found its way close to Zal it would have done more than make him sleep. But you say an elf carried it and used it against you?"

"That's what Poppy—that's what the faery said. But they were in league. She may have lied."

"There's more than elvish magic in it," Sarasilien said, pressing his cut finger gently with his thumb, a rueful expression on his face.

Lila sensed he was calculating what to say so that he didn't upset her, or perhaps for political reasons. Silences within Incon were even more obscure than ordinary elven silences.

"I cannot tell you any more until all of this has been discussed with my masters," he said. "Only that this is not about race hate, or anything to do with the purity of the musical industry. It wears those faces, even through the Daga, but they are only servants of another intent."

"I thought the Daga served Alfheim and its goals," Lila said with disappointment, ignoring the flash of fear that had streaked through her like lightning when he spoke.

"So they would have us believe," Sarasilien said. Now his face was troubled and Lila really began to worry.

"Isn't it so?"

"Possibly."

He was quickly lost in labyrinths of thought, Lila saw. Tentatively she reached out to touch his arm, the hurt one. "Talk to me?"

He looked at her hand and smiled his slight smile that was never truly joyous because it held too many years. "I cannot. I will when I am able."

"Tell me at least if it's personal or business then."

"Both. Come, that's not all you had to tell me."

"Diverter," she accused him gently. "Well, the other thing is that I've tried to find out who Zal is and there is no record. It isn't his real name I suppose, but how do I get further? Like an idiot I already told him mine so I can't even trade for it." The words sounded efficient, unlike the beating of her heart which was far too fast for someone merely sitting in a pleasant room. Behind Sarasilien's shoulder she could see the frozen fire of the vellum and the knife in midair, holding to his word.

He didn't question her research. "So, it's not in the names of the living," he said after a pause. "What about the dead?"

Lila blinked. "You think necromancy? He's not Undead. No way."

"Not necessarily," he said. "Mistakes are made. Elves are hard to kill. Sometimes they are thought to be dead, are buried and rise again, alive, much later when time has healed them. Records aren't always updated. Outright deaths are the only straightforward ones. Even great wounds and sickness aren't always fatal, and the same goes double for magical attacks. Also, the magic of Resurrection does not always create Undead ones, though I am not versed in the Necromancer's art."

Lila closed her eyes for a second to search the databases. When she opened them she was looking straight into green eyes, clear as glass. "Nothing there either. Not even things that look like they could be shortened to Zal."

"It's not a syllable of modern elvish," Sarasilien said. "But it does occur in older languages, when we had more dealings with some of the other realms than we do now. Perhaps it's only a stage name. Did you ask?"

"No," Lila admitted. "There was never a right moment."

He did understand this time. His long eyes narrowed, became hooded. "Lila, are you playing a Game with him?"

"Are you playing one with me?"

His eyes narrowed with a flash of anger he didn't bother to restrain. "You know better than that."

"It started before I knew I was even doing it!" Lila cried in anguish, sorry for hurting him and angry with herself. "When I realised . . . it was already on."

"And which one do you think it is?"

"I'm no expert," she said humbly, picking at a loose thread where the magical messenger had clawed her vest. "I don't know how to read them."

"Lila," he said and waited for her to look at him.

How she hated that waiting! He would wait until sunset, midnight, the next day, until she did what he wanted. So she might as well do it now and have to suffer the disappointment in his face. She looked up.

His serious, intent focus was all on her. She felt like she was being minimised in the bolt of a ray gun, shrinking inside. But all he said was, "Don't pretend to be a fool. You're nothing of the kind. It demeans all of us." Then he let her go and turned away, getting up to go back to the still flames and the blade. "This can still be read, as long as the fire is stopped, but the fire can't be put out, so this will have to do. Not that I need to read it again. Do you want to know what it says?"

"Yes," Lila said, wanting to take on any burden he asked.

"It says that Zal's blood will separate all the realms completely and forever, saving Alfheim from imminent destruction, and that he is the axis of a Great Spell."

"A magical Quantum Bomb," Lila said.

"Just so. The Great Spell it proposes here requires a living sacrifice, to maintain the Spell's power. It also requires someone adept in two opposing magical disciplines, whose nature has been sundered from any purity of line and become a fusion of two or more of the realms. You say Zal healed you with a crow's feather? There is no such elvish magic. That is a thing of Demonia, or Thanatopia, depending on the charm." Sarasilien picked up the knife again from its place in the air, more carefully this time, and with distaste. "This blade was not related to that threat, though. It comes from elsewhere. But it also has two magics on it. Elvish and faery. As well as another, old word I cannot say." He ran into another silence.

After a minute Lila said, "There may be an old faultline running through the east end of town. A Bomb fault. Malachi found it. And somebody's recording everything in that studio. I put a watcher on it. But I doubt anyone will come to collect. I tripped a telltale."

Sarasilien reacted as though he hadn't heard her. "This Game with Zal, whatever it is, must be brought to an end. If these papers are correct, or even if the people behind them *think* they are correct whether or not this spell is what they claim, then the Game will get in the way of you doing your duty, both of protecting him and of protecting the interests of Otopia. So whatever it is, and whatever the stakes are, and however it must be finished—finish it."

Lila bit her lip in silence. Inwardly she rejected his idea as though he'd suggested she drink poison. That resentment was the effect of the Game, she knew, though that didn't make it any easier to resist.

The power of Games derived from wild magic which could manifest in any time at any place, even in Otopia. A Game was made when two players, at least one of them an aetheric Adept, came into conflict of some kind within the influence of wild magic—the raw aether produced by the I-space vacuums—which trickled through the spacetimes of the various realms as water trickles through gaps in the rocks of a streambed. In Otopia raw aether was almost undetectable to humans, being in its least manifest form, and so they were particularly vulnerable to it and often snared, though two humans together, being not Adept but Inept, never formed Games.

Most Games were like traps, some small enough to step right out of on the instant when you realised they were on, and others big and labyrinthine enough that the hapless victim would never find their way free. You might end up in a duel, or promising away your worldly goods, or falling in love, or slaved to a duty not of your own choosing, depending on what situation you were in when the wild magic curled around the deepest and darkest motivations of your mind. Games waited in moments of unacknowledged intent and personal conflict, especially when a person desired something but denied the desire. Wild magic wanted to manifest secrets, to bring the hidden into the world.

All the Games so made had their rules of course, be they known or unknown to the players, and once these were tacitly accepted—once a person made any move at all which confirmed their awareness of one of these rules or their awareness that a Game was on—then they were committed to become a player, and must play until the Game was ended by Victory, Defeat, or Death.

The Great Otopian Downswing of 2020, in which the economy had almost collapsed, had resulted from a faery cartel using Games to dupe wealthy human business owners into selling their companies literally for songs. The fraudulent use of Gaming was then made illegal, resulting in a rash of lawsuits in which losing or bound players sought to sue for damages against their co-Gamers (though this did not release them from the Games they were caught up in). Finally, due to the lawyers becoming subject to Games which required them to lose their cases and to a complete inability to enforce payments awarded, all legal intervention had been abandoned and once more it was Player Beware. Gaming had become the subject of science and was studied in Otopian Universities, though it was practised by the elves, the fey, and the demons more like an art.

One feature that was proven was that the rules were determined by the Opener's intentions, and thus so were the conditions of victory and loss. It was not always clear who the Opener was . . . Lila did not know whether she had started this Game or whether Zal had, only that elves and humans often fell into them whether they liked it or not. Elves had the upper hand most of the time and enjoyed winning. They liked to play though they denied liking it, unlike demons who were crazy about Games. Humans mostly lost, but the Game magic made both sides do their damnedest to win. Sometimes at all costs. You could get murder transformed to manslaughter with Game pleas, easy.

This all ran through her mind in the single moment of her annoyance and rebellion.

Sarasilien caught her arm as she stood up. He was close to her and his *andalune* stung her sharply with the force of his will; a biting cold grip of compulsion, a taste of acid. "End it Lila. Even if you have to lose."

She glared at him and tried to pull away, but he didn't let her. The look he gave her made her sure that he pretty much understood all that losing might entail, and that it was very little short of her life. She had almost lost that before by playing a deadly Game with elves, and he had freed her from it. Now she must free herself, and he was not about to give her any more assistance until she did.

"I understand," she said finally and he let her go. The brief magic that had bound them flared away, silvering mist to either side. Her spirits sank.

"We all know how it feels to lose," Sarasilien said, although his words were no apology for winning this time.

CHAPTER SEVEN

Lila signed out her heavy armour from the Incon arsenal and loaded it into a backpack. She stowed her additional weapons and other items on her vest and in her bike bags. The armourer, a friendly ex-SAS officer, watched her strip and check each of her guns and their ammunition.

"Expecting trouble?"

"My assassination has turned into a likely kidnapping, I think," she said. It was difficult to talk or think because of the reprimand ringing in her ears. Well deserved, she felt, but that made it worse. "I've requested more field support, but I don't think I'll be able to persuade my clients to do the smart thing and cancel their public appearances, so it's all looking somewhat fifty-fifty."

"Do you trust him?"

"Who?" Lila saw the soldier nod his head in the direction of Sarasilien's rooms and the Forensics Unit. Clearly from his face he wasn't so sure. She nodded.

"Good. Got everything you want?"

"I can't carry any more," Lila admitted. "Who knows whether any of this will count anyway?"

"You can *stop* them with this." The sergeant patted her pack, fifty pounds heavier. "Who cares if they die or not, hey?"

"Yeah." Lila gave him a tough grin—at least, she hoped that's what it was. He was trying to show solidarity with her situation, she assumed, but she'd have liked him a lot more if he'd never made the remark. She shouldered the pack and bags on her own, and they were very heavy so that it was all she could do not to stagger. The fleshy parts of her shoulders instantly hurt with the pressure of the straps. "Have a great day, Sarge."

"Sir, yes sir," he said, giving her a friendly salute.

Lila let her discomfort show after she'd rounded the corner. She still couldn't get used to outranking people twice her age, and it was weird commanding his respect when she'd lost Sarasilien's five minutes earlier.

The last thing she had to do was check in with her support crew: the medics and engineers who had built her as their first prototype cyborg officer. In the laboratories on the lowest level of HQ she downloaded reports and they uploaded new programs. Experts in everything from computing to dentistry checked the progress of the way that she and the machine were assimilating one another.

"Got to do something about this. Should get some bushings to fit onto the skeleton to take these kinds of loads directly," one cybernetics technician said, as they looked over the bruises on her shoulders. "Can you activate the gauntlet systems, Lila? Good. Again?"

Lila held out both arms and watched her fingers, thumbs, palms, wrists, and forearms break up and expand into a hundred different functional devices; a silent, silver storm of motion that was a blur even to her boosted vision. Fanned out they looked a little comical, like the ultimate Swiss army knife. Like this they didn't seem a part of her at all, and she was able to look at them dispassionately.

They did the same with her legs and tested the heavy armour connections and the jet propulsion systems in her lower legs and feet. Mostly the technicians didn't seem to notice that Lila had flesh or a head. They worked on their special little bit of her and muttered amongst themselves. She rather preferred that to the physiotherapist's intensive attentions and warm conversation.

"You're overdoing it on the cross-country," said the medical doctor, gently assessing the state of the red tissue where Lila's muscle and skin fused with the prosthetic's engineered biosynthetics and metals. "You're accelerating the rate of carbon uptake into your bone mass. We're risking them getting too brittle unless we slow the crystallisation down. The muscle and tendon cells aren't getting enough time to heal either. Every time you push them they're going to keep tearing because these load stresses are still higher than they can adapt to. It's not bad, but the armour power is always going to give you the illusion you're stronger than your body can take. You'll break yourself in bits if you're not careful."

"Yeah," Lila said, having heard it all before. She turned over, checking the time. "Can we speed this up? I have to go."

"As soon as Doctor Williams says you can," said Dr. Williams, Lila's psych, who had been observing at a distance for the duration of the testing, but had now come to Lila's side. She made the last of some notes with a fountain pen on an old-fashioned clipboard before setting it down. Williams observed the room in an almost bored fashion until the other techs had gone and the two of them were alone. Lila gave the white-haired old woman a smile and began to get dressed.

"I'm fine," Lila said.

"Not what I hear." Williams sat down beside her on the side of the table, hands in the pockets of her lab coat.

"Someone with pointy ears been talking to you?" Lila felt bad, and worse that it was coming straight out of her mouth. She sucked a breath in between her teeth. "I mean Special Agent Sarasilien."

"He expressed his concern."

Williams's observation, the way she spoke as Lila continued dressing, made Lila acutely aware of her underclothes and the way she put them on. She wanted to hide herself as fast as she could, feeling that her body gave her away all the time and that everyone here seemed to think they had a right to take an inspection on anything they wanted.

"Everything still regulation and organised. Routines?" Williams asked, for all the world like a grandmother asking whether or not she brushed her teeth each night.

"I like my routines. They keep everything working," Lila said, starting to pull on her trousers but deciding that she'd be better wearing the heavy greaves and armoured foot coverings of her active defense gear, rather than trying to carry it all, She began to put them on instead, feeling their additions of strength and power expand her awareness, making her lower legs feel invulnerable, like they were in seven league boots.

"Okay. So everything's perfect." The old woman's voice dripped with irony. "Did you do what we agreed and take time for yourself? Did you go and get clothes that are not . . ."

"I have suits. Proper suits. Designer labels."

"Which you wear for work, no doubt."

"Hello? I am *at* work twenty-four seven." Lila glanced at herself in the exam room's full-length mirror and saw an upscaled toy action figure: oversized robot legs, slender silver arms as shiny as stiletto blades, a relatively tiny human torso in a crop top and vest, silver eyes taking almost all warmth from her expression with their harsh statements, and the mane of red hair overcompensating for it, too sexy, too West Coast; a doll in a soldier's clothing. "I had my hair done for this job. All Hollywood. Look, see?" Her hair was dusty, messy, unkempt in spite of the expensive cut.

"You need another trip to the salon," Williams said drily. She plucked at Lila's vest. "You know what I'm gonna say."

"And you know that I think it could wait until this job is finished. Yes, I am still a young woman, despite having no arms and legs to call my own, and I don't think I despise my body any more than those girls down at Glory Beach who diet and pop pills and have surgery to look like faeries and glimms so they get their pictures on the pornopops. So?"

"Start the talking, or I start signing you off the case," Williams suggested. "Your advocate down the hall here seems to think there's something you're not telling him, and he hinted that it was sexual in nature, so he understood you didn't want to discuss it with him, but he thinks you should discuss it with someone, and given the fragile status of you, Lila, not as a project and not as an officer, but you personally girl, I think he's dead right."

Lila couldn't imagine Sarasilien hinting sexual. She didn't want to. "My personal life is none of your business." Lila locked her angry gaze on the gentle, amused expression of the psychiatrist and found herself cracking into a laugh. It was a little hysterical.

"I hear that all the time," Williams confided, and patted Lila on the knee. "Put the rest of all that hardware on and give me a clue."

Lila told her about the Game. "I don't know if it is—what you said."

"Come on Lila! Can't you even say the word?"

Lila hung her head and sat back. The table creaked ominously and she had to stand up again before it broke with her weight. Say that the Game was certainly based on a sexual forfeit? The embarrassment made her feel sick. It would have been like being one of those fan girls, worse, because she was supposed to be beyond and above all that teenage, physical stuff. "No, I don't think so."

The doctor shook her head and shrugged. "Okay. That was reasonably honest at least. I'll let you carry on, unless you'd rather I didn't. Do you want me to sign you off?"

Lila straightened and thought about it. As soon as she imagined it, two conflicting feelings came to her. One was profound relief and longing. The other was resentment at the notion she could quit. Her self-doubts were very strong and having Williams offer her the easy way out only made her more aware of them. "No. I can do it."

"You're not thinking that you're the only one that can? Just because the NSA built you for the price of half an army doesn't mean you have to take on everything for them."

"No. It's like what you'd call—something I have to do. For me.

And for the rest of it." Lila tried to mean it, but there was a knot of resistance in her stomach that made her feel nauseous as she did so.

"Okay." Williams stood up. "You said the magic words of responsibility and autonomy, so you can go. But I want you to carry on with our program just as much as you're doing with the easy physical stuff, hmm?" She glanced at the heavy bag of ammunition. "If I find you're stiffing me with a line, you'll be back here in rehab for six months."

"I'll call you," Lila said, backing away before she had time to change her mind.

It was a relief to get out of the building. Lila wove through the rush hour and arrived at Solomon's Folly at dusk to find the driveway beside the house full of cars. Besides the Doublesafe guard on the door a huge scarlet-skinned demon with impressive horns stood outside, smoking. Lila recognised a fellow bodyguard by his evident relief at having time off for doorstep duty, and his severe suit. The human guards told her that this retinue had arrived two hours ago, unannounced.

"We did all the checks we could," the Doublesafe guard said and the demon bodyguard bared his teeth and growled, indicating that it had been a matter of some contention.

"But you didn't tell me about it," Lila snapped.

"The boss, Jolene, said we wasn't to. Something about no press." He wasn't an Incon agent, only an ordinary Doublesafe employee. Lila ground her teeth and glanced at the bull-faced demon guard over the human's shoulder. The demon mimed peeling a banana and snorted in the human's direction, his meaning clear—you hired monkeys.

Deeper inside the house, on the ground floor where the games rooms and other entertaining areas spread out, Lila found most of the band plus a vast entourage of humans, demons, and faeries sprawled amid a scatter of open champagne bottles and half-empty plates. Music was just quiet enough to permit conversation between people next to one another. The house servants moved among them carefully, bringing and taking away. Lila, still carrying her pack and bag, saw

Poppy get up and hurry towards her. Eyes and faces turned quickly onto her with this attention and through the aid of her sound filtering she was able to hear everything that was said about her.

"Who's *that*?"

"What *is* she wearing?"

"What's she *doing* in here? I thought all the chaff was being left outside."

Lila ignored the comments. She put her bags down beside a seated demon and his friends and glanced briefly down at him as he looked her up and down with great interest. He was about to touch the bulk of her leg armour with one scarlet finger.

Lila put on a stiff British accent, "I don't think you're ready for this kind of jelly." She went back to scanning the room. The finger retreated.

"Whoo hoo, man!" one of the demon's friends said. "What the hell?" Which was a kind of demonic approval, but Lila barely heard it. She was looking for Zal, excusing herself until she moved around the corner and saw him and the explanation for the massed courtiers.

He was standing in close conversation with a female demon in a glittering black bodynet and little else. Her coruscating crimson and black skin glowed and shone with the lustre of a fresh conker. Lila knew her immediately, for her sensuous dimensions, fiery cascade of flame hair, and delicately lovely features were plastered over every billboard on The Avenue and in every magazine on the stands. It was Sorcha, queen of pop, and that was why the door demon had looked so familiar—he was on most of the paparazzi snaps that Lila had seen Sorcha in, always there, minding her, staring out of shot.

Zal's cool, elfin poise and Sorcha's vibrant, dynamic energy were complete counterpoints and they were so close and secluded that there could be no doubt as to their intimacy. Lila stopped in her tracks but Zal must have heard her because he lifted his head from where it almost touched Sorcha's and looked up. Lila was aware of a degree of rubbernecking starting up behind her as the room's hubbub quieted a little and music became audible over the heavy drumbeat. She wondered if Zal was about to order her out too, and was getting ready to fight over it, when he excused himself and came across to her over the empty margin that he and Sorcha had to themselves.

In her heavy armour Lila was now taller than he was, and well aware that she must look freakish. Zal was grinning by the time he reached her. He touched the back of her gauntleted hand with his fingertips in a curious, fleeting gesture.

"Is this what you went to get?"

"I read your letters," she said, considering that adequate explanation.

"I need to stay here tonight," he countered. "Anyway, I thought you read them before."

"Oh yeah, the elvish stuff on the surface all about the way you're bringing the race into disrepute and corrupting the magic of the old kingdoms. Death to the infidel bringing shame on all their houses. And then I read the other things. I think you and me need to have a talk, don't you?"

But in the time it had taken for them to get this far Sorcha had followed her curiosity. She slid in under Zal's arm and wrapped her long tail around his waist. "Who's this, Zal?"

Sorcha looked Lila up and down much as her followers had done, and Lila was surprised by the interest, approval, and admiration she saw there. She hadn't met many demons, and then only before her accident. They had a universal adoration of strange, occult, or unusual things and now Lila realised that she must be one of those things.

"Hey girl," Sorcha said to her with a respect that confused Lila even more. She'd thought someone like that, so famous and powerful, would brush her off as invisible, or worse.

Sorcha's eyes were red fire, surrounded by yellow glowing lava where white would have been. Her mouth covered beautiful, sharp white teeth. She really was astonishingly sensual. Nearly naked, she purred up against Zal's side and moved closer to him, teasing.

Lila kept her face completely still. She felt angry at Zal and angry with herself and could not, would not admit that she was hugely disappointed. She suppressed a blush with a self-administered shot from her resupplied internal medic system. She wouldn't give way. No way.

Zal's smile broadened as he looked into Lila's face. He took his hand from Sorcha's shoulder and slapped it on her bottom, giving her a pinch and making her squeal. "Sorcha, this is Lila, my new shadow. Lila, this is Sorcha, also known as Sorcha the Scorcher. My sister."

CHAPTER EIGHT

Lila was still reeling over the revelation an hour later. She had communicated with Sarasilien about it and to begin with he had not believed her. He said that it must be some publicity stunt. But Sorcha insisted it was true. The conversation had taken them out of the party room and up to Zal's, where they continued talking as he packed.

"Don't you have opposed magical . . . I mean aetheric . . . I mean, aren't you antibodies or something? Elf and demon . . . like . . . ?"

"Angel and demon?" Sorcha laughed and snarled at the same time, quite a feat. It showed her pointed little teeth. "They can't be blood related like you mean by the word brother and sister, no. For sure not." She rolled her eyes and shook her head at the idea, laughing and snorting. "No."

"So he isn't your brother."

"Yeah he is so, and anyone who says otherwise or treats him like he isn't of our estimable kin incurs my family's eternal vengeance." Her tone left no doubt that she meant it quite literally.

"Family of choice?" Lila suggested, not beginning to imagine what choice that was from Zal's point of view.

"Hell no. How could some elf live with demons and what demon would want to claim relation to one of them?" Sorcha stared at her as if Lila had suggested bestiality. "How could we have kinship? Are you out of your mind?"

"That's what I'm asking you," Lila said patiently. "I never heard of anyone being . . . adopted . . . across species. Especially not across your two."

Sorcha grinned and a little steam rolled off her. "Well, I ain't gonna tell you, sister. You have to find it out for your bad self. It's not something that can be told. Only known. See?"

Lila did not see. "It's a secret, then?"

Sorcha shook her head and narrowly missed igniting the curtains with a dismissive flick of her hand that sent small jets of fire from the tips of her fingers.

Lila nodded and sent her findings back to Sarasilien. Finally, rather desperately, she asked, "So, are you going to be . . . are you an elf sister, then?" The demon froze and Lila braced herself, eyes squinting, in case she was about to be barbecued.

Sorcha peered at her with blazing eyes. "Do I LOOK like an elf to you, baby?" Then, relenting, she shook herself and laughed. "Me, get into all that health food and macramé? You have to be joking. I'd sooner cut off my left tit." She jerked upwards with one talon of a thumbnail and made a slicing action, snorted, and stamped her foot. A fine tremor ran through the floorboards and the carpet suddenly gave off a singed smell. Sorcha hummed a little tune to herself, chuckling, "What demon would ever want to do that? In fact, what living being of any soul at all? Hah!"

"So, it's rare," Lila said.

"Far as I know, sugar, he's the only one," Sorcha said. "Only one with any brains at all but that don't mean he has many." She sighed. "I'm so into him. Isn't he great?" After this point Lila was only there to listen, as Sorcha didn't seem to need responses and had no intention of returning to their subject. "I love Mode-X. So dark and bad. So funky. I might do some of it myself. Hey what is taking you so long,

Legolas? Is all this stuff going with you?" Sorcha gestured at the room's furnishings.

"None of it's mine," Zal said, placing some worn-looking clothes into a carryall. "Except the painting."

"Oh, "Titia gave you that? Hah. Pity she's a faery." Sorcha paused and confided to Lila, "Elves put faeries to sleep in close contact. It's the aura thing, y'know?" Then she continued to Zal, "And all your girls here the same, it's like a freakin' nunnery. Are you getting rootsy for Alfheim now you've left home? Going puritan on me?" She kept darting little glances at Lila as she spoke, full of mischief. That was in between the time she spent opening drawers and sniffing around the room, trailing her perfectly manicured fingers along the surfaces, restlessly moving. Finally, she seemed contented and curled up like a cat in the middle of the bed.

Zal ignored her with filial contempt and went into the long, walk-in dressing room, closing the doors after himself.

Sorcha instantly turned to Lila, rolling over onto her stomach. "There's a Game between you two, isn't there?" Her hair waved around her face in tendrils of living fire that was only prevented from burning the house down by careful enchantments.

Lila refused to confirm or deny it. She was trying to retain a professional detachment with which she could vaguely impress Sorcha, but it was a pointless effort since demons were known for their affinity to wild magic. They couldn't control it any more than anybody else, but they could sense and read it with unmatched aplomb.

Sorcha's grin of delight intensified, "Oh, my, you have it bad! What is it?"

Lila shrugged, suitably ignorant for a human.

"Ah, you don't know yet. Want me to find out for you?" Sorcha's long, pointed tongue was out, licking her glossy lips in anticipation. "Go on, before he comes back. It might give you an advantage. I'm really good at these things. Quick, give me something of yours." She bounced across the bed to Lila and held her hand out.

Although Lila could think of a hundred reasons why not, she found Sorcha's enthusiasm and personal charisma impossible to withstand. Worse than an elvish glamour. And her care for Zal was indisputable, oddly, for demons and elves generally were well known as having no time for one another. So, despite her misgivings, Lila found herself opening a zipper on her jacket.

Sorcha was dancing with excitement as Lila handed her a flechette round from her pocket. "I like you *so* much!" she exclaimed, turning the bullet over in her fingers. "Personal weapons of grisly death! And now something of Zal's. Oh!" She leapt over and touched the round to the painting and hummed a note. A faint werelight grew between the two objects. As it strengthened into wavelengths even Lila could see Sorcha gently move the round away from the picture frame. A fragile skein of near invisible tendrils stretched out in the air between, and the spider's web of lines briefly moved into letters of the demonic language before they vanished.

"Aaah!" Sorcha squealed. "Zal you bad, bad dog!" To Lila she turned around and gathered herself and came and sat down, pulling Lila close to her. Her red eyes zipped with glee. "Girl, didn't your Momma ever tell you never play with the elves?" Her changes of mood made Lila feel dizzy. Sorcha was now as concerned and intent as a kind mother herself. "This is the oldest Game there is, honey. You know what I mean?"

Lila didn't know how to respond at all. She was out of her depth. She kept a thoughtful silence. This increased Sorcha's pity, which Lila could have done without.

"Let's see what the Victory condition is." The succubus slowly turned the round in her hand and sang a few notes to it. She listened, her blazing eyes closed for a moment. "Ah. Not too bad," she gave Lila a wink. "The loser is the one who cracks first and begs the other one to end the Game. The oldest ones are the best. Now the Forfeit."

"Forfeit. Isn't that it, when somebody wins?"

"You really washed in on the last tide," Sorcha said. "There's always a Forfeit, though most humans don't know that until it's too late." She went to the painting. "I can even tell you who started it. D'you want to know that too?"

"No," Lila said. "That's enough already." She was wondering what the Forfeit had been on the other Game, and if it had been avoided. Surely Sarasilien would have told her of it? Was there a compulsion lying on her now that she didn't know about? She couldn't believe he would cross her like that.

"Honey don't be down." Sorcha pressed the round gently into Lila's hand. "People are playing this stuff all the time, it's no big. What? What's the matter? You're not thinking of *quitting* are you?"

Lila glanced at the dressing room but there was no sign of Zal. She decided, on an impulse she might well regret, to take Sorcha at face value. She told her about the letters. "I'm obliged to lose," she said. "It's in the way. So, if all I have to do is . . ."

"No no no no," Sorcha rapped smartly. "You have to *mean* it. That's the condition. It has to be genuine lust that makes him beg for your favour, lust over sense with every last shred of personal pride biting the dirt. Otherwise it isn't worth the entry charge, is it? Trust me. I've played this before a hundred times. Loser cracks first and then the Forfeit—well, no, *then* the rooty, unless you're playing a real bastard, and *then* the Forfeit. Forfeit could be anything. You have to watch those."

"Doesn't matter," Lila said, biting down irritation at the wretched binding rules of the magic and her ignorance of them. "Can you lift the Game?"

Sorcha waved her hand dismissively. "No. Don't look so worried. I have four or five on all the time. Life's no fun at all without them. Sometimes I can't even remember who's playin' what on whom. Look though, before you lose, if you *could* lose even, don't you think you're better off knowing the Forfeit at least? No sense in suffering agony over a tin of kitty food, and no sense giving in sight-unseen on eternal banishment to Zoomenon or something. Here, let me." And before

Lila could stop her Sorcha stood up and spat onto the polished wooden chest of drawers beneath the painting. She sang a complicated melody and extended one of her fingernails into a claw. With this she scratched a mark into the saliva. It shaped itself and froze into a tiny lens like a magnifying glass. Beneath it the forfeit could be read, as though it was stamped into the wood in clear letters. Lila bent close.

"Still wanna lose?" Sorcha asked, clearly surprised.

The spit window frosted, and deliquesced to nothing with a few greyish flickers. The Forfeit it had shown her was etched in Lila's mind: the loser will live a lifetime never being able to love anybody else.

Curiously, she found the idea almost comforting. She might have to suffer a brief and difficult short-term period of fixation on Zal, true, but he'd leave as soon as the Game was done, and she was used to living far away from people she cared about. Very used to it. It wouldn't be so hard to put another picture in her pocket and, after that, have the security of knowing that she'd be in no emotional danger ever again.

Sorcha was staring at her. "You scarin' me now," she said. "You can't be serious."

"Oh come on," Lila retorted. "The alternative is having your brother love me for the rest of his life, and he's going to live for centuries, and then . . . gods know what."

Sorcha made a warding sign at the mention of gods. "You listen to me, Metal Molly. I've seen a hundred girls looking for the right angle or minute or chance with him, and I never liked one of them as sister material. But there's something about a human girl who's been made over into a death machine with the fires of hell driving her . . ." She gave Lila a long glance and Lila knew that Sorcha was talking about the reactor—something she shouldn't have known anything about at all. It was one of the many things she would have questioned her on, but Sorcha hadn't paused to let a word in. "And that makes me feel for you, makes me like you, and I can think of worse fates that might be riding much closer to him than that, can't you?"

Lila almost gaped with astonishment, but managed to turn it into talking. "What do you know?"

"I know that you're supposed to protect my brother from these maniacs and I want you to do that job and I think that this Game is working well for me, honey." Sorcha's delicate, supple body rose up and her tail coiled suddenly. Venom formed into a drop at its dartlike tip. She put her face right into Lila's and Lila smelled fire on her breath and felt a sudden, blistering instant of heat. Sorcha's voice was the quiet sound of a distant furnace roaring, "And I'll tell you this for nothing. If you fail, then I'll hunt you down with every demon this side of Tartarus and eat your head."

Lila simply stood there, astonished and slightly singed.

Sorcha was already off, sitting down playfully on the bed again. She flicked a slender golden card out of the narrow belt that was all that held her bodynet in place. "Anyway, ten million dollars for you *if* he loses." She grinned, reached out, and tucked the card down the front of Lila's armoured vest. "I like seeing him squirm. He gets all High Elf and sanctimonious, and his ears get right back like they're welded to his head, and he gets really intense and kinda mad. Still as a statue, just frozen with rage, can't do a damn thing." She laughed at the thought. "Never tire of that. And trust me, he's *so* gonna lose."

"Don't be ridic—" But Lila bit her words back because Zal returned, gave them both a dark look, and threw his bag at the bed where it thumped against Sorcha's side.

"Ship out, Sorcha," he suggested. "My shadow and I have stuff to argue about."

"Don't I know it." Sorcha got up and gave Lila a wink as she moved to the door. She looked at Zal over her shoulder and said something in demonic to him. Lila could hear it but, unlike other languages of the Realms, demonic sounded like music instead of words to ears it wasn't meant for and she had no idea what was said.

Sorcha blew him a kiss with a flicker of yellow fire between her lips and left the door open after her.

Zal walked across and shut it with a kick before turning to Lila. "I'm not leaving here tonight."

"You have to," Lila said primly. "It's all arranged."

"Un-arrange it."

"I'll carry you out if I have to."

"You will not." He folded his arms and planted his feet.

"I will so." She found herself copying his stance.

He dodged her, jumping across the bed and out through the adjoining door into her room. Lila was so taken aback by his speed, and so grounded in the posture, that she didn't even move for a good couple of seconds. As she ran after him she could hardly believe it had come to this.

All the other intervening doors were open. She saw him hurdle the one sofa that stood in his way as he crossed the ocean-view room and then he was onto the balcony and over the rail before she had time to shout out. If there had been a Severed Realms Olympiad the elves would win all the running events, Lila reflected as she watched Zal land with cat-precision, roll, and keep running in a leap that would have broken the legs of any ordinary human being. As she landed from her drop she felt a sharp and sudden pain and heard the whine and grind of machinery as motors worked to protect her. Darts and needles seemed to be pricking the inside of her legs and along the inner surface of her spine. She realised her mistake in not ditching the armouring of her legs, though it wasn't so bad yet, she could run.

But Zal was fast over the track into the hill woodland and Lila felt her new pain increase steadily as she pursued him. Her AI-self implored her to stop, informed her that an increased effort could result in serious tearing between the new layers of flesh and system. But Zal's training had obviously worked well for him and she could see that if she even slowed down he would lose her. Lila ran on, burdened by the excess weight of her weapons.

Slowly she gained on him until they reached the summit of the hill when she lost sight of the flag of his pale hair. He had turned off the path and into the dense woodland there. Lila turned at the same spot.

A blast of icy air and wind suddenly hit her in the face. Leaves and earth pelted her skin and went in her eyes, blinding her. She couldn't stop fast enough and her left shoulder struck the stiff trunk of a young oak tree, spinning her around and knocking the breath out of her. Invisible hands pushed her down towards the ground and she was off balance and fell beneath them as earth elementals tried to bury her.

She'd never seen them cluster and work together so fiercely before. Although it hurt and made life difficult, once she realised what it was she was able to stand up and step back to the path to clear her eyes. When she had she was able to look into the shadows.

Earth, air, and stone spirits clustered thickly beneath the trees' protection, shifting restlessly from form to form, from mist to nothing and back again. Eyes that were empty spaces in nebulous bodies glared at her, ballooned, and vanished only to reappear a moment later. Somewhere close by a wood ghost clattered its flutelike bones against living tree trunks. Lila heard an eagle cry out from far above her, alarmed by the presence of so much primordial force in one spot.

She put her foot off the path and immediately they came together again, all the small spirits rushing to create the semimaterial body of a giant elk, its rack of antlers lowered against her. Lila could only think that Zal was getting away from her and her chances of catching him up or even finding him must be vanishing with every second.

"I'm sorry," she said. "But you're in my way." She stepped forward, braced her arms against the peculiar sponginess of the elk's form, and pushed.

The resistance was ferocious. Lila had no idea that flitting things like elementals could band together and create something so physically strong, not in Otopia anyway. She dug her feet into the ground for more purchase, but the soil began to shift under her as it was pulled apart from below. In a few more moments she'd have nothing to stand on.

Lila engaged full power and shoved. Pain like raw fire flared along her spine and in her hips as the elk's insubstance held for an instant and trapped her in a vice between implacable machine and immovable energy. Then all resistance vanished as the elk form fell into pieces. Lila fell forward with a surge, tripping and sliding on the turbulent ground, feeling like a rider on an uncontrollable horse. She just managed to keep her footing and weave between the trees, moving fast enough to keep the elementals from coalescing again, although they harried her as best they could. They tore her hair, threw leaves, sticks, and small branches at her, tried to move the stones under her feet as she ran.

Zal must have been tiring, because there were clues for Lila to see: a snapped twig, a footprint in flattened grass . . . And then she came out into a little glade very unexpectedly. She slid down a short embankment and into the low point of a dip in the ground, stopping just in front of Zal. He was sitting with his head thrown back, gasping for breath, sweat running off him. There was a strange silence and stillness—Lila realised it was because the elementals had stopped their pestering.

"What the hell are you doing?" She'd finally come to the end of her patience. Her vision was covered in red warning readouts which were completely unnecessary because she could feel the damage the run had done to her.

Zal glanced at her, slightly grey beneath the flush of effort. For the first time she saw his cool crack at the edges. "I have to be here," he said shortly. "I'm not going anywhere else. I suppose you can hang around and watch if you want to, but I'd prefer it if you stood outside the circle. I'm sure you would too." He got up and brushed himself down with something like self-consciousness. Then, without asking her again, he started talking elvish. Or rather, he didn't speak it, he sang it, as though it was demonic, and the lilting peculiar harmonics of the two combined to make the hair on Lila's neck stand up. Suddenly she had no problem at all getting out of the way—none of her flesh and bone wanted to be inside the space he was creating with his spell.

Outside the range of his influence, the elementals returned in force, but although they crawled and clawed over her with semisolid fingers, their real interest lay beyond the heat shimmer of the magical barrier Zal had sketched around himself. Like her, they watched with avid curiosity.

The peculiarity of it didn't strike her immediately—Lila was not familiar with magic in a user's way—but then it dawned on her that probably, if he were going to do anything important, she should have been *inside* the circle, surely, and not outside where she was unprotected. But on the heels of that thought she realised that she was protected after all, because he'd reversed the normal order of things. The circle that Zal had cast put the world inside it. He was the one outside.

"Hey!" she said, moving automatically into a state where what weaponry she had was armed. "I say again—what the hell?"

But Zal wasn't able to hear her, or more likely didn't care. Then, one by one, the elementals of the forest began to slip past Lila, into his space. From their touches she could sense their eagerness to obey the summons of his song. Once they passed the barrier their manifestation changed. On Lila's human Earth, the fifth world of Otopia, elemental beings had wispy and ethereal presences. But Zal had taken his circle out of Earth's domain. It was part of the elemental's home system now—a part of First Realm: Zoomenon.

The elementals came into their true form and power. Wood, metal, earth, water, air, fire. From her studies Lila knew that these beings didn't exist as separated entities in Zoomenon and this was true, she saw now. They united instantly into a multicoloured rainbow haze of energy, which pulsed and danced like the Northern Lights on a dark winter night. She saw Zal through the brilliant light, bathing in it, his head thrown back in abandonment, and belatedly recognised that what she was looking at was the junkie's hit.

The elemental forces coiled over him eagerly and poured in through his nostrils, mouth, eyes, and ears, exiting through the palms of his hands and the soles of his feet to circle around and fly at him again. Zal shook where he stood, fell to his knees, and then over onto his face.

Lila was numb with shock when she heard the arrow whip past her ear, saw it rebound from the magical field of the circle and fall at her feet. As it touched the ground it became a snake, yellow and black striped, and coiled swiftly away from her into the undergrowth. Then her radar found the elf assassins, one coming through the treetops, the other, who had shot, making its way along the ground.

She cancelled all her fright readouts and set out for the ground walker at a dead run, flechette clips arming, switching her body's gross and fine motor controls over to her AI-self's superior communications speeds: it could outdo her natural neurons by a factor of two. Her reactor increased output and she became instantly faster and stronger, so when the arrow that was meant for her came flying towards her she was able to bat it aside without losing momentum. The enchanted flight turned back to search for her, but found the armour on her back suddenly too hard, too electromagnetically polarised for its magical fields to penetrate. It blew into dust as Lila saw her quarry step forth casually into full view with the aloof poise of every miserable High Elf she'd ever known. Cold fear drenched her inside, but the machine parts of her didn't care about that; they gave her more power than she could handle.

At least, she consoled herself, she didn't know this one personally. The elf woman's long ears were pierced and decorated with hawk-feathers and her hair had been tamed with dark wax and braided tightly into a queue that hung across her shoulder. Her earth-toned clothes flickered with the shadows of forests that grew in Alfheim, not the Otopian woodland she stood in now.

"Lila Black," said this monstrosity, as though announcing the name of a new and particularly unsavoury insect species she had just discovered.

"Haven't got time," Lila said, breaking the conversational charm. She knew that this one intended to distract her while the other waited for Zal's circle to break down. That would happen if he lost consciousness and, having seen what he was doing, she didn't hold out much hope of that being anything other than a matter of time.

The elf agent's blue eyes flashed disdainfully, and with insouciant ease she crouched and made a six-metre vertical jump, making for the higher branches of the tree she stood beneath, where a heavyweight like Lila would have no chance of following. She was lithe and trained. Lila was nuclear-powered. She matched the jump and grabbed hold of the elf's shoulders without making any effort to remain in the tree. As they fell back down they wrestled fiercely, but Lila was much stronger and when they hit the soft forest floor Lila ended up on top. She heard the breath whoosh out of the elf's narrow frame with satisfaction. The woman struggled to get out from under, but gave it up when she realised she couldn't budge Lila's mass.

"What are you going to do?" she hissed. "Sit on me all night?"

Lila didn't feel like talking. Part of her attention was focused on tracking the other elf and it was very close to the circle glade. She had no way of seeing magic, so she didn't know what was happening to Zal. She had no ropes on her. Although she felt something like a qualm it was short lived. She extended a needle from her right thumb and injected the elf at the vein in her neck with a short-term shot of a gengineered knockout. It was the kind of technological weapon elves despised the most, but Lila didn't care about the woman's honour at this moment.

She ran back towards the glade and then began to notice other, peculiar changes in the wood. It was becoming misty and a new breeze from the sea had come up in the last few minutes. Gulls shrieked overhead, although she couldn't see them with ordinary eyes. Then, aside from her new target and to her left, she saw an animal spirit in the shadows. The elf she was fixated on saw it too. It moved around and put the circle between itself and Lila. Lila knew Zal wasn't out yet. She could see him, lying on his back, laughing in the delirious way of people who don't know if they're happy or sad, or are much too much of both.

The animal spirit, not of any of the Seven Kingdoms, a curious, Interstitial being from the gaps where ghosts and other lost traces lingered, approached the circle. It was huge, a Megaceros, with a rack of antlers so large that it could not have moved in any ordinary wood, but the trees and rocks presented no obstacle to its passage. It didn't truly walk in the space and time of any of the realms. A thick forestal mist was emanating from its flanks in huge, stately billows. Rain fell from its antlers. Its eye sockets, like those of all ghosts, were black and empty.

Lila was more worried about it than the elf now. Ghosts had the cold breath that killed everything it touched, if they chose to exhale. There was no scientific nor magical ward against it. There was no way to talk to a ghost—it was supposed they were beyond time. There was no way to know what ghosts wanted, or needed, or what might turn them aside from the things which came to interest them. Although the elf and its weapons could not cross the circle that protected the world from Zal, the ghost could.

It moved with a stately progress. Its head tilted to one side as it listened closely, although if Zal were still singing it was a song Lila couldn't hear. She ran as fast as she could, breaking small branches that were in her way and vaporising a stand of elder that stood between her and the circle wall with a light-pulse charge, crashing through the remains in a dust of black particles and smoke. She threw herself headlong at the magical barrier, not knowing if she could get through it, or what spells made it. At the last instant she flung her arms up, elbows forward, to protect her face, picked up her feet, and relied on her weight and momentum to do the rest. As she closed her eyes the last image she'd seen remained impressed on her. She could see the elf on the other side of the circle. His face was distorted by the hazy water effects of the aetheric wall, but she rather thought that improved it a great deal, as did the expression it wore—a mixture of dismay and surprise—which she would have given anything to see two years ago, before its porcelain beauty became a regular feature of her nightmares.

Then Zal's forcefield caught her and she felt the struggle between its grip on her flesh and the robotics that it couldn't command, because they weren't alive. It began to tear her apart. Her head filled with a scream of light and pain but she was too heavy and too much metal. The elf magic was repelled by the metal and silicon and coiled away through skin and bone, fleeing back to its place in the wall as she hurtled through in slow time.

She felt like it had skinned her, but when she landed and rolled up next to Zal's twitching body she could still move and most systems, even though they were all redlined, were still working. She fetched up on the edge of Zal's hollow, and lifted her face out of the dry ground, feeling steam rising from the earth under her face, smelling the healthy, mouldy odour of the soil. Sensors on her back relayed the cause—she was under another sun and it was beating down, hot as hell, baking her under an indigo sky.

She looked up. The animal spirit was moving close, the barrier visible through its aethereal form as it passed through. She saw the sweat on Zal's skin beginning to freeze where his hand was flung out close to the wet nostrils of its muzzle as it put its head down towards him, ears cocked, replying to some demand he was making as the elemental rainbow coruscated in and out of his open mouth. He was smiling, and his eyes were shut, but she didn't think he was unconscious.

Lila tried to get to her feet. Pain seared her back and legs so badly she couldn't. She issued silent commands to her med units to numb her but they didn't respond. The muscles in her torso were useless, but they hadn't the strength to lift the prosthetics of her legs and arm by themselves anyway. Only the motor systems that controlled her limbs could do that, and they weren't reacting. She looked down, unable to make sense of the peculiar readouts that flashed in her mind, and saw that she was covered in silvery metal elementals. They were consuming her power, revelling in the taste of the alloys and pure metals, undoing the energy locked in their crystal form. They were rotting her. She could only lie there and watch the ghost place its unself beside Zal, into Zal's hand where streams of elementals were still pouring forth.

The face of her opponent, the other elf agent, appeared close to the window of the magical wall and watched too.

Lila saw the ghost draw breath in Zoomenon. It inhaled the elements from Zal's unprotected hand. She saw the Jayon Daga agent's face looking down at her, not even contemptuous, not even curious, waiting. And all the time Zal lay there like an idiot, grinning, out of it, as happy as a sand boy, as the ghost breathed in and left his hand empty at the end of his wrist, as transparent as glass.

There was only one thing left to do, though she felt no sense of hope in doing it. She didn't trust it. She didn't like it. She never wanted to use it. All her ambivalent feelings about the people who had made her tried to stop her.

"Battle Standard," Lila whispered. She mentally apologised to the metal elementals who were temporarily blasted apart by her body's response to the command as it switched current phase from her reactor. But she thanked Sarasilien for having the wit to add such a defensive capability to her AI-self in the first place. Field tests had proved BS, as Lila called it, to be anything but reliable, barely even functional, crammed as it was with knowledge her superiors wanted kept even from her, but it was all she had that might work before the damned ghost breathed out and finished them both. The command reset her AI-self into a new mode. Her armour reconfigured. Processes that kept her alive switched over their power to defensive units. A cocktail of drugs and hormones surged into her system and her pains and worries vanished as neural connections were closed down and everything redirected according to the strategies of her defensive programming.

She was on her feet before she had time to think, aware very dimly of horrible things happening to her body but not caring now, not able to feel it except at a distance, as though pain was only a notion, like an idea, which carried no weight and made no difference to the physical world. Lila was distant, soaring like an eagle, strong as a lion, a centre to a storm. She saw herself pull Zal towards her by an ankle, away from the ghost, pick him up, and put her gauntlet over his nose and mouth, pinching them tightly shut. His eyes opened wide and a stream of multicoloured fire poured out over her and ran harmlessly off her, unable to do anything about the phase shifts she was able to perpetuate. The circle disintegrated abruptly and Zoomenon vanished as the elf Lila knew as Dar, barely five metres away, loosed his arrow.

Lila turned and ducked. She was faster than the dreamy speed of the ghost, but not faster than the arrow. It thudded into her shoulder, through her shield and her armour. The point emerged just below her armpit like a reproving finger, bound with magic that even now fizzed and sparked on its point. She looked down in anger and saw the silver tip scratch the skin of Zal's shoulder whereupon it instantly vanished as though made of moonlight. Dar was already away, dodging into the trees, racing to his fallen companion. Whatever his mission was he had completed it, Battle Standard concluded, and therefore she made no move to counter his action.

Zal slumped in her grasp, a completely dead weight.

Things became blurry to Lila, fuzzy, as though the world and her thoughts were all radio stations that couldn't be tuned in. Nothing matched up. She thought she might be dying, but as long as she was still moving the best thing must be to get back home, to where she was safe. Yes, she would go to where there was help or someone who could, if not fix her, at least switch her off. She would like to be off because everything was very very bad indeed.

She went home.

CHAPTER NINE

"Let go, Lila," said a kind voice she recognised, but Lila couldn't.

"Bloody BS system," said another voice wearily, from someone trying to plug a jack into a port on her leg. "Locked again on the exit clause. I'm going to purge it and debug. *Again.*"

"Can you hear me, Lila?"

Yes, she thought, from very far away. *I think so*. But it wasn't important. She had Zal, and she had come to a safe place. There were no more combatants. There was no zone of fire, no defence necessary. Everything was in order with the system. The mission was complete.

"She can't hear me," said the kind voice somewhere out in the light beyond Lila. "Maybe she'll let go if he wakes up."

"He's been out twelve hours. Nothing wakes him up."

"If she doesn't let go soon he could lose one of his feet. The circulation's going, and what's wrong with his hand?"

"Some kind of magical thing. You hit with a magic bullet, eh Lila?"

"What's his real name, d'you know? That might work."

"Haven't a clue."

"Call his agent."

"No need. Who do you think that schmuck in the purple fur coat is? Malachi brought him in and told him this is a private hospital. He bought it, if you can believe that. Guy with him is the producer. Apparently they're surgically attached or something."

"Get him in here. He might know something worth knowing."

"You're kidding."

Lila listened and smiled inside. She had Zal and everything was concluded to her satisfaction. Then Buddy Ritz came in, and Jelly Sakamoto with him, who started shouting in a high voice.

"What the hell you doing to my motherfuckin' star, freak girl? Put him down! What you think you're paid for . . ." It went on a great deal, like a fit in a word factory, expletives building up like explosives. But Jelly didn't get too close.

Now that Lila looked at him from her beautiful distance she could see herself reflected on his eyeballs, and she could see his point. Her fully activated battle armour made her a steel colossus with a woman growing out of its torso. Blood had run out of her eyes, mouth, ears, and nose, and from the places where she joined the metal. She was naked and coated in mud. Her arms and face were locked solid. Her face bore an expression of the kind of euphoria you sometimes saw in religious icons. Zal lay across her arms, his head hanging loose, his hair a flag of defeat. Various people, who looked small and puny beside her, were struggling with cables, keyboards, and remote controls, prying fruitlessly at her arms and legs, and warily watching her weapons-ports. There was a long, black elfin arrow shaft sticking out of her left shoulder.

Lila wanted to tell them not to be silly, but she couldn't move. She felt weary, and that she would like to lie down.

Jelly went off and sometime later returned with Sorcha, all covered up in a black cloud of coat and dark glasses, her high heels sounding like the crack of doom on the hard floor of the emergency room.

"Flown back from goddamned Vegas!" Jelly was screeching. "*Vegas* and are you listening to me, C3PO? He is on stage in *six hours*. Can't you people pull your fingers or your power out of her ass? We're talking millions of serious dollars."

Sorcha walked up slowly, her face set and serious. Lila wanted to smile.

"You look bad, girl," Sorcha said quietly.

No, I'm fine, Lila tried to say, although nothing came out. *Everything is fine.*

Sorcha put her hand up, up, up to where Zal's head hung and touched the tip of one, long, pointy ear. Already on tiptoe with the heels, she leant forwards, closer, closer, so that Lila could feel how warm she was, and smell her perfume. She whispered something that even Lila couldn't hear.

Zal twitched and jerked suddenly, so strongly that he nearly fell from Lila's hold. He made a noise of pain and struggled to claw his way upright, but Lila's arms automatically closed more tightly, to prevent him falling. She would rather have let him go, because she was exhausted now and she had started to hurt, but the more he fought to get free the more her arms and hands drew him closer, tighter, safer.

"Stop, for hellsakes!" Sorcha hissed at him, her tongue a strip of red flame. "She'll crush the life out of you. Something's gone wrong with her. She's broken. Stay still."

Zal stopped. Lila felt him take hold around her neck in an effort to move to a less agonising position. She was glad he was ready to take his own weight. Even something as light as an elf got heavy after a while, and now she could barely stay awake. Only the growing news of discomfort and worse pains coming through to her from the great distant plain of her body kept her from falling asleep. She longed to be able to yawn.

"Shut her down! Reboot! Power cycle her! Reverse the friggin' polarity!" Jelly shouted encouragingly.

"Shut the fuck up, man," Sorcha snarled at him and he jumped aside from the dart of blue energy that came zipping out of her mouth with the words. Sorcha turned back calmly, "Zal, are you cool?"

Lila couldn't see what Zal did but Sorcha chuckled and said, "Sure, you cool. Now don't go anywhere. I got to take me a picture of your ass for the guys."

Then someone took the world and put it back in Lila's head. Her arms collapsed and Zal fell hard against her, dragging her head down and forward. She lost her balance and staggered and screamed with agony. She felt Zal let go, and the natural recoil as she was freed broke something important in her back.

When Lila woke she saw the familiar ceiling of the Incon hospital—a bank of foam tiles set in a light metal frame with recessed lights that shone on her but avoided her face, like eyes that couldn't bring themselves to quite look at her. She smelled antibac and other chemical compounds in the air. Although she felt fine she soon realised this was because she could feel no physical sensations from the neck down. A sadness and sense of defeat crept through her, so profound that she felt she would never be warm again. Tears ran, betraying her with their heat and the softness of their touch, but she couldn't wipe them away.

She was plugged into the Central Intelligence Tree, the AI which operated all of Incon's communications and data traffic and provided informational support. It responded to the flush of blood in her face by opening the windows. Lila couldn't speak, but her AI-self asked it in machine code:

Where is Zal?

Zal is not within the CI Tree span, it told her, obliged to notify her of Zal's uplink status as a matter of protocol. *He was discharged two hours ago and taken from here to the Coke Arena at Bay City Center by Buddy Ritz, Jelly Sakamoto, and Jolene Duchovnik.*

What time is it? Lila asked.

It is ten PM Pacific, the machine said.

Patch me to the Coke Arena coverage of the concert, she insisted.

The AI switched her out of its disconnected security to the Incon servers that were connected to the Otopia Tree and gave her TV.

Zal's support act was still on. Lila let her mind wander through the system and found the internal CCTV units. She started to search through the crowd, and at the same time to look for Zal in the dressing areas. She saw Poppy and the other faeries with headphones on, warming up by singing old R&B melodies. She saw Luke and DJ Boom drinking lite beer, their feet up on the table in the green room, watching the support band and flicking broken potato chips at each other.

Then there was Zal, sitting a slight distance apart on the edge of a table, drinking something out of a styrofoam cup, both his hands in gloves, although that went with the general High Elf woodlands look the designers had given him. His slanted eyes were glittery with a bigger than natural kind of high, she thought, but it could have been the lighting. He looked as though he had been transported in from Alfheim, like he carried it with him in a forcefield that could repel all Otopian influence. The white cup seemed bizarre by contrast. He glanced at the camera, into Lila's eyes, then looked down at the cup in his hands and casually crushed it flat.

Lila made herself switch gear and start working for real.

All the rig reports were in order from the road crews, all the security features functional. The guards collected mundane and magical weapons at the gates.

How badly damaged am I? she asked the Incon Tree, knowing it would never lie to her or try to make her feel better. *When will my insystem be on again?*

You are expected to recover sufficiently for insystem to be returned by five AM *Pacific*, it told her in its neutral, sexless, diffident voice.

What happened to me?

You were in wet-surgery for an hour and a half. Surgical nanoware packs are still operative at the sacroiliac site, at the arrow puncture, and at the major junction bodies within your leg prosthetics. Your reactor core remains undam-

aged. You are receiving a rebuilding nutrient structure through blood transfusion. The magical detection device has recorded a significant alteration in your energy pattern which is consistent with exposure to high-count Zoomenon radiation. The effects are so far unmanifested, and unknown at this time. This has been added to your permanent record. You have been cleared to continue operations, but you will not be permitted to operate without support in the field.

What's the delay then? Lila wondered at the five AM deadline. It seemed a long way off. She pushed aside her resentment at being downgraded. That meant the Incon special agents team were watching her, because they didn't know what the Zoomenon exposure might do, or how it could change her. She didn't know either. She didn't want to.

Your brainwave readouts are erratic, and follow a nontypical pattern. Engram restoration therapy has been recommended before insystem renewal by Doctor . . .

Yeah, well, screw that, Lila said. *Switch it on.*

I am obliged to inform . . .

"One hardly needs to be telepathic to know what you're thinking," Sarasilien's voice said quietly beside her.

Lila would have jumped if she could have. She hadn't known he was there, but he must have been sitting there the whole time at her side.

The tall elf leaned forward so that he came into her line of sight. "It does you credit, but you need to rest and recuperate. Now is not the moment for another attack of heroics. We have deployed other agents to watch Zal while you recover."

She couldn't even turn her head. Sarasilien stood up, and Lila felt the air move as he bent over her. His long hair hung forward, like her mother's used to. "Lila," he said with gentle affection. "Don't cry. You'll be fine in a few hours."

Lila worked hard to try and talk. She could barely move her eyes to meet his. It was exactly the same as it had been on the awful day she woke up here the first time, two years ago, after Lila Amanda Black had officially been laid to rest, missing on assignment in Alfheim.

Then she couldn't feel or move either, and the only things that passed through her head were the replays of the final moments of her old life with the elven agent who had ended it—Zal's hunter, Dar.

Again she saw his face as firestars arose from the words he was speaking and fell onto her, blasting her apart in a shock of white silence.

Sarasilien had talked to her throughout the months of her physical rebuilding and the longer months of her mental recovery, and listened to her screaming silently, able to hear her thoughts through magic when no one else could. She remembered those times with resentment and gratitude, the latter winning out.

"I'm fine," she whispered finally, although the words were mangled in her dry throat. "I saw him. Dar. He was in the forest at Solomon's Folly. He shot me. He shot Zal."

Sarasilien had bent close to listen. His hair pooled over her neck, tickling her. She smelled the clean, evergreen scent of his skin, drank it in. "Are you sure? Zal was unhurt when he was released from here. I could find no magical traces on him."

"The arrowhead scratched his shoulder after it went through me. It self-destructed. And his hand . . ."

"Yes?" He waited for the long age it took her to draw breath and process it.

"There was an animal spirit, an I-space ghost. It drank from his hand. He was . . . we were in Zoomenon. Before Dar shot. Zal was in Zoomenon, outside the circle, drawing elementals. He was . . ." But she didn't know the name, used what she could find, "He was shooting up with them, and the ghost came."

Sarasilien drew back when she had finished. "This is a serious twist. I suspected that Dar might be involved. He's the senior Jayon Daga agent in Otopia." He paused and then added, "Elves have a history with elementals which may explain the source of Zal's apparent addiction, though I can tell you from my brief examination of him that there is a lot more to Zal than any high-caste elven magics. I cannot say what, as he was extremely resistant to my attention. But the I-space ghost is most unusual. Do you think its presence there was a coincidence?"

"No," Lila whispered. But she didn't say why she thought so—that the combination of demon magic and elvish words in the song had called it out of the Interstitial. She felt like protecting Zal from Sarasilien's intellect, for the time being. Instead she flicked her gaze inward, to the cameras at the Arena, and saw The No Shows going on stage. "Maybe it has something to do with the demon connection?"

Sarasilien nodded, "Maybe. If that is true . . ." But he got lost in thought.

They opened with a version of "Mama Told Me Not to Come," treated with heavy expanded Mode-X bass, funky rock guitar and curious disco backing. They started in the dark until Zal sang, "Don't turn on the lights . . ." and then, in a blaze of photonic glory, the crowd went mental at the still unusual sight of a High Elf singing and dancing like he grew up in a Queenstown ghetto bar.

She flicked back to reality. "Who's at the Arena?"

"We sent Malachi." Sarasilien hesitated as Lila watched the band shift into one of their own numbers. "He's really very good, isn't he?"

Lila blinked. "You can use magic to listen to the concert?"

"It is on television," he admitted and touched the side of his head where a slim Fruitfly was pinned beside his ear, feeding images and sound directly to him. "I have Bluetooth."

"Oh." She took in this unexpected adaptation of his, decided it was okay, and watched Zal, wondering if there was going to be some larger shift of elves into the waters of technology. "He's okay." She thought Sarasilien was going to make another Finish It crack, but he didn't. He stood beside her and absently rested his fingertips on her forehead. She felt a trickle of magic, like cool water, run out of his *andalune* and down through her skull into her head. Suddenly everything seemed much calmer and lighter, and the burden of the Game and the last few hours of strange violence lifted.

"We have arranged to move your gear from Solomon's Folly tonight," he said. "It will be on the tour bus when you join it later tomorrow. Jolene put up a fuss about your absence and Mr. Sakamoto was extremely vociferous in his complaints, although the threat of a peremptory audit by the Otopia Revenue Service has dampened his ire. The official story is that you pursued Zal into the forest on one of his marathon training runs and were injured by a fall into a hidden ravine." He sounded less than impressed.

"Ravine?" Lila whispered.

"You called for help and were taken from the accident site straight to hospital. Zal went with you."

"That's ridiculous. My cover won't hold."

"It is still holding, Zal and Sorcha notwithstanding, although they have no interest in outing you. Money has spoken to Mr. Sakamoto and well-placed lies multiply faster than flies."

"They have to take Battle Standard out," Lila pleaded.

"They're debugging it," Sarasilien said. He squeezed her hand, a gesture she could feel but not reciprocate. "It's out of my jurisdiction anyway."

"It *is* a bug," she said, but she was too tired to say more. She watched Zal dance and prance and leap and shriek and sing like the devil himself. She could see what the elves flinched at in his expression. He was sexy, and he showed that he knew it. It was the second part they didn't care for.

She scanned the crowd and there, of course, like the cool creature he was, ears concealed by a bandanna and eyes made up to look human, she saw the unmistakably aloof features of Dar. He was midway back on the ground floor level, a little taller than most, and strangely still and tranquil in the general mayhem. His dark eyes were fixed intently on the stage.

"Dar's there," she croaked.

"I see him," Sarasilien said and took his hand from hers. "Malachi will too."

But Lila wasn't so sure. And there wasn't just one agent, there were two of them. Where was the woman?

"Rest, Lila," Sarasilien ordered. "If you want to be useful again, you have to get well enough first."

But she hadn't got a choice, because they wouldn't return her insystem anyway. She watched Zal, and she watched Dar watching him, and slowly, with waves of sleep struggling to drag her down, it came to her that there was more in what was going on than she could make out, something that tugged at the edge of her consciousness but would not come forward into the light.

Nothing happened. Zal sang and the words of his songs filtered into her dreams here and there, like a secret code appearing and vanishing from the noise.

> ... sorry that I'm not calling you,
> Didn't get the things you ask me to,
> A thousand disappointments building up into this wave ...

The music gave the words power they would never have owned alone, but when the alarm came at five AM and her insystem woke her up, those secret meanings which had seemed so profound to her at the time dissipated like smoke.

CHAPTER TEN

In spite of her inclination to do the contrary Lila didn't rush to join the tour en route up the coast as soon as it was light. One part of her training had been in the subtle arts of fine-tuning ordinary human intuition, because the near-instant subconscious processes of the mind were often as effective as any lengthy study, and her intuition kept putting pressure between her shoulder blades every time she thought of the bug she'd found the other day. She decided to take one more look, even without knowing what for.

After checking through medical and getting a clear from Dr. Williams, she put on jeans and a T-shirt and rode her bike back to the recording studio. She parked three blocks away this time and walked through the grey dawn, taking a slight dog's leg that brought her up behind the bugged sedan. As reported by her subordinates, nobody had come to replace or claim the data tape. Lila figured that the cat charm must have alerted them to the discovery and could have even identified her using that hair it snatched, so they probably were never going to come back.

She picked the locks and sat down in the driver's seat, leaving the door ajar and her foot on the sill. She extended metal pincers from the fingertips of her left hand, created pliers and got a grip on the radio.

With a jerk that barely jolted her sore muscles she ripped the whole unit free of the dash and then glanced around, but the noise hadn't attracted attention. The street slept on. As if anybody there would have got up for a radio theft anyway.

Lila took the tape out of the wrecked unit and checked the wiring over for any unusual features. It was simple recording gear. The only addition was the fix that set it to listen in to the old bugging device. She powered the system off a port in her arm and played the tape, stopping at random to try and find anything that might be worth hearing. There was the usual stuff—people in the studio, talking, setting up equipment, playing. Nothing they said seemed important outside of the immediate moment. She speed-listened as the voices came and went and the light in the sky grew stronger, brighter, cloud clearing to the west. She listened as the studio went quiet and everyone left for home.

Lila heard the static shuffle of the tape wheels turning, and the sounds of the building, soft like dust, and the sound of the tape itself brushing the pickups, and beneath all of that a faint trace, like the imaginary echo of a million-year-old voice talking intently in a language long forgotten before the human race or the quantum bomb had been devised. She remembered what Malachi had said about the possibility of a bomb fault in the area and took the tape herself, leaving the radio on the passenger seat and the door open, so that her break-in resembled a simple theft.

Her shoulders bothered her less as she walked along to the main street a block away and bought a Krispy Kreme donut and some coffee. She put the donut in the pannier of her bike when she got back to it and drank the coffee there, resting her foot on the kickstand as she called Sarasilien with her discovery.

"Good work," he said, as standard. "Send the tape to me and I'll process it for you. The buses have already arrived in Frisco, according to Malachi and the team, so you can catch up there anytime from now on."

"Any more sightings of Dar?" she asked.

"He left with the rest of the crowd. Our agent lost him after about two hundred metres. I think you can expect to see him again."

Lila pulled a face. "Okay. I'll keep an eye out for him."

"How are you doing?"

"I'm fine," she said. "Could use more sleep like you said, but fine. Gonna blow the webs out of my head now. See you later."

"Travel safely," he said in elvish.

Lila put the tape into a smartseal pack and rode it across to a local bike courier company to get it taken straight to the Incon Agency drop. Then she put her visor down and made for the coastal highway. The inland freeway was faster, but she wanted some time to herself and to play with her fears as she laid the bike over in the tight corners where the road traced the shore.

It was lunchtime when she arrived at her destination in the hot, sun-scorched lot outside the Cherry Park Hotel. No tour bus duty for Zal and the others, strictly hotels with security and every luxury money could buy. There couldn't be a room in the place that didn't rent for more than an average weekly pay packet.

Lila left the bike in the shade of the new post-colonial-styled building and met up with Malachi in a tiled courtyard at the heart of the complex, where palm trees and fountains shaded the big outdoor pool. He promised to look into the faultline personally when he got back to town, but then pushed down his trendy fly-eye sunglasses and said, "I did some background checks on the Faery fellowship of song there. Sandy's all cool but Viridia and Poppy aren't straight gemstone darlings. My old ash-tree heart tells me that one or both of them are Each-Uisge, but I can't prove it. That's one tough act Zal's got backing him up."

"Ek Ooshkah?" Lila repeated quietly, not making the pronunciation of the strange Faery name very well, despite some AI assistance. "What's that?"

"Like kelpies, only more so. Kelpies like to drown victims but Each-Uisge are the kind who eat everything but your liver afterwards."

Malachi shrugged, his compatriots' extreme and varied idiosyncrasies as unremarkable to him as a liking for peanut butter was to Lila. "All faeries have pretty faces and walk wingless in Otopia, but not in every realm. You'd have to see them at home or in their element to be sure."

"You got secrets, Malachi?" Lila teased him gently. She was reasonably sure she was not imagining the fact that the plants near to him in the decorative border were leaning in his direction.

"Many," he assured her, feet firmly on the ground

"You think they're dangerous?"

"Hell, no. As long as you don't show them big lakes or the sea. And even then, you're probably all right here in Otopia. It's a pretty juiceless kind of place, y'know?"

Lila glanced at the pool, remembered Poppy kissing Zal by the last one.

Malachi shrugged, "Pools won't do it. Too many chemicals and not enough deep, dark water. Trust me. And in their human forms they'll be their fey, sweet selves, even on more pixie dust than you can eat."

"All right."

"Everyone else is doing okay. A few minor drug raps, some parking fines, a bad credit history, and a few misspent youthful moments. Nothing to get worked up over. And before you ask, no sign of those Jayon Daga agents, but that means nothing. Unlike most faeries in Otopia, bad news elves stay bad. I gotta go get onto that tape situation. Zal's all yours again. My tip this time—trip him up before he gets to the door and hold him down."

"Thanks," Lila said, making a gun of her right forefinger and thumb and shooting him for his insolence. She checked in and found Jolene in the reception area, two Berryphones and a Fruitfly commset on the go. With sign language Lila attempted to explain that she was back and was going up to Zal's suite. Jolene looked irritated, but it could have been from any of the conversations. She handed Lila a security card. Lila picked up the pack Malachi had taken from Solomon's

Folly for her, considered the elevator, and then hauled it up the stairs. She didn't like having to explain that she and her bag tipped the scales beyond the elevator's capacity every time she reached a floor.

The penthouse was rented for the band for the duration of their stay even though two of the members both had homes in town. It had four suites, and Zal got his own. Lila's card opened the door but after testing that she knocked and held it closed. Poppy answered it with a dazzling green smile and a squeal of delight, standing back to examine Lila's new biker clothes.

"You're all back, Li! *Like* the leathers." Poppy ushered her in and offered her a glass of some cocktail from a big jar on one of the tables where several brightly coloured pitchers lay in ice water.

"Hey," Lila said, glad to see her, whatever Malachi's suspicions were. "You were great last night."

"Yeah, yeah, just warming up," Poppy hummed. "Heard you had a bad fall. Okay now?"

"Sure." Lila hung onto the strap of her bag to show it was heavy.

"Sorry, sugar," Poppy said and pointed. "Go right in there. I'll get you something cold."

"Thanks, nothing strong," Lila said and went where she was told.

It was the master bedroom. The bed was messed up and she could hear water running. Trust Poppy, Lila thought, getting some sharp words ready and starting to lift her bag back up when the water stopped. She didn't mean to exactly, but she found she was still standing there when Zal appeared, wet and naked except for the short towel around his waist.

"Agent Black, don't you people ever knock?"

"Poppy told me this was my room. And you can knock off the Agent Black stuff. I think we deserve first-name terms, don't you?" Lila surprised even herself with her tart response.

Zal grinned. "You're so bolshy. I like that. I should thank you for this too." He turned and showed her the dark blue-black bruises on the backs of his legs and under his shoulders where she'd gripped him so hard for so long. But although they were bad, they didn't catch her attention at all compared to the liquid fire tattoo that covered the back of his shoulders. It fanned out in demon licks and tapered along the length of his spine until the tail of it vanished into the green band of the towel. It looked like it was a clear window of living skin beneath which burned a yellow and orange fire.

"What *is* that?"

"Oh that." He made a slight shrug. "It's a demon thing."

She got the clear impression it was so familiar to him that he'd forgotten about it, and that he wouldn't have shown her if he'd been thinking more clearly.

He seemed annoyed with himself as he lay back on the bed and turned the TV on with the remote control. "So," he said. "Not your room. Next door."

His hands looked normal. Both of them.

"Are you okay?" she asked, letting the bag slide down to the floor. She went forward to see for herself.

"Fine." He held them both out for her to see. "Apart from my hangover. How are you?"

"Fine," she said, keeping a polite distance. "Tired."

"Want to sleep with me?" He gestured with one hand at the massive expanse of linen and pillows beside him. "I mean sleep too. Sleep. Switch off. Although that biker gear is nice. I like leather and big zips on a woman."

"*Zo na kinkirien*," Lila said, glancing at the towel. "But you and I have some talking to do."

"We have all kinds of things to do," Zal said. "But if you don't mind I'm going to do mine horizontally. My head hurts." He slid down into the sheets and pulled the towel off, throwing it onto the floor.

"It can wait a couple of hours," Lila said. She felt the noose of the Game around her neck tugging with all this back-and-forth play, and hated it. She would have liked to stay, so she made herself pick up the bag and go out into the smaller room that waited for her. She gave Poppy a glare on her way through but the Faery simply smiled and shrugged.

"What? I pointed to where you wanted to go."

"You're in trouble," Lila told her. She closed the door and changed out of her bike gear into casual clothes. A message icon arrived in the upper right quadrant of her vision to tell her that the tape had arrived safely in the audio lab. Lila took a deep breath and a few minutes to look through her personal effects and check them—everything was in place and somebody had put the silver framed photo of Okie in the bag as well, assuming it was hers. She took the picture out, placing it in between clothes in her bag, and put the frame into one of the empty drawers on her dresser, then called the pet resort to find out how Okie was doing in her absence. He was fine. She felt slightly disappointed, and to get back her self-control after that and Zal, she made herself go through a full and unnecessary systems-check.

Dr. Williams called her in the middle of it. "You shouldn't be back out there," she said wearily. "I recommended against it. But you heard all this as you were leaving me in a cloud of exhaust fumes early this morning. How are you?"

"Perfectly well."

"Never worse news to my ears," the old woman said with a sigh. "Sarasilien told me that you encountered Dar again. How was that?"

"He shot me." Lila could say it without a single flinch. She smiled, proud of herself.

"Is that all? My my, how disappointing for you."

"What's that supposed to mean?"

"It means what it says on the tin. How is Zal?"

"The usual obnoxious two-tone reactions."

"To which you haven't reacted a bit."

"I'm keeping everything professional."

"Lila." Dr. Williams became kind. "Could you tell me about what happened in the forest, please?"

"I did a report. And you downloaded the rest from my AI-self. It's all in there."

"My eyes are old and tired, my neurons weary of the cool logics of AI analysis—indulge me."

"Indulge me indulge me, or, *you're busted fool, now indulge me?"*

"That kind of thing."

Lila closed down her shooting array and watched the guns vanish to their places inside her leg cavities. She rolled her sleeves back down over the scars on the remaining flesh of her arms as the synthetic skin reassembled itself over the hidden components beneath. Although it didn't hurt she massaged her shoulder which had become stiff, though it was well healed from the arrow. "All right. Zal ran off into the woods. I followed him. He drew a lot of elemental forces to try and stop me, or, well, maybe they tried to stop me on their own, but I passed them okay. He made a circle and got high on elemental action somehow. I don't know how or what that was about. Dar and his partner were hunting us down. I neutralised her. A ghost came and threatened Zal so I broke the circle and . . ."

"That's enough of that," Dr. Williams said. "Could you tell me about the elf agent?"

"Oh, she was Jayon Daga's usual. Red hair, blue eyes, full of contempt, hated me for all the obvious reasons."

"And you did what to her?"

"I shot her full of gengineered Pentothal and left her all asleep in a shady grove. She'll be fine."

"And Dar shot you?"

"I think he meant to hit Zal," but Lila wavered as she stated the obvious. She started to doubt whether Dar was that bad a shot, even under the circumstances—or else it was the only shot he could get, and he took it no matter that she was in the way. It occurred to her that perhaps Dar had deliberately shot through her. A shiver ran across her skin, real and synthetic.

"Are you sure it was Dar?"

"Of course I'm sure. I'd know him anywhere," Lila said shortly.

"And then you carried Zal away."

"He was unconscious, or something like that. I . . ." But she didn't really remember anything other than a blur. "There was a . . . I went down along what I thought was the house track and I . . ." Unaccountably, Lila felt that she was about to cry. She didn't know why, only that she had this feeling when she remembered flashes of clarity about running down the hillside. She tried again. "You can get across country to the NSA Incon building because it backs onto the Wildlife Reserve on the edge of town, so I went all the way around because I couldn't be seen."

"You went thirty klicks out of your way," Dr. Williams said. "You carried Zal for thirty-nine kilometres, with an arrow through your shoulder as your body tore itself apart."

"It was the stupid program," Lila said. "It wouldn't reset itself. I would have gone back to the house otherwise."

"Yes, of course."

But now Lila wasn't sure about that. "I won't be using it again," she said.

"Would you like to know the status of the debugging report, Lila?"

"No," she said. "Why are you telling me all this?"

"Because I want you to come back alive and I want Zal to survive you," Dr. Williams said. "And as long as you think everything else is at fault, that gets less likely."

Lila cut the connection and sat, listening to Poppy and Viridia talking in the main room, the clink of their glasses and their easy laughter. She was insulted, frankly, that Dr. Williams thought that she was in the grip of some big psychological trauma that could drive her to do something as crazy as take Zal on a cross-country run in the middle of a fight. The woman was obsessed. How could she make a last remark about Zal surviving her? That was ridiculous.

Lila contemplated making an official complaint about the devious manipulation of psychologists, but of course that would only go through Dr. Williams, so what was the point?

An elegant full-length mirror with a gold Baroque border standing in the corner of the room showed her sitting bold upright, rigid as a post. The magical stain in her hair and skin looked like a splash of blood. Lila's own silver eyes stared at her, reflecting the mirror's reflection into an infinite regress. She got up and covered the mirror with a towel from the bathroom, unable to suppress a shudder—she was an idiot to think that Zal flirted with her. A cold, noxious feeling ran through her and she felt ugly and angry.

She walked back into Zal's room and snapped the TV off.

"What's the matter now?" he said, rolling from his side onto his back. "I thought you'd done the decent thing and left me to suffer in peace."

"I have drugs that can fix that," she said and sat down on the opposite side of the bed to the one he was on. She held up her hand and showed him the hypodermic which she'd used on Dar's partner, glad to see him look quickly away. "I want my answers."

"Do you? About what?" He put one hand behind his head. His flaxen hair was drying. It was longer than she'd thought and his skin was paler, although it had some hints of Otopian tan about it on the face and hands. His large, dark eyes ignored her effort to engage them and stared up into the princess canopy which draped and belled over the bedhead. She felt no hint of glamour from him at all. He did a pretty good impression of being utterly uninterested. She had never seen anyone more attractive than Zal at that moment, and it felt like a punch in the face.

"Let's start with why you ran off to the woods."

"Let's say I'm not going to explain it. Perhaps I think it's enough that you see me in all my weaknesses without having to label them for you so that you can put them into your case file and think you know me, Agent."

"Well, will you be doing it again? Can I expect to get shot more times because you put us both in positions of needless danger?"

"No doubt," he said. "And no doubt I will be lying here thanking you for saving me more times. I believe that's how it's supposed to work, isn't it? And after a few more sessions you can pity me and fall in love with me, and I can feel grateful and emasculated and throw myself into further extremes to prove my virility."

"You know the whole script," Lila said, well aware that he was diverting her effortlessly. She felt as though she was a runaway train and at the same time was trying to change the points on her own tracks. The Game magic wanted to trip her up every which way. She had to think twice about every word she said. "We can change it. Let's finish the Game for a start."

"Here I am," he said and this time he did look at her with that wicked glance that glittered and was up for anything, the one no elf ever wore. He grinned at her hesitation. "You can't bear to lose, can you?"

"I'm in no danger of losing," Lila said. "I was ordered to finish it."

"Oh, well, I think that Sorcha told you that's no good. We'll have to live with it, then, for the rest of our lives. I hope you're not the jealous type. I don't like being alone all the time."

"Can we get back to the woods for just a moment?" Lila insisted. "The elf agent shot you in the shoulder. Don't you *care*?"

"They're out to get me." The tip of one ear flicked dismissively.

"And I can't find you in the records."

"Bullshit," he said. "You're looking in the wrong place, Sherlock. You're looking in Alfheim, and you're looking in Otopia, but you aren't reading the Demonia listings. I'm right there, next to Sorcha, under the family name, Ahriman."

"You're an elf. A High Elf, by the looks of your face."

"Yes," he said. "I am that too. And you, pretty robot? What are you apart from a half a ton of metal and attitude?"

Lila checked his claims on the records via Incon Tree and saw that it was true. Zal Ahriman. "But Zal isn't your real name. Ahriman isn't either. Not the first name." The record did not show previous names, only the nickname.

"Of course not. How stupid do I look? You think I'd survive ten minutes in Demonia under my real name? Elves are their favourite torment-toy."

"So, you weren't born there?"

"Well, duh."

"Is that how Sorcha woke you up from whatever Dar's arrow did?"

"It wasn't the arrow. It was the elementals. And yes, that's how. And no, I will not tell my name to you. And no, I don't know what the arrowhead did. And yes, I do care, but I can't do anything about it. And no, I will not stop the tour. And now I will not answer any more of your annoying questions because you can't be bothered to do your homework."

Lila felt so angry she couldn't speak. She mastered it with stillness.

"Come on, Lila girl," he said, in the same way that Sorcha spoke. "You've got a bit of the devil in you, you know it. Sometimes you should let her out, or else she'll go bad on you when you least want her to." His *andalune* body touched her suddenly, invisibly. She felt it like a feather against her face, where the scarlet stain met her ordinary skin. It ran under her clothing, down her arm, over flesh and metal. It had the most peculiar qualities; the lightness of strength, the coolness of intense desire.

"Leave me alone!" she stood up, her head pounding suddenly. She didn't know what she wanted to do, but she wanted to do something violent and powerful and physical.

"Okay," he said and the touch was gone. "But anyway. Were you shitting me about the drugs? I drank way too much last night."

"Oh yeah, why's that?" Lila did have things that would work for Zal. Being an elf they weren't the same things that a human would take for alcoholic poisoning. "Intravenous, or by mouth?" Lila thought of the elf agent's face when Lila had injected her, the woman's obvious disgust mingled with fear and loathing.

Zal considered it, then held out his arm. "Spike me," he said.

Trust him to be cussed about it, Lila thought. She took hold of the offered hand, his left, the one that had been emptied out by the ghost and was now perfectly whole when it should be dead or missing, yanked into I-space. She tried not to notice the way his skin felt as she examined the inside of his elbow. She ran her finger over one of the green veins close to the surface. A spark travelled up from their point of contact into her chest and she felt something inside respond, as though a living thing jumped inside her rib cage and the space around it was a big empty cavern. Wild magic. The stupid Game.

She found herself staring into Zal's eyes.

Instead of directing the medicine to her arm, she directed it as if she was going to give it to herself, into her mouth. It was all the Game. She didn't care.

"Just nod if you can hear me," she told him as he looked surprised when she let go of his arm and took hold of his jaw in her hand. Or maybe it was the Pink Floyd lyrics that surprised him. "Relax. I need some information first."

"Just the basic facts," Zal replied, smiling with bemusement and leaning backwards until he was all but lying flat on the tideline of pillows that covered the bed.

"It's just a little pinprick," Lila said. She bent down and kissed him. She expected all kinds of tricks. She didn't expect him to kiss her back as tenderly as he did, nor to feel his hand against her face, which made her in turn let go of her medically effective hold on him and slide her hand along his neck where she felt the smooth action of the muscles there and the blood beating in the pulse below his ear as he opened his mouth to her.

The medicine trickled out below her tongue, bitter and sweet, its synthetic macromolecules copying the fancy tricks of real Alfheim plantlife. Zal looked directly into Lila's eyes as he tasted it and she felt both his hands on her head as he deepened his kiss.

His transparent enjoyment and the depth of his immersion in the experience of the moment shocked Lila. She couldn't escape the strongest feeling that what she'd meant to be a tease and a joke, a needle of a different kind, was an act equivalent to what she'd seen him do in Zoomenon—a sacred thing. Wild magic rippled in an electrical fizz along the conduits of her spine. She saw it in Zal's eyes as he pulled away from her, lips wet, mouth open, pupils expanded into dark horizons bigger than any human eyes. He was panting and she was now completely immersed in his aetheric body—a full embrace of such sudden intimacy that it confused her utterly.

Lila didn't know any words now but she didn't like the feeling inside. It was too much, too big, too strange and connected to the Game, connected to him and to the moments she'd been thrown back and poisoned by Dar, connected to Sarasilien's cool hand on her forehead.

She pushed away from him and stood up quickly. She was so hot, she had to get out. Stupid. She was stupid to do that and think it was anything but ordinary lust and human need reacting to simple High Elf glamour.

"Comfortably numb," Zal said softly, eyes glazed, his touch all gone from her. He lay still, spreadeagled in the sheets.

"Is that what you do with the elementals?" she asked.

"I'll show you, next time," he offered, and she had no doubt he meant it. There was a complete change in him. His attitude had gone, replaced by this terrifying sincerity and that Alfheim cool assurance she couldn't stand and couldn't stop wanting to watch.

Lila brushed her hands across her mouth and swallowed the traces of the drugs. They made her feel heady and too energetic. She looked anywhere but at him.

"Well," he said after a moment, sitting up. "I hope that taught you not to go starting fires."

"I did not start the Game," she snapped. She noticed that the main room had gone quiet and knew that Poppy at least must be ear wigging for all she was worth.

Zal raised one eyebrow. "I was talking to myself. I'm going to get up. Thanks. I'll be sure and get drunk more often." He waited, pointedly.

"Oh right!" Lila said in exasperation and turned her back. She used sensors in her back to watch with instead and caught him smiling to himself, at her, in that annoying patrician way of someone who thinks they're winning. She was going to try for a smart retort but found herself looking at the tattoo again as he turned his back. It burned incredibly brightly, a yellow that was almost white. "What is *that* supposed to be?"

"I should have known you'd have eyes in the back of your head," he said and walked back into the bathroom, closing the door.

Poppy was waiting for Lila in the lounge.

"If you say anything, I will kill you," Lila told her before she had time to open her chrysoprase green lips.

The faery smiled and crossed her legs in midair, floating easily as she rattled ice cubes in a tall glass, "Juice with your ice?"

Lila shook her head and tapped her temple. "I have a call to make," she said and went into her own room.

She called Williams. When the woman answered she said with less awkwardness than she felt, "I want to talk to you about Dar and the mission in Alfheim."

"Okay," the doctor replied calmly. "Go ahead."

CHAPTER ELEVEN

"We went into Alfheim as part of the diplomatic corps," Lila began, when she was convinced that their secure link couldn't be eavesdropped upon. "I was one of three agents for the NSA Otopia who went to the embassy in Lyrien. We did all the usual work there. I was never good at elvish really, so I didn't do much contact— you know how sniffy they are if you get a consonant out of place. Well, I was in the offices and I used to deal with all the border control documentation. We'd look over it all very carefully, because there was a suspicion that someone in Alfheim was collecting big game magical artefacts and using couriers to bring them in.

"I used to check all the records as closely as I could and then go and try to verify them by following up on some of the items that were listed, and some of the ones that we thought had come in without customs declarations. I'd pose as a courier for Otopia Postal Service and say that some box or other hadn't been checked and that I wasn't allowed out of Alfheim until I'd got proof of purchase or an invoice or some other piece of information. Sometimes I just asked for a picture of the object and took that with my camera. Anything to trace where the stuff was going. Plenty of it was perfectly legit of course.

"Then Customs and Excise got a lead on one of these couriers when a packet of magicopharmaceuticals she was carrying internally burst and killed her. She actually gave herself up as she was dying. I saw her talk to them. She wasn't making a lot of sense—it was a necromantic drug meant to let the users travel through Thanatopia without dying. Weird because you don't get many elf necromancers obviously, what with their feelings about life and death, but she'd got far more than a single dose and she was walking two worlds and her body was packing up by the time I got there. Nothing could have saved her. She hadn't known what she was carrying until the drug took her into Thanatopia. Well, she found out and met up with some other of her ex-associates in Death—they'd been murdered by their masters you see, after finishing their deliveries—she decided to go along with their wishes and tell the authorities what was going on, try and undo what was being done. But there was a spell on all of them which prevented them from talking about it directly. So she wasn't much help.

"Before she died we managed to figure out that the stuff was being taken beyond Lyrien, into Sathanor. At that time there was a diplomatic mission going out to Sathanor on a rubber chicken visit to cement the trust that Alfheim wanted to show in Otopia now that the immigration acts had been sorted out at last. So I went as part of the cortege into Sathanor, as a PA to the Ambassador.

"There was another agent with me, Vincent De Palma, another Otopian spy. We were under instructions to look for anything that looked like it might link up with what this woman had said. He was very keen." Lila paused for breath, then carried on.

"The thing about Sathanor is—it's very beautiful, like you dream that nature intended, like Eden. Everything is more itself there, even than in the rest of Alfheim. When you go you can see how the elves and the elementals are related magically. Skies are bluer, trees more majestic and individual, stones are more solid, rivers wilder—everything has its own spirit that you can feel, like ultra-authentic. We used to call it whiskey-country, you know? Because it was distilled from hundreds of gallons of ordinary things into this incredible, rich, sensual, spiritual stuff.

"So, we were in whiskey-country and we were kind of drunk on it, and all the elves were a bit too, but they were used to it, so they'd laugh at us because we were all stoned the whole time and that made spying really hard. When you were there you realised that in Otopia, though the elves have aetherial bodies that you can sometimes feel if they want you to, they're just disconnected there, but in Alfheim you realise that they're not disconnected any more. The *andalune* is a part of them that's connected to the land and the sky and the whole place, like my AI-self connects me to the Otopia Tree. Except in Sathanor it's not an interface. In Sathanor the elves are part of Alfheim—there's one big *andalune*, I suppose. I could see why it's called the water bridge—*andalune*'s meaning in Otopian. It flows between everything. It makes all relationships potentially very intimate in ways we humans don't have at all.

"Well, we were at this big party thing in one of the mountain halls—all so gorgeous, I can't tell you—and Vincent overheard some elf princes talking about a necromancer that they'd heard of, operating deep in Sathanor, at some place very remote. They were jumpy about it, not paying attention to much else, and he thought this was a good lead, so we decided we'd pretend we were going out on a hiking trip for a few days whilst the rest of the talking was going on, and we set out and tried to find this place. We had an elf guide with us, an ordinary Alfheim agent, who'd agreed with our bosses in the regular NSA that we should make a joint trip to find out what was going on in secret. Harad, her name was. And we made a long journey into the big country but we didn't get as far as the place we were going. Dar and the other Jayon Daga agents came after us.

"I didn't understand all the distinctions then. I couldn't see why they weren't exactly on the same side as Harad, though they clearly didn't think themselves her allies. Sarasilien told me later that they're a kind of law unto themselves, like a priest caste, the grey eminences behind a lot of the apparent Alfheim ruling classes. Anyway, they intercepted us in the mountains and ordered us to go back in no uncertain terms. We agreed of course, and Harad was very worried about them being there and knowing where we were, but Vincent and I didn't understand the situation and we thought it was such a good opportunity that we managed to persuade her . . . Well, we didn't go back. We went on and then the Daga came after us again and . . ."

Lila faltered. This was where she wasn't sure of a solid narrative any more, only of isolated events.

"They used magical weapons. I think there was some kind of struggle between Harad and the first of them. They captured her, and she was sent away with some of their number, I don't know where to. I never saw her again. The rest of them, under Dar's command, decided that they couldn't let me or Vincent go and they discussed what they were going to do about it. While that was happening the one who had been set on to guard us fell asleep. Something came out of the trees and he just—it emptied him—he keeled over on the ground just like that. And then it got to Vincent, because he was closer, and it was some kind of . . . I think it was a ghost of some kind: an inhaler, not an exhaler . . . um . . . I didn't really see it, just something greyish and our guard falling over. Vince and I had been tied up, hands and feet, and I managed to roll away, but he couldn't do it in time because he had his back to it, and he just . . . I guess he must be dead. I don't know. I was trying to get away and I didn't want to shout because I thought they were going to kill us anyway, but then Dar saw me and he must have thought I'd done whatever it was to his soldier and to Vincent. He was furious.

They picked me up and ran with me. I don't know where. Then they threw me down." *Fire.* "Dar cast this spell and it hit me and it burned . . .

"I see his face a lot in my dreams. I saw him then just a few times, different times. And there was this pain. And he was looking at me with that cold face. It must have been different times, because the backgrounds were different. He never did anything else. I heard him talking to the others and asking me questions but I couldn't answer them. And then I don't remember anything, except the hospital here.

"But that's not the worst. The thing I wanted to say was that what burned me was Dar's *andalune* and it burned me with hate. I felt it because it was everywhere and the spellcast came from it and it carried it into me. I could hear him in it. The way he despised humans, loathed demons, feared . . . he was afraid of a lot of things. He was afraid of the magic he used to stop me. He was revolted by what he saw happen to me. He made himself sick. Every time he looked at me afterwards I could see how much he wished I didn't exist. He'd ask me questions about what we saw, and I'd say nothing because we didn't see anything, and he'd be furious. I would have told him anything. If they hadn't wanted to keep me alive to ask me questions, I'd have been dead. I'm sure of it. Dar kept me alive. As long as I was conscious he never stopped asking questions."

Lila stopped. She glanced around the hotel room. Next door she could hear music and voices. She looked at the time and saw an hour had passed.

"Did he recognise you in the woods this time?" Dr. Williams asked.

"Yes," Lila said, grateful for Williams's calm, able to be calm in return. "And then he shot me. And I meant to say it was worse because Dar is very—handsome—but that sounds ridiculous. Why would that be worse? Only it is. When I looked at him, all I could see was how beautiful he was, and all he saw was how horrible I was. He could feel me, because the magic in his arrowshot carried the charge of his *andalune*, and he couldn't stand it. It made him physically sick." Lila bit out the last words and then clenched her jaws shut. She felt as though she had swallowed acid. At the time, in the thick of the action, she hadn't even noticed it, she thought, but now that she had to say it aloud, her mind was only too keen to supply clear details.

"Thank you, Lila," Dr. Williams said. "You should rest now. You must be very tired." She had put her kind voice back on.

"Yes, I will," Lila said. She didn't really suspect the doctor of hypnotism, but the suggestion seemed so welcome. She went and lay on the bed's cover and then pulled the pillows into her arms and shut her eyes as she closed the phone link down. But this didn't work. She didn't feel better. She felt worse. She could hear Poppy laughing: no happier sounds than faery laughter, kind of crazy and twisted as it was, and Lila felt a smile turning up her own mouth against her will.

She looked at her internal pharmacy registry. There must be something here that wouldn't hurt to take; something that would do what her silly song-lyric game with Zal had been meant to do and leave her feeling like she was in control. Nothing too strong, nothing that would slow her down or make her mad—she looked at the CNS stimulants, an array provided for Full Armour situations when she had to drive her human self to the limit to keep up with the machine. She could take those.

"Hey Lila," Poppy said from the door. "We're gonna order takeout. You want some?"

"No," she said. "I mean. Yes. Sure. Whatever."

"Are you okay?"

"Yeah. I'm glad you came in," Lila sat up and swiped at her face, clearing it of tears.

"Bad news?" the faery said, tentatively coming closer.

"Just work stuff. Really. Nothing to worry about. I'm tired. You know."

"Sure, honey," Poppy said. "He's difficult."

For once Lila didn't bother trying to correct her. "You have a soundcheck in an hour."

"I know. We're gonna eat and go. Sure you don't want a drink?"

"Water."

"I'm on it."

Lila used the time to wash and fix her face. She felt a strange kind of high after all that, because she hadn't taken anything and was still functional. She avoided Zal for the rest of the day, accompanying him with her dark visor on like every other idiot bodyguard, keeping people at a distance and doing the dull things with Jolene that had to be done; scheduling, cars, bike, green rooms, backstage vetting, meeting up with the rest of the security for the site and making sure they were all briefed on the kinds of negative attention that the band could get and who to look out for.

Lila handed out pictures of Dar and the other known elf agents in Otopia, some straight and others with them made up as human. "If you think you see any of these people, you need to call me straight away."

"Are they like, dangerous?" asked one.

"Yes," Lila said. "But they won't give you any trouble if you don't approach them directly. They want to get in. They don't want to attract attention to themselves."

"I heard this band was having trouble with extremists," another added. "Are these the ones?"

"Maybe," Lila said. "You'll see that in *The Herald* this morning they reported on the kind of hate mail that Zal's been getting. Humans, demons, faeries, and elves; all send it in various kinds. The loud ones, in my experience, aren't the ones you need to worry about. If you see the people pictured, don't try to stop them, just call me."

"Man I hate this shit," she heard one guard mutter. "Stupid race-hate bigots. Ruin the whole fucking world."

"Amen," Lila said under her breath. She found herself looking through the stadium camera systems, looking for Dar. She didn't see him.

She located the other NSA agents and went through the call signs with them for the evening show and then caught up with Zal, taking a seat in the front row of the auditorium as they walked a rehearsal with sound and light cues. She practised tuning her ears to block out the band sound so that she could hear around it, picking frequencies and neutralising them. They messed about with dance beats and silly covers of other people's songs. She envied their easy virtuosity.

As they finished up, Lila checked everything she could think of that might matter; weather reports, police radio, traffic, communications. She didn't know what she was looking for. Then Malachi called her from Sarasilien's office.

"I got some early forecasts on your tape," he said once the security encryption on their link had authenticated. "That subaudible signal is definitely coming from a bomb fault that runs under the studio."

"So, not band-related at all?"

"Could be bootlegs with this other thing piggybacking by accident, can't say. Anyway, the 'leggers have legged it, so I'm going to go back and see if I can find out more about the noise trace by taking better samples. The lab monkeys think it sounds like some library recordings of theirs which go back to the Fallout. Someone mentioned the words Seventh Realm, but they always say that when they find stuff they don't understand."

"Okay. If it's not directly Zal-related then I'm going to have to leave it with you," Lila said. "We're good here so far. But I've got a bad feeling. I don't know. Maybe it's the stadium architecture. There's a lot of hiding places around here for anyone with an ounce of magic."

"You'll have to wear the full kit then," Malachi said cheerfully.

"I intend to." She hung up and stretched. The work had done her good. She felt tired and wrung-out, but no longer out of control.

She shepherded the band back to the hotel and took only enough time out to open her bag and install the remaining armour that she'd checked out days ago. She treated her skin where it hurt, swallowed the nasty, slimy goop that contained the nanocytes to maintain her integration with her machine body, and took the doses of drugs that were marked up in her system-vision to support the extra load of the arsenal she was carrying. Her exhaustion paled and her attention sharpened.

There was a knock on her open door.

"Yeah," she said, zipping the bag closed.

"Cool suit," Zal said. He did not come in. "And didn't you used to be shorter than me?"

"Maybe," Lila said, at eye level with him. "What's up?"

"Nothing." He held out a can of Coke. "Thought you might want this."

"I have a fridge full of Coke."

He reached through the door and put it down on the sideboard where an unnecessarily large and ostentatious display of flowers used up almost all the space. His tone was dry and ironic. "I know. I understand that the offering of a dead badger is a more traditional symbol when apologising to mere humans, but hell, there aren't many badgers left in Frisco. The elves have insulted their way out of this town."

"What are you apologising for?"

"Ah see, now you're pushing me too far." He walked forward, fully dressed up in his ordinary elf clothes, as handsome as the sun in spring. "Nice room. Bit small."

"You don't care about my room."

"No." He closed the door behind him and locked it.

Lila looked at him questioningly.

"About the elementals," he said. "It's not what it looks like."

"What is it then?"

"You have a very intimidating stance, has anyone ever told you that? All right. It is what it looks like, but it's not an addiction like heroin. It's part of the way I learned to survive Demonia. Zoomenon is like ultra-Sathanor, you must realise that from being there, right? And I haven't been in Alfheim for a very long time. I've been in Demonia, and in Faerie and in Otopia, and all of those places are fine but they're not . . . me. It's like you said, I was born elf, and I *need* to be in Alfheim sometimes. Do you understand?"

"So, why don't you just go there?"

He glanced down to the right and adjusted the position of an orange gerbera in the flower arrangement. "I don't like other elves that much these days, and they rarely like me. I enjoy not being strip-searched and interned for two weeks while they try to get their heads around me not wanting to live in Alfheim like a good forest-loving, mountain-running, pole-up-the-ass son of the trees. Anyway, there's nobody there I want to see."

Lila watched the flowers behind him open to their fullest. Zal didn't seem to notice or care. He glanced at her. "You must wish you could live a normal life, now and again."

"I do live a normal life," she said.

"Sure you do, Princess Zirconium." He grinned this time and gave her a mock bow. "Your every word is iron-clad with truth."

"Haven't you got an exciting crowd of fans to wave to?"

He placed a hand over his heart. "Ouch. She dismisses me and throws my badger in my face." He backed up to the door and opened it. "Until later, mighty metal maiden."

The door closed with a quiet snick.

Lila glanced at her reflection in the mirror. "Stop smiling," she told it sternly. "You are at work."

CHAPTER TWELVE

The show ripped at midnight but by then the buses were already on their way north along the coast in a land train with the equipment trucks. Lila waited behind for Zal, who wouldn't travel on the buses even if it meant arriving too late to party anywhere new. Zal had hung around with Luke, drinking Mimosas, until Luke had reluctantly dragged himself off to his appointment with a Winnebago Xpress. He had still not appeared when Lila and Buddy Ritz were left alone in the backstage area, with the security guards who wanted to lock up.

Zal's agent rubbed his face and kept checking his phone. "I have to get back to Bay City for morning," he kept saying. "I just wanna be sure, you know, that he leaves here okay at least, and then you're all on your . . ." The phone rang. "Hey Jolene. Yeah. Real soon." He hung up. "What the hell is he doing?" He strode forward to the door but Lila blocked his way.

"Leave it."

"I was only going to say hurry up," Ritz objected, pushing her hand away from the collar of his purple fur coat with a squeamish flick. She recognised that coat from the other night, last night, and let him go.

"I'll make sure he arrives on time," Lila said. "You can go."

"I can go, can I?" he blustered, although she could see he was itching to get gone. Then the door opened and Zal stood there, much the same as always, a little too High for any fashion this side of Lyrien, a little too cool for any celebrity off duty.

"Hey Buddy," he said casually. "Sorry to keep you waiting. They put that glitter on my face and it wouldn't come off."

Lila could see some of it now, caught in his long, carefully braided hair. "Mr. Ritz is anxious for us to leave now."

"Sure," Zal said, as ordinary as you please. "Let's go." He did cast a slight glance sideways at Lila when he saw that she'd brought the bike right up inside the access corridor, but he got on the back without another comment.

"He should really wear some kind of head protection," Buddy started. "The insurance . . ."

The bike started as it felt her stride across it, legkick forwards. The engine's throaty growl in the confined space drowned out every other sound in creation. Lila cued the security system to open the artistes' access door and took them forward in a smooth glide of ever-increasing speed. There was a curious, perfect moment, just before they burst into the night, when she felt that everything on earth was balanced and whole and true and that the pieces of life slotted together neatly inside her, a puzzle finished and done, a charm completed, a talisman charged. Then the light was gone and they were in the cool wind on the road. Zal slid forward and put his chin on her shoulder.

"Did you feel that?"

"What was it?"

"Don't know. Ride faster." His head pressed against hers and her hand turned gently on the throttle in the movement of a dance and her foot tapped for a higher gear and her fingers released and they flew, dodging cars like kids on a stolen ride because she wanted to and it was all her, the bike, the dark, it was all him.

They leaned and glided out of town and onto the coast road, Lila taking it for the bends, for the hills, for the giddy hit of barely making it over loose stones in the tight anticamber on the heights of a cliff where moonlight shattered on the surface of the sea and shone like jewellery. She could smell the ocean, mixed with the scent of little, low-growing night-blooming flowers, and petrol. She did notice when Zal rested his head on her back, and that his arms went around her. It was part of the great ride and the machine.

They caught up with the landtrain and passed it in the quiet traffic of early morning. Dawn met them as they reached the most deserted part of the road, where it ran far from civilisation, along the edges of beachfront parks and the remote edges of millionaire's estates, beside the rough grass of preservation districts where nobody was allowed to build or wander except the animals and birds.

Lila heard their engines before she saw the other bikes racing towards them across the rough terrain of the empty land. Both were light, fast motocross machines, and both riders had the elastic quality and poise she recognised with instant apprehension: Dar and his partner.

Since when did JD agents get funky enough with machinery to ride bikes?

They were coming in at angles which would intercept both her past and future course. Lila curled her lip and felt Zal lean forward again.

"Where's your input jack?"

"What?" she shouted back, sure she was mishearing him, then felt him jam an earpiece over her left ear. She heard music—a heavy metal power ballad with a strange dance funk undertone.

"Never go into battle unaccompanied!" Zal shouted over the wind noise and the riff as Lila pushed her right wrist all the way down and her suspension systems into full sport mode.

Lila out-accelerated Dar, passed the female elf while she was still fighting her way onto the hardtop from the dirt track, and left them in a cloud of pale dust.

She felt the curl of magic against her bones and the peculiar inner pressure cast of a magical footprint as someone fixed a spell on them.

In the growing light all the colours of the world were blue and grey, but for a moment they went green. Lila took a slow, deep breath and ignored it, focusing entirely on the road, laying the bike down almost flat and praying for a good surface as they rounded a small headland and slid gently and decisively out towards the single metal rail of the safety barrier.

She righted them with inches to spare and was feeling the first wash of relief when she saw the twin square blocks and eight huge tyres of two heavyloaders blocking both lanes about two hundred metres in front of her. The road had gone into a low-walled canyon. There was no space either side and nowhere to go.

Lila squeezed the brakes as hard as she dared, to protect herself and Zal from a summary ejection out of the front door. She felt her insides drag her forwards as they bled speed and when the needles looked about right and they were fearfully slow, like snails, she hit the power and the front brake simultaneously and slid around, aiming them both square at the two bikes just coming around the turn.

She opened the casing on her lower right leg and bent down to take out a metal baton. As the armour fused shut into unbreakable plate, she connected to the pikestaff with the sensitive cells in the palm of her hand and swung the short metal stave in the air to her side, avoiding Zal's leg. The baton telescoped out into a sturdy carbon and alloy quarterstaff almost two metres long.

"'kin hell!" she heard Zal say approvingly.

Lila smiled in grim satisfaction. She turned all bike controls over to her AI-self to free her hands and, with the staff tucked under her arm, sat more upright. "Hold tight," she shouted back to Zal and gunned the engine.

The engine spun the back wheel but the intelligent tyre surfaces changed properties and seized the road with limpet tenacity. They surged forward, Lila pressed back against Zal, and Zal resisting until the acceleration faded sweetly into a ninety kph surge. They met the two riders on a short straight. Lila held the quarterstaff like a medieval lance, across the handlebars, braced against her side, and aimed it at the chest of Dar's partner as they closed, but at the last second, with both elves starting to move out wide, she flipped the staff around, faster than the eye could see, and braced it across her waist, its single long arm now stabbing out to the left.

Even Dar's superhuman reflexes were not enough to take avoiding action. The baton missed the bars of his bike by a millimetre and slammed into his upper arms and chest, knocking him backwards instantly. Lila felt the horrible impact as a soggy crunch that tried to tear the bar out of her hands. She let the right hand side go so that part of the force dragged the staff cleanly around to the left, saving her arms and sparing Dar much of the blow's potentially lethal force. But saving her own arms was more important. She saw him twist in midair with catlike desperation and hit the road on his shoulder as his bike went sliding and skidding away. His speed took him rolling in the wake of the other bike, uncontrolled.

"Fuck!" she heard Zal shout with exhilaration and not a little fear.

Lila had kept their balance only because she had calculated the forces in advance and compensated during the attack. Now she recovered the staff and slid it into short mode, accelerating again without turning around to see what was going on behind them. The wind set her face into a ferocious mask. She didn't think this was likely to be over and her long-range sensors began to prove her right almost immediately. No sooner had they put a headland between them and the blocked canyon than she picked up a strange heat-signature in the sky.

A firebird stooped towards them from the haze of twilight blue. It was faster than an animal, as fast as a guided missile, and it tore Earthwards with the accuracy that Lila recognised as signal-oriented. The monster was a kind of missile, and they were locked in as the target. Maybe the earlier spellcast had singled them out . . . in any case, it hardly mattered. She had only a second in which to decide what to do.

Lila slammed on the brakes and laid her beautiful bike down on its side for the last time, trusting Zal's elf smarts to make him copy her move and get his leg out of the way as they went over. He was good enough for that at least, hanging on to her as they rode the machine along and ground it into the dirt, creating a huge plume of billowing dust around them as they finally came to a halt.

Coughing, Lila got up and hauled Zal to his feet, her hands on his upper arms, finger sensors verifying his physiology as intact even as she shouted, "Cast a circle!" She could barely see him through the falling dust though her helm protected her eyes and nose. "Anywhere! Now!"

A flicker of something hot ran across her hands, a tiny flame, but she was already letting him go. He nodded. Lila saw his *andalune* body clearly then. The dust glittered inside it and was spun around as though in the glare of a private sun. It drew suddenly very close to him and then vanished. He pulled part of his shirt over his face to take a breath with his eyes screwed shut, everything about him turning the soft beige shade of the earth. Then Zal sang the circle, just one breath, a few elvish words, a few clear notes that made Lila aware of the junction between her flesh and metal body as cleanly as if they were being cut in two.

She felt a change in the air, in the temperature, and the quality of the ground but she had no time to put these things together before they were surrounded in a boiling yellow gale of fire. Lila flinched automatically from what she thought would be blistering heat, but the air against her skin was cool. Through a gap of a few inches she stared into a roiling heart of flame and felt nothing of it.

Zal coughed and spat. "This won't hold for long against that. And whoever is its master."

"Why not?" Lila asked, looking down at her feet and seeing they were standing on lilac-coloured sand, looking up at the sky and seeing the most delicate of rose clouds against a turquoise blue. She and Zal, alone inside a column of fire, standing in another world.

"I can feel how strong that thing is," he said and to her questioning gaze gave an awkward shrug. "Who were you expecting? Mithrandir?"

"How long?" The fire curled and licked at the invisible barrier greedily. Lila would not step away.

"Minutes," he said, closing his eyes. Suddenly he yawned.

"What are you doing?" Lila was alarmed. She couldn't believe he was relaxed enough to feel like yawning.

"I'm tired," he said. "And holding this is very tiring. You wouldn't understand. I'm sure you'll have another plan by then. That jousting thing was very cool."

"Can you take us to where this circle is for real?"

"No," he said. "Not nearly."

"Can we walk and take it with us?" she asked, starting to feel desperate.

"No. I didn't think about that. It's fixed on the earth. Part of earth elemental magic. I could have done it in air but I wasn't . . . it wasn't what I did." He shrugged and peered more closely at the fire. "I think we're inside a phoenix. That's interesting. I didn't know they were fire all the way through. I thought they were hollow, like those disappointing chocolate Easter rabbits."

Lila pushed thoughts of impending death and strangling him to one side, "Zal, do you know why these people are out to get you?"

"Don't like me."

"The Great Spell," she prompted.

Zal was very serious now. "Yeah, that. I do somewhat fit the recipe for global disaster there. But they don't really want that. Might think they do. Who knows?"

"Someone clearly thinks so."

"Yeah, no prizes for guessing who they are."

"Enlighten me."

"Nobody wants to cut off their kingdom from the pollution of other races and their ideas more than those bastards in Sathanor."

"The High Elves?"

"The High Elves," he said, his ears flattening to his head completely. Lila saw that he was starting to struggle to stay upright. He folded his arms across his chest in determination. "Not all of them. Some. All it takes. And by the feel of this, they've been building their strength a long time. We've got another two minutes, maybe one and a half."

Lila bit her lip and thought. If this was down to who he said it was, no way would they want Zal dead. She decided to take the gamble and quickly stripped off her bike jacket.

"Is this my two-minute charity window?" Zal asked, frowning.

"Put it on," Lila ordered, pushing the jacket into his arms. She stripped off the trousers too, leaving herself in her military-issue shorts and vest, all metal exposed. "And these. Move!" Her boots would have to lie wherever they were forever, lost in time and space when the circle expired.

"Why?" He obeyed her. He was more dextrous than a human man, and more graceful, even when stuffing his Elf sleeves into her clothes.

"We're getting out of here," she said. "And it's going to be very hot, and then very, very cold."

"And how does your not wearing anything of note . . ."

"Nuclear reactor core," she said absently, peering at their surroundings. She could feel heat on her arms and shoulders, face and chest now, slowly increasing. "How you doing?" Zips and poppers sounded like flame crackling.

"Thank god neither of us likes cakes," he said, but without any zeal.

Lila turned and saw him swaying on his feet. She caught him before he fell and braced him against her. At the last minute she grabbed hold of all his long blond hair and twisted it rapidly together, jamming it down the neck of the jacket. "Stand on my feet. Go on. Do it. Okay, let the circle go."

"Hmm?"

She glanced at him, mistakenly, and made eye contact. As the ports on the soles of her feet were opening onto the lilac ground, she lost herself in a deep and puzzling warmth and darkness. The jet systems in her ankles came online and she felt the fire's heat wash away in a sudden cool, like mountain water, as Zal's aethereal body flooded out of him and leapt free of the tight control he had kept it under during the casting of the Zoomenon circle. It gushed over her like a tide, before falling back to its normal place a half an inch beyond his own skin.

It didn't mean anything, she told herself, though she inwardly registered it as a definite embrace.

She shut her eyes and allowed herself only the smallest of interior smiles at the vision of all-leather-clad Zal in her arms. Timing was everything. She had to get it right. She felt the subtle vibrations coming up through her skeleton as the intake vents behind her calves opened up and she felt the ground move away, heard the sheet and scatter of sand being blasted, being made into glass under her toes. "Now!"

The cool air of their envelope met the inrushing hot ionised gas of the phoenix and its oxygen gave the fire a sudden white brightness. It licked around Lila's legs and singed the leather of her trousers and the soles of Zal's boots, but it was confounded by the huge wash-out of her jets as she and Zal rose straight up on their own blazing trail. The phoenix recoiled from them as she had hoped; happy to imprison them, but afraid to damage what it was guarding.

The spell creature turned its massive head to watch them, beak opening as it spread its wings again and took to the air. But Lila was very high, too high and too fast. She navigated the bitter cold jetstream above the cloudline and felt Zal's physical shock at the sudden change, the loosening of his hold on her as his hands lost their strength. Condensation was rapidly turning to frost in the tendrils of hair around his face. And still the firebird climbed after them.

She saw an eagle, as large as the phoenix, coming out of the west. She glanced at Zal's face—his lips were pale with cold, almost white, but he was grinning at her.

"Did you notice how we're always together like this?" he said. "And there's an eagle behind you."

Lila cut the jets. They fell like stone. The eagle swooped after them, folding its wings into an arrow shape, but it was too big and the air resistance would not let it pass quickly enough. The phoenix, a conjuration that was seriously challenged for sustenance in unmagical Otopian space, was diminishing, its power fading as it literally burned away the magic that kept it alive. Such a thing could only be temporary here. Lila looked down at the fast-approaching earth and saw two dark figures on a single bike riding to the spot where her lovely red machine had died and become a blackened, deformed wreck. Finally her call out was answered.

"We can't get to you in time," Malachi said. He sounded awkward, but Lila didn't have time to think about that.

"Fuck," she said under her breath, and then to Zal. "Can you swim?"

But her final, desperate sea-ditch plan flew out of her head as they were suddenly hit by a terrific side impact. Another eagle, the size of a roc, had swept in lower and it struck them at an angle, seizing them in its huge claws. If she and Zal had been close before, they were crushed together now in the force of its grip. The sharp claw tips barely scratched Lila's metal skin but they cut into Zal and he gasped in pain. His breath didn't come back easily either.

Lila employed power hydraulics and levered the claws apart around them, but she didn't have the span to create a gap big enough to free them, only enough to create breathing space. The eagle righted itself into a smooth gliding arc and bent its head down, looking at them with one, great golden eye and then, in a move of great deftness, used its other foot and pressed two sharp claws around Lila, pulling her away from Zal. She clung on in resistance, the yellow scales of the foot that held Zal easy to grip, only to see one huge sickle of horn curve in easily towards Zal's stomach.

"Let go, if you want him to live," the beast said clearly. The claw punctured Lila's leathers effortlessly. Zal had frozen with the absolute stillness of mortal fear. She trusted his assessment of the magical creature's intentions, although it made little sense to her.

"You need him alive," she retorted, neither letting go nor struggling back.

"There are others who will do," the eagle said. "Shall you see me prove it, little toy?"

Lila looked once into Zal's face. "I'll come for you," she promised.

He gave her the slightest of smiles, "I should think so. It's your job."

Lila let go of the eagle's foot and without a second's hesitation the eagle let go of her. They were out over the ocean. She radioed her position in as she fell, watching the bird soar high and beat its way steadily north, towards the nearest Alfheim gateway. The pale effluvia of the firebird's remains had scattered over the desert like marshfires. She saw the two elf agents watching her fall. She saw the tankers that had blocked their way start up and drive away, faeries at the wheel.

Faeries? She glanced again at the elves and saw them signalling to her. The eagle was a dot in the sky. Lila realised that she could not simply go barrelling into Alfheim after it. They would shoot her easily. Instead, she took a deep breath and descended, coming to land a safe distance from her old bike. Her jets blew up more dust into the gleaming morning air and she had to walk through it alone this time, furious and ready to fight.

Dar was sitting on the ground next to her bike when she approached the two of them. One of the dirt bikes lay close by. He was clearly in considerable pain and his breathing was so shallow it was nothing more than rapid gasping. A pale red foam had gathered at the corner of his mouth and he was too hurt to brush it away. Both his arms were strapped across his chest. He glared at Lila, but without the fire of anger she expected. His blue eyes were the same colour as the clear sky. His partner stood at his side, her face taut and grim.

"Agent Black," she said stiffly. "The time has come for a moment of honesty between us."

"I'm all ears," Lila said.

"We do not seek to murder Zal, nor to harm him. We are trying to protect him."

"You've got a funny way of showing it," Lila retorted.

The female elf's face was impassive, but her fingers strayed to Dar's hair, touched it briefly, and Lila realised they were in aethereal contact, talking to one another secretly. The agent mastered whatever she felt about Lila and said, "Zal would have been taken to a safe place, beyond the reach of those who have captured him now. Your efforts have had the opposite effect to the one you desired. You have made it quite impossible for us to do what we must. Such strength and cunning are to be congratulated, and your feelings are clearly—involved."

Lila opened her mouth but the elf cut her off smoothly.

"Curb your anger, I mean no slight by it. We are all prisoners of the heart. Still, this has become a very difficult matter in the last few minutes. Dar would ask me to ask you if you would ride with him now, back into Alfheim, to pursue your mission. He will soon heal, once you reach Lyrien, and then he and those loyal to the true Jayon Daga will help you."

"Forgive my scepticism, but in that case how come you were sending all those poison pen letters and messages by arrowshot?" Lila demanded.

"We did not send the letters," the agent replied icily. "The Daga has enemies within. We have compromised them in Otopia, though we could not stop the Lady's eagles. Unlike her party we wish to keep the Severed Realms attached to one another, for the interests of Alfheim will not be served by separation. Time runs short. You must decide. Go with Dar and take a chance at saving Zal, or go on your own and be lost in Sathanor, hunted by the Daga, consumed by the dangers of the land, or vanquished by our common enemy, for the Lady is mighty and in Alfheim none of your strength can match her power. You did not match it here."

Lila glanced again at Dar and he met her eyes. It took all her resolve not to break first. He took a desperate, difficult breath and his voice was full of whistles and bubbles, "I apologise to you, Lila Black, for causing your present incarceration in metal. Be assured it was no choice of mine."

"I remember who chose what," Lila hissed. "I was there, and there was nothing wrong with my mind."

"No. You are far too clever for your own good," he whispered and closed his eyes, unable to speak any more.

Abruptly his partner sank to her knees and supported him before he fell. Her eyes were narrow and dark with anger as she stared at Lila, "He will soon die here. Go now. This bike will take two, but not three."

"We're not going to make the Alfheim gate on a dirt bike," Lila said. "It's two counties away, back in Bayside."

"There are other ratholes to fit through," the elf said. "He will tell you where to go. You can make it easily. Once you are there, other means will come to you."

"I can get my own means here," Lila insisted. "My field team is on its way as we speak." She hated the idea of saving Dar, in any way. She couldn't stand the idea of having him so close to her, even as vulnerable as he was.

"Do not waste more time!" the elf pleaded with her, and Lila saw tears form in her long eyes. "Dar cannot wait." She took a breath as if she would beg more but then held herself back. Pride and anger fought to take control of her features. She was fierce, Lila thought, and she was desperate. It was not good to be the object of that gaze and it made her feel like a total jerk.

Lila went forward, sun shining off her metal armour into her eyes, and knelt on one knee beside Dar. She moved slowly and gently in spite of her reservations, and made herself touch his shoulder. The *andalune* body she had been dreading had either subsided or was contained. She felt nothing but the cloth of his jacket. She glanced up at the female elf, "What's your name?"

"Gwil," the elf said, almost spitting in her haste and frustration.

"Okay, Gwil. I'll lift him on the bike in front of me. You have to tie him to me so that I don't lose him on the way, yeah?" Unwittingly, Lila found herself gazing longingly at the lump of tarry machinery that had been her bike. The rockracer that Gwil gave her instead was pitiful by comparison. Still, even though they taxed its suspension and power to the limits, it would do.

Lila turned her attention back to Dar and crouched down with his back to her chest. She took hold of him under his strapped arms, bracing against the lower part of his rib cage, but getting his elbows involved anyway. She felt the faint judder of broken bones shifting as she lifted and he made a pitiful sound, a soft shriek, that would have been a scream to anybody who could breathe. He made no resistance or effort to support his own weight, because he couldn't. As she released his weight onto the bike, things must have got worse for him because his contained *andalune* released. Its unique touch was exactly the same flavour as it had been in the moment he had maimed her years ago, but now she could sense only weakness and suffering where it seeped against her human body. It was fragile and evaporating rapidly. To her surprise and chagrin Lila felt sick at the thought of the pain she was causing him and in that instant her hate for him left her. He became simply a casualty, and she his ambulance driver.

"A moment." Gwill put her hand on Lila's as Lila kicked the engine into life. She spoke over the sputter and fizz. "If he is not conscious when the Daga find you, they will not believe your story, given who and what you are. Tell them that Gwilaren Amanita of Lyrien has sent you."

"Amanita?" Lila said, surprised by the name's connection to deadly poison.

The elf grinned mirthlessly, "Not all elves are lovely in name and aspect," she said, stepping back. Dar slumped against Lila's chest, his head on her shoulder.

Lila glanced back once, "Gwilaren Amanita, I will get him to Alfheim."

"Do more, Lila Black. Your ambition insults us." Gwil shouted after her, with uncanny acuity. "Finish your Game with Zal, and discover the truth of your own making."

Lila's ears burned at the elf's words. How could *she* know about the Game? Or did she mean something else altogether? Her embarrassment shamed her, and her responsibility for Dar's state did also, in spite of all the rational rules of combat that she tried to deploy against the feeling. But she soon forgot it as she felt the touch of his *andalune* focus where it touched the exposed skin of her shoulders. Through its agency she found herself able to hear Dar's voice in her mind, soft but clear, as he directed her into the wilderness beyond any roads, deeper and deeper, until they were quite alone among the rocks and the brush and the strange, small plants that lived in the desert.

There, where a wind-scoured archway of old tufa framed the blazing midday sky, Lila rode up confidently across a plain of ascending rock towards thin air which looked to be nothing more than a leap to certain death.

They passed through a strange and silent sheet, a moment of liquid potential, and emerged instead into a thick, rich, dripping green forest. The bike snarled to a halt in a narrow glade, spraying mud and water up over Lila's legs and splattering her arms and face.

CHAPTER THIRTEEN

Lila looked around her into a muggy twilight, filled with the soft-falling cool rain that she remembered from the low hills of Lyrien, the second kingdom of Alfheim; a signature weather mark, like a tradestamp. Her skin drank it greedily after the burning dryness of the phoenix and the scouring of the sands, and she felt Dar shudder in agony and heard the rasping gurgle as he took a breath. A short distance away a wooden shelter stood between two pines on a clearly elven-made area of elevated and flat dry ground. Massive trees of every type crowded the little clearing, covering all but the tiniest chinks of sky from view with their massive leaves. It was extremely quiet, and Lila realised this was because of the sudden loss of Otopia Tree, and all her network connections. There was no Incon now, no contact with Otopia at all, and in Alfheim, nobody listening or broadcasting a single thing; not in the electromagnetic spectrum anyway.

She switched off the engine and, enveloped in the sonic caress of falling water, dancing leaves, and drinking roots, she lifted Dar off the machine and carried him towards the A-frame building. The door was only on a latch. Inside it was dry and quiet, big enough for up to eight, with cots and mattresses set out. She placed Dar on one of these. He was deathly pale and finding his pulse was mostly a matter of good imagination. Where Lila had felt his *andalune* hands guiding hers on the bike, she could find no trace of that body now. She ignored all thoughts of pursuing Zal and demanded only professionalism as she undid the tight strapping of ripped-up shirt that bound his arms across his chest, in the hope that this might help him breathe. It didn't.

As she had suspected from the impact of the bar, both his upper arms were cleanly broken but these, although nasty, weren't life-threatening injuries. His rib cage was another story. Lila didn't bother searching out the elf first aid. She didn't have any confidence that she'd apply it properly. But she could do a reasonable job herself, in spite of a small reservation that Dar would no doubt heavily object to what she was about to do.

Her AI-self had only the scantiest of information on the elf response to x-ray radiation, but she guessed that would be too dangerous to try. Lila quickly pulled her own field kit out of the inner compartments in her thighs and stripped the backing off an ECG sensor, opening Dar's tunic and shirt to place it gently on the skin of his chest, over his heart. She tuned her AI-senses into the instruments and immediately the spike and sine of muscular electrical activity flowed into her sight—a blue line over the top of her ordinary vision. She didn't know what was normal for elves but she could see that, if nothing else, it was regular. Far too regular for her liking. In humans and all Otopian mammals a signal like that meant death was very near.

"Shit!" She didn't understand. Where was the great healing power of the wretched land now? Gwil had suggested simply being here in Alfheim was enough, but it clearly wasn't.

Lila recalibrated the sensors in her left hand and opened a sachet of lubricant gel with her teeth. She spread this over her hand and Dar's chest, where the dark marks of superficial bruising showed red and black. No sign of deeper damage had risen. That was another bad sign. She ran her hand across him, and switched her vision and hearing entirely into her hand.

Echocardiogram, then ultrasound.

It was now clear what crushing damage the bar had done. Dar's sternum was broken and several ribs fractured more than once, creating what was medically known as a flail rib cage, where a whole section had become completely detached and ineffective, moved only by his slight breaths but not aiding breathing. There was serious bleeding around his lungs, and also into the pericardium surrounding his heart, hence its regularity and weakness. Lila blood-tested him as fast as she could, but she wasn't even sure she could wait or should wait for the gas analysis. She looked under his eyelids—almost white, becoming blueish. He was cyanotic. He needed more oxygen.

"Jesus Christ!" she said, several times, rather loudly, to nerve herself as she broke open sealed packs, hunting down the really big needles. On its prompt she allowed her AI-self to activate a cortical shunt that bypassed her emotional responses, leaving them as a minimal experience that could thoroughly inform but not hamper her physical precision. Now her AI-self could cue its surgical procedures and run them effectively. Although she'd never done what she was about to do, the hands of hundreds of expert surgeons informed the movement of her own fingers and thumbs.

She watched herself from a quiet meditative state as her left hand guided and her right hand punched the chest drain into the wall of Dar's body between two ribs. Her hands could see what they were doing with their own intricate sensors. They positioned the needle tip in the cavity full of blood surrounding Dar's heart and switched on one of the minor motors in Lila's arm to power a small negative pressure pump at the other end of the drain tube. Dark, russet-coloured blood began to flow. Unfortunately, Lila had nowhere for it to go, so it began to spatter and pool on the pretty hardwood floor.

Moving with care she inserted another drain for his left lung and attached that to a secondary pump with a minor power line feeding from one of her weapon ports. And there they were, she thought, tied neatly to one another, blood trickling around them, rain falling outside in the quiet, quiet forest. The idea made her smile.

Mercifully, she saw the ECG readout begin to break its rhythm into the less distressing irregularity of tachycardia as his heart began to recover. She felt his pulse strengthen at the same time. The blood gas response came up finally—low ox, high carbon dioxide, high nitrogen . . . whatever. Anyway, she'd done the right thing and she sat back on her heels now to pick out a suitable painkiller with a sense of satisfaction. She administered several shots, placed as accurately as possible, so that there wouldn't be any sedative effect when he came to. She needed him to tell her what to do next, since her human-med skills, involving metal as they did, possibly were not doing him an awful lot of good, although perhaps saving his life would smooth things over on that front.

As a chaotic pattern established itself in his heart, Lila cautiously and somewhat cheekily took the chance to examine his physiology much more closely. If anyone asked her she would say it was for Otopia's files. In spite of pleas to the contrary Alfheim had not divulged most of its medical knowledge to Otopia, nor the bulk of its magical expertise; all of these things were protected under weapons-class security restrictions. It was one of the features of that treaty Lila had gone in to witness as a diplomat years ago. But she wanted to know from genuine curiosity too. She wondered greatly, in her surgeon's mind, what kind of medicine they had and how their bodies differed from those of humans. Not so much in some ways: she found all the organs to be just about the same in relative size and position though they were, with respect to the physiology of their muscles and tendons, superhuman.

But there was a significant difference. Elves had a lot more neural clusters surrounding their major organs and even in their muscles, as though their brain was distributed more fully throughout their bodies than human nervous systems, which had their secondary centres around the heart and gut alone. And she noticed, as she explored this with soundwaves, that the progress of her survey created a reaction in the ECG: Dar's heart responded to the frequencies.

Working on intuition she placed four more sensors on his head and took a scan of his brain activity. That reacted too, even though he wasn't conscious. The response was what she would generally consider not good. Under her exploration the signals of all of his various neural sites became dissonant. His heart juddered.

Lila stopped. She examined her information and then placed her hands back on Dar, this time transmitting electrical impulses targeting specific clusters, copying what she calculated to be their normal function frequencies, in the hope that she could induce a state of harmony. It worked beautifully, and she finally had a good reason to understand why elves were so susceptible to fluctuations in their surrounding electromagnetic fields, and to sound itself, as she restored Dar to a synchronous neural state: everything working together. A few seconds later his eyes fluttered open.

Lila had seen people master pain with difficulty and also succumb to it without shame. Dar's eyes flashed wide as it hit him, and then he paused, and in that pause Lila saw a change in his face moving instantly to self-possession. His *andalune* rose at the same moment and her sensors slid off him in a blurt of static as his skin rejected them. She waited, poised to hold him down if she had to, in order to prevent him yanking the drains out, but he didn't try to move. He drew a breath through his teeth and one of his eyebrows moved up in surprise that it was so easy.

"Be still," she said. "You're not out of the woods yet."

He almost smiled at her weak humour.

"Your arms are broken," she told him. "But you probably knew that. Your heart and lungs were full of blood. I had to take it out. That's what you can hear dripping on the floor. The hiss is the pumping system." She didn't say that he'd lost a great deal of blood, now mostly around her knees, and that she didn't know how much more he could lose.

"The pain is not as bad," Dar said quietly. "You must set my arms."

"I did that when I put them down. Clean breaks. They'll be all right. But they aren't splinted yet. I can't do that, because . . ." And she held up her right arm to show him that they were joined. "As soon as I can, I'll take them out."

Dar closed his eyes. He was quite different looking to Zal, although until recently all elves had had a kind of sameyness for Lila, mostly based on ears (pointy, long), hair (lots of it, long), and expression (aloof, controlled, pole-up-the-ass). There was also some stuff about decoration, manners, and couture which had seemed almost indistinguishable from human gay culture, if less camp. Now she felt that her estimation of them revealed much more about her than it did about them, and that it did not present a flattering portrait of her at all.

She found also that, since Dar had been at her mercy, she no longer hated his face. It was an extreme face of a kind she considered ultra-elven, as though it had been stretched upwards from its strong, slightly squared chin and the tip of his nose, so that the lines of the cheekbones and the features were elongated and slanted: the kind of thing that might happen after one too many facelifts. It gave his mouth at rest a strange almost-smile, which is what she had always thought of as a smirk, but now saw was only the way his face was made. Zal's face was less exaggerated, with flatter brows and a more squared appearance, although he had the same large eyes that Dar did and the same long, thick eyelashes, equally dark. You could see a species resemblance, but Dar had dark brown hair and his eyes were intense and nearly black. His skin also had a peculiar quality that Zal's did not. Now that she looked closely he seemed much darker than she remembered, not tanned like a human but as if he stood in deep shadow. She didn't think it was an effect of his condition.

Lila wondered if Zal were a bleach blond.

Dar opened his eyes again. "Maybe you would consider us even, now."

"No, not nearly," Lila told him amiably. "Hello: half my body missing forever."

"The new one seems to be working out for you," he rasped. "And to my advantage. I am very impressed."

"Ah, come on, make me not want to rip this out and leave you to rot," she said, without any great anger, but some irritation that he could lie there half dead and still successfully bait her.

"Your honour is great," he said. "I thank you."

"Go me," Lila said. "How do I get your lot to come over here and fix you better?"

"I don't think that's a good idea," he whispered, trying to lift his head and then deciding quickly against it. "Also, we need to move soon."

"What are you talking about? Gwil told me . . ."

"I do not trust Gwil, whatever she told you," he said. "And I have no idea who in the Jayon Daga is with or against me."

"You as in just you?" Lila asked.

"No, us as in just us." He smiled a little. "But all the same, better they not come here and find you. Some of them may be my allies, but others will not be, and we can show no brotherhood to their faces, or else our efforts to mitigate their ill-notions will all be wasted in the discovery."

Lila admired the fact that he could get a sentence like that out with only one functional lung. She didn't know what he meant, but it seemed to boil down to the fact that they weren't going to get reinforcements. "So what, we're going in against the big bad to save Zal from immortal torment with me carrying you on your deathbed?"

"No," Dar said. He paused for a minute, to breathe. "You will help me get better more quickly."

"Oh, I don't know," Lila objected. "You're in serious trouble with your chest. Even if it's all fine when I take these drains out, you can't go anywhere or do anything useful for months. Your bones are pretty much shattered."

"Yes, I can hear that," he said. "But this is not Otopia. And we have our own technologies for getting over things like this in a hurry, if we have to."

"Teleport it on over then," she said.

"I was rather thinking you could drag us both across to that cabinet where you will find our medical supplies."

"Typical man," Lila snorted. She was glad she had put him on the closest of the cots. "Hold on then. This is going to be unpleasant for you."

"No doubt that will please you," he said.

She frowned. "Actually it won't. How about that for a turn-up for the books?" She pushed the bed and it skidded over the unpolished floor with only a slight vibration and bump. Nonetheless, Dar hissed horribly and almost immediately passed out. Warm blood splashed on her legs. She adjusted the drain tubes so that she could move around and went to open the cabinet, but the doors would not budge to her hands.

When he woke up for the second time she said, "I'm going to have to up your painkillers."

"No," he said. "There will be something better in there for me."

She held up one hand, "Not for me though. How do you get in?"

"Take my hand and touch the door with it," he suggested.

Lila didn't argue or make any more suggestions. She took hold of his damaged upper arm in her left hand and fixed the bones in place with a power-assisted grip, so tight it made him cry out. Then she moved his arm with her right hand. As soon as his skin made contact with the door, it opened.

"It will be fine now," he said as she replaced his arm on the bed.

"Hope so." She began taking things out—bark boxes and other, manifestly unhygienic-looking containers. Although they were all remarkably similar, each was made from a variety of materials, with a different fold and unique ties. Dar told her to look for something in autumn beech leaves with a linen tie. Lila found and opened it. Inside were slender bamboo tubes, sealed with wax. She opened one and

ultra-fine needles of crystal fell out into her hand. They were so delicate they could only have grown like that, over extreme lengths of
time. "Acupuncture," she said after a second's thought.

"Yes," Dar said. "It's good you are familiar with the technique. The
meridians . . ." He coughed and momentarily passed out, recovering a
second or two later.

"I know where they are," she said confidently. "I sneaked a peek
while you weren't looking."

"With what?" he rasped.

"Ultrasound," she said. "And I can look again to be sure."

"That explains it," he whispered, his voice bubbling slightly. Lila
checked the drains. The heart had stabilised, but his lung trauma was
still leaky. Drops of vivid scarlet thickened on the floor beside her knee
and coloured his lips. She glanced up and saw Dar smile faintly.

"Explains what?"

"All elven aether is responsive to sound," he said. "Do it again."

Lila put her sticky hand over his abdomen and scanned his midsection. "So?"

"It feels good," he said and smiled briefly. "I thought I dreamt it.
A strange dream, to feel pleasure in pain. But it was you."

"Human beings don't feel anything with this." She took her hand
off, aware of her face reddening, and angry for that.

"No," Dar said. "I imagine not. And I don't feel it in my flesh
body. I feel it in the aetheric. It is extremely pleasant. The *chi* pattern
is most interesting. You may find other uses for that in the future while
you are here."

"Are you being filthy?" she asked, selecting a needle and tapping
it down through his skin with a careful blow of her fingertip, her AI-
self effective and detached.

"In the circumstances I have perhaps gone too far," Dar admitted.

"I was going to use x-ray," Lila informed him and her prompt was
answered, after a moment or two and another needle.

"I am grateful you did not," Dar rasped. "The wavelengths are extremely hostile to our aetheric selves."

"So, two weapons from one med kit: x-rays and ultrasound," she said. "Not bad. I'm liking it here already." She moved along, placing needles through his skin carefully, concentrating on his forehead, ears, and in his hands. After the sixth one he sighed and visibly relaxed. Colour started to return to his face and she put her hand briefly over his chest, picking up a heart trace. "That's impressive," she said.

"Now the pain has gone I am able to look and see what is wrong with me, except that your anaesthetic has dulled my ability somewhat. But we can proceed. I suppose you are not a human with magical skills?"

"You suppose correctly," Lila said. "I didn't even think there were any."

"We must make a connection," he said, as though he hadn't heard her. "Something that can unite us, briefly, in spirit."

"I'm an atheist," she informed him. "Machine and soulless. Thanatopia is only hearsay to me and, until I get proof about it, I'm devoutly with the scientists. What you see is what you get."

"Stupid. But whatever your opinion on the matter, it will make no difference," Dar said, his voice louder and more musical, almost at an ordinary pitch. "You and I should be in a coherent state for the duration. That is a physical phenomenon you can measure, if you wish. It is best established through some kind of mutual empathy."

"That's not going to be easy, considering." Lila had to bite back a retort to his insult—stupid! He didn't know how hard it was to be against the Otopian tide-turn back to major religion every time the media came up with some new revelation about Thanatopia.

Dar, thankfully, could not hear her thoughts. "Do not tax me with your talk. If you want to save Zal, you must learn to speak correctly."

"What do you mean?" Even Lila's AI-self couldn't entirely keep a smother on her strongest feelings. She was annoyed.

"To save me, you must speak correctly. Listen carefully . . ."

She gave him a sarcastic look. "You're going to say it only once?"

"Thank you for your cultural quip. It is not lost on me. But you are wasting time. Listen to the elf with two chest drains, because it is hard for him to talk."

He had to pause and rest then, and Lila felt another wash of shame. She didn't much like being herself in this hour. She wanted to punish Dar for bringing her to these feelings, and for all her nightmares of the past, the pain and the hospital, her metal body and her weakness, her foolish pursuit of Zal. And she felt absurdly thankful, that they were both here and alive. She listened to the drip of blood and Dar's laboured breathing and looked at the damage she had done to him. "I'm listening."

"Doctor," he began. "It is like this. Speaking is action. A spoken judgement, such as your statement that our empathy could not be easy, is a sword and shield between us. It makes success much less likely. Your speech is peppered with casual assault." He had to pause again.

"It's just the way we talk in Otopia," Lila began defensively. "It doesn't *mean* . . ."

"You see?" he said, pausing often to take gurgling breaths. "I accused you of aggression, and you have given me aggression back. You had to. You felt that? When speech is careless and labels people, instead of simply stating what was done, when speech is used as a weapon, there is nothing we can do but fight. It is not simply the way you talk in Otopia. Speech defines the world. But be aware that in Alfheim these matters take on even greater weight, because our magic is tied to sounds, and no sounds are more powerful than those of words, except music. Music unpolluted by words is the strongest of all. But you are not a musician, and neither am I. We will confine ourselves to the inadequacy of words for this connection. I will tell you something of my heart: when you hit me with the quarterstaff, I took no offence at it. It is not a matter I hold against you personally. But I believe from the way you speak about me that this is not the way you feel about my attack on you in Sathanor."

"You're bloody right it isn't," Lila said with a venom even she did not expect. "You tried to kill me in cold blood. And then you spent days torturing me by forcing me awake to ask me those *pointless* fucking questions. You never showed me any feeling at all, except cruelty, and you were always . . ." She had been going to say smiling, but after her recent reassessment she didn't want to say it now. She bit her tongue. The faint ECG trace she still had on Dar through her hand sensors showed flickering reactions in the beat of his heart His face didn't change, but his body reacted to what she'd said strongly. She said without thinking, "I'm sorry."

"Sorry is useless," he said. "You hurt me. Sorry does not make it better. Sorry is for you, not me. But truly. What I did I did in order to save you from certain death. That must be difficult to believe."

"Gwil said that," Lila informed him.

"In that then she has the right," Dar whispered, forced to cough and trying to do it gently, but failing. His eyes rolled up in his head briefly. Lila waited until he came back to himself and carried on. "I had to continue your interrogation to convince those with me that I was of their party. All of them are agents loyal to the Lady in Sathanor and until now I have always maintained a position of allegiance to her as my cover. If I had had to kill you, I would have, because as their leader they must not doubt me. Surely they must never suspect I am secretly loyal to the Resistance. As it was, I decided that I could both save your life and impress them with my commitment to their ways by demonstrating more cruelty when I delivered you home in pieces instead of executing you. Though we knew perfectly well that you had no information, this was a plan they all agreed to easily. Their corruption is mighty indeed and so was mine that day. You wear the mark of that deed forever. As do I, although my scars are not visible to the eye, for which I must be grateful. And I am grateful to you, for saving my life now, with so little pain. It is, as you guess, much more than I deserve."

Lila had never felt more sober. In explaining his part of her maiming he was describing a job. There was nothing personal about it, though that didn't make it any less awful. He was describing *her* job, in actual fact, because they were the same. "Making it hard to keep hating you here."

"That was the general direction I was heading in," he said, in an almost human cadence, and then he reverted to elf normal, all careful diction and no contractions. "But it is the truth."

"I know," Lila said, curious. "I can feel it in your electro-readouts."

"Then we are in synchrony," Dar said. "It is time to rebuild me. We will begin with my heart. Please remove the drain."

"Technically it's too early," she said. "But you're in charge. Before I do, care to brief me on the procedure?"

"Forgive me, I thought it obvious. You will raise your *chi* and place it in your hand over my heart, whilst concentrating on your own heart. I will muster my energy and do the same. We will visualise the heart as whole and healthy. We will open our spirit fusion to the aetheric limbs of Lyrien and allow . . ." He saw her doubt and scepticism and accepted it. "Just do it," he said. "Please."

"Don't we need circles or candles or crystals or . . ."

"Of course not," he said, betraying pain and impatience. "You are alive. It will suffice. Your hand."

"I don't even know what *chi* is," she started to protest, but relied on her AI-self to find some instructive materials. She removed the drain carefully, sealing the wound between his ribs with one of her own emergency stick-ons because she had no idea what the elf version of the same was. He didn't seem to mind. *Chi* was, her AI-library said, the life force or spirit energy of living things. There was a lot of argument about its role in the aetheric dimensions (perhaps it was the same as aether itself and perhaps it was a special form, the human verdict was not sure) and whether or not it was metaphysical, or imaginary. It was nonetheless proven to be an effective concept . . .

"Breathe with me," Dar said. "Put your heart in your hand. That's all."

"Okay, okay." Lila closed her eyes and tried to feel anything other than pointless and mundane. Her AI-self decided to help her with a gentle, cheerful piece of music she'd always liked. It was childish, and twinkly, and something she used to play years and years ago, in the summertime at home. The effect, as these things often have, was instantaneous. The words ran through her mind—*surely no greater king has ever lived, no one with the loving kindness, strength, and courage of King Raam*. Lila's awareness of her surroundings fell away. How she loved to hear the song! How she longed to touch those old days and be with Dad and Mom again, with Maxine, Julia, and Okie.

She put out her right hand as the soft notes burred in harmony and pleasure through her mind. She held onto the feeling of how much she had once been loved.

Dar's *andalune* hand surrounded hers. A current shot through her arm and out of the palm of her hand and down into the body underneath it. She could feel it and her sensors could too—pure electromagnetic energy in a strange pattern, at frequencies she wouldn't have expected from a simple human body. Her metal amplified it.

Then she felt Dar's heart *pull* on hers, like a weary horse lagging behind is pulled forward by the stronger one in the front of the traces. Readouts behind her closed eyelids showed her pulse slow down to his pace and then respond to the demand of this strange healing, accelerating them both with her leading this time. She remembered to think of Dar's heart, the four chambers, shaped almost identically to a human's, just larger. She saw the strange energy field in her hand snap into the shape she imagined. She felt Dar's heart in her hand. And then she felt Dar's heart in her heart.

Lila began to understand the nature of magic then. She saw that it was aetheric energy shaped by the shape of the maker, and that the maker was more than a thought or a mood or a word or a body. It was all those things at once. Her breath and Dar's breath, their hearts in one another's hearts, sharing space and time for a moment, the stronger becoming weaker, the weaker stronger until equilibrium. Then both gained strength as another force, utterly unknown to her, came pouring in through Dar's *andalune* self.

The power of this was colossal, like being suddenly plugged into the mains. For the rest of their time together she knew nothing at all, washed away in its force and the reckless vitality, thinking that maybe she could sense the whole of the forest, and the rain, the land and the sky, the water and air . . . that she was Dar and he was the strangest, strangest creature under the sun, drawing power from the life that ran and jumped, warm and animal, through the trees, across the sky.

When they parted it was a natural movement that they both made at once, because they were one and there was no impulse one had that the other did not.

Recklessly, giddy with success, slightly wired on desire and the euphoria of such a strangely tender intimacy, Lila carried on, Dar carried on, to the lungs and the ribs and the bones of his arms, where Lila felt his bone become her powerful metal skeleton and her finely crafted alloys become living tissue. The circuit between them fluctuated as it encountered their profound differences, energy from Lyrien and from Lila's reactor matching each other like for like until the resonances eased and the conjoined will of Lila and Dar brought all patterns into phase.

Then, without warning, she felt the two of them and their separated natures wound inexorably into a single form. The current of electrical and aetheric energies escalated suddenly, jolting Lila from bliss to alarm. In her mind's eye she saw a fuse burning, a flash of coming light . . .

"It's okay," she heard Dar say calmly in the centre of her head. "Take your hand away from me."

She moved with the reflexive speed of fear and the connection broke abruptly. Lila felt that she had been flung from heaven, and the landing was nasty. From her warm, cosy, beautiful place of strength and exhilaration she found herself kneeling on the bloody floor with her head resting on the side of a hard bed. Sweat was pouring off her and she'd expended enough kilowatts to run a small town in the last few seconds. She was shaking, but even though she was exhausted there was a peculiar rightness to her that she couldn't remember feeling in years. Belatedly she realised there was no discomfort in her body. Not one bit.

"Fuck me," Dar said with perfect Bay City intonation.

Lila could feel the bed shaking. She realised he was laughing. It was an infectious sound. She found herself joining in, not nervously either

"Oh god!" she said, and seemed to be referring to herself as she slid onto the planking. She had forgotten what it felt to be this tired and this full of pleasant, whooshy, relaxed feelings. "Elf sex must be amazing."

"In my limited experience it possesses all the thrills and boredoms of any other activity," Dar said. "For one thing most elves do not run on tokamaks, unless I have mistaken them. But I do not wish to belittle your experience, nor mine. It was as unusual for me as for you."

"No," Lila said from the floor. "I get it. In fact, I don't think you need to explain anything like that to me ever again." And she didn't need to ask how he was either. She knew that. He was fine. Exhausted, but fine. "That bioluminescent drawing-on-the-source-of-life thing really takes it out of you, doesn't it?" she said.

"Knocks off a year of your life every trip," he said in another flip revert to the Otopian style. "But who's counting?"

"Is there time to . . . ? But before she could finish the sentence, Lila was asleep.

CHAPTER FOURTEEN

"They're coming. Get up."

Lila woke to find Dar shaking her and a peculiar zap running the length of her arm where he touched her, which she belatedly processed and recognised as a kind of bite or nip from his aetheric self. She got up from the floor and ran a full upgrade at the same time, so that when she had made it to her feet she was awake, alert, and feeling fine. Dar pushed handfuls of wet plastic tubing and first aid at her.

"I don't know how to pack these. You must carry them. They shouldn't know you've been here."

Lila took them and saw that they had been flushed reasonably clean. The floorboards were drying from a scrub, but they were stained. She worked as fast as she could to put everything together and back in its place. She caught Dar staring openly as her leg compartments opened and closed with soft whirring and clicks, a silvery blur of motion that made her hands look slow, a whisper of sound like leaves stirring in a light breeze. He was fascinated and there was no trace of his earlier repulsion towards her on his face. She smiled. "Want me to sand the floor for you?"

"No. There is no time, even for you. If you are ready then we must go." He stood by the door, tall and straight in new, clean clothes, a variety of bladed weapons stored across his back alongside the sweeping curves of a bow and two quivers full of arrows. Their fletchings were of various hues of brown, grey, and green, notched and nocked in varying ways her master-at-arms system identified as being intended for a wide variety of purposes besides simple killing.

She found herself glancing at Dar's face uncertainly. His eyes, now the colour of noon sky and nothing like the midnight of earlier, were clear and full of the need for urgent action. She glanced at his skin— it was pale, like daylight through flat, thin cloud.

"Ready," she said.

He looked at her for a long moment. "Mmn, not quite." He went to another cupboard and pulled out some clothing. "Your armour will reflect too much light, though I do not know if this will fit."

"It's done," Lila said and he turned, frowning, as she changed the surface of her metallic body parts to partial camouflage. Microscopic scales in the metal structure turned to reflect exact wavelengths of light, each different, to produce perfect reproductions of flat colour, very similar to those of her surroundings. It was a step down from full camo, which resulted in complete invisibility for her metal parts and the disconcerting sight of her head and torso floating around unsupported. She took a long shirt off him and put that over her khaki underwear.

Dar almost grinned. He put the rest of the clothes back. "Your hair will need some mud before long, I regret to say. It is a very un-elven colour."

"Not yours?" She found she was teasing him easily, as though they had been the best of friends for some time.

"Mine is close enough to mud," he said, listening for a moment or two before opening the door.

Outside, the forest still dripped, although the rain had stopped some time ago. It was so lush and green that Lila paused to look at it, to smell it, to feel the peculiar intensity with which things got on with growing. Leaves showed her that plants here were the same as those in Otopia, but here they were bigger and more healthy looking. When she listened and tuned out her own and Dar's sound, she could hear everything growing; a susurration of slow but immeasurable power. It was disconcerting. In a way that no Otopian forest could have been, this one was alive. It wasn't intelligent, nor even particularly aware—she didn't feel watched—its biology simply dwarfed hers in scale and appetite. It thrived, and her flesh body responded to that with joy.

They travelled fast, like Zal used to, running at an exhilarating pace through the trees and across open clearings, along the banks of streams, across rivers, through dry gorges choked with old glacial rocks, and up moorland hillsides where the heathers grew higher than their knees. All the time they ascended and, when Dar stopped to point out the views, Lila could see more and more of Lyrien, a beautiful green map, rolling out from her feet like the most sumptuous of carpets.

Lila marvelled at Dar's recovery, and her own. She had never felt better. With the sweat running down her face they came to a rocky outcrop which Dar called the Star Rocks. This tower of stone stood out from the surrounding land which had eroded around its harder substance. It held the two of them balanced on a finger of granite five thousand feet above the lowlands and Lila could see back into Lyrien and forwards, to Lilirien and Sathanor, hidden by clouds.

"Sathanor is a valley landscape within a ring of mountains," Dar told her. "The place you last came to here is a village set against the foot of those mountains, where the pass into Sathanor begins. You can see it from here, right on the eastern edge of the range. Those lakes mark where the river runs out. You remember their shores? I saw you walking there, taking the rowboats out on the last day of that conference."

Lila nodded. She did remember. It had been sunny and warm, the lake still as a mirror, all the boats graceful and smooth as everyone took turns at pretending to be good with oars. She had no idea that Dar had been there then. He could have been anyone. She hadn't been able to tell who was what, there were so many strange faces, and, anyway, all the elves looked the same to her then.

"We cannot go that way. We will cross the land as directly as we can from here. Quickly, we must get down from here." He led the way back, across steeply sloping grassland and into the line of trees which crept as far as they were able up the knoll. Lila looked back as she descended and saw the heat trace of three human-sized bodies far back across the hills they had covered.

"Someone's following," she said.

"No doubt," Dar agreed.

"Dar," she said as they began to jog downhill. "Do you know Zal?"

"Not personally," he replied. "Though I have watched him a long time."

Something in Dar's voice made Lila hesitate. "You're a fan?" she said, unable to believe her ears.

"We are not so far apart, politically."

So, not exactly the kind of fan Lila was used to, screaming and knicker-throwing, but still. Fan. "Is he from Alfheim?"

"Of course." He snorted with what may have been a laugh.

Their descent levelled off and Dar led her sloshing upstream through a narrow gully. She could see a high sandbank far ahead, pocked with the holes of swifts' nests, although it wasn't the season for them and the holes were empty. Another small way-hut stood atop the bank almost hidden in a drapery of vines. "Wait here," Dar said. "I'll go steal the things we need."

Lila stood up to her knees in cold flowing water and shivered with pleasure. Soft green leaves danced above and around her in the light breeze. She wondered what was going on with the agents back home, and how poor Jolene was going to manage when Zal failed to show up for Frisco. Her clock showed her that she had two hours left to get Zal there on time. No way. And she wondered if Malachi had found any more out about the peculiar recordings from the car back in Bay City.

But it was a relief to only be able to wonder, and it occurred to her as she stood alone there that these few minutes, in which nobody knew where she was and couldn't contact her, were a gift of freedom.

Dar beckoned her silently from the top of the sandbank and she started forwards obediently. It was already over.

Lila climbed to meet him and followed his lead into the depths of a vigorous holly thicket. There was a small hollow inside the bushes, covered in flat, brown leaves and dry. They sat there and ate furiously. Lila's hunger was overpowering from the second she smelled the food and, even though it was dry rations that had to be chewed with a lot of water, they feasted.

"No lembas jokes, if you please," Dar said when he could swallow and not bite again immediately. "I have heard them all."

"Wouldn't dream of it. Perfect," Lila said with her mouth full. As she slowed down and recovered her senses from the delicious intensity of filling her stomach, she realised how close they were, actually pressed shoulder to shoulder in the tiny place, knees bunched up, like kids hiding out. She glanced at Dar and found she didn't hate him one bit any more, even if she tried. It made her smile. "Do you do this often?"

"All the time," Dar said dryly. "It is my continual misfortune to languish thus whilst dreaming of white-tile bathrooms and luxury king-size vibrating-massage beds and four-hundred-thread-count Egyptian cotton sheets and five-star room service."

"You're kidding."

"I am." He licked his fingers and swallowed and listened. Lila saw his ears move. The long, pointed tips free of his hair made micro-fine adjustments in their position. It was rather comical, but she didn't laugh. She realised that he was filtering some magical dimension she wasn't aware of. But his humour had surprised her and she didn't feel like laughing at him.

"We have to go." Dar slid out of the bush hideaway on his stomach and waited for her. "The ones who pursue us have tracker elementals working for them and it's possible there's nothing we can do to conceal you if there are metal elementals among them. We will have to keep running."

He paused and drew a small packet from a pocket inside his jerkin, shaking some dust from it onto his hand. Lila flinched, remembering that he had once overcome her that way, knocking her out with a word and a single breath that blew the dust in her face. This time he blew it more gently over the holly trees and across the path that led to the little hut. She heard him whispering elven syllables she couldn't quite pick up.

"That should slow them," he said but he didn't look happy. Lila avoided touching any of it and went the long way around to follow him uphill again as he kept to the contours, trying to place solid hillsides between them and those who followed.

"What was that?"

"Zoomenon dust," he said. "Elementals dislike being removed from Zoomenon. They can only be run like pets by good elemental hunters. The dust is like catnip to them. They will not be persuaded to leave here until they have gathered it all back. The spell will tell me when that is done."

Like the animal spell in the car boot, Lila thought. She asked him about that kind of magic.

"Such cats are fey agents," Dar said, shrugging as though everyone must know that. "Or they are Thanatopic messengers."

"Forgive my magical dunceness," Lila said, "but what about cats that change into rats, or mist?"

"That could still be either. Unless it was a ghost or a spirit."

"No," Lila said. "I don't think so." She remembered the animal spirit at Solomon's Folly with a shudder. The cat in the car had been nothing like that. "Do elves have any affinity with Interstitial creatures as a rule?"

"No," Dar said. "But some demons do. Not any that you would wish to meet however. Why, have you seen one in Otopia?"

Lila didn't answer at first. She wasn't sure how much she could really trust Dar, although she felt a bond with him now that made it too easy to talk to him, and his apparent candour made her want to tell him everything. She had to remind herself that he worked for a foreign power, and was no doubt highly trained in the art of faking sincerity. And so she told herself that, but it sounded a wrong chord in her heart which didn't believe that Dar was lying. Her heart felt confident in its judgement, had done so ever since the moment they had—well, what had happened?

Lila was brought up short by the realisation that she didn't have an explanation, in fact did not know what to call it or how to think of it. She had simply brushed it aside as irrelevant to the moment at hand. But now she had nothing to do but yomp along, watching Dar's back, and it hit home just how far she was from what she knew in any direction. But on the bright side, her aching bones and sore muscles neither ached nor burned. When she concentrated, she couldn't even feel a hint of pain where the medics had struggled to heal the junctions of metal and flesh mere days ago.

Now, as well as stopping mentally and emotionally, she stopped in her physical tracks. Dar turned and looked back at her, questioningly.

"Did you hear something?"

"No," she said, taking a deep breath. "Nothing."

He glanced at her with curiosity but didn't ask what was on her mind. He waited.

"How long would you wait?" she asked, turning the moment to test her heart and its judgements.

"A long time," he said. "Questions are always leading. So one never asks a question, if waiting will suffice, otherwise one gets the answer one expects, which is not generally the truth. What you want to say will reveal itself, if it is going to, when it should. You humans tend to think of it as some kind of superiority complex, I understand, when we keep our silence and give you our full attention. To an elf such a thing is a natural courtesy."

This was not the response Lila had been expecting. She felt conciliatory. "You must find humans most prying."

"It has been noted. But I think our curiosity levels are well matched. It is simply the case that we have different ways of dealing with it." He wiped sweat from his face with the fabric back of one of the archery bracers which encased his forearms. "I am glad that you have stopped, as it happens, because we are about to step onto the foot of the true mountains which mark the border between Tyrien and Sathanor, and these are places where wild magic collects in great abundance. I wanted to warn you to be on your guard for its presence in whatever way you can. It would be very difficult for us if we were to become trapped in a Game, even a trivial one."

Lila's high spirits sank somewhat. "I never saw the last one coming, and I was watching for it. Sort of. Anyway, I knew it was a risk. You lot always . . . I mean, you're well known for catching humans in Games." She stumbled over the end of the sentence in shame. Words that wouldn't have seemed even slightly dubious a few days ago now made her sound like a galloping racist. Because that's what she was. Or had been. She looked up, thinking she would see a flash of the real, haughty Dar now all right, but he only shrugged.

"We are guilty of many foolish Games with Otopians, romantic gambles being only one. But do not say you are not pleased by it, or I think you will make yourself a liar."

That told me, Lila thought, and did not deny it.

"Come," he beckoned, looking back and glancing at the sky where the sun was going down. Shadows lengthened. "Night falls like stone at this time of year in Alfheim. We should find some shelter and rest soon. Some hours are not good to be abroad in this part of the country, and one of them is fast approaching."

"You make it sound extra spooky when you say it like that," she grumbled gently, following him closely. "Why can't you say, *it's getting dark, let's take a break, and by the way the neighbourhood could use some work.* That sounds much less imposing, you know?"

"I . . ." Dar stopped. Lila felt the faintest prickle across her skin and a scent, like lemon, in her nostrils.

"Oh," she said, realising the sudden presence of wild aether. Then, suddenly, from a childhood moment she'd never recalled until now, "White rabbits, white rabbits, white rabbits . . ." She said it seven times.

Saying the silly words broke the charm that she could feel forming between them, the one which Dar would have contracted for them both if he had answered her question. The air around them twinkled with tiny, firefly lights and she felt the prickling more strongly, almost as though she were being nettled. It swirled and she thought, for an instant, that it formed something like a face that pouted crossly into hers, but then it was gone, and the breeze became an ordinary breeze.

"It worked," Lila said with honest surprise, stunned. White rabbits never worked on anything. It was something you said on the first day of the month to ward off bad luck . . . she couldn't imagine it really *doing* something.

"Good," Dar said, almost silently. He called her on with a nod and she concentrated on her step. The twilight had darkened, become blue. His skin had taken on the same hue, making him difficult to see. Around them the trees on this high ground had trunks that looked like pillars of ash as Alfheim's moon rose. Its thin sickle shed barely any light at all. Dar became shadow, and then Lila switched on her night vision and stopped in total shock.

Among the trees on the high hill, now restored to full detail and reprocessed by her AI-optics into realistic colour, she saw drifts of rainbow watercolours flowing across the landscape. Not like cloud, not like water, something of both, the transparent, delicate traces wound around objects, eddied and pooled. Sometimes they formed limblike shapes and darted swiftly as fish, sometimes they diffused into thin air or fell in showers. They were everywhere. And then she looked at Dar and saw him encased in a blue and lilac and emerald radiance, clearly of the same material—his *andalune* body. It had a distinctive outline many arm lengths away from his body. She saw that he was holding it diffused and that its edges helped him navigate the land. He paused to look back, wondering what had stopped her this time, and with his intent to locate her she saw an indigo streak dive towards her almost as fast as an arrow. It brushed her torso, so lightly she couldn't feel anything, and his gaze fixed on her at the same moment.

"Hell's bells," she said to herself quietly. She'd never realised she could have seen magic just by shifting the sensitivity of her vision to different spectra. The wild aether followed Dar's interest, clustering around the slender string of his regard. Now she began to see how it latched onto things. As he walked back towards her, he trailed vast floating banners of it in his wake. Where it touched him it took on the colour of his *andalune* for a moment before furling softly away.

"I can see it," she said. "On the full electromag display. I can see aether. I think."

"I . . ."

"Wait," she said. "There's a lot hanging around you."

"I know that," he replied, whispering. "We should not talk. The safe place is not far from here."

Lila smiled. "I can see you." A gout of sparkling pink seemed to leap forwards from her and pose just in front of his face. It looked as though it was waiting for him to reply. "Hey, d'you see that?"

Dar shook his head and started away again, not looking back.

Lila ignored his irritation and resumed the journey with a new lightness, recording as she went. This was so incredibly—well, she hated to say it, being a top spy with a mission, but—it was so cool! But then other thoughts occurred to her. Humans must have known about this—surely someone had tested it before? There had been years in which to scientifically address aether and progress was being made. But nobody had thought to tell her about it? She instantly tried to call Dr. Williams to complain but, of course, there were no comms connections. The silence began to annoy her.

She found that trees and patches of ground had their own magical signatures, that some plants were almost as actively involved in the wild magic as Dar was, that they had magical properties, clearly. She found a fungus that exuded a yellow vapour. She saw hidden animal dens by the gentle miasmas of green that surrounded them. It was a beautiful, unexpected delight. She didn't turn around and look behind her until Dar led her up a steep and difficult path to a hidden door in an outcrop of rocks. Beyond him she could see this led into a shelter inside the hill above the woods. As she ducked under the ancient lintel and turned to take the handle and pull the door closed, she glanced back at the forests.

The lovely coloured washes of aether extended up into the sky, across the trees and the open ground. Alfheim under the slight moonlight was as lovely as in the day, but her attention to this beauty was quite lost as she caught sight of sharp-edged silhouettes moving quickly along the path that she and Dar had taken. They were four-limbed, slender, with long tails like whips and strange heavy heads shaped like axe blades which they swung side to side in the streams of wild magic. They had no eyes or ears. They followed in her tracks with the unerring single-mindedness of stalking predators, and they left dark wakes that briefly obliterated even the trunks of the palest trees. She had the distinct impression they were filter feeding off the aether, tasting their way through it.

Dar pulled her sharply backwards and closed the door. She heard bolts slide home and then his breathing, elevated from the running, relaxing now. It was utterly dark inside the shelter. She had to switch to thermal imaging. Dar stood easily close to her, taking the quivers off his shoulders.

She told him what she'd seen in a rush, breathless herself, "What *was* that?"

"Saaqaa," Dar said, setting the quivers down in a niche beside the door, his bow next to them. "Night Prowlers. They were once hounds of the shadow elves but they have become feral in the last centuries. Now they cannot be tamed. They eat flesh, but also some kinds of magic. The *andalune* kind in particular. Elves per se are not at the top of the food chain in Alfheim. I told you there were hours of danger. This is one. The first two of the sickle moon. After that, they will still be there, but their power will be reduced until moonset. Then it waxes again and we must hide until dawn. They are, like their masters, nocturnal."

"And that door will stop them?" She thought that, maybe, if the door stopped the Saaqaa, then the Saaqaa might stop the elves on their trail. It seemed too much to hope for.

He tested the door and leant on it for a moment. "Any barrier of wood or earth or spelled natural fabric with an elemental charge of those types. They will not cross through those materials, but they will transect other substances. Not metal of course. They are not properly material."

Transect! She didn't like the sound of that. "Is there anything else I should know?"

"Many things." She heard the scrape of some part of Dar's body on the wall. She could see him perfectly well from the heat he was emitting, and he looked tired. His body sagged and he made himself stand upright when he clearly wanted nothing but to stoop. "Come with me. There is a room in this warren where we can both sleep. And water is there. And food, I hope."

The tunnel was quickly made but sturdy. Lila got the impression it had been dug in a great rush, and then fortified later in stages. There were no niceties about it. Rough beams supported its narrow roof and the relatively welcoming width of its mouth soon became the height and narrowness of an average elf, which was just about the same size as she was, fortunately. "Is this some kind of hunting lodge?"

Dar snorted, "Hardly. No respectable elf would be seen dead in a lodge as rough as this one. This is a Night Shelter, an emergency post built by the light elves for when they are carelessly stranded in the wild at night. Many are scattered across these regions because of the

Saaqaa. Our Daga pursuers will be in one, unless they have elected to travel under cloak and risk being hunted by the Prowlers. They are three, possibly including a necromancer I believe, so they may think it worth the risk."

"I didn't think elves trafficked in the dark arts."

"Needs must," Dar said, his normally fluid body stiffening. He turned suddenly and vanished. Lila saw from the faintest of temperature differences that the tunnel ended in four chambers and that he had gone through a door. She moved to watch him and saw, with a frown, that he walked directly to one of many niches, the only one which contained a lantern. He lit it deftly, shielding his eyes as he did so, then put it back. She saw blinding white, then changed back to ordinary sight and the dazzle became a soft glow.

"You're nocturnal . . . you're one of the shadow elves," she said wonderingly, pleased with herself, bubbling with excitement.

"You noticed." He gazed at her evenly and his eyes were the exact colour of the night sky.

"But you're fine in daylight," Lila objected, thinking that nocturnal must mean incapable in the daytime.

"Sue the Creator," he said drily, almost smiling at her. "So we are. Though many here would have you believe otherwise. Of late great stupidity has grown up between our two races. All our differences become causes for spite even greater than that we reserve for other realms." He closed his mouth firmly and set about checking the supply cabinets with sudden vigour.

"Surely you can lead us safely through the night?"

"No," he said. "Those creatures will as happily eat me as you. In fact, much more readily. There are many of them here since . . . there are many. And," he paused in his activity and smiled to himself in the bleak way people do when looking at old memories of a great struggle, "they make highly effective traps. They were good learners."

She asked him questions, but he wouldn't speak any more on the subject. It seemed to be too close to him, she thought, too personal. He shook his head.

Lila gazed around the earth cavern and saw the walls had been further hollowed to make beds at waist height from the ground, not unlike cubby hotels she'd seen in Bay City and other great Otopian centres. But these were otherwise a far cry from such places. There were a couple of neatly rolled cotton pads in one or two of them and nothing more. In the lantern's soft yellow glow Dar looked slightly less worn than before, but not much. He went out and returned shortly with packets which he unwrapped in a hasty silence and handed her half.

She took the dried fruit and ate it almost as fast as he did. She remembered now that there had been elves like him in Sathanor during the diplomatic mission. None of them had been in positions of any importance, she thought, but her memory was vague on it. Yet Dar seemed to be in a position of some authority in his own agency. Higher than she was in hers, she thought.

He gave her water from a pitcher that tasted like it was fresh, and then he unrolled one of the meagre mattresses and, to her surprise, offered it to her.

"Suppose they come while we're asleep? The Daga I mean," she said into the soft quiet of the place and even her voice was muted. Nothing of the outside world intruded.

"I expect they will," he said, rubbing his face with both hands. "But we must rest or we cannot cross the mountains and do anything useful on the other side. So if they come, then we will fight." He laid most of his bladed weapons down carefully on the floor with quiet exactitude.

"Are you all right?" Lila asked.

"I am not as young as I used to be, but I will be fine. Will you rest?"

"I'll keep watch," Lila said, taking a tone of command for the first time since she'd come to Alfheim. "I can rest standing up, keep a lookout, and still sleep."

Dar paused, smiling faintly, then nodded. He lay down on the bed himself. "I forgot about all your talents," he said. "What forethought has gone into your making is remarkable. You are a miracle of techno-logical development. I wonder, what does it feel like to be so changed?"

"Oh you know," Lila said airily. "Your mileage varies."

"It must have hurt," he said very quietly. "You never moved so well as you have done since we were united."

Lila almost blushed, thinking of the degree of attention he must have paid her. "I've been feeling very good recently, since our . . . well, since." She felt unaccountably shy and concentrated on practical mat-ters, going over her routines before she locked her body in position for rest. Her AI-self switched into sentry mode, leaving her free to sleep. "Dar," she said after a minute's silence, "who is Zal to the elves?"

"A plague on our house," Dar murmured sleepily. "Our own blue-eyed boy." He was almost dreaming, she thought.

"Zal's eyes are brown," Lila said, remembering them suddenly with a falling sensation in her heart.

"They were not always so," Dar said. "They were very blue indeed, when he was one of us."

"What are you talking about?"

"He was a Jayon Daga agent, our Captain Kurtz." Dar rolled over onto his side wearily, turning his back to the room. He sounded regretful. "You know the story. The colonial officer who went native. But he was not always so. And then again, he was always so, but he never had the opportunity to discover that fact, until he came to Demonia."

Lila thought she detected personal sorrows. She jumped on them quick as she could. "You *do* know him?"

"Not really." The elf sighed wearily and drew a deep breath ready for a lengthy explanation. "Zal is of a higher caste than I am, as well as a different race. It may seem trivial to you, even invisible, but in Alfheim these things are very important. Zal is, was, Taliesetra Caste, of the ancient line of Light Kings, who are most closely bonded to Elemental *chi*. Only the Vialin Caste among the shadow elves is aetherically more powerful than that, and they are difficult beings, not truly elves at all. Meanwhile, I am Dusisannen of the Shadow, and we are not of royal descent, not of the high court or even the unhigh court; not of any court but the fresh air. The castes are magical and spiritual distinctions. The details are irrelevant. The point is that Zal and I could never really treat each other with the familiarity you consider true friendship, not even if we were assigned to the same task, though, of course, that would never happen." His words were thickened with a disgust he was too tired or not caring to conceal.

"What do you mean, never *really*?" Lila pursued, yawning.

"I followed Zal into Demonia," Dar said hesitantly, then, abruptly as if he had decided to tell her against his better judgement. "And I failed to prevent his fall."

"His fall?"

"In caste terms I should have given my life to prevent what happened," Dar said. "But we talked there, in the city of Barshebat: a long talk, a long time, and I came back and left him there unmolested. It was my duty to slay him, rather than do as I did, and my homecoming was less than pleasant. I do not wish to discuss it further. Let me rest."

"Sure," Lila said unwillingly. But then she thought it over and it occurred to her that she might not get another moment when Dar was so forthcoming, or another opportunity to ask anything, if they were attacked. "Actually I think I'll have to insist on some more answers," she said. "But I apologise in advance."

The elf made an unhappy sound. "I would think we were in a Game if I did not know we were not," he said. "Since you shared my spirit I have felt it increasingly difficult not to be candid with you. And there is another reason, namely, that I must consider myself the enemy of the Jayon Daga from now on, rather than one of their brothers. In all of Alfheim there are fewer than five people I could trust, and none of them are near, nor would I wish them to know what I have done."

"Because you didn't kill Zal? I thought you said you couldn't be sent after him."

"I said that he and I would never be sent together. But I was sent to bring him back or end him. No Taliesetra or higher caste would want to soil their spirit with that eventuality. Even in the circumstances, it would be a crime that merited only the harshest punishment."

"Exile," Lila said, speeding through elf data on the justice system. It was arcane and vast, but this was simple to find. "They'd send you to take the fall and then abandon you?"

"Somebody must do it. Low castes are considered expendable in such situations, compared with the waste of a higher order." Now at last Lila did detect some bitterness in his voice and he felt it too because he said, "You must ignore my self-pity. My history with the Jayon Daga is no great account of glory. Death and blood are on my hands and the service of Alfheim is no excuse, merely an explanation. You will understand this, no doubt."

"I'm kinda new to the job," Lila said. "But yes. I'm beginning to. But why couldn't they leave Zal alone? If he'd gone and wasn't coming back?"

"It has not escaped your notice that Zal is a public figure." Dar rolled back to face her, his head pillowed on his hands, eyes blinking slowly in the soft lantern light. "His continued existence risks exposure of the fact of his Fall to the wider elf world and the realms beyond, most likely by agents such as yourself. It is the shame that the elves cannot abide. His action, particularly as a high-caste son, displays that Alfheim's magic and culture is not the living perfection of actualised spirit, a claim upon which all caste power is based. It also shows others in Alfheim that it is possible to reject almost the entire spectrum of elven lore and thrive in other realms. This example most of all, cannot be permitted. Alfheim is on a knife edge, Lila Black. The high castes have long allowed power to corrupt them and naturally they claim it will save Alfheim from inevitable destruction. They have hoarded knowledge and power for themselves over the centuries most recently passed, and what was once a fair division of learning between all castes, neither high nor low but differentiated in talent, has become regulated by the hierarchy of absolutism. You have seen this many times in history. Nothing is new. But all those who believe in the cause will speak as though this time it is different. They claim secret knowledge that they cannot share, which tells them that cruelty and manipulation, early vengeance, and defensive posturing are the only way to prevent a terrible catastrophe. These are the people who have captured Zal. He serves a twofold purpose. It is possible he may be one axis of a great Sundering spell, if such a thing exists. But it is certain that there are other things they would much rather he did while he was alive, and we cannot delay in prising him from their control, although I fear it is already far too late."

"What other things?" Lila asked.

"What do you think?" Dar closed his long eyes. As he relaxed, Lila began to see that he was considerably older than she had first thought. He was in excellent condition, and elves mostly looked youthful, even when old. Dar's age was not so physical as it was emotional. He looked as though he had carried a great weight for too long a time and it was this, and not any running or fighting, which caused a profound exhaustion.

"Recant," Lila said, the word springing to her mind intuitively. "A public denouncement of what he did from his own mouth."

"Good," Dar murmured, almost asleep. "You understand."

"But what about you?" she asked. "What happened to you when you didn't kill him? You're still in the Daga."

"I was given the opportunity to try again, once Zal entered Otopia," Dar said and his body stiffened and he drew his knees up towards his chest, curling up. "And a friend and sister in our cause prevented my first sentence of death from being executed upon me, dependent on my second effort becoming successful. I was given the time and means to achieve this goal, but of course, I had no intention of carrying it out. I made it look as though I was committed to his end, whilst in reality I followed Zal closely only to protect him from other Daga agents, and then, some days ago, that stay of execution expired. My friend will have paid for Zal's survival with her life, as will Gwil, I do not doubt. It is almost certain we will pay also, for my mistake in underestimating you."

"Me?"

"Better Zal die on the road than stand up and take back what he has done," Dar said. "If I could not have maintained his freedom, I would have killed him. Although he is a . . . clever bastard, you would say. There is magic in the music and in his changed voice. Where he sings is as important as what and to whom. I do not mean that metaphorically. It is our magic. I will explain it some other time to you."

"And his songs are everywhere," Lila said and thought to herself—propaganda!

"Even in Alfheim," Dar agreed. "Though they are much murdered on the flute and tabor. Now you must sleep. Or everything will be wasted. If you are my friend, let me also rest."

Friend? That was the word actually, Lila thought, inducing alpha waves across her brain to speed her into sleep. Yes, since yesterday's strange fusion, they had become somehow more like each other, or maybe only understood how alike they were, but it didn't matter which. In that moment they had become friends.

"Goodnight," she whispered.

"*Inaraluin*," he said—be dreamless.

CHAPTER FIFTEEN

Lila woke into full power two and a half hours after she had gone to sleep. Before she was aware of what she was doing, she was padding quickly along the tunnel, a gun in each hand, her AI-self in control. After being still for so long she felt twinges and aches now, but she ignored them. Beyond the door she could hear sounds of terrible fighting from further down the hillside. She heard elven voices shouting, and they sounded desperate. For a moment her hand lingered on the door.

The clash of metal on metal and the grunt of hard effort and pain, the whining buzz of magics, and a horrible background noise she couldn't identify reached her senses as she flung the bolts back and looked out. Flickering faint light danced a few metres below the treeline. The awful noise was like distressed metal screaming, but she felt its timbre in her bones, what was left of them, and knew it for some kind of fell creature she didn't want to see. A scream sliced the night in two and fell silent in its course, harmonics enough to damage ordinary human hearing. One elf at least was dead.

Lila used sensors on her hand to sweep-clear the area around the door before stepping out and closing it behind her, in case there were any of the Night Prowlers still around. She didn't consider waking

Dar. Better he stayed where he was less likely to pull attention from the Saaqaa. Instead, she ran quietly downhill towards the fighting, concealing herself carefully with camouflage and stealthy moves until she was almost on top of the scene. Her effort was wasted, since nothing there was looking out for her.

She saw an elf body on the ground ten metres away in a dappled pool of faint starlight. Over it the gigantic form of a black, bipedal animal crouched. It had long arms and savage claws. Lila didn't know what it was. Like the Saaqaa it was eyeless, its long, narrow head merely jaws with ranks of dagger teeth and a bony crest running side to side across its skull. A long tail balanced the head's weight and long legs, short at the thigh but lengthy in the shin and the foot, which was perched delicately on the earth. She was amazed to see that in one hand it held a short, decorated spear and with this it was fighting another elf, standing.

It was extremely strong. The wooden spear point struck the elf's sword with the force of a wrecking ball each time the elf blocked an attack and the elf was failing. Lila saw the fighter's *andalune* body close and tight, weakening as the black creature came close so that it dealt not only physical punishment but drained the energy from the elf at the same time. The *andalune* body was torn off with every pass of the creature's hand as if it were tissue paper.

The third elf of the party was casting the strange werelight Lila had seen from the doorway of the shelter. Its peculiar intense green made the black creature flinch backwards each time it flared, but it was clear that this was not enough to do any real damage. And then Lila saw one of the four-legged types of Prowler stalking around behind the sword-fighting elf, and knew that their time was up if she did not intervene. The light didn't hurt the Saaqaa enough to deter them completely, and whatever the sorcerer whispered in between light bolts was drowning in the dreadful screech that the Prowlers made, a noise, she realised as her AI analysed it, that was geared exactly to disrupt the sonics of elven magical senses.

Around the whole scene wild aether swirled and gathered. The black creatures' tails actively swung around, searching for strong currents, and these they seemed to drink into their skins, becoming darker as the aether vanished, and more violent.

The elf with the sword missed her footing at last. Her energy body was almost gone. She was as magically undefended as Lila was. The creature's spear struck her shoulder as she missed her block and she spun and fell on her face without a sound. At a speed Lila would have had to work hard to match the huge two-legged Prowler pounced on her and stabbed her through the back, pinning her body to the ground. It let out a shrill, terrible scream of victory and its doglike companion leapt forwards, head close to the body, weaving as though dancing as it drained the final aether.

The werelight vanished. She lost track of the third elf as the bipedal Saaqaa straightened up and yanked its spear free with a bloody wrench. All this happened in a few seconds, no more.

Lila felt the odds turning bad. She could go now and leave whoever was out here, yes. It would be smart to do that. It would be the spy thing to do, the agent's business dealt with by nature, not even her fault, not her guilt.

She set a Starlight flare for a low altitude long burn and launched it from the gun in her forearm. Suddenly the forest lit up like daylight. The elf spellcaster whirled towards her at the sound of the gun and cracked a small branch in doing so. In the burn of the rocket glare he stood out against the wooded hillside like a white statue, as brilliant as an angel. The Prowler turned its attention instantly onto him, shadows gathering around its head like a cloak of darkness. It flung its spear and the cast drew a black line across the aetheric mist, gathering momentum as it went.

Lila shot the wooden weapon out of the air in midflight with a flechette round that made it into matchwood before it got halfway to its target. Other fragments of the tiny grenade struck both prowlers, inflicting stinging cuts which confused them so that they leapt back into the darker regions, leaving the dead and their defender temporarily free. Without hesitation the surviving elf ran straight towards Lila.

She caught his arm as he reached her and accelerated both of them even faster up the hillside towards the night shelter, their retreat accompanied by the triumphant screech and scream of the Saaqaa as the flare burned out and fell to the ground.

Lila bolted the heavy door behind them. Immediately her captive attempted to slide along the tunnel away from her, but he didn't know she could see his every move as clear as day. She easily caught up and in the darkness used her excess of strength to pin him against the wall and bind his hands behind his back with a plastic arrest tag. His breath was hot and fast in the confined space, much faster than her own, and she could feel that he was shaking, although he did everything he could to stop it.

Dar was awake and sliding his second sword into place, its hilt above his shoulder at his back, when she came in, pushing her prisoner ahead of her. In the lantern light their visitor's wide eyes showed green, his hair as fine and blond as Zal's, skin a fine porcelain white. He was Light, Lila thought, pleased at being able to classify him. He was not very good in the dark. Maybe that was why his party had been caught.

Dar's eyes widened in surprise and then narrowed. He glanced at Lila, displeasure evident all over him, "What is this? Are you mad?"

"Dar," the prisoner called in elvish. "Who is this? Why are you here?"

"Do not seek to explain yourself," Dar told him, his eyes never leaving Lila's face.

"He can talk," Lila said, sticking to Otopian in case it was an advantage and the other didn't know it. "The others won't be so forthcoming. Something's eating them."

At these words the blond elf jerked his bound hands out of her grasp and staggered forwards, away from her and towards Dar. "You will not speak of them so lightly," he hissed in perfect Otopian, glancing back at her. So, not an advantage.

"Shut up," Dar said offhandedly, still not looking at him. "And now what are you going to do? Torture him? He won't talk. Well, only to lie." His gaze to Lila was strangely desperate, she thought, almost afraid.

"We were trying to reach you, in order to warn you that the Daga have completely split," the captured elf said rapidly, switching to elvish in an effort to exclude Lila. "It is openly in conflict over the Lady in Sathanor."

"I said shut up." Dar stepped forward and kept his gaze locked with Lila, returning to Otopian and the first streak of sarcasm Lila had ever heard from him. "Do you hear him? Good news. The Resistance is unmasked." As he talked he worked at unbuckling the other's weapons and carefully drawing them off him. Lila put her gun away.

At the sound of her armour rebuilding itself the strange elf looked around in spite of himself and flinched visibly. He gave her the look she'd long been expecting from Dar, the one that said, *that is disgusting!* "This is the Otopian agent," he said to Dar. "The one you . . ."

Dar's backhanded blow cut his voice off. He staggered and Dar snatched something from around his neck, a talisman, Lila thought, jerking it clear and almost dragging him off his feet. Dar was glaring at Lila, in a real rage as he stalked around to her behind the other's back and hissed, "You should have saved one of the other ones. Do you see this?" He showed her the silver amulet he'd torn clear. It looked like a Greek letter omega to Lila. "This necromancer is more dangerous than twenty other agents."

"Ghalada of the Dark is dead." The elf turned around. Blood ran freely from the side of his mouth. He fixed quickly on Dar and Lila saw Dar flinch inwardly and guessed that this was the name of his conspirator, his friend, more than a friend perhaps. "She died to save you and Zal. I can help you free Zal from Arië. You know it is true. Without me you stand little chance. You have fair skill in magic, but nothing like hers. And she has an army of sorcerers with her. This machine cannot help you, even if it feels no pain and suffers no magical bond upon it."

"This machine saved your sorry one-candle ass," Lila said quietly in perfect elvish, adapting the words to her natural style in a way she hoped annoyed him. "And it can put you right back with your friends." She met his gaze with an even one of her own and enjoyed his obvious discomfort when he did not know where to look—the surface of her eyes having no iris or pupil upon which to centre attention. He lifted his head and looked down at her.

"They were not my friends in this campaign, even if they were friends of my heart. Do you think I would have let them die in the grip of monsters if they were?" His emerald stare was piercingly direct, viciously sincere. "No. I led them into danger and I watched them die. As you did from your hiding place before you chose to act. But they will not have thought you should help them as they suffered. I know they thought it of me, for I saw their faces full of heartbroken surprise." He turned to Dar, leaning towards the taller, darker elf, licking his own blood from his lips. His voice was clear and heartfelt, "You know me of old, Shonshani Dusisannen. You must believe I am your ally."

"You were ever the Lady's slave," Dar said shortly, still facing away from him, and from Lila. His hands twitched. "Such allegiance as you claim would be the best hidden secret in all Alfheim."

Lila wasn't sure of it, but she thought she detected a moment of weakness in Dar. She could tell from his tone that he longed to believe. She watched their prisoner lick his lips again—was he doing something magical to add weight to his words? She couldn't feel it on herself, but perhaps it wasn't directed at her.

"Everyone kept their colours hidden until the last days," the fair elf insisted, ignoring Lila as he moved past her to come easily within *andalune* range of Dar. "We all had to. You know that is the way it has always been. Nobody can be trusted when the stakes are so high for individual and caste alike. It is the way things have been since the demon wars. Sila and Elyn lie dead and consumed behind me. Not because I did not love them, but because we are in a war for the future of the realm, and they would not take my side, nor I theirs, though they did not know it until now."

"You were freaking out," Lila reminded him, determined to push a wedge into whatever charm he was managing to exert on Dar. "If you had power, you didn't use much of it."

He glared at her with a loathing that almost made her step back with its force. "Have I not said? They were my friends. Silalio was at one time the woman of my heart. You saw what I did. Perhaps you could have done it with more courage than I and slain them yourself?"

Dar glanced at Lila, looking for confirmation. She shrugged, deeply concerned now by the scale of his doubts and the way that seeing this shook her own conviction. There was a moment when they looked at one another and she felt that all the trust they had ever shared was slowly beginning to crack. In a moment it would break apart, pressed down on the block of uncertainties by the considerable exertion of willpower emanating from their captive. She switched to aetheric sight, wanting to touch Dar's aetheric body for some reassurance or at least know his state, but instead she saw the *andalune* of the necromancer reach towards Dar's and touch it briefly. Dar jolted as if he had received an electric shock and his face contorted with anguish which was suddenly mastered. His face became smooth and hard.

"This is why you must never let him talk," Dar said finally, and with a speed that Lila could not block he spun around. There was a knife in his hand and it buried itself up to the hilt in the blond elf's chest.

Shock and pleading crossed the other's handsome face as Dar let go. The vivid light in his grass-coloured eyes went out. His body hit the ground with a dull, soft thump, his bound arms preventing it from rolling onto his back.

Lila turned to Dar, sick in gut and heart, and he screamed into her face, a sound of shrieking, intense agony that wasn't even a word. He silenced her shock and doubled it in the same instant. She was paralysed with the sudden turn of events, could hardly believe them.

"What did you think this was? Some game?" he cried hoarsely at her, though she felt that he was saying it as much to himself as to her.

"Was he lying?" she yelled back, frightened and momentarily out of control with the sight of Dar's own loss of it, though at least this broke her free and let her start acting again.

"I don't know! I don't know!" He stared down at the body and abruptly bent down to pull the knife out of its chest. It wouldn't come and he had to wrench it free over several tries. As soon as it was out he dropped the blade as if it was on fire and buried his face in his hands.

All sense of adventure and pleasure that she had felt earlier in the day was gone now. She felt a fool for even having lost her concentration that long. Lila bent down and picked the elf's corpse up. It was a little lighter than Zal, a little heavier than Dar. Its golden hair hung free and brushed her legs softly as though it didn't realise its change of state. "Sorry," she said quietly, pushing her emotions aside, like she had to when she thought of home. She would never get used to this, she thought, never do anything but hate what she did in those moments where the job had to come first.

She glanced at Dar, wanting him to see that she shared the burden of it. After a second's thought she said quietly, "They don't go easily into that good night. I guess elf necromancers are no different to demons or faeries or humans in that respect."

"No," Dar said. "And he will be no easier to deal with if he comes back from Thanatopia, though that will change him in ways we cannot know." He took a deep breath. "We are not thinking. He is the same size as you are. We should use his clothes and weapons to make you less obvious here, though at close range your metal structure will always give you away to us."

They worked together to strip him down. Lila said, "It feels very wrong. All these are his own things." She found vellum in the inner pockets and handed it to Dar. She found a sprig of heather, old and flattened. She found a piece of Otopian silk crepe de Chine, patterned with beautiful Chinese dragons. All its edges were neatly hemmed by a tidy hand—a loving hand? Each item deepened the discomfort and hurt she felt for the dead elf, enemy or not. They left him his undergarments, more delicate and well-fashioned than even the most expensive treat Lila had ever gotten herself from Agent Provocateur. Blood had ruined them.

Lila folded his arms across his chest. She glanced unwillingly into his face and saw that his eyes were still open a fraction, as green as Poppy's hair. He was very handsome, and his face had the same kind of shapes and angulation as Zal's. They might have been brothers. She missed Zal suddenly. He wouldn't be dead. Maybe he was in a worse state.

Without thinking about it, she bent down to brush the corpse's eyes closed and found herself kissing the smooth, ivory forehead. A zinging tickle ran across her face and a warm, vibrant sensation like a tiny and concentrated swarm of honey bees darted down her throat and lodged in her chest. She leapt back, but it was too late.

Dar stared at her, aghast, as she clapped a hand over her mouth. "What did you do?" he asked, his voice faint. "What have you done?"

Lila's AI-self did not recognise the situation, running diagnostics and finding nothing, but Lila's much-abused human heart knew the truth immediately. It was as obvious as a clear green day. "His *andalune*," she said, staring at Dar and wishing it was not so, unable to believe it. "In my chest. In my—heart—that *chi* thing there, whatever it is." She could hear the dead elf laughing at her, but from the inside, where her laughter came from, only she wasn't laughing at all.

She grabbed hold of Dar's jerkin and pulled him so close and so hard that she lifted him off his feet, "Get it the hell out of me! Right now!"

Dar's blue eyes stared into hers, appalled and afraid. He didn't even try to make her let him go. "It is beyond me."

The honeybees chuckled in tones of grass and leaf and swirled in upon themselves, to a concentrated mote of unhappy triumph. After a second or two Lila released Dar and conducted another, much more intensive, survey. X-rays and ultrasound, she remembered, and put her hand to her chest, emitting first one and then another. The bees' response was immediate and furious.

Out, she instructed, *or I'll irradiate you to nothing. I mean it.*

Then you will kill me twice, said the blond elf's voice, as clear as a bell inside her mind. *I cannot live outside you. So if you are going to exterminate me, do it quickly.*

"He's talking to me!" Lila repeated what had been said, filled with revulsion and wonder in equal parts. "What should I do?"

Dar groaned and his grief turned to anger. "He was ever trickier than even Zal, this one. Long he was beloved of me, before these days became so short and the light of Sathanor so dim inside him. I thought it was too easy to take his life with a simple blade. I should bear the diverse pleasures of his possession, if any should at all. He had a sweet and passionate nature once, but ruled by a cold mind which grew to perfect ice after his mastery of the dark arts. Such a combination is quite deadly when combined with the tasks of a Jayon agent. He agreed to it of his own will, for the service of Alfheim and to demonstrate the depth of his loyalty to the Lady."

During this speech Lila handed over mostly to her AI-self, keeping just enough of her feelings going to keep her sharp. She rerouted her panic and decided to roll with things. So, she was possessed, how bad could it be?

"Necromancy isn't evil," Lila said, attempting to soothe Dar, longing to believe it herself, still shocked at the strange but not uncomfortable burning and thrumming she felt inside. Her AI-self didn't even recognise the presence of anything untoward. She wasn't exactly being harmed. Her words came from a book her AI had read. "It's only very very stupidly dangerous."

"It is the most difficult road and an invitation to wake the evil within, because its powers are very great," Dar said. "And for that alone I would never have seen him touch it. As for what this means for you and us and for him, I have never come across it before and know not."

"Me neither," Lila said. She felt so isolated and scared that she wanted Dar to hold her suddenly, but could not and dare not ask it.

Tell gentle Dar he was always too sentimental for this work, the spirit said, the voice's sudden appearance in her mind jolting her with fresh shock. But her AI-self was processing at top speed, and it kept on finding peculiar advantages in each new discovery, ones which Lila didn't personally like at all, though she saw their sense. Even if her inhabitant was a liar, he was potentially extremely useful.

Lila said aloud to Dar, "He doesn't blame you for what you did. He thinks it was the only smart thing to do." She felt the bees vibrate crossly and added to them, *Can it*. It roiled with anger but said nothing.

"Do you say that or does he?"

Name, Lila demanded coldly of the *andalune* in her chest, *or nuke*.

I am Tath.

"Tath says it," Lila said quietly. She let her hand fall to her side, removing the threat as she realised the extent of the aetheric elf's dependency on her.

"Tath. He keeps his true name from you and gives you his use-name only," Dar observed wearily, his hands still full of Tath's clothing.

"You must know it," Lila said. "The real one, I mean."

"I do. It is not something I would use lightly, but use it I will to defend you if he tries to command you against your will. Do not give yours to him either. It may not have the same effect on you as it would an elf, but he will use it against you if he can."

Tath had curled up into a still and silent emerald jewel inside her heart. With great misgiving Lila realised that as long as he was present there she would never know how much he was able to spy on her. Perhaps it had been a lucky break for him, when Dar's nerve held. She might never know peace again.

Lila was not sure of the extent of true naming's power in Alfheim, only that it had a greater power in this realm than any of the other magical realms, and none at all in Otopia, unless you were an elf. "One minute you love him, the next you talk about him like he's born evil," she said.

"I do not know what Tath's real nature is, any more than I know yours, and in any case, affection is rarely ruled by such distinctions," Dar said with guarded weariness. He handed the clothing to her. "Here. You have run around in your underwear long enough."

"This isn't really underwear," Lila said defensively, alert for any reaction from her new passenger, and finding none. "This is army-issue vest and pants. For work. Under all the heavy gear. It's not like my personal smalls."

"I feel better for knowing that." Dar watched her, and she thought he was finding it more than amusing.

As she dressed she was continually aware of the new feeling of carrying Tath. Her heart felt stronger, lighter, brighter, with its new resident bees and their greenish gold finery. She was on her guard for more invasive measures, but she sensed that this was beyond the power of the spirit. It was not of her body and it could not possess it. Just as well. She didn't want to be run around by a crazy elf.

At that thought she felt an angry zap shoot down into her diaphragm. *Only kidding*, she said, and then to herself thought, *What the hell am I doing?* But just as she and Dar had changed as they shared the experience of Sathanor's healing, it seemed that she and Tath were in a new relationship now, well, in a one-way dependent relation, as opposed to being in a situation of wishing the other did not exist. She could feel Tath's appalled, revolted displeasure at having her as his host, and told him firmly, *You can put up or shut up. Were you lying by the way?*

The reply was affirmative. But it was unclear which part of it was a lie. Not all of it certainly, for the green spirit was full of grief. It recognised this in her own feelings, and was both distraught and comforted. In spite of his regrets and anger, Tath could not but be in some degree of sympathy with her, and she with him. They were too exposed to the truth of one another.

I don't want or like this, she told him firmly.

Neither do I.

I won't exploit it if you don't.

Accord.

Lila was in tears as she straightened and closed the buttons on the outer tunic. It was still warm. Magical sigils fluttered to the surface of it and submerged again. She didn't know what they were. Then she began equipping herself with Tath's weapons. Each one was a fine piece of work by human standards, but she knew from experience that the arcane crafting of them made them objects she might never wield to their full power, if she could wield them at all. Incon training had not run to daggers and bows in the last century, but her AI-self assured her it had the knowledge of how to use them. She reached for his dagger . . .

Wait.

She obeyed his voice. Dar watched her uneasily.

They are all bound to my spirit. They will burn you. If you are to use them you must let me make contact with them.

Nice, Lila said. *Just like genetically coded guns.*

Dar, guessing correctly the reason for her hesitation, said, "Only he knows the power and use of those."

Spill it, Lila told Tath and flexed her x-ray hand.

There was a moment of silence. The bees went quiet.

I will not use them against you.

Lila stood up and moved away from the weapons. "Not good enough," she said. She accessed and armed her flame gun. It was a pity to waste a fuel cell when it was one of the few useful weapons she actually had here. Still—she stood back, Dar copying her, and clicked on the pilot light.

No! I need them. You need them! They are the only useful tools you have here you stupid, ignorant human! And they are the only weapons you will ever find that you can carry beyond death . . .

Lila let a line of fuel run at low power out of the nozzle. It ignited as it vaporised and a narrow stream of yellow fire appeared, as long as a forearm, from the tip of her middle finger. She relayed to Dar what Tath had said and added aloud, "I don't believe in Beyond Death and I doubt I'll ever get there so you'll have to do better than that."

She extended her line of fire another half a metre. The light from the flames danced over the silver dagger blades. She adjusted her oxygen stream and her torch became fiercely blue, flutter of flame changed to single cone of extreme heat. "I don't care who forged them or what they can do. In ten seconds they're solder." She said it with conviction, though she didn't know if they could be melted, not here anyway. She had heard of such efforts failing in the past. But the bow was made of natural materials, bone and wood, and surely it would catch fire. Actually, as she looked more closely she got the impression there was no wood involved . . .

A vice closed in her chest. Her heart stopped.

Is that better?

There was an instant of failing, terrible weakness. Then her AI-self switched on its auxiliary pumping system. She felt the cold pleasure of the green spirit become tainted with surprise and a kind of grudging admiration. He restored her heart.

At least, she thought, he knows when he's beat. To him she said, "Killing me would be a mistake, surely?"

In any other body you would be long since banished to Thanatopia and I would be master of your form, he informed her calmly. *How ironic that it was you and not sweet Dar who took pity on me. But I think I could only command the flesh of yours and being a hopeless cripple does not appeal to me.*

Lila set the torch flame to the bow.

Stop! I will do as you wish, without trickery. I give you my word.

"He gave me his word." She watched the bow's grip starting to singe and blacken. Golden and black signs like words seemed to rush to the point from within its structure.

"It will be good," Dar said tonelessly.

She switched off the torch. The bow smoked slightly but it was not on fire and had sustained no real damage. Tath snarled at her internally, unable to speak he was so filled with loathing. His spirit furled and stormed. She felt him suddenly unfold and spill like liquid out across her chest and down her arms. He paused where her flesh met the prosthetics, a pause of extreme repulsion and dread . . .

"Do it!" Lila screamed, hating him at that moment with all her strength.

There is elemental strength in this material, Tath said. *You did not come by that in Otopia. It is vile to me but I can intersect it. How lucky you have been to find Dar. Few healers in Alfheim are able to remake metal into a thing able to carry aether. Did you know what he has done?* He was taunting. She hated him more. *And he did not tell you about it, nor why someone of his low stature could rise so high in the ranks. How little you know of him.*

Tath's *andalune* suddenly surged down her arms like a fall of cool water. She felt her hands tingle. *You can touch them now*, Tath said scornfully.

Lila set the daggers on her own shoulders, his lovely composite bow in its quiver at her back. Tath withdrew immediately after, his presence lingering where the items lay close to her body, watching over them, comforted by their closeness. She had not detected anything unusual about them. After a moment's hesitation she picked up the silver amulet.

"You will forgive me if I ask you not to wear that," Dar said.

"It's okay. I'm no zombie. It might make people think twice before attacking us if they believe I'm a necromancer." Lila soldered the broken

chain closed with a quick arc shot from her finger and put the necklace
on, hanging the sigil at her neck where it showed clear against the dark
green of Tath's jerkin. She bit back thoughts of Tath's statements about
her metal body, his feelings. She couldn't afford to listen.

"If you insist." Dar seemed to sink under the psychic burden of the
situation and she was sorry for him.

"Dar," she said and waited for him to give her his attention. Then
she didn't know what to say. She touched his arm and he just looked
at her with that elfin, waiting look, but his *andalune* self flowed eagerly
upward over her hand until it found her natural skin. Lila felt the
faintest, lightest breath of it caress her neck.

Then she felt a sudden surge of a very peculiar, delicate sensation,
as of being washed through by imaginary water as Tath's spirit rose
hungrily, expanding through her human body towards the contact
point. It was quite different to the feeling of a moment before when he
had been completely guarded. In his impulse and diffusion now, made
vulnerable by his need to be open to try and touch Dar, he was unable
to conceal much from her.

She understood that Tath loved Dar, among a complex set of other
feelings about him. She knew it absolutely. She thought that she might
too. She wondered if Dar could feel anything different, but he broke the
contact between the three of them at that moment and slipped away,
closing in on himself. Lila was left confused by the welter of emotion,
its nuances and meanings so similar to and different from her own.

"We need to dispose of his body. We can't leave it here." Dar said.

"Outside . . ." Lila suggested.

Tath was appalled all the way as they carried his cold form through
the tunnel, through the door, and down the hill. The battlefield was
deserted and the creatures were gone, though Lila could see them not
far away, feeding in the deep pools of aether. It was a dark hour.

Tath grew furious and agitated but calmed as he saw his physical
self placed on the bloody ground where his friends had fallen. Lila felt

him shrink and withdraw deep, becoming both still and silent. His quiet sadness was very heavy. Her horror at the idea of him being left there was no easier to bear. *Sorry*, she said to him, inside, and touched the pocket of his tunic at her chest, where she had replaced his personal effects. He did not respond.

Dar and Lila made their way back to the shelter and waited there until dawn. They lay apart, uncomfortable in their full gear, and Lila slept only after drugs and alpha waves had nuked the feelings in her body down to a low, dull level. She dreamed, but the dreams were foggy and difficult and she didn't remember them when she woke up. She was glad when Dar came and said it was time to go. He looked in a terrible state, but she tried to smile at him. As they left the warren and turned uphill again, she did not look back towards the forest.

CHAPTER SIXTEEN

The enchantment keeping Zal unconscious let go of him after a period. His enforced insensibility had been so deep he had no sense of time having passed since the eagle had spoken the binding charm. It could have been seconds, or years, or centuries.

He was inside water. A lot of water. One hell of a lot of water. The water was rich with life. It teemed. Vegetable empires abounded, surging, blooming, drinking, dying. Fishy awareness darted. Greater bodies, further off, sang quiet songs of freshwater. He felt the distant presence of many elves, and aetheric adepts of other races, their notes jarring with the rest. Farther away still creatures of greater and lesser power lived and hunted and hid in light and shade. For a moment there was the faint signature of another kind of being, but it was like a flash, there and gone before he knew it.

He rolled over onto his front, opened his eyes, and stared down through the miles of water. He realised that he was not only close to the mighty lake in Sathanor, but a good way under it. The only thing that separated him from its vast tonnage and pressure was an enchantment—the Lady's for sure. She was water adept and had many students who no doubt assisted her in maintaining the enchantments around the clock. But he wasn't interested in the miracle of his prison, only in the trace of the alien mind he thought he had felt in that first instant of connection to the world.

It was gone. In its place now he could only see the hypnotic depths of the abyssal fault that lay beneath the pretty surface of Aparastil Lake.

"Gazing at the navel of the world?" said a voice in the sweet and gentle tones of a much nicer person than the one who was actually speaking. "The source of Alfheim's aether is closer to you than ever before."

"Piss off, Arië," Zal said without getting up. Arië was not there in person, only her voice. Her actual presence would have been tangible and he felt only strangers close by. He was pleased to find himself still filthy dirty and wearing Lila's black leather jacket.

The moment of silence was rather sweet. He wished it would last but it didn't.

"I see you have slid further into the delinquency of the demon world."

Zal yawned. "I see you're still spreading that bullshit about a Great Spell. End of the world required to save our lovely homeland from corruption and exploitation by incorrigible foreigners. Very nice. Must've taken you at least ten minutes to come up with that."

"The Spell only awaits the opportune moment. Your belief in it, or in the reasons behind its use, is not required. But enough of these pleasantries."

Four strong hands suddenly grabbed hold of him and lifted him upright. He was surprised but tried not to show it. He didn't know that Arië's guard could be stealthy enough to sneak up on him, but obviously they were better than they used to be or his sensitivity to the constant murmur of the Alfheim aether was much worse. Probably the latter, he thought with grim resignation. The guards didn't meet his gaze—they wore bone-plate helms in any case which shielded their faces almost completely. They wasted no time in stripping the jacket from him and searching him for amulets or weapons. He couldn't detect *andalune* from either of them, so they were adept enough to keep it away from him. He wasn't sure whether that was out of respect for the danger he represented or just revulsion at the changes wrought by his altered nature.

Arië's voice said quietly, "It is time you faced your elders and betters, Suhanathir. In the name of all the Houses of Alfheim, I arrest you for treason."

"My name is Zal," he said, pointlessly, to the empty air. He wished that the sound of his given name had no power, but Arië knew both parts of it, his life name and his caste name: Suhanathir Taliesetra. The only mark in his favour was that she did not know his true name any longer. Once, when he was still an elf through and through, she had known it, but that name was lost when he was in Demonia and he had a new one now. Then again, he did not know the full version of hers. Arië was just a part of it, as Zal was just part of his. Without being able to say all three parts in sequence, they could not command one another.

The guards silently braced his arms behind his back. One stretched out a gauntleted hand and touched the wall of the cell. It shivered and suddenly ballooned beyond his gesture into the darker, deeper waters of the lake, creating a corridor. In this way they walked through the water in their tiny pocket of air and it stretched out just ahead of them and closed just behind them.

Presently something other than a waterquoia tree loomed out of the thick green gloom. Zal saw another bubble like their own, but larger, and beyond it even more of them and more still, clustered like oversize frogspawn, netted and held in the branches of the underwater forest. The silvery globules were everywhere, above and below. Their bubble drew close and joined its skin to one of these. Where the cell walls met they stuck fast and a door formed. Without ado he was marched forwards.

The palace of Aparastil had been much extended in his absence. He remembered it as a house on a lake, fine and rather too large for the resident Family of Water but still no more than a mansion. These halls of trapped air with their falls and fountains lit by charmed sun and moonlight were all new to him. Like all such show, the waste of power put into their creation spoke of extravagance and strength way beyond his personal resources. It was meant to make outsiders feel puny. It did a good job, he thought wryly as their journey ended—that and the big guards and their massive enchanted broadswords and the astounding size of an entire courtroom full of Alfheim's noble lineage, ranked in tiers, robed and standing solemnly to attention, all looking down at him as he was taken to the centre of their vast oval and left there.

He looked straight at Arië, seated above him in the Magus's position; a place of ultimate jurisprudence which he knew she did not deserve. He was vaguely aware of empty places to right and left in various positions and knew, without having to look further, that these were all where his family and caste family should have been. Occasional other absences marked the positions of friends or people whose loyalty he had trusted.

Arië was as lovely as enchantment could make her, and she had been lovely in ordinary ways before that with her blanched-almond complexion, deep auburn curls, and soulful blue eyes. She exuded youthful beauty, glamour, and sweetness. It was a terrible shame.

It was no moment to be shy. Zal put his hands on his hips and took a very obvious turn, looking at all the faces present before turning back to Arië. "Tie me kangaroo down, sport," he said with the full power of his voice, words dry as a desert. He knew full well nobody there would have a clue what he was quoting, but at least it was amusing him and he needed amusement desperately because otherwise he was going to start feeling afraid. "I'm hoping we can skip the part where you talk self-justifying shit and just get straight to the guilty verdict."

His speech created an icy silence in response. Even those souls who had been ambivalent, perhaps sympathetic to him, recoiled from the lash of spite in them. Here, if not in any other realm, words literally hurt and his could hurt more than most. But the Lady was not affected.

Her *andalune* lay around her like a gleaming shield. The minor charm simply bounced off her and the only thing it might have done was disrupt her sense of decorum. That was something, at least.

"The fact of your treason is indisputable," Arië said. "You have betrayed us to Demonia, and most likely to Otopia as well. You disobeyed orders. You cut yourself off from your masters. You withheld information. Shall I go on? The only matter of interest remaining here is what the sentence of the court shall be. In ordinary circumstances it would be death, but you have made yourself a creature of unusual abilities that render you potentially more useful than a corpse so we consider that you may redeem yourself one of two ways. Either you return to the service of Alfheim by command of your true name . . ."

"Not a chance," Zal said without waiting to hear the alternative.

"I think that it is at least possible you are open to persuasion," Arië said and made a slight gesture with one hand.

Zal did not turn to look but he heard several pairs of feet enter the room and walk towards him. One pair dragged and shuffled.

"What I want to know is why the rest of you are here," he said, ignoring the sound. "Why would you ally yourselves with this idiot, when the only solution she has to offer you is isolation and subservience? For centuries she has dragged power into Sathanor, away from every other region. She has fostered needless hatred against the Shadow . . ."

"There is an Aetheric Gate beneath Aparastil's water," said a strong voice from the gathering.

The massed *andalune* of the gathering was a huge force, united, against him. Zal could feel it like a weight in the air. It was smothering. Within it those hearts that were guilty about their complicity in something they found repugnant (and there were many) were held back by its colossal inertia and the sweet, constant soothing of Arië's personal glamour. She groomed them and they would not resist. Feeling it made him sick. Where many *andalune* were voluntarily bound like this they were a psychic force almost impossible to fight against. Whatever he had to say was pretty much irrelevant at this point. They went on . . .

"Its energy is limitless. Once it is open we can restore the decaying lands and begin to reintegrate our society. These measures are temporary," said another.

"It would not be safe to open it whilst connected to the other realms."

"Alfheim is in crisis . . . the land falls into darkness. It cannot be denied. The Prowlers . . ."

All the old stories about the decline of his homeland: he knew them by heart and their reasons. The voices came in ones and twos from all over the room, old and younger voices, some less forceful than others. They were sad and grieving. They hated what they were doing, but still they considered it a strong and right manoeuvre. Zal could feel everything they did, because only a few chose to shield their intent. They wanted him to believe. They wanted him to join them. Their invitation was almost overpowering. He had been away for so long. The idea, the proximity, of being held again in the continuum of *andalune* that was the natural state of communion where minds and spirits ran so close! And not just the poor substitute of elemental companionship . . . he felt that he was just one step from heaven. One tiny step. Just agree. Just say yes.

And it was true, Alfheim was declining, rotting, its aether changing in unpredictable ways. It had been happening over long ages, though at rates that until recently were almost undetectable. But he had never believed it was because of the workings of the Shadowkin or even of the other aetheric realms, as many theorists did. His demon self *knew* it was not so and he used not to be the only one.

The great gestalt of the noble horde around him brushed at his awareness with the sorrowful acceptance of a family looking at a prodigal son.

Zal's back prickled. He fought with his disappointment at how many people he could feel in solidarity with the Lady. He took a deep breath and looked up at Arië. "Nice parrots. All you need now is a wooden leg."

Arië did not flinch but she did remain stock still for a moment. The wave that had reached out to welcome Zal back withdrew. The room brimmed with anger.

Zal could tell that one of the people behind him was gravely ill. Within the court there was enough healing knowledge and power to do all but raise the dead, but nobody moved. He felt genuine disorientation—this could never have happened, even a few months ago. Who in Alfheim, even the most conservative, would let someone feel like that and do nothing?

Not one person stepped forward, although their anxiety and distress became palpable in the aether, increasing until he could even hear it as a faint whine all around. He stared at their faces. Most of them were looking away.

Arië beckoned. She was effective, cold. He hadn't realised how cold until now. She was the frozen surface keeping the rest under control. He didn't understand how she had taken so much to herself. He'd been away too long and it was too late. Zal didn't look at the suffering person until they moved into his line of sight.

The dying elf was Aradon. He had served with Zal in the secret service, been in various operations with him. He was friendly, loyal, a little introspective. He was one of the first to join the Resistance years ago when the extent of the High Light hegemony had become clear and the Shadowkin pushed out of Sathanor. Here, in the days of High Light rule over all Alfheim with its lore of purity and healing, he was a bloody mess. Someone had beaten him to the edge of extinction. His face and hands bore marks that Zal knew were torture inflicted, not just the result of a desperate fight. He was barely conscious and that was a mercy. Zal reached out to touch Aradon's *andalune* body but the guards moved between them. He got the impression Aradon no longer possessed an *andalune*, but without necromancy that was not possible.

"Many of your coconspirators have talked a great deal, Suha," Arië said to Zal. "Even of your ridiculous plan to prove the nature of every person in the realms as equal. But they have been unable to tell your name, and finally I believe that none of them know it."

"Help him," Zal said, pointing at Aradon. He tried to make eye contact with the people nearest him but they refused. They stared through him or past him. "What's the matter with you all?"

He had thought that after all he had been through there could be no more things able to terrify him and he was right. He was not scared. But he had never imagined he could find himself so disgusted with his own kind. He'd never really believed they could become like this. And here, look. They were. Their outward silence said it all.

Zal tried to push past the guard. He was held back by two of them. Their bone gauntlets dug into his arms. He reached beyond them. His *andalune* was different to theirs, and they were not keen to touch it now, tainted with demon aether, but he could not reach Aradon anyway. There was no more to him than flesh and bone.

"Tell me your name and we will restore him," Arië said. "And all those presently under arrest will be released to pleasant confinement in a civilised place."

Zal looked at Aradon's swollen face, all but unrecognisable, at his hands and their bloodied nails. Everything he had ever known about elves, humans, faeries, demons, and their machinations in the complicated world of politics and power ran through his mind in a clinical stream. His name was all he had.

"After him how many more will there be?" he asked.

"All of them," Arië said. "But not you. There are other tasks you must do. Either you will do them as our loyal bound servant or we use your blood to access the hidden well of aether . . ."

"It is no well!" Zal shouted at her, unable to restrain his anger, aware that it only made him worse in their eyes. "Fifty years ago we researched every possibility that the leaks from this lake may be some free source of aetheric energy and the conclusion from elf and demon alike is that it can only be some faultline or weakness in the realm that gives onto nothing but the Interstitial. The aether coming in is wild, but the lake moulds it by the time it reaches the surface so it seems like it's Sathanor energy. It requires some reinforcement, not weakening with your efforts to mine it."

"We have found a way to cap the well," Arië said. "I am confident. It is expensive but it will be worth it. And this is not your concern. You have your friends to think of, Suha. Your loyal brothers and sisters surely have much more knowledge they have garnered and hidden against us. It can be left to them and they to themselves if you are willing to surrender to us. Come, we are not partial to witnessing this pain and you delay its end."

"The energy will make you invincible," Zal said quietly to her. It was true. He was sure it was her major motive, but she would not think so.

Zal made himself look at Aradon again. He had no aetheric presence, as if he was already dead.

"He will stay alive this way, beyond light and shadow, unable to connect to the *andalune*, for the rest of his life unless you surrender. They all will. Of all people, you will know what this is like and it will be even less than the pitiful contact you are still able to make with us. Communion will be only a memory. The spirit is dead."

Zal lifted his head and looked at Arië. He didn't know how Aradon had suffered or what had been allowed to tear out his spirit; maybe it was some captive Saaqaa. It was not important. All that Aradon was proof of was that Arië was beyond any kind of appeal to mercy. He could tell that the sight of Aradon revolted Arië, it hurt her and she loathed it, but she was able to master her natural impulses, and she was able to ignore them completely. For her there was a greater good and in the service of that good she was immaculate. The horror, and her own ability to withstand it, only increased her conviction.

The room's silent agony stretched out. Zal made it stretch longer.

He studied every empty seat in turn and thought of all the others, not knowing if this was a bluff of hers or if the entire project to prevent Alfheim's decline into tyranny was over because every person involved had been cut down.

He could end Aradon's suffering himself, he knew. But if he showed his demon power, then Arië would ward against it and any use it might be later, if there was a later, if there was a chance to get out—and there was no chance here—would be lost.

He turned his back on Aradon and gave his head the smallest shake—no.

"Very well," she said. "As you wish."

CHAPTER SEVENTEEN

Lila, wearing Tath's boots now, was glad to run as soon as a safe hour came with dawn. She asked Dar where he thought Zal was, how far it was, how long it would take to get there, what they could do . . . He just shrugged and said they must run. She thought about Tath, but whenever that happened she ruthlessly directed her thoughts somewhere else.

To prevent herself dwelling on unwelcome feelings, and with the presence of Dr. Williams consistently appearing in her mind like a vengeful ghost, she concentrated on learning and copying Dar's style of motion. He ran on the ball of his foot and leapt with catlike grace over small obstacles, coming to a halt with a perfect lightness of balance even when he was very tired. All day she followed him, the pleasure of the previous day's journey much dulled by the events of the night and the constant awareness of Tath's presence. Lila found herself longing for radio contact with Sarasilien, with Malachi, with anybody, even Poppy. She would have given much to have a faery alongside her to lighten her mood. She even missed the silly, trivial world of the music business, and had begun fondly to think of purple fur coats and melodramatic speeches about download sales and marketing budgets by the time Dar chose to take a rest.

"Have you any music with you?" he asked her as they sat high in the mountains on a bare strip of rock. The view was spectacular. Below them a huge, bowl-shaped valley spread green and luscious, its far side of uniformly steep walls barely visible in the clear light. Grasslands and woods covered the ground below them and Lila could see lakes and streams sparkling in the high noonday sun. She took a piece of stale bread that Dar handed her.

"What would you like? I never much went in for classical, except Mozart and Vivaldi," she said apologetically.

"Play me what you like," he said. "Anything." He went to fetch water. They drank and he sat down finally, unshipping his bow so that it did not scrape on the ground. Lila did likewise and then sat behind him, her legs on either side of his.

"Ear ear," she said, putting the palms of her hands gently against the sides of his head. "Haven't got any speakers so you'll have to make do with this. Shouldn't be too bad through your skull. I've kept all the levels low." She played the music through the smart metal and multiple synthetic sheets that made up the structure of her palms, allowing them to act as speakers, and listened to it herself internally, direct to the brain from her AI-library. Together they sat overlooking all of Sathanor, hungry and heartsick, and listened to The No Shows doing "Time in My Hands."

"Now all we need are some smokes and we're sorted," Dar said to her softly with a Bay City accent, but his attempt at good humour didn't last more than a moment. He sighed.

"I can do you an aspirin," Lila offered. Dar leant back against her, to her surprise. It wasn't entirely comfortable because of all the weapons between them, not least the grip of a sword pressing against her jaw, but she didn't move. She saw that his dark brown hair was streaked with silver here and there, and with strands that caught the sun and made themselves into glowing amber.

Tath, she thought, was awake but barely aware of her, folded over his own thoughts protectively. In the hours that had passed since he hitched a ride Lila was sure there weren't only stings but honey in Tath, although there couldn't be any telling which one you'd get on request. Her fear had peaked early and now was all but spent and continued to fade the longer that time went on and he did nothing. If she didn't concentrate on his presence, she could hardly feel it.

The song ended and Lila took her hands away and rested them lightly on Dar's shoulders. The wind freshened and she caught the scent of lilacs and other flowers rising from far below.

"Time to go," he said abruptly and stood up. He held out his hand and she took it, getting to her feet with effortless ease. Dar pointed down into the broad valley. "Beyond the first woodlands the valley deepens and forms a great lake, not unlike the lake you visited before in Lyrien. It is there that Arië has her home, below the waters of Aparastil. I would be certain we will find Zal there."

"Shouldn't you be in a bad place for a bad spell?" Lila asked, taking a last look at the panorama, memorising the location.

"You should be in a safe place, where you feel most secure," Dar said. "And there is no more difficult place to get in or out of than Aparastil Lake. It is guarded by all the elements, by the lake itself and its denizens, and by the full force of Sathanor's magic bent to Arië's will."

"Oh good," Lila said faintly. "I like a challenge."

"You will find one," Dar assured her, jumping down the side of a steep human-height boulder with no more care than he might have stepped off a curbstone.

"We need a story," Lila said.

"There is no story which will fool the Lady of Aparastil. The truth will do in a pinch, though she probably expects us. I do not anticipate a great deal of trouble getting in. It is what will happen then which is beyond my skill to guess. But we may get somewhere if you could become a more likely elf."

"I'm workin' on it," Lila said. "Sorry. I mean, I am making every effort to become a more effective spy."

"Try harder," Dar said, not even looking back. There was a peculiar ring to his voice which made Lila experience the comment as a tantalising clue rather than a stinging criticism. She puzzled over it and then realised that Dar was obliquely referring to Tath's presence.

During the next few hours they dropped lower and lower down the steep sides of the valley walls. Their progress was agonisingly slow. When she did not have to concentrate on her footing too much Lila tried speaking to the gold and green presence in her chest.

If you were truthful about your allegiance, she said, *now there's a chance to prove it.*

He did not have anything to prove to her. He didn't even speak, or need to. She could feel the answers as if they were her own thoughts before she put them into words. He remained grief stricken and appalled at the idea of what she was, let alone who she was. He found her repellent, because of her robotics which he found alien and threatening, because of her humanity, because of her Otopian allegiance, especially because of her fusion reactor which frightened and revolted him equally. At the same time he was grateful for her kindness and his continued existence, in a stiff, typically highfalutin' snobby elvish way. It took all of Lila's self-restraint to forgo responding to this rush of emotions whenever she tried to address him. But her own emotions were also there, whether she restrained them or not, and the elf felt her fury and her dislike of him without the mediation of her thoughts. They were, for better or ill, two spirits in one heart, and they could not hide from each other.

Tath coiled tightly on himself as she attempted to get him to talk. Lila knew him horrified and hurt, willing himself out of the situation as much as she did, resenting her like crazy. The situation made her so angry she shouted out loud and with a single blow of her hand struck a reasonably sized branch from a tree she was passing.

"Lila?"

She found herself staring at Dar. She wasn't sure he had ever called her by name before. It was effective, if unmagical. "Sorry," she said. She picked the branch up and pushed it back towards its old position but then let it fall to the ground. The sap smelled rich and sweet and soon filled the warm afternoon air around them. Bizarrely she noticed she was standing in paradise. She scuffed paradise's grass with her foot. "My fellow traveller doesn't like the idea of helping out."

"Then you had better leave him alone." Dar glanced at the branch. Insects were already gathering at the break in the trunk, to eat the sugary sap. Dar bent down and took some of the sticky stuff onto his hand, licking it off his fingers. Lila ignored it. She felt hungry, but she had the tokamak. Dar had nothing.

"How do I get rid of him?" she asked quietly.

"Exorcism," came the reply. Dar took his knife out and stripped the bark from the branch expertly. He tore away the inner layers and started eating them, then used part of the outer section to fashion a cover for the wound in the trunk. He trimmed the wound on the tree itself, hacking it into the right shape, and then patched it quickly. "They die," he said. "Trees like this die of a bad wound, and Tath will die if you root him out unless he can find another willing heart."

"Willing?" Lila repeated, taken aback. "I wasn't willing."

"It was a Game," Dar said, chewing carefully. "You played it. You lost it. You were willing."

"There was no Game!" she protested, furious. "How could there have been? There was no wild magic. There wasn't time."

"Elves carry the wild magic in their *andalune* when they have passed through it recently. It takes time to wear off. Tath had the skill to control that. He might not have wanted to play with you in his mind, but his *chi* was stronger than that. It saw its chance when he knew that I was likely to kill him, and it took it. You must have felt the sting of it when it happened."

"But I didn't agree. I didn't know the rules . . ." She trailed off and shut her mouth firmly, swallowing the rest of what promised to be another worthless excuse. One day, she thought, she must remind herself to stop making them. But she couldn't stop raging at herself for her stupidity. The presence inside laughed at her.

Dar looked at her with what she thought might be sympathy. "I keep forgetting how young you are," he said. His gaze was very intent and steady.

Just when I need another button pushed, she thought angrily. "Why, how old are you?" she demanded.

"Old enough," he replied in a strange tone. He stepped forward, holding out a strip of the white, dripping bark to her. "You must be hungry. Taste it. It will make you feel better."

Lila found herself looking into his slanted blue eyes. They were exactly the same brilliant colour as the Sathanor sky. She was surprised to see that they held hunger of quite a different kind. She began to lift her hand to take the bark, but stopped, uncertain about what his offer really was. She was alert for any zing of magic, but she didn't feel it. She felt the strangest pressure from inside, still hating herself, and from outside the opposite, as if Dar was offering her a road out of its miserable flat plain. She was on the cusp of some inner movement she didn't understand and it was all balanced on her decision to accept one or the other version of some verdict on herself. She said no and Dar said yes. She scowled and stared at him, all her senses on overdrive trying to suck more information out of the moment so that she could calibrate it and make a decision based on solid logic, using her AI-self to its utmost to judge. But that didn't help.

As she continued to hesitate Dar reached out and put a piece of the soft bark against her lips. Her heart was racing. She felt her skin flush but her lips moved of their own accord and opened. He pushed the strip gently into her mouth with his fingertips. In taking it she inadvertently brushed his fingers with her lips and tasted the salt of sweat and earth and the sweet sugar on them. Lila felt lost in a world she hadn't noticed was there until now. All this sensing and feeling, all this strange intimacy . . . she thought of Zal and saw him lying on a bier, stone cold dead. She stood beside it and there was a torch burning in her hand and she could not light the fire. She stood and the torch burned down to ash in her hand and she stood forever until she was a statue of metal and bone. She heard Zal's voice in her head, as though he could see the image too . . .

"You silly fool. I'm not dead if you do. You're dead if you don't."

Dar's eyelids closed and he staggered as if he was drunk. Lila knew the feeling—hungry intoxication—because she felt something surging in her veins and it wasn't the sugar. She couldn't help herself. She licked his fingers.

They were in each other's arms in a heartbeat. Dar's lean, hard body shook, very like Tath's had, but this time it wasn't fear doing the shaking. Lila felt Dar touch her face, tracing the line of the magical scar in her skin. He was intent and serious as he let his finger touch her lips again, very lightly, following the shape of the top lip across its bow and then pressing more firmly against the lower lip.

Lila swallowed and watched his blink rate decreasing, his heart speeding up to match hers. He pressed harder, watching her mouth. As she let it begin to open she saw his face mirror the action unconsciously, lips parting, his eyelids lowering.

Lila took his finger in her mouth up to the second knuckle and closed her lips and tongue around it gently. She caressed the hair at the side of his face and stroked the strange, angular line of his cheek, surprised when he took hold of that hand, synthetic skin or not, and placed her palm against his mouth. He closed his eyes and kissed it, then slid his tongue up between her fingers as she sucked his. It turned her on more than she'd felt before, even more than Zal, and she didn't understand it at all. The cool wash of Dar's aethereal body spread across her skin and became warm, became almost muscular. And then she felt a strange opening sensation in her chest, a feeling of unlocking and springing back, and from the centre of her being Dar's soft touch was matched by Tath's unfolding.

Dar felt it; she saw his surprise, his confusion just like hers, the sense to stay away from each other completely swamped by the heart's drive to join, the body's need for contact to soothe itself. In that instant Lila remembered all she'd forgotten in the last forty-eight hours, all her trauma and her loss, her self-hate and her fear for Zal. She realised she hadn't missed it and how good it had felt to be running in this wild place with a friend, even if he'd been her mortal enemy until . . . whenever. She took his hand, removing his finger from her mouth and placing his palm against her breast instead, moving forward to kiss him on the lips. She felt an all-over kiss that was *andalune* as the two elves synchronised and merged across the surfaces of her skin in an intimacy she was unable to share. This might be enough for Dar, even for Tath, she thought, but she didn't have an aetheric side and it wasn't enough for her.

She slid her hands strongly against Dar's waist and down, pressing his hips against her, then in the next moment leant back to get rid of some of the hardware getting in the way. Buckles and laces caught against each other as she fought with the unfamiliar closures of his clothes and hers. Dar stepped back and helped her out, frequently pausing to replace his mouth on hers and to caress her. His kiss was all hunger. Hers too. They were starving and they were bread to each other. All that she could think of, all that she wanted, was to have him inside her. She wanted to know if this side of her was still alive.

Dar spun her around and backed her up against the tree. She hit it hard, struggling with the wretched clothing, wriggling to make it easier, groaning in frustration when he had to stop and yank Tath's tight leggings further down on her. But then she felt him and it was all right. She got both hands on his hips and drove herself down on him as he pushed back into her. The sensation was as purely divine as anything she could imagine. She heard his gasp of pleasure and the anticipation of more of it. Then they were moving together and she lost awareness of anything but the perfect feeling rising, riding Dar hard and as mercilessly as he rode her, all the way.

Baby, she heard Tath whisper to her, but it was a word formed from a knot of lust and pleasure of his own, so she let it go. She didn't know who he was referring to. She didn't care.

When it was over, they let each other go carefully and politely, no more kisses, only gentle, efficient touches enough to separate. Lila pulled her trousers back up as she slid down the tree trunk, her body liquid and vibrant, warm and suffused with Tath to such a degree that he was a part of her in that minute.

Dar reclothed himself and sat down beside her. He put his hand out onto her booted foot, gripped it briefly, then lay back on the sandy earth under the tree's shade, panting, his eyes closed, free arm thrown across his face to shade it from the sun.

After a few seconds he lifted his arm and looked at her. Lila looked back, smiled, a little self-consciously, and held out her hand. He took it and pulled himself upright. He pressed his shoulder into hers for a moment, letting his head fall towards her, and she let her head rest against his, rubbing her stomach.

"I think without baldrics may have been better," she said.

Dar glanced at her and laughed, reflexively touching the buckles of the sword belts that crossed his chest. "I am sorry."

"Don't be." She showed him that the rest of his carefully picked bark had been ground in the dirt and threw it aside for the insects. "It tasted nice." She felt absurdly happy. Its excess was in direct proportion to her expectations of what lay ahead. "That was . . ."

"I know," Dar said, tightening the laces on his tunic, and they both laughed. "Where is he now?"

"Everywhere," Lila said, shrugging as he looked to her for more explanation.

"Let's go," Dar stood up with an effort. "It's another day's walk at least."

Lila walked across to the steep edge, a few metres away from them, and looked down. There were still hundreds of rough and rocky metres to descend. If she'd been able to plan . . . but there were no hang-gliders here and no suitable materials to fashion one. She picked up Tath's bow and set off after Dar, doing nothing to disturb the well-being she felt, knowing it was going to be short lived. With every step she was aware of Tath's presence, but it was no effort and no intrusion. He was mercifully silent.

It took another two hours to climb down the steep escarpment. They slid on scree, climbed boulder falls, and jumped where jumping was possible. By the time they reached the valley Lila had surveyed it extensively and took issue with Dar's geography. She was certain that Sathanor was not a valley at all. It was a crater.

She didn't mention it to him, part of her spy instincts, abused as they were, kicking in to prevent it. She knew that the only reason Dar had told her about Zal was that he had burned his bridges everywhere else. It was a little weak of him, but she could understand it. And she reserved judgement on its truth. Hot, sweaty, and starving she turned on her coolant system and was glad when Dar saw fit to take a minor detour to get more water. Idly she calculated how far behind schedule the concert tour was by now, and wondered if there were any temporal loops she might use to make the disaster a little less disastrous. It was a science fictional dream. Nobody had ever travelled in time.

Tath, recovered from his psychic liaison with Dar, found this very amusing. She was dismayed to find that the activity seemed to have restored his health somewhat. He told her he didn't think she was going to see the end of the day. Lila ignored him. The Sathanor water Dar gave her was very good. "You should bottle this and sell it," she told Dar, feeling Tath quiver with outrage at the idea. "You'd make a fortune."

"It is sacred," Dar said absently. "The water sustains youth, heals disease, and allays hunger. The fact that I let you, an alien interloper, drink of it would be enough to hang me almost anywhere in Alfheim, and many places beyond its borders. There are those who kill to trade in this water, and die for it. If you have a container, I would suggest that you fill it, because this is the last water until the lake, and I do not think it would be wise to drink of that."

"The water of life: tastes good and it does you good," Lila said, filling her belly with it. "I stand by my assessment. Total gold mine. Just think how many products you could make with it. Beer. The beer of life. The wine of life. The sparkling sugary soda of life. The Sathanor Detox Diet. And failing that, when you get out of here you can take over the black market."

"It is all I am fit for," Dar agreed with amusement. "I pray you do not notice the air or the plants or the animals and see dollar signs in their places too."

"If I do, I'll keep it between me and Tath," Lila said, getting up and patting her chest. "He has a long way to go before his education catches up with the modern world." And then she had to struggle for a moment not to be sick. "Lil' devil," she said. "I feel peculiar."

"It is the water's effect. It will wear off presently," Dar turned and led off through thick grass and beneath beautiful, pale-leafed trees whose trunks were as smooth as polished stone. The trees watched them.

The afternoon passed in a soft focus blur of pleasantly healthy delirium. Later Lila would remember almost none of it, though some things remained. She asked Dar once, when she had imagined both of them storming a palace, "Is there a chance?" He turned and took her in his arms and kissed her, very gently, and then he led her on, her hand in his for a long while.

Sathanor had a curious calendar quality. She couldn't quite connect with it. It seemed not to require nor want human interaction, and she felt strangely detached. She was also aware of Tath watching her responses and wanted to withhold them. He longed to touch everything that was ignoring her. And eventually, after the hundredth simply breathtaking vista full of birds, animals, and insects of unusual and exquisite creation, she found the ability to stop noticing it all and slumped into appreciation-fatigue with gratitude. Once that had gone she found that the more they travelled, the more she felt observed by an attention that used the birds and trees to follow them.

As they approached the lake itself, Dar led her to a grassy, sunlit glade and stopped. "Rest now," he said, sitting with her. "This is the last time we will have, most likely. Arië will know of our approach by now, and be waiting. She, like all elves, will wait as long as we like. Time is on her side. We should fear nothing on her ground. Sleep if you would like to."

"Nah," Lila said with a sigh although she was deeply tired. The sunlight made her more so. "Why don't you?"

"I do not wish to leave this situation only to have to return to it."

"Amen," Lila said. "So, what are we going to do? Walk in?"

"Yes."

"Do you feel like putting it off?"

"No."

She got to her feet again. "Is there anything . . . how many things . . . oh for fuck's sake, never mind."

"Never mind what?" he asked patiently.

"I was going to ask you for all the secret inside info, but what the hell, you shouldn't tell me even if it would make a difference. I'll never pass for one of you in a million years. Look, even if I do this," and Lila got up and used all her skill and AI systems to perfectly mimic Dar's own way of carrying himself.

"You could at a distance," he said. "But the metal is a strong . . . a powerful signal to our aethereal selves. Your hair and face are all wrong. And you have no *andalune*. If someone tries to approach you secretly with theirs, they will find nothing."

Lila pulled at a strand of grass, contemplating the bizarre complexity that must be elvish social interaction. "Could you command Tath to cloak me in his?"

"It would be abomination to him," Dar said, not without a trace of speculation.

"Two points." Lila counted them on her fingers. "One, he had no scruples when he wanted to get a hit off our shag. And two, he's dead, and he should be grateful he's still . . . whatever he is, thanks to me. Even if he won't do it, he could at least shed some light on a few issues, couldn't he? And I'd rather know if the spy inside was going to try and fuck me up at some critical point when he sees a way to do it in the service of Lady of the Lake there."

Dar smiled at her with what she thought was grudging admiration. "Fair points all. If you will ask him nicely first, I will command him second."

"Is that naming? Command?"

"It is absolute," Dar said, "Absolute, and for that reason no elf would use it against another."

"Except in situations like this one, right?" Lila said. "I mean, you stabbed him to death. This seems—I don't know—less aggressive than that?"

"It is more so. With naming comes obligation. I killed him and that was that. But when I name him he will regain a sort of hold over me. I will owe him protection because he has no defence against me, and whatever happens to him as a result of my command is my responsibility and I will have to pay for it."

"With money, or favours, or that horrible aetheric direct debit thing where it just sucks it right out of your soul?"

"The last," Dar said. "But since it is unlikely that there will be a lot left of me to pay with then, as you say, in this situation, why not?" He was almost lighthearted.

"No, then I'll do it," Lila said. "I don't see why you should. Tell me his name and I will. There's magically pretty much nothing of me."

"Which is why it will not work for you nearly as well as for me," Dar said. "No credit, no shopping."

"Fuck!" Lila said and the ears of both elves twitched; Dar's visibly and Tath's gnostically.

She addressed Tath, "I know you've been listening. Come nicely, or we'll make you."

He did not come nicely. He wanted to get his figurative hands around Dar's throat. He coiled up into his emerald self, small and hard as a stone in the deepest chamber of her heart.

"Hit him," Lila said to Dar.

Dar shook his head and took a deep breath which he savoured. Lila saw that he considered it figuratively to be his last, and she opened her mouth to stop him but he was speaking already, "Ilyatath Voynassi Taliesetra, glamour this woman your host with the full power of your conviction to appear as yourself, and convince all that she is as you once were for as long as you both persist or until this command is undone by her intent or by mine."

For a moment Tath did not respond. Lila waited—she felt she was learning this trick well by now. Then there was a silent explosion in her heart. A shockwave spread through her, flesh and metal both. She felt Tath's anger and his resentment at death suffuse her with all the charm of a bucket of iced vomit. But above that soared a peculiar joyous rush and an intense curiosity. He wanted to recoil from the technology of her, but he couldn't because the charm did not permit him to hesitate. He was sure it would harm him in spite of the moment in which he had helped her to pick up his swords and bow. He was amazed to find that his aetheric body could properly transect her metallic self and not be destroyed by it.

This is because you are no longer made of the spiritless elements of Otopia, Tath said. *You are like metal that has been mined and forged by the Shadowkin; half alive. You are a curious charm, like an amulet, or a weapon. I see why Dar was so keen to weld you close to his side.*

That was friendship, that was, Lila told him firmly but suddenly she wasn't sure. She checked to see that she maintained full control of her body. She did. *You said before I was changed by Dar. Now I'm changed again right? Or the same as before?* She felt furious that Tath could still so easily hold her to ransom this way, with his magical intuition and his skill.

Different again, Tath said. *You should be careful about intimate relations with elves. I thought they taught you that in Spy School. But if you are confirmed in your wish to change, you could ask me . . .*

Shut up, Lila said. *That wasn't about control.* She wanted to have words with Dar. The techicians at Incon had laboured hard and unsuccessfully to enchant technological artefacts. Her changes were apparently miraculous to Tath, who could not hide his surprise, but at the same time she couldn't detect any change except that she wasn't in pain.

No, you are right, Tath said. *What you did with Dar was not about control. It was the pact of suicide. You will never make it alive out of Aparastil. I salute your honesty and feeling.*

His sincerity was worse than his taunts, she thought.

Dar blinked and looked carefully at her. He spoke quietly and bowed his head for a moment. "Death has not diminished your light, Ilyatath."

"Do I . . ." Lila began to say and stopped in astonishment. She didn't hear her own voice. She heard the elf's, complete with all its curious harmonies and tones. The words and intent were hers, the sound was not. For a moment Tath's envy and hate almost overpowered her. He considered her completely unworthy of his presence. The words his voice said were not his and he was violated. She felt nauseous.

"Lila." Dar looked back up, lifted his head. "It's time. Are you ready?"

"No," she said. "If I screw it up . . . If I speak out of turn and spoil the illusion, or show my ignorance at the wrong moment, I apologise now."

"We enter the gates evenly matched." Dar got to his feet. "Except in the matter of name. I know yours but you do not know mine."

Lila jumped up and put her hand across his mouth. "No," she said. "Spies can't use what they don't know. Don't tell me. It's bad enough if Tath knows it."

Oh, I do.

Lila put her arms around Dar in an awkward hug. His embrace was quick but strong in return, strong enough for her to wonder if she was being stupid in passing up such a weapon as his name. Tath's words echoed in her mind—changed again.

Then they set out and within a few minutes had come to the lake shore. It was sunset and the surface of the water reflected the rose and soft orange tones of the sky. Lila looked down and saw a slender blond elf where she stood: Tath, right up to the tips of his mobile, nonexistent ears.

Now Dar said words that Lila couldn't catch. They slid from her understanding like fish slithering quickly out of a careless grab from above. A breeze lifted and blew her illusory elfin hair.

"Consider yourself invited," Dar said after a moment. "Follow me and do not show fear." He walked forwards into the water.

Lila frowned but followed—she'd come this far, why not further? The water felt unnatural as soon as it touched her. It didn't run into her boots or soak her clothing. Glancing down she saw that she was protected by the extent of Tath's aethereal body which was projecting a few millimetres beyond her own. Where it made contact with the water a surface formed, like the surface of an air bubble, and the water kept away. She wondered what would happen when it reached her nose and got ready to engage a gas recycler mechanism, but when the water closed over her head she found that she was walking downhill beside Dar as though they were both on dry land, though they moved with the slow grace of divers and had to push the water's weight around them. They did not float and they did not drown.

CHAPTER EIGHTEEN

Lila and Dar walked slowly, wading, slightly afloat with every stride, like swimmers who reach for the ground with their feet, each stride a bound, their hair in clouds around their heads, the water like a heavy air they could breathe, though it was a struggle to breathe it. The water itself was green and the light which fell through it was quickly smothered, leaving them in a khaki umbra where all colours became green. Lila saw the silver shapes of fish dart close in curiosity and then flash as they turned their sides and flicked away with a snap of tailfins. She felt her boots catch in clumps of weed as they slowly trod a stone-paved road, sinking ever further by its guidance down and down into the depths.

Soon it was so dim that Lila had to use infrared to enhance her vision. As she turned it on she felt Tath's permanent low level of contempt for her vanish in a moment of surprise. Dar saw well, even in low light his elfin vision had a much greater range and colour capture than Lila's, but by the time they reached a huge stone door that barred their way Lila could tell by the way his movements grew more tentative that he was finding it hard. The barrier before them was a smooth block of stone, a monolith carved and decorated with a low relief of animals and plants and words in an old form of elvish that even Lila's AIs didn't recognise. But they did recognise the simple frame and its scale as something that must be a door, though there was no sign of a handle or a keyhole or even anywhere for a guard to look out.

Lila watched Tath's pale, aethereal hair sliding around her face though she could not really feel it, and gave Dar a questioning shrug as they came to a halt one arm's length from the stone.

Dar said something and his words went up in bright bubbles from his mouth. Lila heard a soft sound, felt a vibration that seemed to come out of the stone under her feet. It was an ominous sound, and soon it came again. She felt Tath's focus attenuate—his listening felt like her nerves expanding and lengthening into the cold water that pressed them on all sides. It made her nervous. But she remembered that Dar had told her to show no fear, and so she stood and did nothing, concentrated on relaxing and tuned into her AIs. The vibration soon became distinguished enough for her to identify it as the drumming of more than one drum. Together three instruments wove a syncopated beat which she could feel passing through into her body from the water. As the drum beat became stronger the water shivered.

A shadow, darker than the simple sedimentary gloom, crossed them with a distant cold touch as a large, sinuous, long body slid past somewhere above their heads. Lila felt the turbulence of its wash press her clothing against her. Movement, infrared and heat-based vision fed through her AIs and told her in a clean readout at the left of her vision exactly what she'd guessed just by the size and power of the creature. A water dragon had passed them by. Its sensitive whiskers would have picked out everything it needed to know from their scent in the water, the disturbance they made in moving, the sound of their breath and heartbeats, the magic or lack of it that ran through them. Lila glanced at Dar, but he was watching the door. Tath's *andalune* prickled throughout her body. She wanted to scratch, but she wouldn't have known where to start.

The door moved, the hairline gap between it and its frame suddenly darkening as it shifted position, moving straight back into the

stone itself before rolling aside. Before them a circular entrance led
into a new subaquatic darkness which none of Lila's senses could penetrate. She wanted to object, to confirm the impossibility of there
being such a space but Lila didn't need to. Tath did it for her.

Do try, you won't succeed, he said, silently, from his safe place inside
her heart. *Your hesitation will only make her think you unworthy. The magic
that guards the palace is primal magic and not even your mechanical
appendages will serve to do what it will not allow.*

He was pleased when she believed him—and she had to, because
she would have felt it if he lied. She felt his pleasure in her fear which
rose up suddenly at his words and made her shiver in a tiny, convulsive
motion she couldn't help. Lila knew the water was simply transmitting
everything she did to all the watchers hidden in the silty murk. She
didn't feel that she could cope with dragons, internal hostile agents,
and the rest of it all at once. Tath in particular was in too close a contact to her true feelings all the time. She decided, with misgiving, to
allow her AI-self to execute the routine to bypass her emotional centre
and replace its decision-making finesse with cold calculations.

What was that? Tath demanded, able to feel the change but not
understand it. He had no links to her AIs. Well, that was something,
she thought. A red warning icon flashed in her upper right vision, to
remind her that this was strictly an emergency procedure and that she
should return to normal as soon as possible to avoid lasting psychosis.
It was very distracting against the black background of total nothing
in front of her. Lila switched it off.

Dar led the way inside. As they stepped through the circle they
passed out of the lake and into air. Lila found herself unexpectedly
plunging forward into the dark as the resistance fell away. She quickly
got control of her feet and then stood firm on the stone road.

"Now we follow the air," Dar said from a short distance away. "The
entrance to this palace is via the primary elements. Water is the first.
Void will lead us to the Air Gate. Air's the third."

"What's the second?" Lila asked, hearing Tath's voice speak where hers should have been. It almost died completely in the strange space they stood in. She expected to feel uneasy but she felt nothing, only a calm kind of mild interest in what was going on, the all-pervasive calm of Nirvana. In spite of her orders the AIs signalled her regularly to turn it off—Nirvana was highly psychologically addictive, bad for the brain, bad for the nerves and with many other possibly unpleasant effects including sudden death. But Lila wasn't alarmed, of course. She tried to use the echo of her voice to map the space so that she could locate Dar, but all her readouts came back zeroed, even though she could hear him perfectly well.

"It is the Void," Dar said in answer to her question. "The nothing in which you now stand. It is the fundamental in-between, the gap between one breath and the next, between last and first. Tath would know more about it. Necromancers must cross the Void to enter Thanatopia."

Lila had been studiously ignoring Tath. She found that at maximum capacity on all sensors and using as much power as she dared, she was able to use her sonar system to trace a picture of Dar when their voices bounced off his body. She could also decipher a large hole not far in front of them. It was an irregular and ugly shape. Paths which seemed to offer good passage to either side quickly became useless ledges and smooth wall. There was a way across, set in widely spaced stepping-stones which moved in a snaking trail through the empty space although they seemed to be floating in midair. In Nirvana, this was all right.

"There's a big hole here," she said confidently, noting Tath's annoyance. "I can see it."

"I can feel it." But Dar did not object when she moved closer to him and touched the edge of his hand.

"We can go this way, to my side," Lila said. "As long as we keep talking, I can see the edges. There is a path of stones."

"I have been here before," Dar told her coolly. "But if you like you can go first." She heard him getting something out of the bandoleers and then heard the tones of a chain of softly sounding glass chimes. Immediately, the sensitive nerves in her skin began to decipher the strange pathway much more clearly. It looked almost like a computer rendition of a series of platforms. If elf ears could pick that up without technology or magic, then they were much more sensitive than she'd thought.

Lila led the way out. The steps were sturdy, but no matter how hard she tried to, she couldn't see anything between them. "What if you fall here? Do people fall here?"

"I don't know," Dar said. "Nobody came back to tell us." He sounded tense and Lila left him to the chimes and concentrated on her footing until she was across. As she waited for him she peered into the hole, which was beginning to look much less like a hole and more like something perfectly flat. She thought she could detect the slightest traces of electrical activity, either big and far away or very slight and close at hand, but then Dar landed beside her and they were safe. His *andalune* touched hers and Tath's briefly and, with a keenness as though it were her own, she felt the truth of Dar's fear in the contact. It pulled at her, as though he wanted to catch hold of her. Tath flared on the instant with a brief, victorious contempt and Dar instantly stepped aside as though burned.

She ignored them. "The air," Lila said in a strong voice to counteract the Void's giant swallowing mouth that strove to eat the sound. The Nirvana icon blinked at her, scarlet, alarmed. Whatever emotions she denied now, using its artificial bypass, had not gone away. They were simply active in a place where she couldn't feel them. After a certain load stress, if she did not reengage her experience they would begin to emerge in unpredictable ways. The red light was telling her that this moment was not far away. She glanced at the numbers and deleted it. Even if she went back right now, she didn't think she'd stay as frosty as Dar could, not with Tath waiting like a scatter of crows to descend on her every weakness. "Which way?"

"Wherever the elemental is," Dar said. His voice was composed, cool and confident, nothing like what she'd felt second-hand through Tath.

Lila turned her face this way and that. There was a distinct wash of air moving in a steady, cool stream which she could easily follow.

"Not that way," Dar said as she set off.

"You said . . ."

"An elemental is a being," Dar said. "And we need its help to get through the Hall of Fire. Air and fire work together here." As he was speaking, Lila began to see him with her own eyes. The presence of light made her search for the source and she saw that the walls and roof of the cavern they were in were giving off a faint, lichen-like, glow. Behind them, where the Void had—had not—been, there was a flat, ordinary rock floor. Their stepping-stones were scattered boulders lying on it. Dry sandy earth spread between them like any ordinary piece of ground. In the gloaming, Lila saw Dar reach into the bandoleer he wore again and bring out a whistle. It was fashioned from a pebble which had been hollowed and carved with a patience Lila could barely imagine into a slender ocarina shape with a perfect mouthpiece though it had no finger holes. Dar blew it and it made no sound.

"What is that?"

"A whistle for bringing down the wind," he said. "Blow hard enough to hear anything and you get a hurricane." He started to put it back.

"Can't I see it?" Lila stepped towards him, holding her hand out.

"No," he said.

"Well, who made it?"

"They're not made, they're found . . ." He glanced meaningfully at her. "Are you quite all right?"

"I'm fine," she said. "I was just curious, that's all. No reason. I never saw one before."

Dar narrowed his long blue eyes and his ears flattened close to his head like a horse's do when the horse in question is feeling vicious. "As you say."

"What do you mean by that?" she asked, intent on becoming very clear about everything before matters progressed any further. Was Dar being deliberately obtuse? Tath glowed like a smug beacon in her chest.

Dar's left ear tip came forward again, though his facial expression didn't alter. "Air elementals are curious. It will either let us through this hall, or it will not. It would be wise to be quiet and allow it to question you."

Lila felt unpleasantly dizzy and slightly seasick. She could see the door they had come in by, just, if she squinted past Dar. For some reason her thinking seemed to be getting foggy. "What hall?"

Dar took hold of her shoulders and turned her around. Behind her a series of dark tunnels led off in different directions. He pointed at the central, largest tunnel, which was carved smooth, perfectly cylindrical and straight, and through which could clearly be seen a disc of brightly lit space across which figures moved easily. The round mouths of each end—magical gates—Lila could understand. The cylinder itself was quite empty.

"Throw something into it," Dar suggested.

Throw? She didn't get it. Perhaps it was a signal and if she did it then the game would be up and Dar would betray her. Or it was a dare.

Tath, watching from the inside, tried to make a kind of contact with her AI while she was distracted in the act of looking through his pockets (her pockets) for something to throw. In the end he couldn't quite bring himself to touch the machine in the way he would have had to. His repulsion was too intense. Lila hacked and retched suddenly.

"Are you quite well?" Dar said again, with a touch more concern as Tath said simultaneously to her, *Much as it pains me to observe this, I do believe you should undo your binding spell upon yourself, Agent, lest both of us soon have cause to regret it.*

Lila's fingers closed around a small item in the close-fitted pocket of Tath's jerkin, over her breast. She pulled it out. A tiny flower lay in her hand, a white daisy. It was old and flattened and quite dried, though it had kept its colours surprisingly well. She tossed it, vaguely aware as she drew her arm back that Dar had started forward and that a sudden knot of anguish was unleashing itself inside her with startling acuity, making her gut spasm and her legs suddenly become weak.

No!

The flower was very light, almost featherlight, but Lila's AI-self had calculated perfectly and it crossed the magical boundary set in the stone just as it began to fall and tumble erratically in the air. As a warm tongue of air wound around her and curiously lifted the aethereal masses of Tath's glamoured hair, Lila saw the daisy burst into brilliant yellow and white fire. It was almost instantly embers that flared to red for a microsecond before a few motes of pale ash fell to the floor of the Hall of Fire.

Dar caught hold of her arm. She saw that he was greyish white with shock for some reason and noted that even though he was holding onto her his *andalune* body had entirely withdrawn, as though he was in mortal danger and must hide. Within her body Tath recoiled and she felt the glamour flicker and fade. She saw the metal and synthetics of her hands begin to emerge from beneath Tath's illusory knuckles. Her moment of deadly anxiety had drawn back from her like a tide from the shore. She felt Tath poised, silent, waiting, as though he was a held breath.

The Nirvana icon returned and would not be banished. It had gone black and beneath it the load stats informed her in cold blue digits that she was now on an automatic countdown to a return to fully authentic experience, whether she liked it or not. A report would automatically be sent to Headquarters for the attention of Dr. Williams. It would not be favourable.

"You told me to throw something," Lila said calmly. "So I did. The

Fire Hall is obviously pure oxygen and the elemental in there ignites everything it doesn't think belongs in there. If we go in like this we'll burn up just like any other remotely flammable material. I get it. I'm working on a solution. Why are you acting like that?"

Only the compulsion of his naming kept Tath anywhere close to competent as he continued to project his aetherial self through her. Lila felt as if she were contained in an emotional storm, lit by bursts of strange lightning, as if emotion itself had a unique energy and Tath was generating it. His anguish created real static charges that built in her prosthetics and caused her senses to flicker. Meanwhile from the outside world micro-gusts of various forces lifted her clothes, wound beneath them, even blew through her lips and into her mouth, up her nose, and across her eyes in tiny flicks that made her blink furiously. The same thing was happening to Dar. As he stood, his arms held out to his sides to permit the frisking by the air elemental, his gaze met hers. It almost looked as though nobody was home.

"Don't move," he whispered. "Don't do anything. Air is very sensitive."

Lila was deeply, deeply puzzled.

4 . . . 3 . . . 2 . . . 1 . . .

She opened her mouth, drew in a huge breath, and screamed at the top of her lungs. It was a raw, terrible sound and it expressed an equally raw and devastating onslaught of feeling which Lila was powerless to deny. All her senses were blotted out by the internal storm as though it was a tornado which ripped up her nerves and shredded them into chaff. Her heart faltered and the life-support systems came on with all their alarms in silent flaring yellow. Her reactor powered up. Most strangely of all the clear division between Tath and herself blurred. His emotions and hers were very similar and in their collision she saw what he had seen and realised what it had meant.

She saw the little white flower burning.

She saw the ashes falling.

She heard the magic in the bloom die, and felt the spell it had held fast break up and shiver away to nothing though she didn't know what it was.

She saw Dar's face as he had seen the daisy in her hand, in his hand, in Tath's hand. His eyes not looking at her, but into Tath's face, at Tath.

Tath had been telling the truth. Tath *was* Dar's ally. More than his ally. There was some kind of choice-brotherhood between them founded in silent spirit, a bond and a relationship that Lila had no name for.

Dar's devastation became more plausible.

There was something else too—about Tath's magic—but she lost that as her scream came to an end. The external world came rushing in. She found herself upright but no longer standing. Dar was below her and she was aloft in a maelstrom of air currents that held her suspended several metres above the ground close to the cavern roof.

Tath separated out from her as Lila was turned slowly upside down. *Give me control if you wish to live and have a chance of saving Zal*, he pleaded from the leaf-green place inside her chest. *There is no time for explanations. The elemental knows that we are not what we seem.*

The air that held them up began to swirl and eddy. It spun Lila around. Tiny zephyr slivers ran under the tips of her nails and darted down through her mouth in between her teeth and gums. It felt like needles. Lila fought it, trying to bat it away, to rub it out, to fight free, but her thrashing made no difference whatsoever. The air would have its way.

Lila gave control to Tath. She felt blown apart, like there was nothing in the centre of her except the strange concentration of his green energy. Tath bloomed outwards as the gyre of wind that held her up began to spin her around in a circle, building velocity steadily. She had only the vaguest awareness of Dar below her, the stone whistle in his hand.

Tath-in-Lila was as agile as her AI-self, but with an instinctive bio-logical grace she'd never had. Lila felt her arms and legs moved, drawn into a shape that was sympathetic to the currents as they shifted around. Where she'd fought the wind, Tath flowed with it and almost immediately the worst of the turbulence stopped. Belatedly, Lila realised this must be the way to talk to the air. Tath opened her mouth and spread her fingers. The air rushed into her lungs and out again, it drew her along with it and held her up. The gyration slowed down steadily, becoming a lazy swirl. The needlepoints had gone. Only tem-perate currents ran against her skin and through her hair. They pene-trated Tath's outer shell and felt their way along Lila's magical stain, along her face, everywhere on her body that flesh was marked forever by charm and bonded to metal.

Are you going to cast a spell? Did you? Lila asked Tath as they were gently lowered.

I know none that can hold the wind, he said. *Only Dar's whistle has that power, and then, it is not so great a power. The elementals are charmed by who they will, and there is no magic, even wild magic, that can command them against their inclination. Mere magical circles and barriers are insufficient. Air is the most curious of all the elements. This individual is in chosen service to the Lady of the Lake. Now we must wait and see if it is satisfied to let us pass.* He hesitated a moment. *Is that really a nuclear reactor?*

Yes, Lila said as Tath unobtrusively handed her back her body, only his *andalune* glamour remaining unfolded within her. She lowered the reactor's capacity to normal levels and saw the last of the yellow alert icons blink out.

Lila felt her feet touch the ground. She became heavier, then her full weight was down and the curtains of air were withdrawing, rushing around Dar one more time before calming to almost nothing. She was about to speak and apologise, but Dar wouldn't meet her eye. He looked strangely chastened and then he turned.

"Time runs short," he said.

Lila glanced back. The walls and roof of the cavern seemed closer than they had before. In fact, it was less than half as big as it had been when they crossed the stones. As she looked back at the Hall of Fire the other open mouths of the tunnels narrowed, closing. "Do they go anywhere?"

"I don't know. I have little hope of that," he said. He looked down at the whistle in his hand and then dropped it on the ground. "Perhaps this will buy some time. What power I do have I will give back now," he said to the air, and then stepped on the delicate thing. There was a crunching sound as he crushed it completely with his foot.

Lila didn't need Tath's dismay to tell her what a sacrifice that was. She felt Dar's *andalune* body touch her fingertips briefly, unconsciously, for he retreated a step when he noticed it himself. Around them the quiet breezes died away entirely. The walls and roof drew closer in a smooth, silent drift that would have seemed gentle in other circumstances. They walked closer to the Fire Hall's gate, as close as they could go and not risk accidentally crossing it. The Water gate came sliding towards them. The roof paused its descent as it reached the height of both portals, leaving them a few centimetres of clearance.

"Did this happen before?" she asked.

"No," Dar said. "We are out of luck."

"There has to be a way out."

"The only way is through the Hall of Fire, but the air will have told the fire that we are untrustworthy and we will not make it through there. I am sorry I did not get you further . . ."

Lila took hold of Dar's jacket with both hands, pulled him close, and kissed him on the mouth. His lips were cold. The walls drifted in, world shrinking. No air moved. Dar drew back and they shared a look that didn't require words for communication. If this was it, then neither of them wanted to leave without doing something.

Lila contemplated nuking Alfheim's most sacred spot, envisaged the mushroom cloud, the devastation, the destabilising effect on the interdimensional sheet, the shocking, complete sundering of the worlds.

Dar's hands slid around her head as she felt rock against her back. He put his head beside hers as the closing space pressed them together, gently at first, then with a terrible authority. Lila's AI-self ran through a thousand attempts at escape, none working. Dar's heavy hair brushed against her cheek and pieces of metal began to bite their way into her ribs. She knew that she would be the last thing to break, or burn. She kissed Dar's ear as the breath was pressed out of them and the Water Gate arrived and began to slowly push them up to the Fire Hall's waiting maw.

She put her arm outside Dar's, her leg outside his. Her sleeve went through first and caught immediately. The pain was indescribable. She couldn't help but tense against the tall elf body. "Hold your breath and close your eyes," she said feeling the strain in his body as his bones began to suffer badly under load. Her arm was burning, skin and synthetics in a conflagration, but the temperatures weren't yet high enough to spoil the action of her right arm gun system.

The outside edge of her foot passed the barrier but she had no real flesh there so it was only Tath's boot blazing for now. When it got hot enough steel was a fuel, and in pure oxygen it would continue to burn until it was nothing but iron oxide, but that wasn't going to happen. Lila configured the grenade shells in her arm for maximum burn and thrust her whole forearm suddenly through the shield. It caught with an explosion that incinerated her nerves and superficial transmission systems so fast that she felt almost nothing, but the gun assembled itself and discharged the full round into the hall as she used her considerable physical strength to keep Dar and herself from going through the invisible circle.

Her gamble paid off. The grenades went off about halfway down the tube in a glory of blue and white fire which flashed out instantly, filling the entire hall with a conflagration so extreme that the rock wall began to glow and melt. But the magical barrier prevented it burning them.

Dar groaned in pain.

"Press your hand over your eyes!" Lila commanded and felt his pelvis against her metal one starting to crack and one of the ribs she'd healed before broke again as she pulled free, dragging him with her into the Fire Hall and through the few seconds of near total vacuum and scaring heat that was all that remained The grenades had consumed the oxygen and rendered it into part of their crumbling pale ash and molten slag. The pain of the heat and the pain of near-explosion in the vacuum vied with each other.

Lila hadn't given any thought to whatever was at the end of fire. The oxygen level was rising fast as they ran, their boot soles burning, hair smouldering, skin scalded by the heat radiating from the walls. She put on a spurt of speed. Dar couldn't keep up with her, so she turned and lifted him, as she'd lifted Zal, throwing him across her shoulder in a fireman's lift, hurting him no doubt as the shear forces in both their bodies racked up terrible loads. She felt pieces of her tearing free of other pieces, but it was minor damage. At the same time Dar and Tath's combined aethereal bodies provided a kind of barrier against the rising oxygen concentration.

The rock surface slid under her disintegrating boots and then hardened, mercifully, but the temperature was so extreme that the oxygen didn't have to build up to its previous levels. Though the vacuum was gone, now things wanted to ignite readily. Lila felt Dar's clothes starting to catch light under her remaining good hand. She set her jaw and put all the power to her legs, making the last ten metres in a single leap which found them both alight as they fell through the empty rock ring and landed sprawling and gasping on the unyielding cool of a jade floor.

The floor dropped them. Lila found herself plunging into cold water. Still holding Dar she kicked strongly, but the weight of all her metal was making her sink. She couldn't swim with only one arm. Then she felt Dar's hands pulling her up, saw silver bubbles dashing past her, moving down. Abruptly several more pairs of elfin hands came and hauled them both out of the lake water and, as they drew level with the floor, the water itself seemed to solidify, becoming the jade that had caught them before. It lifted Lila clear.

"Tath?" said a voice Lila didn't recognise. She dashed water from her eyes, struggling to get to her feet. Tath's spirit body and this other's were in contact.

Astar, Tath informed her with sadness. It was someone he missed.

"Astar," Lila made herself say though she could hardly see for the pain in her arm. But Tath's glamour covered this. She didn't even look particularly singed.

"What an entrance, My Lord," said Astar's soft, feminine voice. Lila looked up at the person helping her stand and saw an elf woman with black hair that curled and coiled around her shoulders in waves of night. A single diamond shone from a silver circle on her brow and beneath that her eyes were more than a little concerned—not for Tath's health either, Lila thought, and her suspicion was confirmed as she heard another woman's voice, this one even softer and more melodious than Astar's.

"Tath and Dar, who would think to find you lacking in elemental kudos? There were days you would have danced to my door."

Lila jerked her hands back from Astar's gentle assistance before the other had time to feel a difference and straightened up, fighting to stand. "I have spent too long across the Void in Thanatopia," she said, hoping this would be a good excuse to explain the situation. "Some changes are . . . inevitable." She glanced quickly at Dar, who had also gained his feet though he looked both burned and drowned. Two strong male elves were on either side of him at a fastidious distance. Both of them were supremely well groomed and beautiful in that way that set Lila's teeth on edge; they reminded her of salesmen. Thankfully none of them looked like Zal.

Then Lila turned to see Arië.

The Lady of Aparastil had eyes of the most intense grass green. They shone from within as though they were made of stained glass and were set before a gleaming morning sun. Her face was the pale cream white of fine porcelain framed by a waterfall of coiling amber hair. A circlet of silver sat around the Lady's temple, and her ears were set close and elegant alongside her head, at a neutral angle. She wore watery, aqua robes of surprising practicality—Lila had expected dresses but Arië favoured britches, boots, and strong, forest-suited gear, all of which she made look infinitely more lovely than any piece of couture. Delicate silver leaves that twinkled threaded here and there through the fabrics and across the leather, so it looked as though she had been dressed by the forest, spiders her tailors. Her features were of a different cast to Dar's, the ones that Lila had grown used to looking at. Once all elves would have looked identical, but Lila recognised the High look now she saw it again—Zal's look. But before she could think on it she was staring up around them, at the room in which they stood—the Lady's Hall.

They were in a bubble beneath the lake. The walls and floor, and the roof itself, were made of water, water held aside by magic and charmed into the soft arches and parabolas of elfin architecture. The light that lit the place was sunlight, though Lila thought it must be channelled from the surface because her readings told her that there was about a fifth of a kilometre of lake water over their heads. Great thick stems of lily and giant water hyacinth rose beside them out of the dark green gloom. And below—the floor that Lila had taken for jade was simply water that refused to let them through its surface. She was amazed, trying to consider what possible conditions existed on that surface to permit her to stand on it and wondering how aetherial manipulation could create such a thing. For a moment she was struck totally dumb.

But Dar was far from being so impressed. He shook himself off, grimacing with the effort of concealing his wounds, and bowed deeply to Arië. "My Lady of Aparastil, I am your servant. Tath's glamour is but a trick. He was slain in Sathanor and his ghost inhabits the human against his will. It was a necessary evil I had to permit in the name of achieving delivery of your prize, Agent Lila Black."

Lila felt her jaw actually fall open. She was speechless with shock, aware only of Tath's amusement inside her skin. "You treacherous fuck," she said to Dar, in Tath's voice.

Do not be so upset, Tath said to her. *The Lady would see through me eventually and though there are few elfin necromancers in all there are none who use flashbombs*. A grudging admiration seemed to spread across the inside of her chest as he said this and Lila got the impression that Tath had rather liked the gun. *This is the only way for one of you to remain at liberty here, and Dar is no good friend of Arië's, which she well knows. She will be far from happy, whatever her demeanour. Trust me. And whatever happens do not release me from the glamour. If she sees you her reaction will be less than kind. She knows only that you are human, not that you are a machine.*

"Trust you!" Lila said aloud, only realising that she'd spoken when all eyes turned to her.

Tath reminded her about the daisy. She recalled her insight—even under the dulled effect of the Nirvana shunt—that he was an ally of Dar's. That he must be opposed to Arië. She had no idea whether or not she ought to trust either of them. No, she had a perfectly good idea that she definitely *shouldn't*, but there was no choice for the time being. She quickly covered up her slip . . .

"Trust *you*!" she said, slightly differently, stabbing her good finger out at Dar. "I don't know whatever made me believe that I could trust you!"

Dar drew himself up to his full height and did a very good impression of haughty superiority. Lila couldn't help flinching back—he looked exactly as he had in the instant before he had almost killed her. If she hadn't had Tath's insistence she would have counted herself completely betrayed. She was awed by his ability to dissemble, if that's what it was. She wasn't sure.

"Tath!" exclaimed Astar softly from behind Lila's shoulder. Lila could hear tears in the voice.

"It is most unseemly to wear your victim as a disguise," Arië said, although she could have been reading poetry for all the alteration in temper she showed. "Do us all the honour of releasing our friend from the hold of his name and we will look less unkindly upon your plea for fair trial after you also release his spirit to our care."

Lila ran through scenarios in her mind, implicating Dar, not implicating Dar—she didn't have time to play them through. Her arm and portions of her back hurt fiercely and she released as large a dose of cocodamol into her bloodstream as she dared.

As you love Zal, do not give Arië anything now, Tath said.

Sure you're not just pleading for your own life? Lila shot back as the silence grew in expectancy within the lake hall. Aloud she said, "My hostage remains as he is. If you want him back, then you can arrange safe passage for me to Otopia."

"So bold," Arië' said, moving closer. She placed her hand on the pommel of a sword that hung beside her hip then drew the blade from its scabbard and held the tip out, placing it precisely in the notch between Lila's collarbones at the base of her throat. "Yet I can kill you now. I have no use for you. In fact, you represent a considerable danger. Why should I let you live?"

Lila used her good left hand and took hold of the sword point between her forefinger and thumb. She began to move it aside. "Because if you do then your beloved Tath dies with me on the spot." She felt Arië resisting her actions quite firmly but that the elf would not exert enough force to show that she was actually losing to Lila's insistence as Lila forced the weapon tip away from herself. The edge of the blade altered subtly as Lila continued. She felt it grow harder and sharper until it was like a razor and marvelled at the speed and ease with which the substance changed to the elf's will. It turned and cut through the remains of her burned fingers right to the transformed alloy of her bones, but even so it was no match for Lila's brute strength. Blood dripped freely down onto the jade floor and ran back along the blade, over the ornamental guard and onto Arië's fingers as Lila pushed it away to arm's length.

Lila heard a satisfying and astounded gasp from the collected audience ringing them and turned her head to look at Dar. His lips parted and one side twitched upward for a moment. Then she looked back at the Lady. Although they both appeared to hold the weapon lightly, there was a great deal of force running through it in both directions. Lila glanced into Arië's eyes and wanted so much to destroy the cool hauteur there. With a small movement of her finger she bent the sword point to a ninety-degree angle.

There was a moment that Lila felt was adequately interpreted as a pause for thought. Tath was a cold pleasure in her heart, enjoying every minute.

Arië released her effort and Lila let go. The Lady watched the blood running over her own knuckles like a cat watching a mouse and then handed the sword aside to the elf at her shoulder—another of those big Nordic blond types, all angular features and disapproval. Lila ignored him.

"There are magics," Arië said in the light, conversational tone in which true hatred is best delivered, "which Tath will know of, that are useful in dislodging the possessed. They would be hard to endure."

Lila felt Tath shudder eloquently. *Now you tell me!*

"Perhaps you would be so kind as to await our decision elsewhere," the Lady continued. Her Nordic type and another who might have been his brother stepped quickly to either side of Lila. Lila looked back. The elf Astar had her face in her hands but she looked up now.

"I would speak with Tath," she cried. "My Lady, let me talk with him and perhaps I will be able to decipher some knowledge to our advantage or persuade this human to mercy."

"You may have half an hour," Arië told her kindly. "For that is the time it will take me to make preparations for his extraction."

The elves took hold of Lila's arms, flexing their hands uncomfortably against Tath's glamour, feeling him in spite of the fact they suspected something different underneath.

You'll never know how different, I hope, Lila thought. She struggled and twisted so that, as Arië addressed Dar, Lila could spit in his face with all the conviction of the fear that she'd been holding back. One thing Lila was confident above all else in—she was a good shot. She hit him square in the eye. Dar's return glance, blinking, held all the condensed loathing she was pretty sure he could genuinely feel.

Then Lila let herself be taken away.

CHAPTER NINETEEN

Zal lay on the floor of his cell, singing a little because he could think of nothing else to do. From time to time he heard Arië's voice. She would just say the name of someone he knew and for a moment his memory would fill in one of those blank places at the court with a familiar image. He guessed she meant him to realise that she was listing the people he had condemned with his silence, maybe mentioning them as she punished them. Or he was meant to think so.

He was reasonably sure that Lila was in Aparastil. It was just a feeling, but in Alfheim feelings were unusually trustworthy about this kind of thing. Aether was everywhere and it transmitted information instantly, even faster than the Otopians' electromagnetic waves. He wondered how she had got here, and how long she would last. He sighed as he thought about the reception she would receive.

He thought about the songs he had been going to write and the hope that the charm in the music and the words could effect some kind of shift in awareness among a wider population towards a new kind of openness between the races . . . it seemed very silly to him now. Trying it in Otopia of all places where the humans had so little use for other ways of seeing the world was manifestly dumb. He should have stayed in Demonia where they were open to ideas—too open, but open nonetheless . . .

He realised he was singing "A Hard Day's Night" and stopped with his mouth ajar. Thinking about Lila was why. He wished she was there in the room. He wished he hadn't lost her jacket and his bruised arms ached.

Of course he could not have stayed in Demonia, doing nothing. Aggravating Alfheim's wavering would-be radicals by pissing them off with music and cavorting in Otopia was exactly the thing to do under the circumstances . . .

Way out in the lake, something looked at him.

The same flicker of awareness he had noticed before was there again. It was faint, and very, very strange. He thought it was ghostly. Its attention was like the laying of a cool butterfly wing against the inside of his forehead.

All elves carried wards against ghosts; bones with eyes on, stones with naturally made holes in, small circlets of thorn wood, snippets of cloth once soaked in children's tears. Ghosts could not always be turned aside even by these. They came and they took in silence.

Zal had long since discarded all of these trinkets, even before Demonia, when he decided it was better to know than not know, and he had let go of any hope of eluding fear. He just hoped that he not be paralysed by it when it was strong. But that was all. And even this wish was only a necessary little bit of flag waving. He recalled Lila's battle stance function with a wince and a smile—at least she could switch fear off and act in the face of it. He worried less about her suddenly.

The thing looking at him was not a ghost. Zal knew ghostly touches. When the ghost of Forgotten Forests touched him on the hill above Solomon's Folly it had felt—it had been the absence of feeling. This was alien but not absent. It was almost the opposite of absence. He couldn't identify it but it had, yes, *presence*.

It turned away.

Zal sang another line.

It looked back. It was so deep and far away he was not sure it wasn't imagination on his part. But who cared?

He carried on singing, one song and another, whatever came into his head.

From the dark it drifted upwards beneath him. He saw little gas bubbles and old leaf silt rising on a new current, passing his prison as water was pushed upwards at some speed. The thick stems of the waterquoia trembled. The cool wing under his skull folded itself closed and left with what impressions it had gained. The water stilled. It didn't come again.

Dragons, he thought. In elven lore they were lucky creatures. Tales mentioned a time when dragons and elves talked, but then again, tales mentioned a time when elves and demons were one race so . . . that was probably too long ago to be of any use today. And if you went back far enough there were records that stated the worlds were made by dragons spinning words like silk, as if dragons were spiders and the universe their web.

In modern times it was well known that dragons were creatures of the Interstitial, of the space between worlds. The Otopians had even attempted to tag one and radio track it. Of the research team nothing was ever found except a rather nice handbag containing some fortune cookies. The cookie fortunes were classified, so Zal had never discovered what they said, although he believed the rest of the story when his informers didn't. Dragons were inexpressibly strange. No doubt Arië considered its presence the final commendation on her status. To attract a dragon was the ultimate pride, a mark of absolute sorcery or innocence.

Zal didn't think it was his innocence doing the trick.

Arië just said the names. Zal sang songs and waited and hoped Lila had some kind of discreet yet incredibly useful weapon hidden about her person that he hadn't yet seen.

CHAPTER TWENTY

Astar trailed after Lila and her guards. They passed from the hall through walks glimmering with wave-lensed light, beside gardens of weed filled with incredible varieties of fish curiously nosing up against the air world of the interior. Rooms filled with fountains, walls tumbling with falling water . . . Lila only looked to notice entrances and exits and to map the way. She tested the strength of her guards, pulling this way and that, and realised they were tough, but much lighter than she was in spite of their bigger size. She fought the urge to vomit with the nauseating pain of being held around her burned right arm. To distract herself she talked to Tath and tried to discover anything that might make it more likely she could get into the same room as Zal.

Now that we've bought some thinking time, tell me, does Arië know that I was Zal's guard?

Unless Dar has told her so I would think not. She has little interest in your function, although if she ever found out that Zal had caught you in a Game, that would be a different matter. A lever against Zal is something she would value more than my life or Dar's, that is certain. She will not accept your mastery of me at all and I believe she would sooner kill us both than suffer the continued embarrassment of that, for she sees me as her prop-

erty, but she would gladly spend Dar and myself in the achievement of mastery over you. Like us, you must decide exactly how much you value the lives of those with whom you must deal and how much you value the greater good of your people.

This was good news of a sort. As long as Lila played things right, she at least could survive long enough for an attempt at escape. Tath's statements about his relation to Arië made her cringe however. *Her property?*

Arië is the leader of the light elves of the Valar inheritance, among whose number I count myself. As she is our leader, according to her authority I am hers to spend. It is why I became a necromancer. If not for her engagement of me, why would I pretend to such a loathsome office?

Lila guessed elf loyalties in the spy business might run to extreme altruism. *For the Jayon Daga?*

Even they cannot require such a sacrifice of service.

Lila was turned to face a door. Like all doors in the lake palace it had no solid barrier involved, being a magical barrier which vanished at the her guards' touch. A small room lay beyond encapsulated within a dark area of weeds which overgrew the sides of the bubble walls. A bed, a table, and a minimum of other furnishings graced it, looking as though they floated in midair from most angles. It was hard not to stagger when she walked because it was so hard to judge depth of space. Astar followed her inside and watched as the magical wall shut itself at their backs.

As soon as they were alone, the graceful female elf turned Lila to face her and held her hands, pleading, "Say it is you, Tath, and this some dreadful Game playing and not the truth!" Her elongated eyes were rimmed with red, their dark irises huge in the low light. As she finished speaking she made to dab her tears with a filmy handkerchief out of which fell a scatter of flowers, as though she had been picking them at some point in the past, and forgot them within the handkerchief's folds. She bent quickly to pick them up, a slight pressure on her hand drawing Lila with her. Among the pretty things one white daisy . . .

Inside her, Tath doubled in intensity, sad, his *andalune* over Lila becoming strong enough to reach out and touch Astar's carefully restrained aethereal form. His sadness was worse than the burning pain in her arm.

Lila picked up the daisy and held it towards the black-haired elf. "Sadly, it is the truth, but hardly all of it."

Astar held Lila's hand but she felt Tath's fingers as she took the flower carelessly and then drew the hand to her lips and kissed each of the knuckles gently. "I have missed you so much. Say it's you that speaks and not the impostor."

Lila had been about to attempt soft politeness in the face of this sympathy but found herself grating out impatiently, "It's the freak, not your brother."

Astar put Lila's hand away from her but stared boldly into Lila's face. "You wear him well, then, whoever you are, for his *andalune* is his own where it and mine are joined, and he is not suffering because of you. Will you let him speak with one who holds his heart dear?"

How many girlfriends have you got, exactly? Lila said to Tath.

One exactly, though she died as I did, upon the hillside where you left us. I have three sisters.

Hell, oh hell, Lila thought. *If you're lying to me* . . . She let Tath have the whole show. Give the elves their due, she thought, as Tath used her body to embrace his sister, they're fey and strange but they know who's who and they don't freak out like I would if I could go back to my family and hug them one last time. A stab of pain in her heart made her wince.

But there was no point in thinking about that. She concentrated on lining up repair systems, prioritising, cueing up harmonics in the nerves causing her the most discomfort so that their efforts to tell her she was in trouble became simple information in her AI-self rather than a sensation of pain in her body. Probably Dar would be okay, she thought as she wondered what she would do with the largely destroyed surface of her right arm. Sathanor was that kind of place. Probably he would be better already.

Lila quietly mended the fingers of her left hand as Tath used it to hold Astar close to him. They sat down together on the narrow bed.

"Can we persuade this person to release you?" Astar was saying. "I would hold your spirit within mine and release it to a child of your heart . . . Give me the flower. Where is it?"

What the hell? Lila thought. *Elves* clone! *Are you crazy? Is that what she's saying?*

It is extremely rare. Aloud to Astar Tath said, "I do not wish to leave my host."

"What?" Astar and Lila said simultaneously.

Tath took the handkerchief out of his sister's hands and found the white flower again. He would not give a reason aloud although to Lila he said, *If I leave you and Arië discovers what you are she will not kill you. It will be worse. Arië loves Sathanor, but beneath her love lies fear, and the thing she fears most is technology like you. It is quite irrational. She will continue with her disastrous plan involving Zal, and she will certainly kill Dar, very inventively I expect. There is nothing good in any of that.*

What did she mean about the flower? Lila insisted.

The flower bound me in life to my true friends. All necromancers carry one. Without it, if one of us dies, we cannot be restored by any means. Thus it is when you burned it that I became bound to you, Lila, because without it I cannot cross over. If you die, I die, and when Arië tries to separate us, if she succeeds, then I certainly will.

But if you still had it then you and . . . whoever . . . they could have resurrected you in some way and . . . does Dar know? Lila was outraged at being kept ignorant about this, especially by Dar. Letting her think he'd slaughtered Tath when all along there was this chance of resurrection—she was furious for a second, but Tath was still talking.

It does not mean the same thing to Dar because it is also a mark of the Revolution, but yes, when he saw you burn it he did know that whatever chance there was for me to survive was gone. When it went, he had effectively murdered me most surely.

Oh, so now it's my *fault?* Lila snapped, though she didn't get an answer.

"You are talking together," Astar said quietly. "I can feel your attention shifting."

"Oh crap!" Lila said, not meaning to speak her sudden fresh doubt in Dar aloud but unexpectedly finding that she had command of their voice.

Astar started.

"Not you, I mean . . ."

"You are the host," Astar said attentively. "Why does my brother not wish to leave you?"

Do not . . . Tath began hesitantly, full of the delicate subtleties of elven politics, not sure if he could trust Astar or even the water not to betray them, but Lila was watching Astar's face which was soft and sympathetic on the surface but with eyes rather more suited to a patient lizard than a trembling rabbit, and she was reasonably sure that the woman wasn't quite as spineless as Tath seemed to think.

"He can't leave," Lila said. "The daisy soulkeeper thingy he had is toast. He's stuck with me, and if you want to see him alive in any form for much longer then you'd better start thinking of a way to get me to Zal before Arië rips his spirit out of me and feeds us to the fishes. So, know where Zal is?"

Astar, mute, eyes like saucers, gave her a long, thoughtful elven stare.

"Anytime in the next ten seconds would be good," Lila prompted.

Brilliant, Tath observed sarcastically.

"You're most direct," Astar said. "I hope you are as effective in pleading for your life and that of my brother as you are at issuing questions. Zal is far below the surface, where the darkness and cold plunge over the edge of the lake bed and into a chasm of extreme depth—a ley chasm of great aetheric potential where Arië seeks to . . ." She continued to say something about raising power and using it to purify Sathanor and some other kind of semibiblical flood analogy that Lila thought sounded uncannily like a form of Whole Earth fascism. The ideology didn't interest her except inasmuch as it was now clear that Alfheim was about to enter a civil war and that was worth reporting. But the really interesting thing was *A bomb fault!* Lila thought, translating the elfin way of thinking. *Under Sathanor, how peculiar. I wonder if it is linked to the recording studio in Otopia or is the same kind of thing?*

". . . He is contained by a separate sphere which hangs free in the lake water, connected to the palace by a single hair from Arië's head," Astar concluded. "More than that I have been unable to discover. We are not permitted so far below."

"He has to come to us," Lila said, "That can happen how?"

Astar shook her head helplessly. "Nothing but the Lady can command it."

"So she just needs a reason."

We need more help than this, Lila said privately to Tath. *I'll be straight with you. Unless you have any more friends here who are on the white daisy side then we aren't looking so great. Let's say I do get to him, then how can I get Zal out of this place? Oh wait . . . I know.* Her AI-self had been checking possibilities and had decided the best thing must be to wait until they were all united, for any reason, and then to power her way out, carrying Zal. She could certainly make the surface alive, and probably use her internal oxygen systems to support at least one other if it was a long way up. As for how to get together in the first place, she and Tath could most likely break through the charm wall and swim down . . .

Tath picked up her thoughts quickly, much more than he used to. He even clocked the AI-self's neat chart of survival possibilities and its redlined conclusions.

No!

Yes. It's the only way. *And look on the bright side, if it fails and I have to, I can blow us all to doomsday and back. It's a plan. You don't have one. We'll stick with it.*

Dar was quite correct in his analysis that you are poorly placed for diplomacy, Lila.

Lila recounted her explosives, ammunition, and the chances that Arië was insane. Most likely Arië was not insane but frighteningly intelligent and well-motivated, if wrong. It all looked extremely bad.

Astar looked up. Their time was over. "Arië likes to keep what she fears in sight," she said in quiet, rapid tones. "And she would enjoy making a fool of Zal. She has no fear in her own house. Offer her the chance and you may get yours."

You do know that Astar used to turn me in to our father when I stayed out after dark, don't you? Tath complained. *She would betray me for one approving smile and gloat at my punishment. One look from our mother was enough to make her come to heel.*

I'd betray my sister for the promise of a half-sucked breathmint, Lila said. *But not here and not now.*

The door vanished abruptly and her guards stood there.

"Lady Astar," one said deferentially.

Astar stood up and preceded Lila out.

Tath, do you know anything about demons? Do you have any—relatives? Lila asked as she followed, kicking the floor. It bent slightly. She thought that the water must transmit every sound and vibration quite well, and sighed.

You are talking about Zal, he said. *I have heard of his theory that demons and elves are a bound aetheric duality, but it is heresy here, you must understand. I have no idea if it has any truth in it. Nobody in Alfheim knows what he did in Demonia. My concern with this lies in the salvation of Alfheim, from one destruction or another.*

I guess I suit your purpose quite well so far. If we stop Arië you get to save the world.

I guess you do. How does your arm feel now?

Lila hadn't been concentrating and realised that she wasn't feeling even slight discomfort. She tried her arm and found that it was well-healed. The plastic and metal damage was still there, but her skin, her bone, the human parts of her—they were fine.

You may thank Astar for helping me. I hope it is the last time.

The last time for the next five minutes, Lila said, acknowledging Tath's own irony with a rueful smile. *Don't get too sweet now, Tath, or it'll start feeling like we're friends.*

He didn't reply.

I had an idea, Lila said. *I know how we can get to Zal.* She explained as they finished their short walk and arrived back in the lake hall.

It seems a bit convenient, Tath grumbled although Lila could feel a sly kind of gladness in him at the level of trust between them she would have to rely on. *You will have to be very convincing.*

Not me, Lila said. *You.*

Arië and her entourage were seated around low tables there, for all the world as though they were out for a picnic. Dar was close to Arië's left side, changed, dried, and cleaned up. He looked quite the part in his lilac and lavender finery. Lila felt completely sick at heart with what she was about to do because it was, as Tath said, very dangerous. She longed to cry. Instead she gave him a big smile and a wave. It was all she could think of that might act as a warning of any kind; a gesture so out of place that it must carry meaning. She saw Arië's green eyes narrow slightly as she was marched up to the gathering. Astar walked quietly to her Lady's side.

"I regret my entreaties were in vain," Astar said and sat down.

Lila felt the strong *andalune* presence of the guards at her sides withdraw as they stepped away from her. Now was the moment.

Okay, Ilyatath Elenir Voynassi Taliesetra, she said inside. *Sell me down the river.*

Lila Amanda Black, I surely will.

"But the Lady's effort was not in vain," Tath-in-Lila said, as Lila felt her body change the way it moved, to his style. "I have gained the upper hand within our struggle thanks to Lady Astar's strength." Tath dropped the glamour.

Lila had to admit that the look on Dar's face was quite gratifyingly astonished. The rest of the faces however, those that didn't turn aside with revulsion, stared at her with the kind of expressions that it took all her courage not to react to. She supposed that her dirty state, her stolen clothes, her scars, her mangled hand and the metal that showed must be quite something if you were used to the kinds of flawless beauty that decked the halls around here. Still, as the silence rang on and twenty pairs of elfin eyes flicked over her as though the sight of her were poison, it wasn't so easy to bear.

Tath spoke quietly, with a surprise entirely of his own. He was surprised that he was surprised. *I can feel their hate.*

Welcome to my world, Lila said to him, staring straight ahead now, wanting to look at Dar but knowing she wouldn't find any support there, most likely. Couldn't risk it anyway. Then doing it. His face was rigid and intense, the face of her nightmares. *What the hell was that look about?*

That look is Dar thinking at top speed. And . . . But Tath didn't finish. Lila sensed his curiosity burning though she could not decipher its cause. Tath's presence, which had been so all-consuming it had become natural, was now focused on the tiny space he occupied within her solar plexus and he was difficult to read. Suddenly she was on her own.

The Lady of Aparastil was first to rise and, as though commanded in silent languages, the others remained quite still around her as she came forward to inspect Lila more closely.

Arië said nothing but that didn't stop the rest. Lila heard a lot of elvish words that her AI-self unwittingly translated before she turned off that function: hideous, abomination, monster, freak, disgusting, perverted, ugly, repulsive . . . The sly giggles, gloats, and sneers could not be erased so easily.

Lila held fast, as though Tath controlled her, and stared into the distance, into the deep green where the fish suddenly darted and flashed their silver semaphore of alarm. They were replaced by a huge, horned, tentacled face, long and triangular, with colossal golden eyes whose star-slit pupils gazed at her for an instant before vanishing into the water and weeds. She saw golden scales and black scales in diamond patterns winding on and on after it, seemingly forever, long amber fins and powerful, clawed feet: a water dragon. Because they were fixated on her, none of the elves noticed it, except for Tath. He reacted to the sight of it with intense excitement and fear, but he was soon distracted.

At close quarters Arië's allure was almost overwhelming. Lila could feel Tath melting with the very idea of being so close to the Lady. Lila was melting in a different way, every piece of her attention focused on maintaining calm homeostasis on her skin, in her muscles, in her breathing, in her energy patterns, giving away nothing of the seething molten anger that made her want to activate all weapons and bury Arië and her retinue in the muddy bottom of the lake. And as she held the line and gave nothing away, as she burned, she felt Tath inside her chest, a new kind of sensation from him that she didn't expect or look for even in allies at times like these: respect.

Just don't fucking say anything, Tath, either way, she thought. *Don't make it harder than it already is.*

He didn't.

"Are you able to show us what this . . . thing . . . is capable of?" Arië asked.

"Yes," Lila said, quite herself and trying to talk Tath-speak. "Though I advise you to stand aside." With hands that didn't sweat or shake she began to undress.

She took off Tath's baldric and belt, his dagger and his bow. Arië took them from her, holding them reverently. Lila took off Tath's jerkin and his shirt, revealing her stained singlet underneath. She removed what was left of his boots, undid the laces that held his britches closed and took them off—careful not to think of the last time she'd done that, although she would have loved to see Arië's expression if her liaison with Dar were to become public knowledge. She stepped out of them to stand in her regulation underthings, stinking of human sweat, as naked as she ever wanted to be again. The prosthetic arms and legs, the rivers of interrun flesh and metal, their unhappy pairing, the scarlet stain of Dar's magic . . . she let Arië take a long look and thought she saw the stirring of pity in the elf queen's face. She wanted to hit that face.

"What manner of terrible surgery has been foisted on this person?" Arië demanded. "It cannot be intentional that—she—has found herself thus made so abominably malformed. Look at her eyes! Nothing but metal. What could she see with those except the hardness and coldness of things?"

I see you, you trite bitch, Lila thought. She activated all her weapons systems into attack configuration and watched with deep satisfaction as pieces of her arms and legs which had seemed to be a flush surface with her skin lifted out and apart, flicking into new positions, her limbs a blur of moving metal parts, the air filled with the sound of a thousand snicking precision-made components shifting like a storm of mechanical insects taking wing. Battle armour, multifunctional self-adapting guns, missile launchers, an extra five inches of height . . .

Lila watched the elves recoil from her flat silver eyes as her hair activated and became charged sensory and comms transmission systems. Blades grew out of her hands. From her heels, killing spurs emerged, coated in poison.

Arië was the only one who did not recoil. She looked Lila up and down. "Can you operate these things, Tath?"

"I do not have complete access to that. The machine . . ." Tath said in his own voice, trusting that Arië's imagination would fill in the blank.

"How is it powered?"

"I cannot ascertain the method."

"As you were," Arië said thoughtfully and Lila returned to her civilian self in less than a second; the incredible shrinking girl.

"There is something else," Tath added at Lila's prompt, making no move to take any of Lila's clothing back. She turned her head and stared into Arië's green eyes with her solid silver ones, knowing the elf would only see herself in them. "This agent was one of those assigned to Zal in Otopia to protect him from the Jayon Daga. She and he were involved in a Game which is unresolved." It was her final card, the only card she had. If Arië didn't pick it up, they were all done. She had to bet that Arië could not resist using this information.

"What kind of Game?" the Lady demanded softly.

Lila hesitated. Tath took over seamlessly and used her mouth for her, "A love match." Her voice. Her mouth. Tath's words. Suddenly they were too close for comfort and she almost panicked at the notion she would never get out and that he could take her over so easily if he wanted to . . . Tath felt it too. For a second they were on the brink, each realising the other's power.

But if the atmosphere had been bad before, it was as nothing to the depths it plunged to now. Someone actually gagged. Lila saw Arië's face tighten compulsively.

"To the death?"

Tath did not know the answer. He was watching Arië and made no attempt to seize power. Lila supplied it. "The death of love," she said and resumed command, turning her face back to its attention position so that she didn't have to see the triumph and hate and loathing flood Arië's beauty with a whole new kind of vertiginous attraction, every strong mood of hers magnetic and charged with magic. As she revealed her secret she heard Tath say, *You're full of surprises, Lila.*

You should see me on a good day, Lila told him, though it was only words to her, she felt nothing of the assertiveness she pretended to. She longed to be unconscious, to be anywhere but here.

"Such a Game," the Lady mused, the company there hanging on her every breath. "Such a dangerous Game with such as this. Surely . . . but there is no end to his degradation it seems. Truly, you did not return him a moment too soon, Dar. Now come, Tath, you have suffered long enough in such an unbefitting prison. Give me the token of your necromancer's soulbond with Death and I will give you back to your sister, or to whomever you wish. Any of my retinue will serve you."

That damn flower!

Stop moaning and think, Tath snapped.

"I think it would be more interesting if I remained here," Lila said via Tath, passing him ideas as she had them, not even sure how she did it. "Zal will not know that I am not the real Agent Black, after all. Maybe we can be useful. Zal will be difficult to manage. He was at the best of times. But the Game and his affections for this creature may make him ductile."

Ductile? Lila shot at Tath. *Nobody in their right mind uses words like ductile.*

Nobody but me. That is why she is still going along with this madness. You do the thinking and leave the talking to me.

The Lady smiled. "You reason prettily enough, Tath. But give me the token, so that I can restore you immediately if things go ill. Neither of us can trust a being such as this one, whose spirit such as it is has been infiltrated and bound by the impenetrable blankness of metal and electricity." Her smile was like the sun coming out of the clouds after a long, dull day of grey skies. Tath and Lila both felt its warmth and promise of goodness.

Oh crap, Lila thought. She was out of ideas.

I could not have put it better myself.

"I have it," Astar interrupted quietly, coming forward with a daisy in her palm. "He gave it to me for safe keeping." She gave it to Arië and the Lady closed her fingers over the token.

Inside Lila, as she felt a rush of gratitude for Astar's quick thinking, Tath became extremely dense with tension.

"That is well then," Arië said, clearly relieved. "For I would not have you used against me, Tath. I hold you very dear."

Sure, that's why she sends you into Thanatopia against your nature when she won't go herself.

I am aware of my position, Tath said ambiguously. *And if you want her to swallow this you had better leave the rest to me. You have not the graces yet.*

"You do me great favour, Lady," Tath said, and performed the elegant, supplicating bow that Lila didn't have in her. Lila was slightly nauseated by Tath's deference—at the way it made him feel so good. Tath did the *andalune* equivalent of pulling a face at her.

Arië gave Astar Tath's gear. "Please dress and resume your glamour for the time being if you would, Tath," she said. "I must say that I prefer your fairness to this mockery of life and beauty. You were always most comely."

"Thank you, Lady," he said and Lila felt the surge of Tath unfolding over her like a comfortable old coat.

How peculiar, Lila thought, *to be more comfortable as somebody else. How nice to know you are pretty and how nice not to draw the wrong kind of attention.*

Lila looked down at herself as Tath getting dressed. There really was not much comparison. Tath was sculpted muscle and acres of smooth, perfect skin. It was quite startling to see how much the sight of that apparent physical health calmed the others in the room. Even Dar was relaxing and that sense that the whole place was about to shatter had gone. *Beauty junkies, that's what you are*, Lila thought sadly, even Arië, especially Arië, who has never looked in a mirror that didn't like her or a face that wasn't humbled by her.

Is that other daisy a big mojo spell daisy or just a daisy? Lila asked Tath, trying to keep matters practical.

It is only a flower, a sign of her solidarity with us and nothing more.

Too bad. Anyway, you like Arië an awful lot, for an enemy.

My heart is my own problem, Tath said coolly.

Lila took the silver Thanatopic amulet from Astar last and put it on. As she did so, Tath sighed inside her, a heavy, long-suffering sound, and her chest felt as though it sank a degree. The office hurt him. It was a literal weight in his spirit.

"Come with me now," Arië said to Tath. "Tell me of how you came by this robotic nightmare and the spells by which you hold it under mastery. Dar has told me of how it was he came to Alfheim in mortal pain, but I would like to know what happened to the lovely Silalio. Why is she not with you? Her heart would break to see you so."

Tath switched command position with Lila again, as though they'd been a tag-team doing it all their lives. He was graceful about it, and only Lila felt the sadness and the anger as he said lightly, "Her heart lies with my body in the woodlands south of Sathanor. The Lady Silalio is dead, killed by Saaqaa as we travelled fast by night to catch up with Dar. Wild magic was everywhere around us, indeed, I have never seen so great a concentration of it as I did that night. It led us astray from the path and we were surprised by the hunters. She fought," Lila felt a catch in his thinking, in his emotions, like a stumble, "very well, but the beasts were too powerful for all of us. Their ferocity and numbers have grown like wildfire in the last few months. They slaughter across Alfheim with impunity."

Sighs and sounds of grief and surprise broke across the gathered elves around the Lady Arië, not least from Astar, who walked quickly away from them all and left the Hall. The sight of it cut Tath to the core, but he held his position and Lila felt her face change only the slightest amount, sinking at the corners of the mouth. Lila wondered if Silalio had carried a daisy too, forgetting how easy it was now for Tath to hear her.

Indeed she did not, he said acidly. *So put away that pity you were beginning to feel, unless it was for her.*

"I am grieved to hear it," Arië said. Tears stood in her eyes and she displayed her emotions so openly and with such force that to look at her was to feel the epitome of all sorrow. Lila didn't look. She let Tath carry on and tried not to experience the way that Arië's expression tore at him.

"Tath," Arië walked forward and put out her hand, then hesitated
for a fraction of a second, and let it down again. Her *andalune* body
touched his for the briefest of moments and he almost swooned in the
combination of pleasure and agony. Lila felt the strange charge it carried, more than sympathy and more than attraction. She *knew* that
heady, intoxicating rush—Arië and Tath were involved in a Game that
went beyond the obvious one of political struggle! The citrus, efferves-
cent tang of wild magic sparkled in her mind.

She betrayed you with love?

Tath did not answer.

"If you will not be undone from this creature, then I cannot offer
you any further consolation, though your self-command does you great
honour in my presence," Arië said. "Come, before we continue this difficult task, eat with us. There is someone I would like you to talk to."

She turned and her retinue got up quickly and silently to follow
her. Dar hung back, but not enough for either of their aethereal bodies
to make contact, and Tath would not meet his eye.

Lila reconsidered the wisdom of her position as they passed out of
the lake hall and into another glorious room of glassy walls and living
wallpaper. Either of the elves would kill anyone for the stakes that she
was still only dimly aware of, all tangled about them like weeds here
in this room: politics, families, magics, love. She only wanted to save
Zal's skin, not create an international incident. Those two things
seemed impossibly far from her control. And then they sat down at a
beautiful curving table shaped like the curl of a gentle wave. It was
laid out with a feast. In spite of her revulsion at the idea and the knife-
edge they were balancing on she was very hungry, so Lila ate the food
of Sathanor and, just for the moments that she did so and before guilt
had time to manifest, she forgot everything but the sheer pleasure of
being alive. And then she watched and waited, and hoped that Arië
would not be able to overcome temptation.

CHAPTER TWENTY-ONE

She did not have long to wait. After they had eaten and drunk in formal silence and the first course had been cleared away—by servants who were more like Dar than Arië, Lila noticed—then the guards who had escorted her to her talk with Astar opened the doors and escorted Zal into the room.

He looked no different to the way he looked when he was about to go on stage, Lila realised, with a physical shock that made her glad she was seated. Every fibre and electron of her thrummed in a moment of total harmony. Now that she was used to elfin faces she saw Zal's familial relationships clearly written in his face. He was of Arië's kind, although for such a high-caste elf he had stronger, more human features. It was his eyes that stood out the most, brown beneath dark brows. They were not Taliesetra eyes, for theirs came in all shades of blue and green.

A zing of disbelief ran through Tath and Lila felt his convictions waver. *They used to be blue*, Tath said. *I have not seen him since he was in Bathshebat. I had no idea what had happened.*

Zal didn't spare the guard nor any of Arië's court a single glance. He took the seat left for him at the nominal foot of the curved table with a distinctly human kind of carelessness, dragging his chair. He looked once at Dar, though neither of their expressions so much as flickered. He looked once towards Lila and her heart leapt up eagerly though she knew he couldn't see her.

"Ilya," he said, using the part of Tath's name which Lila had come to understand signified a rather frostier relation than the more common version. "What an unexpected aggravation. Still licking the Lady's boots for a living?"

If Tath had still had a body, it would have gone from calm to full, bristling alert at Zal's words. "Still protecting Sathanor from you," Tath said smoothly, though Lila was aware that his feelings towards Zal were highly ambivalent. Tath was experiencing a definite chemistry of some kind, along with a most un-elven burn of curiosity.

"Still conspiring in my death, I believe you mean," Zal drawled. "Got your eye on the throne, or the seat next to it."

Really? Lila demanded.

Hardly, Tath said but she didn't believe him.

During their brief exchange the second course had been served. Zal idly pushed the plate away from him and tipped it over the edge of the table onto the floor where it broke. Food splattered in all directions.

"Oh dear, how sad, never mind," Zal said. "I just love these home-cooked meals and all of us here together like this. Gives me a warm glow, right here." He tapped the centre of his chest with his fist. "And the conversation," he said into the frosty silence. "How I've missed your empty posturing, Ysha, Elwe . . ." He named everyone at the table and gave them each a gleaming and insincere smile as servants hurried to clean the mess away.

Zal rested his elbows on the table and his face in his hands, staring flatly at Arië. "Is that what you brought me here for? To see my old Daga mates and eat here with you so that I never want to leave again?" He ran his finger across the untouched sauce on the plate of the elf beside him and stuck it in his mouth. Judging by his expression Lila could see he really liked it and guessed that he was actually starving.

He pulled his finger out and wiped it on his neighbour's shirt. "Not bad. Had better. Still want to leave. Still not going to entertain you." He pushed his chair back and stood up.

"*I* am the one the Lady has brought you here to speak with," Dar said and for the first time since he came in Zal looked at Dar, thoughtfully.

"Why hello, Dar. It must be all of two days since I last saw you." Zal walked around his own chair and held onto its high back. He had more animation in him than the rest of the court put together, an energy that Lila saw didn't match theirs. There was some kind of *andalune* tussle then, a ripple of power that ran around the gathering faster than thought. Lila caught the tail end of it via Tath. She knew now exactly what Zal had meant on that wooded hillside at Solomon's Folly, when he told her he *had* to be in Alfheim, sometimes. It was home. People of aether could only be at full power on their own turf, but though this had at one time completely satisfied him, it transparently didn't do so any longer. He was changed and they all felt it and recoiled. They didn't want to know.

Lila knew she must get to the bottom of this pattern of magic and relationship between the aetheric formats, but now was not the moment. While she started considering breakout possibilities from the room they were in, Zal and Dar faced off.

"You know that the reason you're here isn't because any of us dislike you, though we may disagree with your chosen path, Zal," Dar began, slightly moving his body so that it did not square against Zal's, but deflected the pressure of attention sideways, less aggressively.

"Spare me," Zal pushed the chair away and straightened up but he stayed where he was to listen to Dar's speech, a curiously pained look on his face which Lila did not trust herself to interpret.

They are friends, Tath said. *Whatever it looks like. Dar is playing to the Lady. Zal is waiting to see what the game is.*

"Every one of us wants Alfheim to recover from the ills of recent years, just as you do," Dar insisted, genuine appeal in his voice. "The wild aether burgeons. The Saaqaa population explodes out of Delantis with every passing moon and we cannot control their spread. Old lunar charms that cast spells for darkness or light have warped, and now break holes in the worlds bringing Thanatopic and faery magics leaking through. All tame creatures are growing wild. Isn't this decay and pollution what the Jayon Daga have been sworn to end since the beginning of the Otopian Age? When the walls between worlds thinned we sent emissaries to the five realms to learn of their arts and magics, to become practitioners or to find trusted double agents whom we could turn to our ends. Wasn't that how you were left in Demonia? And how you came to abandon us, your true friends and brothers, sweet companion of my heart?"

Sweet companion of my heart? Lila gasped. But Dar had said he didn't know Zal personally at all . . . had explained to her that they could never be friends. She could hardly believe that he had told such a barefaced lie— and Zal was doing nothing to deny it. Why would Dar do that? She must have been a fool to trust him as much as she had. What else was a lie?

Trust nothing. The stakes are too high, Tath said and then seemed to catch himself, as though he didn't mean to speak it to her.

As she considered this, Lila's AI-self was rapidly recalculating the scale of the gulf Zal had crossed in going over to the demons. She'd known it was significant but by their reactions here it was huge. He had done the unthinkable, more than breaking some cultural taboo.

Tath filled her in. *Nobody in any realm had previously questioned the distinct separations of the people's natures. Their essential forms are unsympathetic to one another, lethally so at times. Zal has embraced an oppositional magical system and culture which his native land despises and fears, their antithesis. He has come back and shown them that he lives, but they don't know what he is now. They fear and despise him. They are more dangerous than ever. His desire to break down barriers has had the opposite effect. You can feel the truth of it and he can too.*

Yes, but anyway, Lila shot back, fiercely proud of Zal, *companion of my heart*? She didn't understand all the elvish terms of endearment, so many formal, so many intimate, so many degrees of meaning—she searched her AI database rapidly and watched Zal's face. Did she see a flicker of emotion cross its rigid set? His ear tips bent towards the thick blond fall of his hair more closely.

Dar was still speaking, "It has been a miracle so far that the Daga have managed to keep so many secrets from the other realms, not least the Otopians. And if you are not another symptom of Alfheim's disintegration, what are you? Really, Zal, set aside your self for a moment and consider how much of what you have done is motivated by our interests, as you claim, and how much of it is driven by the general illness that is decomposing Alfheim from within. You are sick and you will suffer, if Alfheim continues to collapse."

"Really I think that you'll find Alfheim's problems with aether pollution started around the same time as the High Light Hegemony decided to go for partitioning and all that other separationist bullshit," Zal said. His dark gaze, levelled at Dar like a spear a few minutes ago, had softened, though only a little. "I can't believe you sit here with this unimaginative, frightened woman, who is merely hours away from throwing every value she had to the wind, in a mad effort to save what cannot be saved. But you have the healer's skill so I hope you're going to back me up when I prove to you that the last thing you have to worry about is demon aether and the last thing I am is sick."

Lila and Tath sat as still and fixated as the rest, their food gone cold, as Zal pulled his shirt off and turned around. The fire flare on his back was a shocking blaze of yellow and orange. Chairs scraped and cutlery clanged as there was a universal and involuntary move backwards from everyone present. The massed *andalune* of the Lady's party shrank back and even Lila twitched and pressed against the sturdy frame of her chair as what she had taken for some kind of magical mark opened up and two huge, dripping wings of fire emerged from Zal's upper back.

The guards froze in their forward step, fixated.

Heat beat against Lila's skin. The wings were enormous, batlike but covered in a thin sheen of what seemed to be lava that gave rise to feathers of flame. The laval substance ran and dripped towards the ground in strings and globs of orange. As these little pieces fell they shimmered. Small bits evaporated into the air, larger globs fell right to the floor where they instantly penetrated the charm of the surface tension and dropped into the depths in streams of boiling, foaming water. Steam rose in clouds. There was a strong smell of hot metal.

I can't help wishing he mentioned this before, Lila said to Tath. *Is it show or does it all do something? Think we can bust out of here by force?* Her gun ports twitched.

You will not make it. Arië has at least five mages here and the lake to command. We have to distract her much more.

Zal turned around slowly and said, in a voice so convincing Lila barely recognised it, though she knew it was the start of an old song. "I am the god of hell fire, and I bring you . . ."

Nobody got the joke. Lila told Tath the song lyrics to "Fire"—Zal had recorded a version of it six months previously.

It is well they do not know those words, Tath whispered but his attention was barely on what Zal was saying. What he was seeing was plain impossible; a known high-caste light elf with demon attributes and vile Otopian habits living perfectly well in Sathanor. Lila could feel Tath as suddenly fragile, almost disintegrating. She wasn't sure she was ready to know this truth either but there it was, ready or not.

Zal was having a fine time. He laughed. "Dar, do I look sick?"

Dar couldn't answer. Like the others, he was transfixed. Even Arië was motionless.

Proof, Lila said. *I saw it before but I thought . . .*

Desperation, Tath said after a pause. *It is all he has. It is proof indeed, but that will make no difference.*

Why? Lila demanded.

Because the truth is immaterial in this case, Tath said. *Arië will rule Alfheim and nothing that could threaten her claims can be allowed to stand. Zal is a fool. He still thinks that his original mission has some value and that others in power care for the truth. He holds fast to his ideals and dreams. He has sealed his fate.*

"Desist or I will drown you as you stand," Arië said then.

But this has to be more important! Lila insisted. *Look at what it means . . .*

Your naive ways will get us all killed, Tath said coldly. Aloud he said, "Do as she commands."

Zal turned to Tath. "And you, Ilya. Using your skill to preserve the crap that Arië wants all Alfheim to believe, when you know from your dealings with Thanatopia that it's all bullshit. Serving two masters always; your caste and house, her and the Daga, scraping around accepting their condescension, believing that you are abusing yourself for their good when all the time you haven't the faith to trust your own heart. If you did, you wouldn't sit there waiting for my blood to fulfil Interstitial Warp spells when yours would be just as effective in the task. You could have secured power months ago without me if you had the guts to stand up to her and shove her worthless life into the endless dark. You're not just a bastard but a coward. Did she promise you some family connection, promotion and power?"

"We do not kill kin. You are my family," Tath retorted.

"Not anymore," Zal said, and his talent for vocal command lent his words a chill and regret that made Lila's blood run cold. "We are long lost to one another." He snapped his wings shut and they vanished suddenly, one second there, the next gone. In their absence the room was cold.

Tath's hurt was piercing, old as it was, and his resentment and anger hard to contain.

Lila had to fight to concentrate. *Companion of my heart*—her AI returned to her at last: *friendship affirmation, emotional intimacy (first degree), longevity distinction (adult friendship matches only), sexual rapport (second degree, intermittent), bond strength (first degree), connotation (appeasing, persuading), speaker willingly accepts temporary lower degree of power and kudos in relationship.*

Then they used to be more than good friends! Lila thought. Very good. This gets more and more complicated by the second! How old is Zal? How old is Dar? But she had no time to put everything together, yet. She tried to ignore the stab of jealousy she felt towards Dar momentarily, though she couldn't ignore her rage at his lie. Tath gloated, paying her back for her earlier disapproval of him.

"Alfheim's power and strength all come from Aparastil," the Lady was saying, as sweet of tone and manner as though she were hosting a party for her dearest friends. "As any other realm is likewise compelled, we must protect it with our lives. You cannot doubt that."

"You're an idiot," Zal said, as every other elf in the room winced at his Otopian use of language, "What's happening here is the result of policies *you* began years ago and it has nothing to do with other realms. The more you attempt to manipulate the Interspace, the more savage the reactions will become and they will tear Alfheim to bits. Ask any demon scientist. At least they check their facts."

Arië's pretty coral lips curled with anger. "You have abandoned Alfheim and turned your nature to the service of degraded magic and black arts. Your words could exert no compulsion on my mind. What proof have you of your claims? Does Demonia embrace the otherworlds and rejoice in perfect security?"

"Demonia's borders are open . . ." Zal began patiently.

"Because no sane person would enter!" retorted one of the Lady's companions.

". . . open and yes, it does experience ghost crossings and visits of other creatures of the Interstices, and it's fine. Demonia knows that I-space is the glue that binds us, as your willing little slave Ilya knows only too well. Leakage between all the realms is a proper part of their dynamic coexistence. No place can ever be pure. You can't save Aparastil by refusing contact to anyone not descended from the Valar. You should reopen the borders immediately."

"The Saaqaa were never so bad until the Otopians emerged," Arië said. "Every degradation of Alfheim has occurred through contact with Otopia and Demonia, Faery, Thanatopia, and the Void. In the days of earlier Ages we were many times near destroyed by unwise and ignorant efforts to explore the distant places beyond our borders and our eagerness to bring their treasures home. Other races value what we abhor. They all have their own homes and their own power. We have all seen one another and learned. Let them stay in the places they love the best, and not be polluted by what they so dislike in Alfheim."

Zal pulled the chair back and sat down on it. His manner became weary but his intensity didn't alter. "Look at me. I'm still all right. I'm half demon, and I'm still an elf. I can drink the water and I can breathe the air. I can cross into Zoomenon, like any other elf mage, and the elementals come to me. I can live wherever I choose."

"No elf can be half demon," Arië said. "The magical systems are antithetical to one another. Such a harmony is your fantasy, nothing more. You have sustained yourself with frequent transits to Zoomenon, and you would ever be forced to do the same. You cannot live in another realm forever, you will always be coming home and when you can't you must bring it to you. That vile taint is killing you surely, even though you think it so wonderful."

"I'm not dead yet," Zal said and shrugged. "I'm sure I'll get the hang of it before that happens. It's a work in progress."

"You do not deny your reliance on the elementals to restore you, however," Arië said. "You are dependent on them."

"Not nearly as much as you'd like," Zal said quietly, his head dropping forward and jaw biting shut. The muscles in his face hardened.

Arië made a gesture with one hand and the guards came towards Zal. He stood up and the withering contempt in his words was physically painful, even to Lila, as though the words were real weapons. "Of all our family you were always the most fragile. I'd pity you, if I could be bothered, but my patience with you ran out a long time ago, somewhere around the minute you decided it would be better for all of us to scatter and do your dirty work for you at whatever personal cost it exacted from us." He glanced at Dar and his accusation was no less damaging. "You surprise me. I thought you would have had more character than this."

Dar shuddered and went a pale ashen colour. Lila's heart went out to him, but Zal had already let himself be turned away.

There'd better be another chance, Lila told Tath.

One for certain, he said. *Zal succeeded in pushing her off balance. Me too. I think you will get your moment to be a hero. Do not worry.* He sounded grim and was full of self-loathing. Lila felt sick.

The food, which had all gone cold, was taken away and replaced but she couldn't touch it. The court talked around her, of other matters. Lila watched Dar. He was paler than usual, and if the food had savour for him he showed no pleasure in it, pushing it around almost without noticing what he was doing. He glanced at her with a troubled expression and Arië watched the both of them.

Lila began to realise the poverty of the situation she had stumbled into. Surely the Incon must have had an inkling of this petty tyranny being behind Alfheim's oh-so sophisticated political posturing? They had sent her in blind, she thought, and felt resentment knot her stomach. And they must have known much more about Zal than they let on, especially Sarasilien, he would have known Zal was once Jayon Daga if nothing else, and that whatever he was doing it was part of the decay in Alfheim, and deadly. That hurt.

And then she abruptly thought of her family, for no apparent reason, and her would-be grave on the hill. *I am already dead*, she realised, glancing at Dar. *I was expendable. An expensive prototype, a secret, and here's my test run—they're seeing what I'll turn out like when they let me alone*. But then again, sending her so untried into this kind of storm all to bring back one self-destructive elf—that made no sense at all and she doubted her own doubts and shoved them quickly into one of those mental drawers the AI-self provided for such things. For the rest of the almost unendurable meal she pretended that her dog, Okie, was under the table, and that the occasional brush of *andalune* energy that touched her was the feathery hair of his tail.

At last when the court retired to its preparations for the spellcast, Arië summoned Dar and Tath to her. "Zal's change disturbs me greatly," she said. "I am convinced now that he may pose a great danger to us. Perhaps he will attempt some interference with the spell. But if this Game exists between Zal and the Otopian Agent, perhaps it can be used to maintain control of him." For the first time Lila saw Arië look doubtful and, through that moment, saw how tired the Lady was, and how anxious. "Are you sure that the forfeit is the death of love? If so he would lose all loyalty to anything but this abominable creation."

"I am sure," Tath said, and Lila closed her mind around Sorcha's actual words (you will never love anyone else again). Meanwhile Arië's *andalune* was caressing Tath's, grooming Dar's too; Lila saw both of them struggling against the pleasure of her goodwill and approval. It nauseated her that she could feel Tath's resistance weakening under that touch, and to realise how defenceless he was—all elves were—to such rapport from one of higher social rank, of higher power, of greater kudos than they were. For the first time in her experience of them she began to understand some of their behaviour, their weakness, their smooth ways. And meanwhile Tath groomed Arië the same way, increasing her conviction about his statements. Lila had to interrupt to save her own sanity.

What's your game with her?

None of your business, Tath declared.

Do we get our moment with Zal then?

She did not become the Lady of Sathanor because she is easily persuaded or duped. I would not count anything for what it seems now.

Well, I suppose you have to give convincing her your best shot, then. Knock yourself out, Lila said. She distanced herself inwardly from the elf's experience of the aethereal contacts, sure she could not stand another oleaginous moment.

Springing Zal from here and taking him back to Jelly Sakamoto seemed a bizarre goal now, in the face of what she had learned, although she was certain that preventing the spell and saving Zal were mutually compatible goals which her bosses would order her to complete, if only they could communicate with her at all.

And then there was the way she felt, dizzy and sick, longing to touch Zal again, even in passing, even in the dark, anywhere at all and for any reason, all her senses tuned to one another and waiting, as though he was the catalyst that would make her into something wonderful. She tried not to think of that, but it was impossible not to. Even Arië reminded her of Zal, and Dar's presence reminded her of *their* brief intimacy, in which he had *not* rejected her, nor found her unattractive, even if it was all for the sake of getting her here, and even if everything about him was a doubled, tripled front and he was Arië's servant. She held onto that sliver of truth.

"Very well," Arië said finally, withdrawing. "Tath you may try this tactic and exert what power you can, but beware the wild magic effect and any alterations you may decipher in the forfeit. Dar, come with me, and assist us."

Dar gave Tath and Lila a long glance. His *andalune* brushed Tath's and there was a sparkle of communion, but no words. Tath told her quickly, *Dar is afraid. He says her court will create a tenfold cast in the structure of two and eight. You do not know magic, but such a shell casting will give her power to wield that is an order of magnitude larger than ten elf mages could muster. Her court are all well practised, and I doubt many of them are closeted Revolutionaries. Even if they are, they may not be able to effect any help for us. Once Arië is the pearl of that shell there will be no magic in Alfheim she cannot draw on, and she was always a clairvoyant of great skill. We must keep all our thoughts to a minimum and our words yet fewer or she will know all our intents.*

Fantastic, Lila groaned inwardly, trying not to despair as she watched Dar follow the Lady, his face grim.

Lila and Tath followed yet another of Arië's tame courtiers through the palace, down and down through long halls and fish-lined galleries until they were left in a tiny set of rooms on the outer extremity of the palace. These were set so low in the lake that the water looked almost black—a full two hundred metres down, Lila confirmed with a quick burst of radar. Few fish swam towards the candlelight and glowing mineral lamps which lit their cell. It was like being suspended in green night, Lila thought, as she was left alone with Tath, who undid his *andalune* glamour, leaving her feeling suddenly naked even though she wore his clothes. And now she must pretend to seduce Zal and at the same time try and inform him that this was the best plan for escape and he would be suspicious of course, and maybe, in that way of spies who never know what is true or false really, he might not believe her . . .

She took off Tath's clothes and put them on a chest which rested against the inner wall and was partly hidden by a trailing ivy with pale yellow leaves. Neither she nor Tath had great faith in their ability to maintain such a network of disguises. To focus herself she made herself return to the centre of the room and look out.

In the bubble wall's shining reflections she saw herself suddenly, her scarlet hair, red magical stain, and silver eyes shocking and ridiculous against her tan skin and the subtle forest colours of the room. Her singlet and shorts were grubby with mud and other substances, her burned arm looked like an ordinary arm over which candlewax and mercury had run and set in lumps, and, thanks to the distorting effects of the bubble's curve, she also appeared ridiculously stretched out. The sight had an effect on her as though she had been suddenly drenched in cold water. Although it revealed the peculiarly natural look of her blend with her cyborg body, grown to health in Sathanor better than it ever had in Otopia, she was not lovely. No, not at all. She looked like a circus freak. The elves were right about her. How could she have entertained any dream of Zal?

To her surprise she felt Tath wrap a strong blanket around her self-loathing and it was lessened.

No, he said. *Not true.*

Such an unexpected kindness made tears start in her eyes.

Stop it. Are we spied on? Lila asked Tath, turning away so that he would not also be seeing her. She longed for his reassurance to be heartfelt and true, but she knew that his success depended, as hers did, on hanging together, not coming apart at the seams. It was probably only a necessary sop to her damaged ego.

It is likely. He was alert, curious, and Lila could feel him laughing at her remark because, of course she was spied upon—he was there. And that reminded her of the other times he was there and she felt a burst of embarrassment and to cover it up walked briskly towards the wall and began to test its structure and strength. As she stood there tapping the membrane of cajoled surface tension, and watching it generate curved wavefronts in the water beyond, she saw silt in the lake ahead of her stir suddenly and the shadow of a long, sinuous shape go gliding by just beyond the range of the candlelight.

Dragon, Tath said.

Lila didn't know much about dragons. They were so rare everywhere that almost nothing was known to anyone. Generally they were considered lucky, but this was only if you saw them from afar, like black cats and red sunsets. They were the bringers of storms or good weather, and were said to ride rainclouds and live in heavenly abodes at the four corners of the wind. But directions, navigation, weather, and the rest of it all changed depending on the realm, so imagining you knew what a dragon was there for was a tricky business.

It is curious, Tath said as they both watched the lake. *Perhaps it will talk to you. This one has been here a long time, longer than I have been alive.*

It has never spoken to anybody, but Arië considers it the emblem of Aparastil's purity. She values its presence most highly.

Mascots. Cute. How will it talk? Lila asked him, stopping her taps immediately. *I can't talk dragon.*

Dragons are telepaths, Tath told her. *If it wants to, it can easily communicate.*

Have you spoken with a dragon before?

Only once. A conversation I did not understand and was lucky to survive. He shuddered, making Lila's chest feel as though she was having cardiac fibrillation. She took a calming breath. Out in the murk the flash of golden scales glinted for an instant and was gone.

The reflections on the transparent walls changed suddenly and Lila turned around. Zal's surprise was almost comical as the guard pushed him through the door and closed it after him. He stood fast a few steps inside the room and lowered his chin slowly to look her over, taking in every piece of her, from head to singlet to burnt arm to metal legs. His surprise changed to a grin with more than a hint of the demonic about it and Lila's heart surged into high-speed response, her breath lost to her.

"Why Agent Black, this is a very unexpected disaster."

Lila decided that the feeling of nakedness she had had before was an illusion, compared to the one she had now. Zal's grin showed none of the signs of revulsion that the others had. Lila became hot and flustered, unable to speak as she opened her mouth to explain.

You didn't tell me you were in love with him, Tath said, reproachfully. *And you really never mentioned that he was in love with you.*

He isn't in love with me, Lila told him sharply, told herself. The recollection of her reflection was all too keen. She barely noticed Tath's envy, *We don't even know each other. It's only magic.*

Tath laughed at her.

Lila was still locked in Zal's gaze. She felt as though she was literally melting down. She didn't want to show it and she didn't want it to be true. She was hideous, and only some temporary wild magic effect could make him believe anything else.

Wait a second . . . Tath said, but Lila pushed him aside. His contempt for her needy state of being she could live without. She was supposed to pretend love for Zal, at least the Game of it, well, she could do that, and if it seemed real she'd remember it wasn't, and if it was too much then she'd pretend that it was real and get through it that way.

One of the best things about having an AI-self, Lila decided, was that it could make sense of things like that at a time like this.

She lifted her chin and steeled her spine. "I'm here to rescue you."

"I'm delighted," Zal replied, folding his arms across his chest. "And I take it your imprisonment in this maximum-security holding cell wearing nothing but hideous military issue underwear and various burn scars is all part of a masterly plan?"

"Naturally," Lila said. Clearly they could not discuss the plan, even in pretend, and she was having to fight the urge to go closer to him. Was it her imagination or was there a slight citrus fizz in the air? She switched her vision to aetherial sensitivity and saw the telltale vapours of wild magic spiralling slowly up through the floor.

Zal followed her gaze. His look switched back to her and became calculating. "I suppose Dar brought you here?"

"Yes," she said. On an impulse she ran her thoughts through her AI Tath-filter. She wanted to speak with words right for an elf but wrong for Lila, in the hope that Zal would notice and figure out that something was up. "After you were swept away by the phoenix he and his partner came back and we fought. They overpowered me, and brought me here."

"Tricky," Zal said, mostly to himself, and then to Lila, "I lost your kinky bike leathers. Arië burned them. She doesn't look kindly on the wearing of dead animals, no matter how nicely they've been turned into fabulous body-hugging fetish-wear."

"It is no matter," Lila said in her best impersonation of a girl who had been to finishing school and learned Shakespeare, even though she had no idea what finishing school might be like. "You can replace them with like when we get back to Otopia."

"No matter," Zal repeated carefully, exactly mimicking her voice. His dark eyes narrowed and his ears made that horselike motion that laid them perfectly flat to his head. In horses such a move signalled ill temper and presaged a kick or a bite. Lila wasn't surprised when he undid his arms and broke his casual pose to stride forward.

Before Lila knew what was happening, or rather, some time after she had correctly predicted what his movements intended, and had the near-delirious pleasure of a half a second to enjoy the prospect, he seized hold of her shoulders, pulled her close against him, and kissed her hard on the mouth. At the same instant his *andalune* body surrounded and submerged her completely.

Prepared for the shock of seeing him again, of being close to him, even of touching him, she was not prepared for immersion in his aethereal body, nor the way that the *andalune* sweetly invaded her like a trickle of warm water, cell by cell and conduit by conduit. Though it was not compatible with her electrical systems it inhabited the gaps between wires, the biological components of her mechanoid body carrying it as they carried Tath's; changed but whole. Lila was suffused with Zal and, as with Tath's *andalune* contacts, through it she became immediately aware of his state.

She could sense his physical strength and difference to herself, his energy levels, his emotion. He could hide nothing from her, not the fact that he was giving her a psychic frisk for hidden weapons, not the fact that he knew she was in trouble here and that he was afraid they both might die soon, not the fact that he suspected she was possessed or controlled by another, not the fact that touching her in any way intoxicated him so that he could hardly breathe or think. The *andalune* kiss filled Lila's senses until there was no part of her that was not bathed in Zal. He did not love her. It was more than that for him, it was right out there, something he couldn't explain or master. He caressed her. He sang her. Lila floated on him, in a state of complete bliss. Whatever she had done with Dar or any previous boyfriend was nothing compared to this.

A prickle of wild magic coursed up through her power systems. She saw a gold and black pattern in her mind's eye, diamonds and spots. She heard a voice that wasn't a voice, more like a person listening to her, far away, waiting for something to happen, waiting . . . and then she could also feel Tath and his sudden convulsion of fear, like a pressure on her heart.

As condensed as he could be, Tath was locked down into a green light of brilliant intensity but he was also caught in a two-way struggle with his own desires: to make himself invisible to Zal's persistent aethereal investigation of Lila, and to make himself known to Zal, so that they might be able to communicate in secret.

Lila felt this in Tath, and riding on its back yet another layer of his conflicted loyalties that stretched between the Daga, Arië, Alfheim, and Zal. These all strained in different directions, pulling Tath with them until Lila nor Tath had any idea who or what he believed in. Zal's betrayal of Alfheim was personal to Tath, but Zal's words against him hurt a great deal. Tath longed for Zal's approval, or at the very least his forgiveness. Zal was the elder brother that Tath had always wanted but never had.

Lila was astonished, though this was nothing to Zal's incredulity as he saw Tath through her connection and made all the same leaps of understanding himself.

Longing won out in Tath. He relaxed, expanded, and Lila, delirious with the possession of Zal's *andalune*, felt the two beings meet inside her chest.

Zal snapped backwards in shock and left Lila so fast that she had to fight to stay standing. Her body reeled after him, smarting with grief at the loss of his presence, burning with hunger to have it back.

Tath bloomed outwards, almost to the surface of Lila's skin, in a turmoil of emotion.

Zal didn't say anything. He was panting and his upslanted brown eyes were hugely expanded with pleasure and surprise.

Lila didn't trust him or herself to speak, and the only way she knew or wanted to forestall it quickly was to reach out and, this time, kiss him. She put her hands either side of his head, over the beautifully unfamiliar shape of his long ears. It took less than a second to activate the speaker-films inside her palms, as she had done to play the music to Dar. This time she whispered through her hands, "Don't show that you know about Tath, or we're toast. Arië thinks he's here playing me to get you to lose the Game so that you'll lose all your connection to Demonia and go along with her plan."

Lila felt the full gamut of Zal's astonishment and delight in the revelations. It dampened even his guarded self-possession for an instant. His mouth smiled against hers and she saw him, fully present and laughing in the eyes that looked into hers. "Well," he murmured through both the *andalune* and lip contact, respectful and amused, "fuck me sideways."

CHAPTER TWENTY-TWO

Lila's brief lift of spirit and moment of pleasure were broken by a flash of gold in the corner of her eye. The wall beside them bulged inwards suddenly and then recoiled back into place with a snap. A dull boom and vibration rocked the cell and shivered the lake water. She drew back from Zal and turned in time to see the dragon gliding off into the darkness at speed, its tail driving it strongly through the water.

I think it likes you, Tath said drily, though he was jittery with fear.

"The Game magic," Zal whispered to her, "They're attracted by it. We must discharge it or stop. Didn't your friendly inboard necromancer bother to tell you that?"

"He is *not* my . . ." Lila began but she didn't get to finish. A golden face, as big as she was, loomed suddenly from the depths beneath them and slid up the side of the cell wall. The five-pointed black star at the centre of its eye narrowed as the candlelight struck it. Close-to she saw the hairlike fronds of the beard around its long, saurian mouth reach out and feel the bubble-shield of their cell, tasting its magic. It opened its jaws and a long, black tongue dipped between razor-sharp diamond teeth and touched one of the trickles of wild magic that were rising from the deep lake bed. The eye narrowed again and blinked at her.

An idea, in words and images not her own, appeared in Lila's mind and she saw herself and Zal for an instant, as though through a strange lens, every place they touched one another attracting the snap and tang of the wild aether.

Elfheart machine-woman and demonheart elf-man. Walking four worlds inside the forfeit bond. Sing the two, eight, eighteen canticle, the shape of things, the weird of breaths, the soft hand in hand dance, and, as all water is one across the worlds and sings each to each unbroken the lowest notes of sweet lament, we shall bend our mind to thy curious measure.

"What?" Lila said aloud without meaning to as she snapped back to herself and found Tath churning and terrified, a panicking bird inside her chest.

Zal put his hand over her mouth. "Listen," he said.

Lila smacked his hand away. "I *am* listening to the . . ."

"Not the dragon." His long tipped ears were moving subtly and he let her go and moved back. As he did so the dragon abruptly slid away from the wall, its body flashing past and its wake buffeting the cell so that they both had to fight to keep their footing.

She refined the search and tune pattern of her AI hearing.

Arië has seen the dragon alongside us. Whatever we are about to do, we must do it now, Tath told her, back in command of himself now that the dragon had gone.

"Plan?" Zal asked her, raising his eyebrows, body tensed for flight or fight.

Lila ran everything through her AI-system, making the second she actually had into an approximate minute of ordinary thinking time. Like calculating the moves in chess she played and replayed the possibilities and permutations of the situation, but it was so complex she could not see beyond a second manoeuvre anywhere, could not calculate a significant favourable move. Their original idea was as good, or as bad, as anything else.

"Pretend to lose," she said in desperation, hearing the guards' bootsteps outside and the singing of swords being drawn.

Zal dropped to his knees in front of her. Where his hands caught hold of her metal legs she felt the sting of magic crackling, making the candleflames sputter and shoot high into the air. From the green darkness the dragon barrelled out at them as though it was about to ram the wall, then at the last instant ducked beneath. Its bow wave rocked the room as the guards came in. Lila felt Tath reach down through her and connect briefly with Zal. Tath said some elvish words and Zal repeated them under his breath too, humming them into a desolate melody. The coils of aether surrounding them suddenly drew in, as though inhaled by a breath, and the air snapped fiercely with the spit of releasing energy. After it, the wild magic had gone.

Zal slumped down and let go of her as though defeated.

Party trick, Tath said. He was tense and afraid, as Lila herself was, both of them knowing quite well that some, if not all, of their cover was surely gone. Worst of all, they had never got their story straight with Dar. Any wrong move by him now could undo everything. It was a desperate, terrible situation.

The guards took Zal away, and waited only for Lila to reclothe herself in Tath's gear before marching her off in the same direction. As she went she combined a few drugs for herself, to boost her calm, to stop her shaking, to help her maintain her cool. Her supplies of basic composites were running low. She would have to be careful, she thought, and then she felt Tath react to the influx of chemicals in her blood, as though he was truly a part of her.

What did the dragon mean? she asked him, feeling him calm down.

The forfeit bond it spoke of is the Game with Zal. As for the rest I can gather only fragments. A canticle in Thanatopic magic is a summoning or banishing song to command the Dead. The water reference is really to wild magic most likely, although water-element Adepts, like Arië, say that the water in all worlds is one sea. I don't know about the rest.

He spoke rather easily for Lila's liking. She wasn't sure he was telling her everything. She knew what the numbers meant though, remembering her chemistry classes. Two, eight, and eighteen were the numbers of electrons that completed each shell of an atom with three energy levels. But, even though this gave her a fresh insight into the links between magic and science across the realms, it did not help the dragon's statement make any more sense. The time for puzzling was over however.

They had come to a vast cell like a cavern in the lake's black depths. Above them they could see the rest of the Palace of Aparastil shining like silver spheres, glints and glimmers of light dancing within. To all other directions they saw only their own reflections against a black background, with tiny bubbles of air or motes of silt briefly illumined as they brushed against the walls. Glistening pockets of gases from the deep which had become trapped beneath them moved under the clear floor in silvery undulations. They collected like mercury where the floor had been shaped deliberately into the largest and most complicated series of magical circles Lila had ever seen.

There signs and sigils bristled against one another for space and fizzed and glowed in the air above the ground. Artefacts of power: swords, flails, whips, wands, cups, candles, digital crystals, ropes, and witchlights littered every available inch of space to either side of a clear walk that led directly to the heart of the circles. Shrines to the magical elements of earth, fire, water, wood, metal, air, and space were arrayed around the walls. The room hummed with chant and incantation.

Arië's courtiers stood demurely waiting, clad in black and silver. There was a demon there, Lila saw with shock, his sapphire blue skin roiling with lightning streaks beneath its thick surface, his horns curled close to his head and dripping with grey smokes that trailed around him in the air. He was busy at his allotted station, working over a heavy stone thurible, stirring something with a bone held in the curl of his forked tail.

All her mages are here, Tath said. *That one is Zal's replacement, bought or bribed or coerced into action, or a traitor to his kind.*

Who replaces you? Lila asked as she was pushed on towards the Lady herself where Arië stood with Dar and her entourage of attendants.

Tath did not answer.

Tath? But it had already come to her in a moment of horrible insight. There was no replacement for Tath, because he was here.

Lila tried to exert a compulsion on Tath, to make him speak and admit where his loyalty lay, but he resisted her easily. Meanwhile the dragon's words echoed in her mind. Water, water everywhere . . .

Meantime they had been brought to stand in Arië's presence. Her *andalune* body touched Tath's briefly and he was comforted. "Come, Voynassi," she said to him gently, using his honorific name. "It is time for you to resume a better form and occupy a vessel fit for the work ahead and your life beyond. Your sister here agrees to carry you until you can be made whole."

Behind Arië, Lila could see Astar standing absolutely still with terror, *andalune* body completely withdrawn. Dar was expressionless, his aethereal self barely visible to Tath, it was so restrained. He didn't even glance at Lila but maintained his position among the courtiers. Arië held out a white daisy in her hand towards Tath. "Come, Lady Astar, take the hand of this golem and prepare to receive your brother's spirit." Arië's lovely face glowed with warmth and kindness.

Golem! Lila thought, her anger almost igniting despite the rushing cool of the drugs in her system.

Astar came forward, staring into the glamour of Tath's likeness on Lila with a feverish intensity, searching the face for any ounce of hope. Lila knew there was none now, with the possible exception that Arië may not discover the extent that Lila herself was in command of her faculties and not under Tath's power. She saw Dar look at her, his gaze already the vibrant watchfulness of someone who is striving to take in every part of an experience.

The Lady took Lila's hand and placed Astar's upon it over the daisy. Astar's *andalune* surged forward to cling to Tath's and a swift current ran between them. Lila felt herself freeze as Arië sang a few pretty notes and spoke her charms aloud. There was a moment in which all the room waited for the exorcism to begin its work, where every magical being listened and watched.

The daisy was simply a daisy, so the spell was useless. Lila saw the realisation of their deceit dawn on the Lady's face instantly. Behind Arië, Dar had gone ashen. He gave the most minute shake of his head as he looked towards Lila and Tath.

"This flower." The Lady plucked it gently from between the elves' hands. Her manner remained sweet and she spoke as though personally wounded, her eyes beseeching. "It blooms not for thy ransomed life, Ilyatath. Where is your token, that you have falsely given me this one in its place?"

"It was burned in the Hall of Fire. An accident," Tath said. "My sister gave you . . ."

"I well know what she gave me. Her loyalty to you is a shining example and her betrayal of me an exceptional artifice whose skill must be commended. Yours to me however, I find less worthy of praise. Why would you not tell me immediately of its loss?" She made a single gesture with her finger and one guard stepped to Lady Astar's side and took her arm in his hand.

Tath shivered but Lila admired his grit when he said, "I did not wish you to see me bound in life to this form by my own dire mistakes. I would have you think highly of me. I thought that I would find another way out when the spell was done. And my strategies have not failed yet. Zal is broken and here is your most dangerous opponent, his champion, at my command."

"It is pretty reasoning," Arië said, her voice rising a little at the end of the phrase, as though she was considering his words. She let the daisy fall from her hand to the floor and half turned to look back. "Dar. Perhaps you would remind me of how it was you came by this robot and Ilya, and how the three of you came to Aparastil."

Behind and all around them servants were lighting lamps. The demon thaumaturge and the elves at the Otopian and Faery altars had ceased their activities and stood at attention at their stations. Lila kept on looking with all her senses for any way out, for any useful thing. She saw a server approach with a beautiful red and black lidded ceramic dish and stand alongside Arië, face downcast. She looked for heat, but there was none. The container was cold and Lila could not see inside it.

We are lost, Tath said, though he didn't explain. Dread claimed him.

Lila increased her drug dose, to keep her reactions clean.

She watched Dar lie and had to admit he was, to her eyes, completely and utterly convincing.

He said, "I brought Zal's bodyguard from Otopia with me. We were both badly damaged by our struggle. In Sathanor I was made well, at the overnight huts where the Vale of Sinda meets the woods. I pretended treachery to engage the trust of this woman and made her believe we were coming here to rescue Zal. At the Deeps we were attacked by Saaqaa under a dark moon, and there Tath's band caught up with us and we all fought for our lives. The wild magic was particularly bad that night. Tath and his companions were all killed there but, knowing his magical skills, I deceived this woman into taking on his *andalune* body, so that he might use his skill to gain control of her. At the Hall of Fire we sacrificed the flower in order to maintain his binding upon her, else you would have released him easily and she would have had a chance to kill you before you completely understood her nature."

"It would gladden my heart to believe you. I would rival the sun in splendour to count you my loyal friend but, sadly, in these moments of your close presence I can see inside your treacherous mind," Arië said. She reached out and gently removed the lid of the red and black dish. Inside it lay white, glistening concertina curls of sap-rich bark.

Lila did not feel shame, to her surprise. Instead she felt a spark of gladness, because Arië was both sentimental and cruel, a justified opponent instead of a misguided idealist. Lila glanced at Dar. He was expressionless and did not meet her eye.

Everyone in the great hall had become still and silent.

Arië drew Tath's knife from its position at his side and held it out to him, handle first. "I do not wish to command you, but I will."

What? What does she mean? Lila demanded of Tath. There was a new anger inside him, but a hopeless one, full of self-hate.

Leave me to do this alone, he said. *Or share it with me. It is up to you. We have to finish what we began, all of us, in the end.*

He took the hilt and Lila felt her hand close around it, her machine strength the core of his action. He made to move forward but she prevented him, taking back control of her physical movements from him easily, as she had always been able to do.

She could not let herself believe they had come to such a moment as this *No. I forbid you.*

Let me go, and she may yet believe I have mastery over you. This is why she asks it. It is the only way.

I will countermand you then! You can't do this! Lila screamed at him, but at the same moment her AI-self confirmed his words as the best course forwards, if she wanted to remain alive and potentially enabled to save Zal. In the cool runways of perfect, drug-enhanced cognition, her emotions were swept aside. *This is my fault,* she said, and let Tath have control, but stayed with him all the same so that they moved together in a single forward stride, faster than any eye could follow.

Lila was very strong, her aim perfect, her focus absolute. She looked into Dar's eyes as they stood face to face for the last time, her hand firm against his chest where the blade had pierced between his ribs directly into his heart.

CHAPTER TWENTY-THREE

Dar's hands gripped her shoulders. Lila remembered the night in Sathanor, the bioluminescent night, when she had held Dar's heart in hers. Now they were in synchrony again and the blade that was killing him was in her chest. For an instant she felt the wound's terrible pain and Dar's agonised effort to cling to the last seconds of his life. Through their sympathy she was aware of all his energy scattering, his aethereal body fading against Tath's.

Dar was trying to speak to her, she realised, as she saw his lips move. She routed power from her reactor through Tath into her bond with Dar.

"Surely no greater king has ever lived," he gasped, fighting to draw one more breath. "No one with the loving kindness, strength, and courage . . ."

He was gone. His body, became a deadweight, slid off the knife blade with a grating wrench, and fell to the floor.

"What did he mean by that?" Arië demanded.

Lila dropped to her hands and knees beside Dar, letting the knife fall out of her fingers. "Good-bye," she said, in Tath's voice. His final words had cut her to the heart. How many more times was she going to find that people dead were more loyal and true than when they were alive? She wanted it to feel worse than it did because she deserved to hurt but, because of the drugs, it didn't. And at the same moment her smart AI-self noticed that her hands were flat to the bubble's floor.

She set her speaker films to the lowest frequency they were able to produce—something well below even elvish hearing span—and upped the power to maximum. She sent a message in Sheean, the faery language, just three words tuned to their particular tones and scales: Zal Apastil Help The only faery she knew who might collect the message was Poppy, or Viridia at a push. The only chance she had was if the message carried and if they touched water. If the story was true, if Malachi had been right about their faery natures. So many ifs.

Lila felt the Lady's hand on her shoulder. "Your presence is required in the centre circle, Tath. Come with me now."

What about Dar? Lila was jabbering inside to Tath as she got up to obey and handed him overall control. *What will they do with him? Where has he gone? Can't you do something?*

Dar is dead, Tath said. *But we are not. You must concentrate on the matters at hand.*

And now what? What's going to happen?

Now we are going to bleed Zal and bind him to a ley fracture halfway between Alfheim and Interstitial Space. It will not be a physical prison, merely an aetheric one. He will live here in the palace and Arië will look after him like a sacred son all the days of his miserable long life.

But what are we going to do about it? Lila pleaded.

When a moment arises that I think of anything, I will let you know, Tath said. *Come, there are more vile deeds to execute before this trial is done.*

Anguish and grief tightened Lila's jaw. She clung to Tath's self-possession as the effect of her drugs began to fade; she did not have much left and she must save that. But she dare not let go of their artificial restraint on her feelings. She was sure that she would collapse here if she had to face up to what she'd done in any realistic way.

Then do not, Tath ordered her. *Be strong and do what must be done. Time for recrimination and the rest later. Now you must act.*

Surely no greater king . . . she thought. Dar had been telling her to carry on, just as Tath was, even if they could never have been real friends.

Because it was all he could give you at that moment, Tath said. *And if you do not fulfil that command you will have twice betrayed him.*

Arië and Tath had come to the centre of the circles. The other mages had followed them some of the way, each halting within the ring that denoted their particular shell of influence. Two mages stood in the circle beyond the centre. Eight in the circle beyond that. Lila/Tath and Arië were alone in the nucleus, until they fetched Zal.

As he got closer Lila saw his eyes were dilated and sheened in a classic opiate reaction. He was naked above the waist and his face and body were limned in sweat that was making the magical markings drawn on him run in streaks of coloured ink. He was doped, and when Arië took his arms and pushed him down, he sank to his knees on the floor and sat there, head slightly to one side, completely unresisting. His *andalune* body was quite withdrawn, not even projecting beyond his skin. He lolled against Arië's leg like a ragdoll and she stroked his hair absently with one hand as she signed orders with the other. Lila could feel, through Tath, Arië's great anticipation of relief, the pleasure with which she looked forward to the safety and restoration of a world she loved without limit.

Singers and speakers closed the outer shells of the seal, beginning with the least and outer ring, and then the inner ones. As each was completed they hazed Lila's view of the room, spheres of pale mist and aether leaping into instant life around them until, as the inmost ring was made whole, she and Tath, Arië and Zal were enclosed within an opaque bell whose walls shimmered with all colours like mother-of-pearl. This circle, unlike Zal's casts, did not transport them to another realm. It took them outside all realms, outside time, into the Interstitial. They hung nowhere and nowhen, everywhere and everywhen, held within the tidal powers of all seven regions, balanced as though on the point of a pin.

Finally Lila understood what Tath had meant when he called Arië the pearl, but she did not feel pearl-like herself. As her blood reverted to normal she felt cold and alone. She most longed to go home and to never have come anywhere near Alfheim.

You need not stay, Tath said to her and lifted their hands upwards to his jerkin. Lila witnessed herself opening hidden pockets on its front, lifting out the instruments they had always contained and which, until now, she had never even discovered. *I will do it.*

I *will goddamn well do it. Whatever the hell it is*, Lila said. The only shred of self-respect left in her demanded it. She could not let someone else take the blame.

She saw the things she held in Tath's glamoured hands: a length of bone carved into the ornate handle of a pen, the nib point replaced by an obsidian flake of black glass; a hollow crystal needle, like the ones she had used on Dar, but this one bigger and mounted between straps of fine leather upon which magical writing oozed and ran like liquid. The needle was slant cut at one end, ready to puncture, but the other end broadened and fanned out, the thin walls becoming liquid at their limits, then so thin that they evaporated. They were light to hold, but she felt them weigh on Tath suddenly and her hands drooped beneath the load.

The bone was his bone. The leather was his skin.

You're kidding, Lila said. Tath didn't say anything.

Around them in the ring the songs merged suddenly and became a single chanted line. Mesmeric syllables spun the pearl wall faster and beside him Tath felt Arië's energy suddenly intensify. And then the Lady of Aparastil began to sing.

She had the clear, sweet voice of a young girl. Her melody was sad and lonely, a heartbreakingly lovely lament such as Lila had never heard in her life. What words in High Elvish that she sang were borne on notes of such purity that they seemed to pierce all matter and Lila felt the song in her bones and in her circuits, in every cell and unit, all resonating where they were able, amplifying and harmonising with the spell until Lila was part of the charm, bound to it in synchrony against her will, and Tath with her, and Zal with them. The faint idea she had held of shooting Arië point blank seemed impossibly distant to her. She could never destroy anything like this, and she wanted to listen to it go on and on in any case, to let the song transport her to the places that it promised, so good and far from all this.

Tath bent down before Zal. Lila felt her hands take Zal's right arm and rest the forearm on her knee.

The faintest zip of wild magic, barely more than a flicker, ran down through her leg and up into her body. The note Arië was singing wavered ever so slightly. Zal's dreamy expression didn't alter.

Keep that in check! Tath pleaded. *This must not get out of hand.* He pressed the pen blade to Zal's skin and wrote quickly down the length of white skin from elbow to wrist in a series of flashing gestures. Blood spat from the nib. Zal groaned and his eyes rolled up in his head. The slashes stood out clearly for a moment or two and then began to blur deep scarlet. The characters were all from the Thanatopic alphabet. Where Zal's blood leaked from them it ran a short distance and then began to bubble and evaporate into a fine dark haze. The haze coiled and flicked. It drew wicked faces in the air and they spoke to Tath, though Lila could not understand a single word.

Meanwhile Lila fought the lull of Arië's song, but whenever the urge to shoot came close, the pretty sound pushed it away from her. She used the AI bypass, thinking Arië's magic was working on her feelings, but it made no difference when she locked herself in her AI mind. Only Tath moved, and he let go of that arm and took Zal's left arm up instead and wrote on that too, and spoke to the dark faces that emerged. She had given up hope that Tath would help her now. She doubted he even could, but she was wrong.

Play something. Anything! he said to her. *You must drown her out and take back your will.* At Lila's unspoken question he added, *Thanatopic immersion at least has the virtue of blocking all other charm. If you are to do anything you must do it soon, before her song is finished, for then the pearl will break and whatever is done remains.*

Lila didn't have the energy to search for a song. She simply accessed whatever played last, and turned up her internal systems as loudly as she could. Loud rock music beat through her head. The bass and drum negated Arië's languorous rhythms and the piercing guitar took out most of her midline.

Lila's mind cleared a little. She remained inside her AI-self, and took a long, calculated assessment of conditions. Then she searched every part of her systems.

Tath put the pen nib into her mouth and she felt a burning lick of pain as it cut her tongue.

All Thanatopic magic requires blood. Aloud he spoke again to the twisting figures that danced in the burning of Zal's blood and now the words he used took on form also, and became creatures that walked across the air and danced with the creatures Zal made. It was most interesting.

A wisp of pale green energy appeared at the junction of Lila's leg and Zal's dripping arm. Its appearance made the dark dancers pause and eagerly look its way. One or two of them zipped down towards Zal's wounds and began to burrow back in.

No! Tath reacted instantly, his voice and speech changing. Faster than she would have thought him able he slashed at her upper arm with the pen blade where her flesh met metal, and drew another ghostly djinn from the wound with whispers. At his direction it darted forward and where it touched Zal the blood ran faster from him and the tiny genies were pushed back. They were pushed back, but they grew larger, and stronger. *I told you to keep that in check!* He was almost panicked.

I need my hand for a moment, Lila said, increasing the volume as Zal's voice began to sing in her head, and replaced the pen in Tath's pocket. She put her hand to the floor, where water supported them above the gulf, the lake itself hidden completely by the pearl shell. She channelled the Mode-X music down into the lake in a sequence burst: two, eight, eighteen pulses. If she was right, if she had started to understand it, then magic was the user and their will, no more than that. A canticle was a summons, and she was calling.

Give me that back! Tath reclaimed her limb immediately. He took hold of Zal's wrist in his hand, set the crystal spike against the vein in his elbow, and pushed it through the skin, not very hard. He didn't need to, because as the instrument made contact it leapt from their hand and drove itself home, as though it was alive.

Zal shrieked, a terrible, multitonal cry of agony, as Tath bound the crystal to his arm. Bright scarlet blood ran down into the instrument's tiny pan and where it fanned out into the air its surface ran with bright red and golden flames. No smoke or genies came from it. Where the crystal pen seemed to become thin air the flames did too, vanishing from Alfheim, Lila realised.

Flowing into Interstice, Tath said grimly, watching the Demon flicker. "*All done, brother.*"

Arië's song stopped. There was a sound like the distant boom of a buried atomic bomb and a second later an aetheric wavefront passed through them, momentarily disabling Arië and Tath equally, obliterating the genies that had been skittering around, leaving only the burning flow from Zal's arm. Zal's body seemed to waver, as though it was passing into another reality, and Lila saw a shadow come over him.

It is his Death, Tath told her.

With the passing of the wave the shadow drew away again, lost in the tide.

At the same instant Lila began to rise and ready her guns, all pretences dropped. She felt within her body the cool, insistent pressure footprint of a major spellcast and then, as her metal and machine parts continued their action, her flesh and bone suddenly stopped and there was a blinding and devastating pain. It didn't entirely surprise her. She had suspected that either the energy Arië had had to use for the spell or the wild magic intrusion had given the game away.

Tath read the impact before she could.

Arië has bound your body not to oppose her. She can't command the metals, only the rest of you. If you try to move against her physically now, you'll tear yourself to pieces.

Lila didn't even pause. As she heard Tath, she retargeted, gaining her freedom, and shot the floor. The bullets punctured the tension easily but it didn't break. Where they went through it weakened however, and her foot suddenly plunged downward to the knee into the bitterly cold lake water. She was almost through.

At that moment something struck the pearl shell from beneath and it broke into a million glittering shards.

CHAPTER TWENTY-FOUR

Lila was falling, her feet no longer supported by the water. At high process speed she stretched time out for herself and felt the Lady's willpower, strengthened and aetherised, pushing her and Tath down into the lake. She didn't need them any more. Lila did not attempt to counter Arië's supreme force or struggle to stay within the palace. She simply placed her hand around Zal's ankle as she fell past his sprawled, bleeding body, and locked it in place, dragging him after her into the icy water. Heavier than any human or elf, or any being twice her size, Lila fell like a stone.

Gold and green lights far away winked at her in the instant of silent calm as they plunged into the depths. She looked down and, on radar, sounded the bottom, only there was no bottom . . . She looked up and saw the silver palace of air above them receding gently. And then the water convulsed around them and boomed with a grating, grinding sound like planets colliding. A powerful electromagnetic pulse followed, so powerful that it momentarily knocked out all her machine self and left her reeling inside, alone, with Tath. The ends of readouts and the simple obliteration made for an easy calculation of the cause.

Faultquake! Lila shrieked at Tath.

But Aparastil . . . he began

Sathanor's not on a regular fault or even an aetheric ley, you idiot. Don't you do geology? The whole thing is a crater. This is the Quantum Bomb crater as it manifests in this dimension and we're falling into the biggest nonrecorded fault in the whole history of faultlines! How could you live in this thing and not know?

There was a second in which she felt Tath bristle.

Arië was the keeper of such knowledge and her word . . .

She lied! Lila frantically tried to reconnect with her systems but all of them had died. The reactor, presumably, ran on but she couldn't find it. She couldn't feel her arms below the elbow, her legs below the first few inches, half her spine seemed to be missing, her internal organs felt as though they were being crushed by a deadly, numbing cold, and she was suddenly very, very short of breath, *Tath, you've got to help me!*

Now! Lila screamed at him. Her lungs and body were aching, burning. She didn't know how much longer she could prevent herself trying to breathe. A second trembling ran through the ground and the lake.

Tath's *andalune* surged outwards. Though Lila could only sense it in her human body she could feel the desperate energy with which he focused himself and drove up through her arm and shoulder. At such densities and concentrations the aethereal was capable of becoming corporeal and Tath's form of magic, the lively art, was more able than most to manifest strong forces through the shaping of raw aether. Shaping himself was only a variation. If he had still possessed his own body it would have been routine. Without it he had to spend himself in making the effort. Lila felt his presence flicker and weaken. But his ghostly hand extended up and up, beyond the rigid lock of her manacle on Zal's leg, up to his arm where the flechette was bound. Tath said a word and a darkness, a final shadow, dragged at her heart. She felt part of her life leaving her as the flechette disintegrated.

The binding is undone, Tath informed her weakly. *But his lungs have collapsed. He drowns.*

She tried again and again to find any connection that could operate, counting away the seconds. How could it take so long? There must be a mistake . . .

And then at last she heard her AI-self's voice: **Countdown to automatic restart commencing. Five, four, three . . .**

. . . and then the world shook and boomed again and another pulse tore silently through them and the voice was gone.

Lila opened her mouth and the water of Aparastil filled it as she tried to suck it into her lungs. She failed. Her lungs were too compressed to hold anything. Detached and dreamy, knowing this the final stage of asphyxia, the dream and the hallucination, she wondered what they would think at home when they found out, only they wouldn't find out of course, because she would be falling forever, and in any case, they thought she was already gone . . . She wanted to sleep. Yes. Just for a minute. After so much fighting, surely she deserved a minute? She began to drift, but an annoying voice, an annoying sensation in her chest, wouldn't leave her in peace.

Tath was talking to her, in a stupid foreign language that wasn't remotely like elvish or Otopian. Everything was sibilant, like hissing snakes. The vowels were owlish, hooting, soft.

Shut up, she said to him. *Why won't you just shut up?*

Oolerathan sirssalliel, Tath said softly, coaxing her. The words tied her up and drew her closer to him. They opened tiny doors inside, onto sweet darkness that was not of the lake at all. They offered pathways. She saw lights within them, beckoning her. **Sirmasenna, sir-masenna, abrayuth manmayess.**

Just like the dragon, she remembered. She hurt. She was beyond tired. *Let me go.*

Abrayuth Lila Amanda Black. Abrayuth set imma. Manmayesim.

She saw Dar's face. Not the face of her dreams that had tormented her. The face of his death, stretched in pain. *Leave me alone!*

Countdown to automatic restart commencing. Five, four, three, two, one. Main power online. Auxiliary power online. Automedic enabled. Emergency autorespiration enabled.

Lila struggled against the colossal weight of anaerobic toxins in her blood, against the need to sleep still clogging her mind. Around her the world, which had been no bigger than a mote of dust, expanded into vast, lightless space. They were still falling—more than 230 metres down.

Lila pulled Zal's body against her and held it to her side with her left arm, then ignited her foot jets and began to drive them upward, ascending as fast as she could. As she did so she ordered the last of her drug precursors to synthesize adrenaline, Terbutalin, and other pharmacological agents that aided rapid decompression.

Tath, frail as candlelight, stretched out inside her, and kept up his whispering, to Zal this time. **Abrayuth Azrazal Suhanathir Taliesetra. Abrayuth set imma. Manmeyesim.**

Selecting the biggest needle from her store, Lila activated her wrist injector, found Zal's neck, located his artery with precise ultrasound, and pushed in, tangling her fingers in his hair to stabilise his head and neck against her arm. His pulse was very slow, very weak, heart almost stopped, but the cold and the opiates and Tath had saved him so far.

Lila could run her own blood through a nitrogen scrubber to save her from the bends. The same system was now flooding her with necessary oxygen whilst replacing much of what she would normally have needed with helium, oxygen being toxic at depth. She shifted her hold on Zal and switched usage on her secondary forearm systems, dropping and dumping her gun and its ammunition into the lake, replacing it with another wide-bore catheter which she inserted into the other side of his neck. She shunted her blood back around away from the gas exchange system and ran Zal's blood through it instead, not even pausing to consider the effects of contamination. She had to get up, and she had to get up very soon.

And so they went, breathing alternately with Lila's machine system, stopping often in their ascent as the nitrogen built and dispersed, held in life by Tath's commands against death. As they ascended they drew after them a long, lambent tail of wild magic and after the tail came the golden and black gliding shape of the dragon. Lila saw it suddenly as she held at 210 metres, the palace above her, the water around them full of bodies, and artefacts and clutter, trapped beneath the bubble's silvery bulk. Fascinated in spite of her fear she stared at it as she pumped Zal's blood through her arms and back into him, waiting for him to wake up or show any sign of life, listening to his slow, weak heartbeat . . .

Don't look at it. You know better than that, Tath said, breaking his canticle.

But Lila didn't need to look at it. She smiled as the dragon came up on them and then wound around them, wild magic from the deep streaming off its flanks, sparking on her arms and legs, in her hair, against the metal surface of her eyes.

Zal shuddered against her and only her thumbs locked against his jaw prevented him from trying to breathe the lake. His eyes opened, but she doubted that he'd see much with his unmachine sight, a few gleams. He could feel the cold vice of her around him however, and the pain of his many cuts.

"It's all right," Lila said through her hands into the bone of his skull. "I've got you."

It is not all right, Tath amended gently and, with dismay, Lila saw the dragon's lazy winding around them change into a full-on charge towards the bubbles above.

Something Arië said upset it maybe? Lila asked him, but she rolled onto her back away from their vertical position and drove them away as fast as she could through the water. She didn't see the Dragon or its impact on the Palace, but she felt it. There was a high-pitched vibration, and then a world was falling.

As Lila felt Zal's hands catch hold of her waist the first object struck them. It was the stone altar of Earth. Lila rolled and fell with it, fighting out from under. Zal's grip fell away on the left, tightened reflexively on the right. But then they were in the midst of a storm of falling debris—every piece of furniture, every object, every person who had inhabited the Palace of Aparastil was now within the lake, and those below fifty metres were simply sinking, as bodies will when they reach a certain depth. The heaviest things sank the fastest. Lila and Zal received a battering. Amid the furore Lila felt the water itself surging, trying to tow her with it as it responded to Arië's summons. The lake queen was drawing undines to her aid, huge bodies of lakewater, animated by her will, though they were weakening as the mages who had bound themselves to her drowned, one by one.

Astar! Tath thought, and Lila inwardly moaned with the very idea of trying to do more than survive. To their left and right, back and front, materials fell and bumped and bashed them. Something heavy smacked the side of her head and she reeled, seeing stars. She missed her pump switch and Zal blacked out again.

There was a moment or two of floating weightlessly, beginning to fall again. Through radar and sonar and heat-sensors she saw Arië propelled towards the surface in a twisting eel-like vortex of water, and she saw the dragon's golden arrow tear through that column, its huge mouth agape. It seized Arië in its jaws and, without pause, turned to face gravity and plunged down and down into the dark until it was lost to all sight.

Lila restored Zal's oxygen and boosted the level of it in the tri mix. She added the last dregs of her pharmacopoeia as opiate antagonists and began the long journey up towards the light. They rested at forty-metre intervals, waiting for the nitrogen bubbles in their blood to abate. At 180 metres Zal's hands came back to Lila's waist. It was discernibly green here, and Lila could see him in normal vision as the faintest ghost in front of her.

"It's still okay," she said to him through her hands. "Don't worry about the pain. It's only pressure. You'll be fine." It was a lie. She thought that the pressure and depth would have burst his eardrums—though he should still hear through the transmission of his skull—and the pumping system kept having to speed its game. Zal was bleeding out, right in front of her.

The catheter I used prevents healing, Tath said to her, simply as an explanation. He did not mention Astar again, but Lila kept scanning for her. She could not remove her hands from Zal's neck and head. She kept Zal on an extra cycle and rose through another fifty metres in ten seconds flat, constantly adjusting the oxygen mix. They kept bumping palace debris that sank very slowly or floated. Dead bodies were there, but Lila didn't look at them. She knew Astar must be among them. Knew it. And Tath did too. He became very still and silent.

At fifty metres Zal suddenly moved closer to her, the drift of water between their bodies vanishing, its cool replaced by warmth. His eyes were heavy-lidded, but the corners of his long mouth flickered with the hint of a smile. His lips, blue tinged, parted slightly and she saw him swallow.

Drink the water, Lila, Tath said suddenly. *He is trying to tell you.*

She did. Vigour and health surged into her. She didn't care to think about what would have happened to them if they hadn't been submerged in a lake of such intense aetherial properties. Long dead.

Zal's smile deepened and he pushed forward against her hands. His arms slid around her. She didn't believe what she felt. Here was Zal, cut, bleeding, half-dead, catheterised, drugged, cyanotic, but against her she could feel the unmistakable line and press of a serious erection. His *andalune* body caressed her so lightly she could have mistaken it for currents in the water, but this moved beneath her clothing.

Demons adore such straits, Tath said with appalled fascination.

She decided to ignore it and took them to the surface, turning her face to the light and air as it came down to her, holding Zal away from her as she cycled his blood and rebalanced it to elfin normal. The fresh day broke against her face and she gasped for real, clear air.

In front of her Zal coughed and groaned with pain. They floated for a moment on the power of Lila's jets and then she drew back both needles with a whir and snap. Zal gasped and his head rocked as she let him go and took hold of him more securely around his midsection. Keeping them high in the water she quickly found his right arm and pressed her thumb down on the open wound, sealing it shut. Zal smiled faintly at her, barely conscious.

"Are we at my two minutes of charity yet?" he asked. And then he disappeared.

He was seized so fast that Lila barely noticed it as he was torn from her weak hold and pulled down again. Then something tough grabbed her foot and dragged her under.

She was swallowing water, her hands battering lost items, getting tangled in scarves and clothes, hitting wooden things, hitting dumb flesh limbs. Lila was so tired.

"Battle Standard," she said and felt the elfin clothing of Tath's be cut to shreds as all her capacities and weapons expanded to their maximum extent. The water boiled around her and the grip on her foot vanished.

You called Each Uisge! Tath exclaimed, jolted out of his grief into a breath of hysteria at her stupidity. *Otopian mania! Do you know nothing?*

Zal's friends, Lila amended, diving down and boosting power with grim and certain intent. She could see the two faeries ahead of her, their beautiful black horse forms with their finned feet and streaming hair wrapped fatally around Zal's pale body. His hot blood made a trail that was easy to follow. She had not known about Poppy and Viridia being deadly hunters, but even if she had, they were her only possible allies.

In human form perhaps. In water or their true body they remember nothing but the hunger. You are insane! All this, and now they will drown him and rip him to pieces and leave you his liver as a keepsake.

Like hell they will, Lila said, *Unless I'm mistaken, you can knock them cold.*

In Otopia maybe, Tath said. *In Aparastil . . . no Each Uisge has ever come here. They are of the water, Lila. They are in their element.*

The water horses dived fast but Lila's rocket boots were faster.

As she neared them she noticed that they were slowing, their easy glide becoming sluggish and dull—they were falling asleep, just as they always did around elves when their *andalune* bodies made contact with faery flesh. It would have been funny if she hadn't been so exhausted, and in some other time and place.

She caught the water horses that were once Poppy and Viridia around their fine necks and, as the hair tried to tangle her arms, wrapped her legs around Zal and swept her hands through their manes, cutting the hair clean through. The faeries fought and struggled to recapture them both but they could not get a good enough grip.

This time she took Zal up fast, not looking or caring what they hit, not pausing at the surface but leaping up and out into the waning light of late evening. She set them down at some distance inland, at the clearing where she and Dar had stopped before entering Aparastil. There she laid Zal on the sweet blue-green grass.

The wounds on his arms were all gone, except the single puncture that still bled freely. It was incongruous there, in the delicious peace of the wooded grove, in the scented twilight. Lila tried not to notice how beautiful Zal was, how his vulnerability made him almost perfect, that she wanted him, like this and here, when he was barely even there. She didn't want to be that person.

How do I fix it?

You cannot. I will, Tath said. Even he was a shadow of his former self. Lila regarded with horror the degree to which he had faded. It was only with the greatest effort that he managed to extend his aetherial presence outward through her. He spoke in the dragon's language. The wound in Zal's arm stopped flowing. Lila felt Tath sink lower, lower, shrink down to almost nothing.

Tath!

He didn't respond.

Songbirds swept across the glade, calling their last calls of the evening. A soft blue mist rose among the grass and there was loveliness everywhere, everywhere.

"Zal?" Lila said, kneeling beside his head. He was unconscious.

Like she used to do for herself she went through the routines of checking, this time doing it for him. With ultrasound she located the meridians in his body, scanned and found his deafened ears, some damage to his heart, peculiar resonances that might have been unique to him, or a kind of ruin—she didn't know what. Her hands, multisensory, glided above the surface of his skin and she willed him well. For herself, she felt almost perfectly healthy, in a fresh and glowing way, the way she recognised of Sathanor, that had never been before she had come here. Her own body was well in itself, for the first time perfectly harmonised, biometalloids and flesh seamless, as though they were always meant to be this way.

Finally she had nothing left that she could do. She sat back on her heels and slowly watched her Battle Armour power down and withdraw into normally sized limbs, ordinary shapes. "Please wake up," she said to him, in her own voice. But he did not.

After a few moments she heard sounds from the lake. Poppy and Viridia, getting out to come looking . . .

Lila bent down and picked up Zal in her arms. She held him gently, close to her, and carried him away into the night forest, away from hunting faeries and hunting Saaqaa, wherever the path took her, seeing and avoiding all the soft trails of lemon and lime magic that twisted and danced in the moonlit air.

CHAPTER TWENTY-FIVE

"It's all right, Lila. Lila, you can put me down." Zal's voice was laced with melodic cadences that rose above and sank below the true tone, a curious effect that made Lila feel sleepy, as though she'd been drugged. She could barely understand his words, but the music filtered into her limbs and slowed them down. All her perceptions misted and fogged away from the battle-vision's piercing clarity and she came to a halt like a heavy horse, one last footfall sinking gently into the soft earth beneath them.

Lila stood in a silver place underneath a full moon shining, more brilliantly and through less pollution than any moon in Otopia had ever shone. She glanced at Zal, realised that he was all right, and that she was too, and set him down. The night was very quiet. Around them the trees and bushes soughed gently in a light breeze. Their scents—tobacco flowers and dark jasmine—twined around them both in heady sweetness. There was no sight or sound of other creatures nearby. Everything was indigo, violet, purple, and royal blue; the grass and the trees reaching high above her with their massive span, the thickets of broadleaved plants clustering close in the moonlight, their two shadows inky on the ground.

Zal stood very shakily on his own and rested for a moment with his hands on his knees. His breath was quick as though he was the one who'd been running. "You need to rest."

"Me?" Lila said. "No."

Without motion she felt empty, like a jug that had been poured out and cleaned and set aside. Without direction she did not know what was important in this scene she was in. It was so strangely quiet without the shrieking, screaming elves swimming amid the palace ruins, scrabbling to gather themselves on the lakeshore, staggering around like crazy people, fighting one another in panic. The fury of their grief and recriminations was written on her eardrums in a precise, pretty language that had burned her inside.

Yes, now it was very quiet, Lila thought appreciatively, and her body sang with the vitality of Sathanor and with raw power from the reactor core, machine and flesh indistinguishable to her now. Everything was running smoothly, though things did seem to be at a remove from her. She liked that. She liked it a lot. She liked her cool mind. "I'm fine. Been in the health farm pool. You know, I'm just fine."

Zal straightened up and drew a deep breath, "I know. Me too. But let's pretend."

Lila shrugged. His words made sense enough though he was speaking in a rather exaggerated way. Still, she took no offence— thinking he must perhaps have PTSD or another related issue, particularly after what had just occurred. Why not? She had nothing else to do, no mission goal left, though she would have expected there to be some orders about returning home. There were none however. Pretend to rest. Even so, the sense of something being wrong niggled at her. "Here?"

"Why not here?" he said.

She looked around automatically and then, finding no dangers, folded her legs and sat down.

"Flatter," the elf said, sitting beside her. His voice was very quiet, as if he was speaking to a frightened animal—a thing she almost resented, or rather, got the impression she would have resented, in another life. "Lie down."

"I'm perfectly fine. I'm not scared. I'm not tired. I don't need to."

"I know. But I do, and it would make me feel much better if you did too. So, do you mind?"

"No, I don't mind." It was pleasant and easy to have a direct, simple instruction, much nicer than having no instruction at all, Lila thought as she complied. The ground gave gently under her weight and the grass bent under her skin, cool and faintly prickly. The soil was damp and there was a gathering of misty vapour among the tiny leaves which chilled her a little, condensing on her metals. She liked it here, but it was difficult to lie this way with all her weapons in assault mode. Her armaments scored and cut the earth and separated her from its welcome. Lila downgraded her defensive conditions and listened to the soft whirr and snicker of a billion perfect metal parts shifting back into her civilian body, smoothing her skin, making her comfortable. If only the nagging sensation in her mind would be quiet she could sleep here.

"On your side," Zal said perfunctorily, and she obeyed without thinking—having once accepted his instructions, she found herself glad for more. It was a relief to be told what to do.

He lay behind her and matched his long tall body to the shape of hers, knees bent; spoons. He negotiated a position for his arm around her carefully, avoiding the hard metals of her forearm and outer hip on the upward side. Carefully he undid the front of the elvish jerkin she wore and slid his hand underneath its tatters. She felt his fingers work to push her vest up a few inches, so that he had skin to skin contact with her at her waist and then the soft, warm touch of his *andalune* spread out from there, covering her over in seconds like the world's softest, most intelligent smart blanket. It was curiously asexual, this contact, kind and concerned but no more than that and it made her smile just a little. She predicted its likely motivations, recalled her previous encounter with this, and began to explain that she was quite healthy and in no need of medical assistance. "You don't need to . . ."

"Just shut up, Lila. This is my hometown and I'm going to look after you here," he said, back in his most normal voice, elf in sound, human in word, demon in temper. "Elven hospitality, if it still works after that hook-up with unreality. Here's hoping."

Unreality? Her AI mind didn't know how to process that. Everything was real that could be perceived and there were no immediate threats. She responded to the part she did understand. "I don't need to be looked after. I'm looking after you. That's my assignment and that's what I'm doing."

"Yeah, I got that," he drawled as if he didn't believe a word she was saying.

The gentle, downy sensation of the *andalune* presence began to sink down into her as though it was melting through her skin like butter. There was something weird about it—more weird than usual even, as though Zal was connected to Sathanor, as though all of Alfheim was holding her through him, or more like he and it were temporarily concurrent, like two solutions to a single equation. She didn't like it. It was too big. It was too elfy. Magic ran through it and magic was both untouchable and unpredictable. She didn't want to be there now.

"Stop . . ."

"Stick a sock in it," he said patiently. "And turn off whatever Ninja Assassin program you've got running that's making you act like GI Jane on acid. Do you want that treacherous little shit to live, or don't you?"

For a split second Lila had no idea who he was talking about. Then what he said sunk in and she realised that Battle Standard was operational. She'd forgotten it was on, didn't even remember cueing it. With numb efficiency she executed the commands to disable it.

Virtual Warrior Suite closing down. Normal Status resuming.

Guilt flooded her, but it had a hard time getting anywhere because of the suffused pleasure of Zal's *andalune* body, occupying all the space Tath had once occupied. "Tath?" she said aloud, to him and to Zal.

There was no response from the place Tath used to be. "You mean Tath!"

"Yes, him. Unless there's someone else here I don't know about," Zal snapped, completely unable to disguise how exhausted he was and how angry.

"He saved your life, you know."

"Don't even start, girl. Hold still."

While Lila could not find Tath at all, Zal located the echo of his spirit easily. Zal's *andalune* wasn't like Tath's, or Dar's, Lila recognised. It had a sparky quality to it, glowing at strange, half-glimpsed levels, like far-off cities in her mind where night skies were alight with dark red and amber warning flares. It flowed harmlessly, smoothly, an ocean of potential.

Zal breathed energy back into Tath, though Tath fought it every inch of the way. Tath wanted to die, had thought he already had. The fact that it was Zal reanimating him made him furious and shamed, but as soon as he had enough strength to do it he turned, as fast as a snake, and began dragging on Zal suddenly, sucking energy through him as though he couldn't get enough. He *pulled* Zal towards him through the aetherial current and, with a filament of words, bound them for an instant.

Lila, inhabited by both of them, watched their fusion and felt the triple shock of it: Tath hating and loving Zal, Zal mostly furious with him, the two of them locked in something like a territorial war with Lila the landscape. The energy and the emotion suffused her body, intoxicating. There was a flash and recoil. She smelled brimstone and Tath was once more the bright green burn of resentment he had been in the first instant they were fused together. Zal's contempt for him was blistering.

"Now," Zal said to Tath. "Be a sweet boy and go to sleep." He did something devious to Tath's energy body and Lila felt Tath slump eagerly into dormancy, ready for oblivion if it meant escaping Zal's regard. To Lila, Zal said wearily, "If you poke him hard, he'll wake up. So don't poke him."

"Poke him?"

"You know what I mean." Zal withdrew his *andalune* and sighed. She felt him relax.

Oh, she thought sadly, Is that all it was for? To save Tath? She wanted him to come back, but had no idea how to get there from where she was. But, as it had done before, the conjoined healing therapy of Sathanor left her exhausted in mind and spirit. Lila struggled to stay awake, even though she was colder now. She took some confidence from the fact that his arm was still around her, his hand on her, his body close and warm against her back. "Zal?"

"Yes."

She could tell by his voice that his eyes were closed. That was a strange thing, she thought. Or perhaps it was in the deepening relaxation of his body. "How come you can hear me?"

"Through my skin. It's dull as hell, and everything sounds like we're living in glue, but it works, just like yours."

She thought he was opening his eyes, more awake than he had been a second ago, and then he lifted his hand from her waist and gently brushed heavy strands of wet hair back from the side of her face. Suddenly she wasn't drowsy at all. She was fearful of breaking this moment of apparent tenderness and stumbled somehow in the simple words, "Does it hurt? Your ears I m-mean."

"What do you think, Einstein?"

Be practical, said a voice in her head. Shut up, Lila thought to it viciously. "I haven't got any drugs left. And your heart . . ."

"Is like a sponge, but it's still working." Zal's fingertips caressed her cheek so softly they barely touched it. They traced the shapes of her face with a sensuous gentleness she had never been touched with before, passing over her ordinary skin and the magical stain and the filaments of metal beside her temple without pause. Not even her mother . . .

Without the slightest warning Lila suddenly felt an enormous surge of emotion. It was so overpowering that she had no defence against it. She didn't even know what it was. It was too strong to identify, too intense to bear. Tears welled and burst from her eyes and heat flared across her exposed skin. She couldn't breathe or see anything. She was as rigid with fear and shock as a rabbit about to be run over by a truck.

Zal's flutelike voice seemed to come from another world, one that obviously didn't contain her, because it was one where thought was still possible. "I always wondered what you'd look like if you didn't have your pain locked up in your face."

Lila could not speak. Tears streamed unchecked from her eyes. She hoped he wouldn't stop, and at the same time, if she had been able to move, she would rather have knifed him than have him continue now he'd given a name to her agony and released it into her mind. Zal's touch opened all her self-loathing and her anger, everything she'd never said to Dr. Williams or Sarasilien, everything she'd never ever let make it through from the inside of her to the universe of thoughts, in case it sneaked into words and one day gave her away. "No," she moaned.

"You don't mean it," Zal said softly.

His touch was so lovely, it was killing her. "Please."

"Ah, you mean that," he said and she felt him lean up on his elbow to look at her. His move freed her from her immobility.

"Stop!" She rolled around towards him suddenly. Her hands were locked around his neck and she could feel his pulse under her thumbs and his breath moving carefully beneath her palms.

Zal's face was calm and gently intent on hers. He blinked slowly, soporifically, without the slightest reaction to her hold on him, and continued his exploration of her face and neck on the other side he hadn't been able to touch before. She stared at him, shaking, "What are you doing?"

His slanted, large eyes flicked to make contact with hers, teasingly, seriously. They flirted with a smile, narrowing slightly from the lower edge, and then they went back to work. "Making love to you. I thought it was obvious." He opened his lips and took a thoughtful breath. His fingers drew their patterns on her forehead, around her eyes, across her cheeks, connecting things, solving things. He watched the place he was touching with absolute concentration.

Her hands on his neck became slack. She let them separate, lower, and come to rest on his collarbones. The pungent herbal odour of the grass that was crushed between them filled her nostrils. Lila knew the word for what she felt then. Sad. How could she have been so stupid all these years? How could she have gone along like an idiot, letting her employers mould her and make her, lead her one step at a time from her foolish, innocent life? How had she agreed to all of this—until she was here, with him, disfigured beyond belief, a dead person walking and him so alive in front of her, Zal who had never lost himself.

"The Game!" she cried. It was a stupid objection, but she was desperate to make this stop. Hot, blinding tears streaked down across the bridge of her nose and ran down her temple into her soaking hair. Her ribs had become rigid. Her breath fought in and out between her clenched teeth.

"Be quiet and let me do it, or punch me out and leave me here," Zal said with a tolerant frown, never breaking the flow even for an instant.

"Please," she said. "Leave me alone."

He stroked her brow, "You're okay. See? Elf strong. Demon strong. Make pretty robot girl hero better."

"You don't understand!"

"Don't understand what? That it hurts to belong nowhere, to nobody?" He pressed gently on the centre of her forehead, between her eyes, and then smiled to himself and let his finger trail down her nose and down to where her lips met, where he let it rest.

It was as though he'd flicked a simple switch. Lila felt older, but the fury of feelings had abated and become something past and done. It wasn't gone, it was resolved. Zal yawned and blinked at her with catlike self-possession.

Lila tried to smile but it didn't work. "I killed someone." All the charm of the moment died, and she had killed that too. She regretted it bitterly. Her whole body shivered with intense love for him.

Zal took his hand away. His dark brown eyes, black in the indigo light, glanced down and left, into the infinity of memories before they met hers. "Me too."

There was none of the joking, teasing demon about him in that minute. Lila saw only the elf, older than she'd thought, whole worlds of experience far behind his gaze as he looked first at her, then right through her with the thousand-mile stare she was coming to know so well. His skin was pure white in the moonlight, all the shadows on it and in his hair soft blue tones, pools of liquid shadow. He came back from his sojourning and looked at her again, no further, "And don't it make my brown eyes blue?"

Lila wanted him as she had never wanted anything in her life. She rose up on her hands and knees and turned him onto his back. Crouching over him she took a long look where her needles had pierced him, the points only bruises now, mere shadows in a world of tree shade and cold moonlight. He lay with his arms fallen to either side of him, lax in the deep grass, his face expressionless as he looked up at her. She didn't know what he would do, but for the first time she didn't mind, even if he rejected her, and placed her lips gently on the site of one wound.

His back arched and he made a soft, unshaped sound of pleasure. She felt the feather touch of his *andalune* body against the inside of her wrists, brushing the metal that was antithesis to it, sliding off its unreactive, impenetrable surface. She covered his throat with kisses, licking and biting his warm skin. He stretched his arms out wide and lifted his chin, head tilting back in a wanton gesture that made heat flare through her body like tracer fire. She moved her attention down, over the strong, flat muscles of his naked chest. Where Aparastil Lake had tasted of nothing at all, his skin was faintly salty, sweet, and spicy. When she brushed across his nipple with her tongue and felt his hands in her hair suddenly, drawing her closer to him, she forgot who and what she was and lost herself in sensation, action and reaction, in the bliss of being close to him and his willing submission to her pleasure.

Lila heard Zal's breath come faster. He shivered and moved below her, pushing up towards her whenever she lifted her mouth from his body. His *andalune* body came skating across the surface of his skin, touching her lips and tongue, stroking her closed eyelids with tiny hot snaps and languid tingling blurts of energy. She felt tendrils of it dancing through her hair where it caused static sparks to jump and sting on her shoulders and neck as she bent low across him and licked her way over the hard muscles of his abdomen, lingering in their hollows as they flexed and tautened in response to her touch. He groaned and dug his hands into the ground, holding fast. His body was poetry in her mouth and below her hands, moving inward, back from thought, into all that came before, pure desire. With a snick she opened the switchblades in the index and middle fingers on her right hand.

Zal glanced up at the sound and smiled at her, panting. She spent a minute looking at him, perfectly enraptured with the sight of him, as beautiful as a statue, but real and panting beneath her. His long, pale hair, half dry, half wet, was tangled around his head, making him look like a fallen angel. He returned her gaze and then, slowly, closed his eyes.

Lila took hold of the waistband of his leggings, pulling them clear of his flesh, and cut through in two precise strokes, slicing the heavy silk from waist to thigh down both groins. A flush of heat raced through his *andalune* where it touched her at her throat and breasts as she peeled the soaking cloth away and bent over him again. He gasped as she licked up the length of his erection and then took him into her mouth.

Lila lost herself in him, in the game of drawing him to the edge
and then leaving him there, in the perfection of talking to him in this
way. She watched his body become her instrument, listened to him cry
out, made him do it again, learned how to play. She never wanted to
stop, never, wanted only to be lost, but there came a point where she
heard him pleading in whispered elvish. A crackle of wild energy
rushed up both her arms like lightning and earthed out through his
andalune body.

He came, pulsing strongly against her tongue, repeating her name
amid syllables that were both elven and demonic. Lila drank him, she
didn't want to let him go. Zal ran his hands down the length of her
arms where they were planted against the earth on either side of his
hips and, when he couldn't move her, slid himself along the ground
underneath her and caught hold of her head. His tongue was long and
hot as he kissed her, mouth savage and hungry as he pulled her down
to him, arms locked around her neck.

"I weigh enough to crush you," she warned him, poised with
machine precision on her elbows on either side of his head, her knees
against the outside of his hips.

"Shut up, Plutonium Girl." He slid his hands down, opening the
rest of Tath's old clothes where they hung on her. Defeated by the
strong elastic of her remorseless military vest he kissed her harder and
used fingers that were entirely energy to slide under it and caress her
breasts while his ordinary hands moved downwards.

Being touched by him was an even more intense pleasure than
touching him. Where his hands lingered Lila burned, almost as if he
had touched chilli and brushed the oil on her skin, and when his fingers crossed over the biometal surfaces of her skin they created strange
electricity that replicated the surge and tide of his *andalune*.

When he reached the rags of Tath's leggings, now little more than
shorts where her active armour had ripped them to bits, he simply took
the remains in both hands and tore them off. The delicate touch he had

employed on her face now teased down across her belly and buttocks and up the inside of her long steel thighs.

Zal's angular face lay completely open below her, sometimes kissing her, sometimes not, every flicker of emotion visible; delight and arousal their only two forms. She felt supremely beautiful and powerful as he slid his fingers, warm in contrast to the cool damp air, across her lips and then inside her. She saw him smile at her wide eyes when he used his ethereal body at the same location, licking her with multiple small tongues of alternating heat and cool. They teased her as mercilessly as she had teased him, and his fingers, sometimes one, then two or three, penetrated her in agonising counterpoint that would not settle into the necessary rhythm. Lila wanted him so much she lost her mind, "Azrazal Ahriman . . ."

Zal slammed his hand across her mouth. His eyes glittered. "No names. No pack drill." With a strength and energy she had never expected he could possess he flipped them both over. His *andalune* coated him in a faint red coat of plastic energy, making him momentarily as strong or stronger than any of her machine counterparts, fed as it was with Sathanor's endless, absolute fuel. He burned.

Lila wrapped her elegant chrome legs around his waist and buried her hands in the heavy mess of his hair, touching the long tips of his ears with her thumbs. He made her wait, holding her just out of reach until she lay still on the ground and stared up at him with seriously murderous intent. Then he gave a wicked grin, slid his arms around her, and pulled them both upright, chest to chest. He sat back on his heels, his energy body giving him much more than ordinary power, and then he let her go, very, very slowly.

The sensation of sliding down onto him was purely perfect and exquisite. She heard her own voice shouting out in joy.

His hands slid up across her back and took hold over her shoulders, pulling her, down onto him with rough power. They devoured one another's mouths with abandon. Cold red fire and swift green heat flashed as winding, twisting skeins of wild magic curled through Lila's hair, through her ears and eyes and nose, mixing with the charged envelope of Zal's aether and crackling as it met antagonist charges. Heavy ionisation made the air as freshly primed as the ocean wind. Lila breathed it, drank it, dimly aware of herself changing with its tides in ways she didn't understand or care about because all she wanted was right there in the sinuous flex of Zal's hips, the drive of his pelvis, and the deep, repeating thrill of his body moving inside hers.

His *andalune* tongues passed through her flesh and into the bone, vibrating on multiple wavelengths that effortlessly tipped her over the edge. She looked into Zal's eyes and they were weeping flame like tears. Pale yellow and white petals of fire flecked the surface of his tongue and his passion-slackened mouth. He looked faintly surprised, gazed deeply into her eyes and then a column of white fire rushed up the length of her alloy and bone spine and out the top of her head. Lila was surprised too, and then she was unconscious.

CHAPTER TWENTY-SIX

When Lila woke up it was daylight. She was lying on her back, and above her she could see the azure of the Sathanor sky through dancing green leaves. The first thing she noticed was that she was alone. Zal was nowhere to be seen.

She rolled over and looked at the ground. Apart from the flattened area where they had slept, she was able to pick up their incoming trail, and see that he'd retraced her steps. With the exception of her vest she was naked. Tath's shirt lay where it had been put under her head. She picked it up and put it on, its stained white linen draping her from neck to a third of the way down her thighs. Tearing off the sleeves to use as a belt to hold the thin material close around her hips helped slightly on the modesty front, but that was it.

She climbed up the small rise, looking back towards Aparastil, and expanded her hearing acuity as much as she could. Once the environment had been cleaned from the signals she could hear elven voices, and Zal's among them. They were about two kilometres distant, almost back at the lake itself, and it was very difficult to pick out words but she gathered from the snatches she managed to hear that Zal had found sympathetic company. One of the others had a voiceprint that matched Tath's sister's. They were working hard to help survivors of the lake implosion but were insisting that Zal leave them quickly.

"It is too soon . . ." Lila heard Astar say. "Go back to Otopia and we will contact you there."

One of her male companions agreed. "We will mend matters here as best we can but it will . . . a long time . . . government weakened . . . worse to come. Take . . ."

But then they must have turned away. Their sounds became too weak to decipher. She waited and began to pick up the vibration of running feet coming her way; just the one pair. She was more relieved than she liked to admit when Zal returned. He was fully dressed and carrying light packs in both hands.

"Clothes," he said, throwing her the first one. "Food," he added as he sat down beside her and started delving into the other pack. He handed her a birch-bark packet.

Lila tore it open and found the contents waterlogged and squashed but edible. They didn't speak for several minutes, only ate.

"Thanks," she said when she had a moment that her stomach allowed her to stop and talk.

Zal swallowed. "We have to get back to Otopia as fast as possible. Arië has a lot of friends who are recovered and on the lookout for us, and the only reason they haven't found us is that you flew most of the way here. The resistance are trying to hinder them, but they have to maintain their covers so we can't expect much."

Lila opened the clothing bag and pulled out wet elven clothing—trousers, jerkin. She didn't ask where they'd come from, only shook them out and started to put them on. She saw Zal watching her as he ate, his gaze lingering until he noticed her noticing and glanced down.

"Everything should have changed," she said, referring obliquely to the night before but allowing herself to include the whole of the day before, because it seemed safer.

"Nah," Zal replied. "It just feels like it because you're a liminal being, like me, not one thing or another, able to go anywhere and be anything, without knowing where you're headed. And then it fades away and there you are again, much as before."

"Much, but not exactly."

"Not exactly."

From beyond the rise of the hill which sat between them and the long descent to Aparastil they could just hear voices. Some of them were very distressed, grieving and panicking. They were not coming to hunt Lila and Zal. They were looking for medicine in the rich undergrowth of Sathanor. She heard one shout out when they found the plant they needed.

"We should go back and help them," she said, thinking it was the right thing to do.

Zal shook his head. "We can't help them. They'd only want to kill us. The only people we have to worry about down there are Poppy and 'Dia and with any luck they'll already have had enough of trying to drown her tenth-level zerg mages and be back in Otopia washing their hair," Zal said. He had stopped eating, the pack of food half empty beside him. He rolled onto his stomach and lay, propped on his elbows, plucking fine stems from just below his face and eating the lower inch of them with many dissatisfied micro-expressions. "Grass?"

"I'm through my horsey phase." Lila felt the tension between them stretch taut like a strange polymer. Her confession preyed on her mind. For the sake of her job—for the sake of her mind—she wanted to know why he'd killed someone and she wanted to find a reason why she'd done it so that she didn't have to feel sick.

Zal flicked an eyebrow and twirled one long strand between his tongue and top lip before spitting it out.

"So, who did you kill?" she asked, dissatisfied with him, disappointed in his lack of heroic help, and her own.

Zal shrugged. "A faery man and a human woman. Both duty murders, in the days when I was more able to do that kind of thing."

Lila waited for him to flip back the question, but he didn't. He glanced at her in silence. She said the words to herself in her mind before she spoke them aloud, to try them out, see if she even could say them. "I killed Dar."

"Ah shit!" Zal said softly and dropped his head forwards until it almost rested on the ground, hair sweeping forwards to hide his face. His body hung on the bony axis of his shoulders like wet paper. He bent the crown of his head into his hands and she saw his fingers drag through his hair and pull it hard, tight.

Lila was shaking with remorse and misery. "Who was he to you?" she whispered, dreading the answer.

"My friend. One of the only, in spite of our differences. What a fucking waste." He groaned and collapsed flat, his hands over the back of his head, face buried in the grass.

"I didn't mean to . . . that is, I was doing my . . . I didn't want to do it." Lila felt more anguish suddenly than she had even in the moment she had pressed the knife home, and her voice tightened to silence.

"Yeah, I know how it gets," he said, muffled by the green.

"You were an agent," she pursued him, going back to safer ground, fighting to control her urge to beg his forgiveness.

"You don't have to explain," he said quietly. "I understand."

Lila picked up the empty clothing bag and flung it away from her. "Well I . . . I hate how we're just talking about these things as if they're all part of a great and noble job that somehow excuses them and makes them less than murder and less than people!"

Zal lifted his head and looked at her a long minute. "It's a necessary skill. Push everything under until you can let it out somewhere else, more useful, where it can do some good. Just because you don't see me crying doesn't mean I won't. We're still in hostile territory, and this is far from over. If you want to validate yourself then get up. We both have to." He got to his feet.

"Spoken like a true agent!" she snapped.

"I regret you dislike me because I will not say the words you long to hear. They are not mine to give you." He held his hand out to her.

"Spoken like a true elf." She stood up easily, unfolding her legs with hydraulic efficiency, keeping her hands to herself.

"Fuck you, Zirconia." He picked up the food pack he'd abandoned. He took another mouthful, two, and then threw it away.

"Three's the charm!" Lila said. A zip of magic snapped up through the side of her that was closest to him and she saw a grin flicker across his face. "What the . . . I thought it was gone!"

Zal shrugged. "What? The Game? Don't be ridiculous. I didn't hear you screaming—no, I did hear that—but there was no total surrender moment . . ."

"Not me—*you*!"

"Me?" His smile was pure innocence.

"You were begging me . . ."

He snorted and smiled to himself. "Yeah, I was. But that wasn't my essential spirit you heard talking, only my essential need to get off. And, though I'll regret it until I die, I will tell you that that need has never been so fully answered."

Lila was momentarily thrown by what she decided was a compliment. "Then what . . . ? I felt it. The wild magic."

"Whatever you felt, it wasn't the Game ending."

"And then what about that thing at the end?"

"Strange things happen when you shag your brains out in Sathanor. Especially with metal that's already been fused with elemental forces in the most fiendishly unnatural way."

"When I healed Dar."

"When he healed you. He was good at that." There was no trace of jealousy in him.

Lila felt awful. She felt exultant. Nothing here made sense, the switch from despair to joy, from anger to grief and back again, with all this beautiful living forest around them being nothing but surging, fermenting energy realising itself.

Zal waited. He still held his hand out to her.

She sighed and touched his fingers briefly with her own. "It was a nicer morning, before we started talking, when you were just chewing the cud."

He caught her hands in his own and pulled her down to the grass with him. They rested on their knees. He leant forward and kissed her on both cheeks. "Lila?"

"What?"

"Play something."

"What?"

"A tune. With your hands. I want to hear a song. You choose. Play me something."

She put her hand against his head. As she cued the song she checked his eardrum with a fan of ultrasound and it was fine, perfectly mended.

Beyond the ridge somebody was crying and another several people were shouting names, searching for lost ones. Their voices were piercing and anguished.

"Louder," Zal said, closing his eyes. "Ah ha. Cole Porter. Dar liked his songs, but then, everybody does."

Lila listened to the elf voices through the music. After a while she heard people beginning to separate into parties, one of which started to move in their direction. She cut the feed and took Zal's hand.

He stood up easily at her coaxing, light and graceful with the trademark antelope-poise. He handed her Tath's jerkin and she put it on over the shirt, tightening it up as far as it would go.

Lila signed to him about possible pursuit and he nodded and led off, taking a path that lay in a different direction to the way she had come before. It was only as she followed him at a steady jog, her feet remoulding themselves into broad, flat shapes to leave less trace that she heard Tath say, *Where did the dragon go?*

Still in the lake, as far as I know, Lila replied. She wondered how long he'd been awake. His presence was almost undetectable it was so compact.

I doubt that. Are we returning to Otopia?

I hope so.

Did you hear my sister among those you are fleeing?

Yes. Tath fell into a relieved, grateful silence, and Lila started to wonder what she was going to do about him.

She allowed Zal to pace her through the open woodlands of Sathanor's enormous crater and her thoughts ran with her feet. She hadn't let herself consider being bound to Tath forever in any realistic way. But she couldn't return him to the Daga because of what he knew about her, and for the same reason she couldn't let him out into someone else. She certainly couldn't contemplate killing him. She also had to admit how much their relationship had changed, and continued to change as time went on. She wasn't sure that Tath couldn't hear what she was thinking. He could certainly feel whatever she felt emotionally and physically, whether he liked it or not, and when she let him take control with his aethereal body then she felt him likewise. After all they had been through, though she couldn't say she liked him and had no faith whatsoever either that she knew him or what other motives he may yet have hidden, she didn't hate him.

They crossed a beck and Zal followed its line for a short distance until the vegetation on the bank grew too dense. She calculated their path was leading more or less directly towards the crater wall. She would have volunteered to fly but Zal was keeping to the shadow of the trees. She turned from watching the erotic mechanics of Zal running back to the problem of Tath.

Resent him. *That* she could do. But what the hell was she going to do with him in Otopia? Could she even tell of his existence in her debriefing—should she? No. The NSA would want him extracted. They would compel it. She was certain about that. No way could they let a hostile agent of such unique experience and peculiar magical affiliation, an agent who had participated in an enemy action, run around with a spook like Lila. And how much could she trust him? She knew next to nothing about him, nor his powers. He'd tricked her before. He could do it again. Maybe he was in the middle of some unknown plan of his own serving whoever Arië had served, if such persons existed. Thinking of it all boggled her mind and defeated her. She knew why she would never be suited to running a spy agency, or a government—too hard to anticipate all the possibilities, even with an AI. But one thing she felt strongly: she was a fool to conceal him, but that's what she was going to do.

Then again, the idea of trying to keep him hidden in the face of interrogation and, potentially, forever, made her furious, but what choice did she have? And it was pure pie in the sky to imagine Tath settling down like some kind of internal pet elf or alternative AI resource, even if he'd wanted to, which he didn't. Besides which, he was still a whole person, even if he was corporeally challenged. And his death still felt like her fault. And Dar's death was both their faults. A grim thought that this was the thing that bound them more truly than any other . . . she dismissed it.

And maybe he was only waiting for the right moment to do something. Elves and their waiting. . . .

Wishing I was Zal? Tath asked drily, clearly suspecting her thoughts were centred on his circumstances.

Oh no, Lila retorted. *I like Zal with his own hands.*

I noticed that.

Even though she sensed the edge of desperation in his snide remark, Lila wasn't going to let any precedents get past her. She hoped her nervousness about Tath's true power didn't show when she said, *Let's get something straight. You don't start acting like my Aunt Madge after too many gin slings, and I won't let Incon tear your memory to bits before they send you straight to the Long Ships. I'm not spending the rest of my life sniping with you like some old married couple.*

I cannot spend the rest of my life like this! Intolerable!

All ears, buddy. All ears, Lila assured him, but Tath slumped into a sulk. If he knew a solution, he wasn't about to share it.

Ahead of her the bright shine of Zal's hair dimmed as he passed into shade and he stopped quite sharply on the summit of a small rise dominated by three ancient Lyrien beeches, their silvery trunks each the girth of five men, their elegant branches spread out in a single canopy of copper and magenta leaves. She ran to his side and stopped just behind him to look down. Below the slight hill lay a circle of brown, dead grass, as cleanly made as if it had been marked out with compasses. Tiny, almost invisible green shoots were just beginning to peek out here and there within the ring.

"A Thanatopian gateway," she said, recognising the style from a field guide in her AI library. "In or out?"

Zal half turned towards her, "Tath, did you know of any Dead agents involved in Arië's plans?"

"He says not," Lila reported.

Zal flicked his eyebrows up and down in a flash of cynicism. "Well, there they were, or are, and in the heart of Alfheim no less. It's not more than two days old. I'm guessing they used the distraction of Arië's spell to slip past the defences." He straightened up to his full height, listening. He sniffed and Lila felt his *andalune* body sink down and merge with the earth momentarily. "They're not nearby. Let's go. I don't want to risk casting circles inside Sathanor. Too much unpredictability, too much power."

"Where are we going exactly?" Lila said.

"To Frisco," Zal called back as he ran down the slope. "Before I lose all my sodding fans."

They spent the rest of the day crossing country. Zal picked and ate things on the way: fruit, nuts, berries. He shared them with Lila though she ate less, able to do all her running on reactor power. By the time it began to get dark they had reached the base of the crater rim where the gently increasing incline of the ground became a sudden, near-vertical wall.

Zal, chewing the last of an apple, turned from his lead position and put his arms around Lila's neck as she arrived beside him. "Okay, Rockets. Take us up."

Lila braced her legs into the jet position and put her arms around him. His lithe, fit body was hot and damp from exercise and the way he moved as he panted softly was thrilling to hold. She liked his salacious grin too, as he pressed gently against her. She valued nothing more than his thudding heart and the transmission of his longing and fear into her skin through the contact with his *andalune* self. He was light and fragile in her embrace.

"Don't let go."

Lila jumped into the air, catching an even closer hold on Zal's body, careful not to bruise him with the strength of her grip, They looked up as the machine system lifted them both towards the sky, out of reach of the trees and their high canopies, along the precipitous face of the cliff. Zal grinned at her suddenly and she was surprised when he wrapped his legs close and high around her waist. She realised his intention as he started to lean back and she leaned the other way to keep them balanced.

"You'll burn your hair, you idiot." She released him slowly, her hands behind his waist, and he opened backwards with the supple ease of a reed bending until he hung upside down, his head between her knees, hair trailing. He held his arms in a wide cross.

"To infinity and beyond!" he yelled.

Lila looked down at him, and tickled the sides of his waist where the piratical ragged edges of his stolen shirt and his waistband parted company. He giggled and shook them both so she had to work hard just to keep them upright. As they rose above the level of the crater rim they could both see the pink, orange, and violet streaks of the sun setting, and just hear the calls of birds above the hissing power of the jets. Gentle winds blew into their faces from the heart of Sathanor, bringing the traces of burning and destruction from the lake shores. Lila's hands stopped tickling and stroked across Zal's naked belly instead. He lay calm in his invert cross as they stood and hung, supported on an invisible column of superheated air.

Lila stared at the beautiful sky. Their position, peculiar and unexpected but curiously right for this instant, had severed the moment from time before and time after. She longed to stay there forever.

"Don't stop," he said and brought his arms up and back against his sides. Lila felt his hands take a confident hold against the back of her thighs.

She marvelled at the fierce colours, the skim of clouds that caught and shone with the sun's fire. She caressed the tops of his legs, the curving bones of his pelvis, the length of him where his erection pushed the cloth up against her hand. She set them down on a span of flat, grassy earth on the cliff's edge. Zal put his hands down easily on the ground, unwound his legs from her waist, and put his feet down with a circus performer's grace. He unfolded to face her and shook himself off. The tips of his longest strands of hair were black and frazzled.

"There are a lot of Saaqaa out and about," he said, ears twitching. "Stand still."

He sketched out a circle that circumscribed them both and then he sang a line like the call of an unknown bird from a distant time.

Lila suddenly smelled hot dogs. The air around them fogged. "Why didn't you do that when Dar caught us the first time?"

"Hadn't got any elf juice," Zal confessed. "My fuel stop got cut short by that ghost at the Folly, but now that I've swallowed most of Aparastil I could even get you through to the Dead. Don't they tell you anything at spy school?"

Andalune energy, but this is a demonic spell, Tath said, jolting Lila with the sudden reminder of his presence; he had been so quiet.

We always suspected they had the power to form temporary transits through J-space. I trust you'll be finding out how it works.

And then they were standing in a dark parking lot under a sodium streetlamp. The air was damp with rain and stinking with car fumes and the reek of charring onion and hot fat. With a disappointment that was much more acute than she'd imagined, Lila's AI scan recognised the back of a burger stand, the bumpers of six SUVs, some curious human faces that were rather gaudily made up, and the bulk of the concert hall which had been their destination days ago.

"Don't tell me you time-slipped!" Lila whispered from their partially hidden position behind the bulk of a Chrysler Majesty.

"Of course not," Zal said. "These people are all here to see the Rollright Rolling Stones. Look at their hair. But over there," he pointed across the street to the Victorian magnificence of the Cherry Hill Hotel, "is a suite with my name on it. Let's go."

"Why didn't you materialise us in a room, or the lobby?"

"Steel box girders—bad idea to intersect them, bad geology under the hotel, also media circus as elf appears with robot from thin air." His hand closed more tightly on hers. He tugged and moved forward but Lila found her feet rooted to the floor.

"What's the matter?"

She didn't want to go back. "Nothing." She made her feet move again and they walked past the staring lines waiting for hot dogs and the ends of the crowd filing in through the turnstiles. They crossed the street, and came under the brilliance and finery of the Cherry Hill plaza where the doormen and car jockeys waited, sitting on the low-riding flats of gold-plated luggage trolleys. Zal ran them through it, around the edge of the building and in through the kitchen exit.

"You again," said the chef, adjusting her white headscarf as she caught sight of them. Her sous-chefs barely looked up, although they let themselves gawk when they realised she couldn't see them doing it. "Go round by the vegetable deck and not near my pastry with your filthy selves," the chef added, brandishing the filleting knife she had in her hand.

"Cook something for me," Zal called with the sweetness of an angel.

"Filthy bastard," the chef admonished him. "Out, quickly, before I lose my licence! You look like you've been rolling in the mudflats."

Zal took the room service lift to the penthouse.

"Don't you think there might be somebody in here?" Lila asked him as he starting punching numbers into the keypad beside the overly ornate mahogany doors.

"If there is, I'll buy them out," he said. The doors opened silently inwards.

There was no one there, although the door was signalling the hotel which was signalling the manager that Zal was there "He'll just put it on Jelly's tab," Zal said. "They won't even acknowledge I'm here. Jelly will never know unless his Mastercard starts bouncing."

His words reminded Lila that she hadn't so far made a single attempt to reconnect to the Incon network or the Otopia Tree. The peace in her head had become normal to her, her brief life as a wired girl more like a dream than any lasting reality.

She looked around the huge room with its highly decorated period antiques, beaded lights, velvet comforters, mountains of cushions, specially printed fabrics, and enormous, marble jacuzzi. She looked at her lover, his long, singe-fringed hair, his ruined clothing, his elegant eartips in a questioning forward gesture, a flicker of yellow fire in his dark eyes. "When are you going to call Jolene and let her off the hook?"

"What time is it?"

Lila read off her internal clock, which was picking up an update signal, "Eight PM Pacific."

"Maybe tomorrow," Zal said, stretching, arms above his head. He let go with a shiver. The glass-shaded lamp beside him flickered in the classic electrical telltale of nearby wild aether. "And are you," he waved the fingers of one hand beside his head, "talking to the secret masters?"

"Maybe tomorrow." Lila moved forward and put her hands up to his face, feeling the tingle of his *andalune* wind across her wrists. She kissed him gently on the mouth, exploring all the angles until they both found one that gave the perfect fit.

ABOUT THE AUTHOR

JUSTINA ROBSON was born in Yorkshire, England, in 1968. She studied philosophy and linguistics at University. After only seven years of working as a temporary secretary and 2.5 million words of fiction thrown in the bin, she sold her first novel in 1999.

Since then she has won the 2000 amazon.co.uk Writers' Bursary Award. She has also been a student (1992) and a teacher (2002, 2006) at the Arvon Foundation, in the UK. Her books have been variously shortlisted for the British Science Fiction Best Novel Award, the Arthur C. Clarke Award, the Philip K. Dick Award, and the John W. Campbell Award.

In 2004 Justina was a judge for the Arthur C. Clarke Award, on behalf of the Science Fiction Foundation.

THE NO SHOWS US. CYNIC GURU

Through the agency of arcane powers beyond imagination Zal's band, The No Shows, have been in collaboration with real-world band Cynic Guru, so that together they are able to bring you a free track for your entertainment. Listen live to "Doom,"* at www .thenoshows.com.

You won't find "Doom" or all its musicians mentioned in *Keeping It Real*, but you will discover it in the second story—*Selling Out*.

This page is dedicated to **Cynic Guru** as a thank you for allowing themselves to be temporarily possessed by beings from beyond. They are:

Roland Hartwell (vocals, violin, guitar)
Ricky Korn (bass)
Oli Holm (drums)
Einar Johannsson (lead guitar, vocals)

They also write and record many great songs entirely their own that have nothing to do with channelling the mystical aether of imaginary space-time. More information about them, their tour dates, and their music can be found on their Web sites: www.cynicguru.com and www .myspace.com/CynicGuru.

---

*For the composition of this track, Roland took his inspiration from the highly addictive computer game of the same name, while Zal swears it's all about the thrills of fighting alongside and falling in love with Lila Black . . .